I'VE ALREADY MET THE DEVIL

A Story of an American Family

By
R. K. Price

Published by Quiet Owl Books

I'VE ALREADY MET THE DEVIL
A Story of an American Family

Cover Design by Jennifer Welker

Set in 12-point Book Antiqua

Second Quiet Owl Books paperback edition 2012

ISBN-13: 978-0615593661
ISBN-10: 0615593666

Published by Quiet Owl Books

Quiet Owl Books
P.O. Box 58
Montrose, PA 18001
www.quietowl.com

Printed in the United States of America

Quiet Owl Books are available for bulk purchases in the US at special discounts. For more information please contact the Special Markets Department at sales@quietowl.com.

To Jerry and Cecil and all of those who came before and behind; plus Ashley for her guidance; to Danilo for being my friend and translator, and Janet and Sara for their love and patience.

Based Upon a True Story

Table of Contents

PART 1

Chapter 1
Trees, Dust and Steel

I can say with some certainty that my very first memory of life in my hometown was about the dust. People say you begin to remember things around the time you are three years old. If that's the case, I was about three when I first realized that the goddamn dust swirled around my town all the time, night and day it seemed. The wind blew most of the time in my town too, so much so that my mother dusted our family's furniture at least twice a day. But I learned to put up with it, and gradually I learned to ignore it, because in the dry, arid climate in Southern Colorado where we lived, the dust came with the territory.

Back then, there weren't many trees in my hometown to break the wind and keep the dust from stinging my eyes, scratching my throat, making me sneeze, and landing thick on my mother's kitchen table. Besides a slightly worn pair of light brown Oxford shoes that belonged to my brother, ones he outgrew and my mother handed down to me to wear to Mass, I would say that the few clusters of trees that dotted my hometown was the second thing I remember from about the age of three.

I'll never forget the trees. I was in heaven when I was among the trees. And I'll never forget those shoes. They were two-sizes-too-big and they slipped at the heel and gave me a blister, but I loved them with a great passion, mostly because they had belonged to my brother.

The few trees that I found in my town when I was a boy were clumped together in a small grove in my hometown's own Central Park. We called it Central Park because it was in the center of town and most of the streets that ran through the neighborhoods reached a dead end right there where the park began. As more and more people could afford to buy cars and drive them on those streets, the leaders in town finally figured out that they needed to build the streets straight through so you weren't forced to stop your car, turn around, and go back in the same direction when you ran into a dead end trying to drive to the other side of the park.

Building the streets through the park made a lot of sense, I guess, but after they were built, it made it harder to play there because you had to look out for the traffic, light as it was.

Anyway, my brother told me much later, long after we stopped playing in the park, that even though it made perfect sense to build the streets through the park, it took the city council two years to come to that conclusion and finally build the streets to smooth out the traffic flow. Carlo said the city had the money to build the streets, but the debate was over who would get the city contract to do the work. There were a whole bunch of companies that wanted the contract and were willing to pay to get it. My brother said the council eventually compromised and gave some of the work to a bojon company and the rest to a company owned by a wop family. Apparently that made everybody happy.

Let me explain something.

We called the Slavic and Polish people of Pueblo, Colorado – my hometown, "bojons" back then, and, of course, everybody called the Italians and the Sicilians "wops." Sometimes, for a wop like me, calling someone a bojon automatically meant you were in a fight, and the same was true if a bojon called us wops, wops. If another wop called you that, or called you a guinea or something, that was okay, but that was it, no one else could call you that and get away with it.

In the end, the bojons thought the streets they built through the park were straighter and smoother than those built by the wops, and, true to form, the wops were convinced of just the opposite. A few fights broke out in the park over that issue, at least according to my brother.

But back to the trees. I remember clearly the scrawny little things in that park, mostly oaks, maples and a few Blue Spruce, because going to Central Park when I was three or four, before the streets were built, was the most fun I could imagine at the time. When I was older I learned, and I don't think it was from my brother, that our Central Park was only about five acres square, but to me at the time it seemed as big as the universe. And when you look at the old pictures of the park in the town library today, you can tell there were only about twenty trees scattered about. But to me, that measly grove of trees was as big as Rocky Mountain National Park.

When I was old enough to know how, I counted the trees. I don't think I counted them correctly, because I remember the number I came up with was one thousand five hundred and forty. I did count our park's picnic tables correctly though; there were two. But after awhile, I would not go near them because every time I did, I got a goddamn splinter in my hand or in my butt. The town found enough money to build the roads, but not enough to paint the picnic tables. Maybe the painters in town didn't have enough money to get that contract.

When I was much older I visited the really famous Central Park in New York City. It was a glorious day, the day I walked through that park. It was a day the whole city of New York, actually the whole country, was celebrating, and the park was packed with people, shoulder to shoulder, or as we used to say in the Army, assholes to elbows. I probably should have enjoyed my walk through the park much more, but when I was there, all I could think about was getting home. I'd been gone for just about four-and-a-half years. Sometimes, when I look back, I think I should have stayed in New York awhile longer to get to know the place a little better, but at the time all I could think about was getting home, back to the dust and my little grove of trees.

Anyway, my Central Park was a good twenty-minute walk from my mother's house, the only one I knew until I bought my own. It was a neat redbrick, one-story bungalow that sat among thirty others just like it on a street called Goodnight in a neighborhood called Bessemer. It was called Bessemer after an enormous oxygen sucking, fire-breathing monster, and the Bessemer open-hearth furnace, which made steel. People in my town knew about such things as the Bessemer furnace, and Sir Henry Bessemer, the Englishman who invented the thing, because my town was a steel town through and through.

Steel was king, and every kid on every street corner in my town could tell you about the Bessemer furnace and how it processed molten pig iron, refined by blowing air through it in an egg-shaped vessel known as a converter. It kind of looked like a huge teapot standing upright. They'd pour in the melted iron ore in one end, and out the other end belched molten steel which was shaped into railroad tracks and barbed wire, the steel company's two main products. One time, when I was almost a teenager, Carlo took me on a tour of the steel mill to see the furnace. He told me that it takes hundreds of tons of coal to fire up the Bessemer furnace, which along with high-grade iron ore is abundant in vast mineral deposits found in the foothills south and west of my town. Carlo was real smart and he was real proud of the steel mill where he worked.

Every day, at least eighteen hours a day, railcars filled to the brim with shiny black cargo would rumble in and out of town. I thought the supply of coal had no end. Living in my town, especially living close to the steel mill, we had to get used to sleeping through the constant coal train traffic, even though the vibration from those behemoths shook your bed, and the screeching and scraping of the steel wheel-to-steel track nearly pierced your eardrums. But just like the dust, we got used to the noise.

When I was old enough to go to school and take history, I learned a lot more about steel. We were taught about the discovery of hematite ore and the making of pig iron in the Catoctin Mountains of Maryland, about 60 miles north and west of Washington, D.C., the same mountain range where Camp David is situated, and where today, our presidents of these United States play and sometimes work. Monotone, dreary-eyed teachers who, by the time I heard their lesson on the subject, may have been repeating it for the ten-thousandth time taught us. They told us about things such as Mr. Thomas Johnson Junior's marvelous Revolutionary War-era iron-making contraption, the Catoctin furnace, which mass-produced quality American pig iron, and how from Mr. Johnson's furnace came such wonderful things as the Franklin Stove, Robert Fulton's steamboat hull, the cannonballs used to supply George Washington's Continental Army, and the iron plates on the Civil War vessel, the Monitor.

We learned how the Catoctin furnace paved the way, some seventy-five years later, for a brilliant Englishman to perfect his fabulous Bessemer open-hearth furnace, and how both Mr. Johnson and Mr. Bessemer became immensely wealthy making steel. Mr. Bessemer even earned his knighthood with his patented converter, and stowed away millions of British pounds in the process.

Years later, I remember seeing a sign off Highway 15, north of Fredrick, Maryland, directing travelers to the Catoctin Furnace Museum. I was in Maryland visiting my daughter at the time, and we were on our way to see the Gettysburg civil war battlefield. Seeing that sign brought me back, way back, to my high school days and those sleepy-eyed history teachers and their lectures, by which time much of their enthusiasm for the topic of steel was long gone. One thing that stuck out in my mind from those god-awful lessons was the teachers' repetitive final instructions: "Strive to be like Mr. Johnson and Mr. Bessemer, to love steel and work hard making it, because someday you could be rich just like them."

Yeah, sure.

My town's unofficial motto was, "Steel is better than gold, and don't forget it." This theme was recited over and over until it was pounded in our heads.

That day with my daughter in Maryland, we ended up driving right by the exit for the furnace museum. We had only one day to see Gettysburg, and I didn't want to miss that for sure.

Speaking of steel, there's another thing I remember as a small child that I forgot to mention earlier. And that is the soot. Steel mills make tons of steel, and back then, before there were such people as environmentalists and such devices as smokestack scrubbers, the steel mills covered our town in black, sticky soot. When it rained, which wasn't often, the soot almost turned to tar; it was that thick.

On those days when the soot came, it was real hard for my mother to do the wash and hang it out to dry on the backyard clothesline. Our backyard was only two blocks from the steel mill's front gate, and sometimes she had to wash and hang the clothes two or three times a day, on top of all the dusting. Carlo would tell me that before I was born. On those days when the dust and soot both came and it made it impossible to do the wash, my mother would simply stop what she was doing and wait for the wind to die down and the dust and soot to settle. She didn't mind this little inconvenience. She was a happy person in those days, and to pass the time, she would sing. Carlo told me he didn't understand the words she sang, but that didn't matter; she had a beautiful voice. He said she sang like an angel.

Anyway, sometimes the dust and soot would get so thick that if I was standing in front of my house, I could hardly see across the street. It was kind of like an early morning fog, but this fog stunk. Nowadays, I hear, they advise people to stay indoors when pollution gets that bad, but back then they didn't know much about such things, so on nasty, foggy days I was still allowed to walk to the park. Not by myself. My mother wouldn't think of letting me go to the park alone. But she would with my older brother. I went with Carlo, and my mother made me hold his hand along the whole way. Usually, we would go after Carlo came home from school in the afternoon. He and I first began our walks to the park around 1927, I think. My brother, five years older than me, was just eight at the time, but he was old enough and smart enough to find his way to and from

7

the park. So, it was all right with my mother for us to go by ourselves. Sometimes, I remember Carlo complaining to my mother about having to drag his little brother along, but she didn't listen. She trusted him. She had taught him well, and she just sent us on our way. On those days, I remember being kind of sad at first that Carlo didn't want me to come along, but I soon got over that too. Just like the dust, noise and soot.

My brother Carlo was the fifth child of my father Nick and my mother Angelina's seven living children. I was the last to be born, and five sisters had come along before and between Carlo and me. My name is Archangelo. They call me Johnny. That's the American version, I was told, so it stuck with me. I like Johnny better, anyway.

Despite what the teachers in my town were telling my brother and his classmates back then about getting rich as men of steel, few people in Pueblo at the time were reaping the bountiful wealth spreading across many parts of my parent's new country. The 1920s weren't roaring too loudly in my town. Only a handful of people had captured the prosperity filtering through an economy fueled by an exploding stock market and an Industrial Revolution quickly reaching its peak. Steel was king in my town, but the king's bounty was doled out discreetly to the vast majority in small, weekly pay envelopes. In my town people worked very hard to get what they got. Nothing was handed to them. As it did with my family, the pay got folks by, but only a very few were truly getting rich.

Back then I used to hear stories of some who owned a new DeSoto, played polo, and dined in a decked-out Pullman rail car on their way to the races in Saratoga. There were a few who could dance the Charleston, and a few who frequented the best speakeasies in Chicago. However, in Pueblo, they didn't know how to dance the Charleston, and they called their speakeasies "taverns." But even those who could lose more than a year's average steelworker's pay on the seventh race at Saratoga (and not miss it) would argue that the booze and the music, their kind of music, were as good in my town as they were in the finest joints in Detroit or Philadelphia or anywhere else for that matter.

In my town, the few who knew about some of the finer things in life, like losing big on the ponies, were the beneficiaries of either one of two economies flourishing at the time. They sure weren't the steelworkers. They were the people who owned a piece of, or at least managed the operations of, the steel mill. Or they were the others, those who didn't make their livings, as Carlo used to say, "on the up and up."

Sometimes on our walks to the park, Carlo would tell me stories of our town, pieces of our town's history from conversations he had overheard between my parents, or rumors passed around school. One story that's as vivid to me now as it was the first time I heard it seventy-five years ago is the one about Mr. Rockefeller. Yes, *that* Mr. Rockefeller.

Even though he certainly didn't live in my town, nor did he ever come near the place, John D. Rockefeller Senior, the Titan himself, was one of the few who lived very well off Pueblo's steel mill. His son, John D. Rockefeller Junior, also prospered, and he came to visit my town once. Certainly, as the baron of all oil barons, Mr. Rockefeller also lived well off his oil companies, even after the government broke them up in 1911. But the steel mill in my town contributed a great deal to his and his son's overall well-being.

Carlo told me that Mr. Rockefeller's involvement with my town began after the turn of the century when the steel mill fell on hard times; in fact, it was on the verge of bankruptcy when he stepped in. The way Carlo tells it, Mr. Rockefeller took some small change from his pocket and bought the mill and all of the coal and iron ore deposits in the land surrounding Pueblo for a hundred miles or more. It cost Mr. Rockefeller a few million dollars at the time, but that didn't leave much of a dent in his bank account.

Mr. Rockefeller's purchase, however, saved the mill, and my town. Soon after he bought the mill, the mines, and most of the town, Mr. Rockefeller sent his son to visit his steel mill and coalmines. But the year Junior came to my town was not to look over and admire his properties. It was to make peace. You see there had been some serious problems at the mill the year before, and it was time for the Rockefellers to make amends. The entire town remembers how, during that visit, Junior had his picture taken at the front gate of the mill with about a dozen or so of his partners, and some of his mill managers. They were all dressed in natty suits in the latest styles. No bib overalls in sight.

Looking at the picture, the day appeared to be a rare one, bright and sunny, so more than likely, my mother was hanging clothes on her backyard clothesline some two blocks away. She was probably singing while hanging our underwear out to dry.

The day after Mr. Rockefeller Junior's picture was taken, it was splashed across the front page of the local *Chieftain Journal*. By the time the issue hit the streets, however, he had left town, hoping he had "mended the fences," as Carlo used to say. His tour of the mill and the surrounding coalmines had attracted a lot of attention. It was planned that way. He was there to rub salve on fresh wounds. Neither Junior nor his papa liked publicity, but in this case, neither had a choice. The story they were trying to end was too big to handle other than through their own personal involvement. It was a bold move on their part, and

10

strange territory for either of them to enter. Carlo said he used to hear our father talk about why Mr. Rockefeller Junior came to town, and why he left so fast. It wasn't from the heat of the blast furnace making steel either; it was the heat from the steelworkers themselves – the ones who were still living, anyway.

Quick a visit as it was, after Junior left town in his very own decked-out Pullman sleeper, the whole world knew he had been there. Some of them, many of my parents own neighbors, used to go to the front gate and stand where Mr. Rockefeller Junior had stood so they could have their pictures taken in the exact same spot as the Titan's son. I know many of them brought their children, because I saw the photographs on the fireplace mantels of their homes. Others in my town burned the newspaper clippings in symbolic protest as a final gesture of defiance of their notorious leader. At least that's the way I heard Carlo tell it.

For a few years after Mr. Rockefeller Junior hurried out of town, going to the front gate and standing where he stood was a mandatory school "field trip" orchestrated by one of Carlo's history teachers. So, once a year, Carlo and his classmates went to the gate of the mill, and while they were standing there, they were reminded about the Bessemer furnace, and getting rich, if you worked hard. "If Mr. Rockefeller can get rich, so can you," his teacher would chirp.

Carlo told me once that our father was appalled at the idea of going to the mill's front gate and standing where Junior had stood and having your picture taken. He thought it was downright demeaning. So, no one in my family ever did it (except when they were forced to do so by their teachers). By the time I got to school, the tradition had ended. I suppose it was either abandoned or there were enough fathers like mine who convinced the teachers they were being stupid. I never met my father. I wish I had.

Chapter 2
A Son-of-a-Bitch That's Ours Alone

Even today, if you go into a bar in my town, order a drink and strike up a conversation with the stranger sitting next to you, and that person happens to be a native, I'd advise you not to talk too much about why Mr. Rockefeller Junior came to my town back then, had his picture taken and left as soon as he could. Yeah, that would be one piece of advice I might give you – don't bring up the Ludlow Massacre.

Most people say the Rockefellers didn't like my town much after that dark April day in 1914.

That was the day that twenty innocent people (at least that's how many were accounted for in the official record) died in an inferno and a hailstorm of bullets. Mr. Rockefeller distanced himself from the incident the minute the first shot rang out. Junior took the stage in defense. That's why he came to town. No one ever took credit or blame, and all in Mr. Rockefeller's cadre of advisors denied making the request of Colorado's governor to call out the National Guard and help suppress the striking miners. But suppress the strikers, they did. They were very effective.

After my father and mother moved to town, and my father began his life's work at the steel mill, they rented a house in Bessemer they later realized had been occupied by Mr. Antonio, one of those miners who, to his and his family's terrible misfortune, were residing in the tent city at Ludlow on that horrible day.

The makings of this tragedy began early in the year, around February, which marked the third year of a freeze on the steelworkers' wages. The miners hadn't seen a pay raise in three-and-a-half years, and the average workweek for both groups had been stretched from fifty to sixty hours, with overtime pay banished. Problems escalated when the "troublemakers" tried to meet with mill management to air their grievances and ask for better working conditions. At first they protested privately, or better put, simply griped about it to themselves and their families. When they started talking among each other and to management that meant they were trying to "organize." Then the workers started to slow down their production. First a few, and then a few more got sick and couldn't come to work. And then a few showed up with signs openly declaring their complaints. And then a few more picked up the signs and left work early, and then a whole lot of them didn't come to work at all, just walked in front of the gates of the mill and at the openings of the mines with their signs.

These actions were seen as intolerable defiance. Management would not accept anything less than total obedience.

Right after the protest began, but before there was any bloodshed, Junior was hauled before a Congressional committee to defend an "open shop" workplace. Carlo explained that's when managers and owners don't recognize unions, meaning they don't want more than one guy at a time asking for a raise or better working conditions or they don't want anybody challenging the way they run their business. Anyway, Carlo said Junior did a pretty good job with his testimony and seemed to quell not only the political disturbance but some of the protesting picketers as well.

Yet there were still plenty of disgruntled mine and mill workers who openly defied Junior and his father and eagerly joined the rapidly forming union to man the picket lines.
The miners' and mill workers' protests had turned into the first strike organized by the fledgling United Mine Workers of America.

While Junior was still testifying, all those who had walked off the job that happened to reside in the company-owned Bessemer houses were forced to vacate their homes immediately. The family that owned the house my parents later rented was among those who were evicted without warning, barely given time to gather a few belongings.

Many of those workers and their families headed south of town to join striking miners, and with no other choice, they set up a tent colony for shelter and protection. The problem for the strikers and the excuse to use force against them was the unfortunate fact that their tents were placed on public land. But the strikers thought they had a right to be there. It was public land, after all, and besides, they had no place else to go. And furthermore, this was America, they said, which they thought gave them the right to pitch their tents anywhere as long as the government, not the Rockefellers, owned it. But they thought wrong.

After my parents moved into that house in Bessemer late that year, my mother found a letter written by Mrs. Belinda Antonio to her sister living in Milwaukee. Mrs. Antonio and her husband, Fredrico, had two children. Fredrico had gone on strike with the others, and the "Enforcers," as they called them, had come that morning to make sure the rest of the family was gone by noon. Apparently, Mrs. Antonio didn't have time to mail her letter to her sister, because my mother discovered it in the top drawer of the former tenant's bureau. My mother kept that letter, and the one Mrs. Antonio wrote to her about a year later from Milwaukee where she was living with her sister.

April 19, 1914

My Dearest Mariana,

Today is Tuesday. Tonight we shall be gone from our home. I don't know where we are to go. They told us this morning that we had to leave even though our payment was made on time. Fredrico is defiant. He will not go back to work even though we have no money and little food. He is packing the truck with all we can carry. We don't have time to take the furniture. We don't know where we could take it anyway. The workers are united, Fredrico believes, and he thinks they will win. I don't know. I am frightened. I worry for our children. They can't go to school. The teachers won't let them in because their father is on strike. We hear there may be a place for us south of town. Some striking mine workers are setting up a tent city. But what are we to eat? It's still very cold at night. How will we sleep? Will we be safe? The Enforcers are angry. Some of Fredrico's friends are now Enforcers and they are treating him like dirt. One spit in his face this morning when he answered the door. He wants to fight. I want to hide. Life has been good here – better than it was in Naples, but this is hard now. It shouldn't be this way. This is America. It should be better. I must go now. Fredrico is ready

Your Loving Sister,
Belinda

November 17, 1917

Dear Angelina,

Please forgive my informality in addressing you only by your first name. I do not know your last name and only heard your first name from a friend still living in Bessemer who said you and your family had moved into my house after we left for the tents. You are welcome at my home. I have no use for it now. I am living in Milwaukee with my sister. In fact you are welcome to all I have in the house since I no longer wish to keep those things that bring back the memories. I will never return. My Fredrico and my children are not with me. They are gone. They did not survive the tents. But I survived and often I wish I hadn't. By now, you probably know what happened to us in the tents and how some survived and others didn't. I don't know you if you can somehow understand how it may feel to lose all that means anything.

When the bullets came through the tent, we were lying flat in the trench Fredrico had dug to keep us safe. But we were not safe. The bullets kept coming in lower and lower and finally my children's screaming stopped, and Fredrico, lying across us in the trench would not move. The bullets had stopped, and the fire had begun. I wanted to stay in the trench with the rest of them, but a man came inside to search and found me and made me go with him before the fire took me, too. They left me that day and my heart will ache forever. My house and my life have no meaning. I am sorry to write to you this way, but now you may understand why I don't care anymore.

17

Please use my things for your good, and may they bring you pleasure.

With Respect,
Belinda Antonio

~

Carlo told me years later that when the official reports of Ludlow were released, it said after the tents were erected, and after the strikers had worked their first shift on the picket lines, they dug foxholes in which to lay and avoid the stray bullets from the strikebreakers' rifles that frequently pierced the tent canvasses overhead. But on the day of the siege, the men, women and children taking shelter in those tents watched in horror as a truck-mounted machine gun operator took aim and sprayed fire in all directions. At the same time, a crew of thugs splashed kerosene on the tents for quick ignition. I'm sure the strikers knew then that their fate was sealed.

Mill management totally denied responsibility. Both Mr. Rockefellers were detached from the proceedings and their hands were always clean. Some months later when Junior came to town, he tried to reconcile with and formally recognize the union. After he made peace with the union he got his picture taken with his buddies at the mill's front gate. He did a good job swaying public opinion in his direction. When he left town, he had some friends, but he also still had a whole bunch of enemies.

For many in my town resentment, distrust, and suspicion lingered long after Junior caught his train back to New York. For those people who lived here then, and some who still live here today, the incident never faded from memory. It created solidarity among the steelworkers and miners and moved the union from an option to a necessity. My father became a true believer. He would always be a steelworker, but now only a union steelworker. Even almost a century later Ludlow remains a real sore point in my town. The stories are passed down to sons and daughters. When Nelson Rockefeller, Junior's son, ran for vice president on the ticket with Gerald Ford in 1976, he probably got less than five percent of the vote in my town.

Today, a monument stands where the accounted-for twenty striking workers and their families fell.

Visiting the monument is a mandatory field trip for most high school history students, and Ludlow is taught right along with every other subject. My kids most definitely went there and paid their respects when they were in high school. I can tell you that. I took them myself.

Even though another dust storm might be looked upon more kindly in Pueblo than the Rockefellers, many people believe Ludlow was a turning point for the steel magnates in many ways. After Ludlow, Rockefeller spent the next twenty-two years of his life giving away his money with distinguishable grace and humility. He defined American philanthropy, and more than any single individual before or since, used his money in immeasurable ways to advance education, medicine, environmental preservation, and scientific research. His son and his grandsons followed suit. The irony is that the lost ones of Ludlow may have been the founding of a movement that saved the lives millions of people worldwide. Even after Ludlow and all that happened in my town and among its people, the Rockefellers remained its lifeblood. We couldn't live without them.

When my brother was ready, he, like all the other kids his age in town, went to Mr. Rockefeller's school. The

Titan had built the sprawling structure soon after Ludlow. I went to Mr. Rockefeller's school, too, and so did all of my sisters. It was called Bessemer Elementary and Secondary School. Surprised? I guess no one could come up with a better name. Carlo's teachers, especially his history teacher, were Mr. Rockefeller's teachers. His steel mill paid their salaries. And they became my teachers, too. If it weren't for Mr. Rockefeller's steel mill there wouldn't be any schools, or any town at all for that matter.

Back then they didn't teach about Ludlow in Mr. Rockefeller's school. Even if you asked your history teacher about that bloody day, he would dutifully change the subject. You learned about that dark day in history around your kitchen table at night, especially around the tables of my town's Italian and Sicilian families. Sixteen of the twenty who died that day were Sicilian and Italian brothers, sisters, aunts, uncles and cousins, if not by blood, by spirit. It seems as though we're all related, somehow. We sure felt related to the Antonios after reading Mrs. Antonio's letters.

Nick and Angelina moved out of the Antonios' house soon after my mother received the letter. They left the furniture for the next tenant. The house sat vacant after that for many years until it was eventually torn down. Today a 7-Eleven store sits there. It was in my parent's second house in Bessemer that all of us were born.

Despite the bitterness and lingering anger following Ludlow, people in my town settled into a nearly thirty-year period of relative peace and calm with their employer, and they generally accepted the way Mr. Rockefeller ran his steel mill.

"*Egli e' un figlio di e'cagna, ma egli e'nostro riglio di e'cagna.* He's a son of a bitch, but he's our son of a bitch." Carlo would quote my father.

And up until about the time I was strolling through the real big Central Park on my way back from England, most of my town, its houses, businesses, stores and politicians, still belonged to Mr. Rockefeller. It wasn't until shortly after World War II ended that Junior sold the steel mill, and with it, the rights to control our lives.

Chapter 3
The Polka and a Swinging Steel Beam

So when you're at that bar, say Joe's on the other end of town, and you're talking to that stranger next to you, just so you know, it's all right to ask about my town during the Roaring Twenties. Even though I was just a boy back then, I got the impression that people in my town were pretty happy during the Twenties. They continued to work hard; save as much as they could, and when they weren't working, they cut loose at the taverns, dancing the waltz, polka and the tarantella (but not the Charleston). The vast majority in my town wasn't rich, but they were content. It was sure better than what most had left behind.

In fact, my mother used to tell me she said a Rosary every single day thanking her Blessed Mother for her family's place among the dust and soot in Mr. Rockefeller's town. Every night during dinner it was the job of each of us children to report to her the events of our day. From the smallest incident to the biggest, she needed to hear how we coped with our problems, celebrated our victories, stood up to our defeats and generally played the game of life. The dinner table also was the place to settle disputes among us. We could not go to bed with one or the other of us angry or harboring resentment. My mother was our confessor, our counselor and our mediator. When I look back, she was reminding herself and us that our place was a better place than she ever thought she would live. Once in a while at night before bed I would hear her in her room with her Rosary asking her Blessed Mother to forgive her for doubting her beloved Nick, who first told her about their new home in paradise, and convinced her to follow him there.

The story of my parent's journey to America has been pieced together over the years from tales heard first-hand and second-, third- and maybe even fourth-hand by us children. I remember Christmases in my cramped, cozy living room, when my mother would tell stories about her and my father's journeys leaving out one important detail, we found out later. Other pieces of the puzzle were gathered from my father's brother, my Uncle Pete, who came here first, and persuaded his younger brother to make the trek across the world to join him. In any case, this is what we think happened.

Nick and Angelina left for Nick's paradise around June 1914, so it's unlikely that news of the Ludlow killings had made its way to their tiny hamlet near Palermo, situated along the west coast of Sicily. If the tragic story had made the Sicilian newspapers, the names of some of those murdered may have been familiar to those remaining behind in their homeland. But like Nick and Angelina, those escaping Sicily at the time were free to pluck their family roots the minute they boarded the passenger ships for the West. There were some like my mother and father who had family waiting for them in America, and they were lucky in that respect, but so many more left without a trace and came to America searching for a safe harbor and finding no welcoming party. Very few much cared where you came from in the first place or where you were going once you got here.

As Nick and Angelina crammed onto the ship at Palermo harbor, all Nick cared about was shedding the oppressive world their homeland had become and finding their way to the far-off, mysterious but alluring United States of America. They had to leave their island home, the home of their ancestors, stretching back dozens of generations. They had no choice in the matter.

Post-World War I Sicily had slipped into an unbearable state of poverty, violence, drought, and anguish. My parents belonged to a destitute people fleeing their native land in desperation, and America was the only hope for tens of thousands of refugees like them. Sicily's plight was brought on by a perfect storm of years of failed crops, a broken, backward economy, which existed largely underground, and a government corrupt to its core. What little free market of agricultural products and light industry that existed was blackened by the Black Hand, the clan whose hardened criminals had stepped in to fill the vacuum of power and dole out protection for a price. It was clan versus clan, soon relegated to family versus family and brother versus brother. Language barriers, cultural conflicts and territorial disputes brought on a near state of civil war. Italy was not much better off. It too was strapped in a never-ending series of territorial conflicts that pitted citizens in one province against people in another over land rights, crops, and just about every other excuse to engage in one bloody conflict after another.

In Sicily, Nick finally made the decision to leave their four-room stucco house with its single olive tree in the front yard the day Angelina, (who we would later find out was five months pregnant), was slammed to the ground and kicked by two of the town's twenty or so apprentices of La

24

Cosa Nostra, which is just another name for the Black Hand, the Mafia. The name didn't matter. They were all bolts cut from the same cloth. They were the scourge that had fallen on Sicilian society and the disease they carried was spreading.

The punks got my mother's twenty lire, but that night, they each lost a kidney when Nick's razor sharp stiletto slipped easily into their lower backs, just deep enough to teach a lesson, but not deep enough to beckon Father Benito for last rights.

Even after the beating, Angelina resisted leaving her home. Sicilian women were not supposed to question their husbands, but instead were to dutifully obey and follow. Angelina, I've learned, was different than most women of her time. She was strong-willed. She spoke her mind. And Nick respected her opinion. Angelina was not happy when Nick first told her it was time for them to leave for America. She could not imagine leaving her family, friends and home and living in another place, even when her husband told her about the job his brother had at the place that made steel railroad track, and how, if they made it there, he could earn as much as five American dollars a day, just like Uncle Pete. But eventually, despite her misgivings, Angelina came to appreciate the opportunity. She knew that in Sicily my father was lucky to make that much money in a month. She was soon able to compose herself and outwardly support her husband's decision to leave their home. She understood why, but that didn't make the leaving any easier. She cried every night, and worried about the baby in her belly growing up without her extended family. Once Angelina accepted her fate and embraced her future, she hardly had time to say goodbye to her family and their homeland.

Preparations for their departure were hastily put in motion, especially when Nick came home with the news that the two with holes in their backs were favorite recruits of the Black Hand. In a day's time, their meager belongings were packed and they left for the ship harbor at midnight. Angelina had a pain in her belly the whole time. She could have blamed it on nerves, but four days after boarding the ship, the bleeding came in a rush, and so did the detail my mother would always omit from her stories. Her name was Prudence. My father and his bride cried when they watched the on-board priest bless the tiny body wrapped in the woolen blanket they'd bought at the harbor store in Palermo and gently drop the bundle into the sea as their ship passed through the Gibraltar Strait and entered the Atlantic.

Prudence.

I always think about her and what she might have been like, if she would have had skinny legs like mine, or Carlo's thick, black curly hair, or Sophia's green eyes, or Katrina's turned-up nose and dimpled chin. Angelina fought the infection that set in after her miscarriage, and slowly regained her strength during their three-week voyage across the ocean.

My mother would only tell us about the seasickness, horrible food, grey and putrid drinking water, and the smells and ceaseless sobs from fellow passengers below decks. We knew about Prudence only from Uncle Pete. We never asked my mother about her first-born daughter. I wish we had. I wonder if she would have told us anything, even later, when time had passed to heal the pain.

By the time the ship passed through the entry point toward Ellis Island, she again could walk almost in stride with Nick, matching his long, rapid pace.

After they crossed America's threshold, Nick and Angelina hunkered down for three months in the teeming tenement of Manhattan's Little Italy while Nick scraped together the fifty-two dollars for the train tickets to

Colorado. All the way across the plains, Nick reminded Angelina with a smile that he would soon be making the steel tracks on which they were riding.

After a short time in their new Colorado home, Angelina became grateful for Nick's persistence. She now knew leaving Sicily had been the right decision, and her children would be better for it. She knew those things even on that day when Uncle Pete and cousin Fabio came to her home with the news that shattered her heart and crumbled her world. Yes, she knew coming to America had been the right thing to do, but after that day, with the exception of the weddings of each of her children, she wore nothing but black for the next fifty-seven years of her life.

Nick's final day on the line and the last day of his life were only five short days after his tenth year on the job, and just five short days after I was born.

My father had advanced quickly on the grab lines, using his strength and steady balance to coax the giant, glowing orange-hot thirty-foot tracks from the thousand-degree Bessemer furnace. It only took him three years to move to the head of the crew overseeing the movement of those fat T-shaped steel bars through their final firing onto the cooling baths.

Uncle Pete told my mother how Nick had stooped to reach for the hand of a crew line member who had stumbled while stepping into position, and as Nick moved to regain his own balance, he leaned just inches too far into the path of the swinging two-inch-thick suspension cable. Suspended from that cable was one of Nick's freshly made, shiny new, one-ton rail tracks. He had always told his wife what beautiful, magnificent pieces of fine art he thought they were. This one's deadly path was just right to strike him at the right temple. He fell and did not suffer.

Nick was the seventeenth to die at the mill that year. No one told Mr. Rockefeller. Accidental death reports never made it to his desk.

Carlo told me that Angelina nursed me, her last born, while praying with Father Michael for Nick to find his way to heaven, and for the day she would join him there. And the day Father Michael ordered the casket lowered and Uncle Pete led her away from the gravesite was the last day for many years that Angela spoke a word of English, that I know of anyway. I guess she somehow needed to recapture some of her life before America, and the dust, soot, steel, heartache and death.

Whatever the reason, until the day many years later that English became acceptable in her house, she insisted her children learn her native tongue, and we were forbidden to speak to her in anything but Italian.

Chapter 4
Pretty Girls and Red Brick Bungalows

Carlo used to tell me about the day of the funeral, foggy details, like the black veil covering my mother's face, the pungent smell of the incense rising from the altar, and the shrieks of my sisters when they lined up to see my father's body lying in the casket. But he remembered vividly how our mother came home and spoke to him in the strange language he couldn't understand. He was confused and hoped Angelina would return with her smiles and songs, but he soon grew to understand that that side of our mother no longer existed.

Carlo tried to help as best he could, taking on Nick's tasks at home, and he knew, someday, he would replace him at the mill.

One month before Carlo turned thirteen, he marched off to work. His place was at the cooling baths, not on the grab lines, and far away from the swinging cables. The one-thousand-dollar settlement check from the steelworker union's Death Fund was quick to disappear, although Angelina rationed everything, including her love, as evenly as she could among the seven who occupied our dinner table each night at six o'clock.

She had bore each of us in her bed in her brick bungalow in Bessemer, some in the blistering heat, others in the bitter cold, but all of us in the shadow of the mill spewing out its rancid smells and bad memories.

Carlo's work at the cooling baths meant he couldn't continue his studies, but at the time that didn't matter much to him. He could read the comic books and the dime novels he bought crumpled and torn from his fellow steel workers. Once in a while, he saved enough for a magazine, the ones he hid in the shed out back, with few words but many pictures of women reclining on velvet couches, women who filled his dreams and sometimes caused him to soil his sheets.

He was old enough to realize that the cooling baths would probably be the place for his life's work, and that was okay with him. He was proud of himself, and I knew Nick would have been proud of him too. Each day I watched him strut off to the gates of the mill those two short blocks away with a sense of purpose. He was making five dollars and fifty cents a day.

I know Carlo grew up before his time. He learned how to smoke, to drink a little, to cuss and to fight before he was barely out of grade school. Inside and outside of the gates, out of earshot of our mother, nearly every other word rang with "shit this and fuck that," not that he meant it all that much, but rather he talked that way to earn his place and to mark his territory.

One time, when bojon Billy Padloski called Carlo a "guinea little prick," and said our mother "liked to position herself bottom up," Carlo broke Billy's nose and cracked three of his ribs before the cooling bath workers decided to pull him off. Billy was eighteen, five-feet-ten and one seventy-five, and Carlo was fourteen, five-feet-seven and one thirty five. Soon after Billy hit the concrete floor of the cooling bath corridor chin-first, Carlo was asked to join the mill's junior boxing league. Before he retired from the ring, he became the mill's undisputed middleweight champion, and rested on a record of thirty-three, three and three.

Five-fifty a day meant Carlo didn't have to go to school, but it meant his brother and sisters could.

Taking care of Nick's family was his mission now, and whatever it took, it always seemed to me that he was up to the task. My brother practiced his Italian every night, without the cuss words, and this became one of our mother's few pleasures. He learned the Sicilian and Italian dialects from our older sisters, Katrina, Sophia, Nicole, and Helena. Priscilla had been born between Carlo and me, and was just ten, but already learning the language well since all of us desperately yearned for our mother's approval more than she ever realized.

Katrina and Sophia were seamstresses and very good at their craft, but their combined pay didn't come close to Carlo's five-fifty a day. Together, however, there was enough for flour for pasta, pork from Sammy's butcher shop, and goat cheese from Jimmy's stand, which was one mile down the road and along the river, where, at night, fancy cars were sometimes parked to the side, in the shade of a big willow tree.

Carlo and I, when we got older, shared the clothes Nick had first worn, and Katrina got the first new dress and handed it down after just one year.

"Just enough to go around," was Carlo's view later in life. He was satisfied with the basics. And we waited. Waited for time to pass, for the pain of our father leaving us to ease, and our mother's often dark moods to subside.

Carlo was right about most things then. He had good instincts and common sense. He was the best stand-in for a father our family could have hoped for.

My brother took Nick's place at the head of the dinner table each night. It was his proper place of honor. He liked that role and that place at the head of the table, at the other end opposite Angelina. I would sit to the right-hand of my brother – second in line.

I couldn't understand this positioning, really, either at the table or in the line of succession. Back then, I had no idea of the significance, but that's the way it was done. Our sisters on each side descending by age. It remained that way each night, each of us in our proper seats until, one by one, we all either married or moved out and on. Even when we were adults on the rare occasions when we were all together, we instinctively knew our places at the table. A sacred rule, never violated.

As I said, I loved and respected my brother deeply, and grew to appreciate what Carlo was doing for us through his hard work and dedication to the mill. Strange thing though, after yearning to follow my brother everywhere, as each year passed and the steel mill consumed nearly every aspect of our lives, I realized I never wanted to follow him there. No way. No how. Not in the cards.

For one thing, Carlo usually smelled. He smelled bad from each day at the cooling baths, and sometimes from his boxing matches after work. Damn guy wouldn't take a bath but once a week, and only after Angelina would refuse his place at the head of the table. And he farted constantly, seeming to delight in performing this loud and obnoxious habit at will, especially at the precise moment I would quietly move beside him in the bed we shared in the one room that Angelina allowed us to ourselves.

Don't get me wrong when I call my mother by her real name here. It's not for lack of respect; it's just that I dearly love the name Angelina. I love to say it, and love to think about the person who went by it.

Anyway, I convinced myself over time that I could get used to Carlo's smell and his farts, but I could never get used to the idea of committing my life to the mill. The thought that I was better than Carlo never entered my mind. I knew I could never be as good or as smart as my brother. But early in my life, maybe by the age of eight or nine, I just knew I wanted something different. I guess I wanted something that would allow me to fulfill what I believed had been my mother's bigger, brighter, more vivid dream for her children on the day she boarded that ship with Nick and left Palermo far behind.

Yes, I put my brother on a pedestal and worshipped him at times, but I hated the thought of having to do what he was doing for the rest of my life.

Besides, I rationalized the mill guys only seemed to get the ugly girls. It was clear to me that the guys who worked somewhere other than the mill got laid more often and married the prettier ones around town.

That woman theory evolved in my head over time until I met my brother's future wife. But my adolescent longing to be free of the shackles around which the steel workers so freely fastened their wrists for the rest of their lives never left me.

Chapter 5
Two Missing Fingers and the Livestock's Escaping

When I was fourteen I told Carlo that I didn't want to take the job on the roller line at the mill. In fact, I told him I didn't want any job on any line at the mill. When I told him that, my brother hit me so hard he cracked my right top molar. I think he didn't mean to hit me that hard, but he swung with anger and a prizefighter's perfected right cross. Four years later, while I was on a forced march through an early winter storm in Holland, the tooth became abscessed, and had to be extracted one night with a pair of pliers. I still have a hole in my jaw from that missing tooth.

I knew what the roller line was, and if you had any desire at all to work at the mill, I guess it wasn't a bad job to have. The roller lines were long conveyor belt-type areas where the molten steel came out of the furnace and was actually rolled and stretched into thin, round sections of steel string, extending miles in length. Those strings became barbed wire, "the Devil's Rope," the steelworkers called it. The stuff of legend, folklore, and myth. Some local historians even declared that "barbed wire made the West," and I knew Carlo could think of no better place for his brother to work. Carlo had become a steel worker even before he was fourteen. Now it was time for his brother to follow behind. It was all arranged. The union had made a place for me.

"Ungrateful little shit," he shouted, right before the right cross-caught my jaw.

How could anyone not be proud to join the roller mill? I thought sarcastically as I lay on the floor spitting blood.

Barbed wire, with its "colorful past and its brilliant future," my teachers would say, was a vitally important product from my town's mill. So, naturally, it was a vitally important subject taught by the company's vitally important history teachers at my town's vitally important school. Later, I began to see how it all fit, put together like a crossword puzzle in your mind. As a boy at home you were taught about steel. Your father's life was wrapped tightly around it. So steel became your life, sucking up every ounce of every waking moment. When you went to school, the message was reinforced. More pieces to the puzzle. Your friends talked about it after school. They dreamed of the day they could go and be among the men and come home gritty and smelly to a loving, patient wife. More pieces, until finally they were all in place and you fell in line and marched straight to the pearly gates of steel heaven. Never looking back, never looking forward beyond the next day's shift. Later, after the war, I heard someone describe how the Nazis brainwashed the Hitler Youth, and I found it eerily similar to what happened to the boys in my town, blindly following their fathers straight to Mr. Rockefeller's front door.

Anyway, when the subject of barbed wire came up in school, which happened religiously once a term and mostly in shop class, lots of the guys tried to get some sleep during that lecture. It was a Bessemer School tradition to doze off when barbed wire was the topic. But none of us ever got too much snooze time.

Our shop teacher was Mr. Cantrell. He prided himself in being the scholar of all scholars on the subject of barbed wire. I remember him vividly because one day in class he was demonstrating a new electric circular saw and the board slipped and his hand slipped into the whirling blade. His pinky and ring fingers flew up against the wall, hurled by the blade. It was amazing. He was amazing. He calmly turned off the saw, walked over to pick up his fingers, wrapped his blood-spurting hand in a towel and as he walked out the door told us to go back to our seats. Two weeks later he was back in class, minus two fingers. I guess the doctors couldn't sew them back on.

Anyway his lectures would go something like this:

"Barbed wire dates back to 400 AD. Even in those times the process of pulling hot bloom iron through dies in a drawing plate producing short lengths of various sizes of smooth wire was known and practiced widely."

This was about the time, if we put our minds to it, we could drift off to sleep.

Skipping forward in time some fourteen centuries plus seventy years, Mr. Cantrell would continue:

"By 1860 good, quality smooth wire was readily available in all sizes and lengths. Stockmen used the smooth wire in fencing, but WAIT," he would shout intentionally, the noise yanking our slack necks up like rubber bands. "The wire was undependable. SOMETHING HAD TO BE DONE. THE LIVESTOCK WAS ESCAPING."

He would have this almost deranged look on his face and his three-fingered hand would pump the air as we blinked in the harsh light of the classroom.

"The answer came," he would continue in a calmer, more soothing tone, "when in 1868, inventor Michael Kelly perfected a practical wire with POINTS which gave birth to this wonderful device."

In his full-fingered hand he would hold up a sample for the class to see. I had seen miles of barbed wire made at the mill, as had my entire class, but that didn't matter to Mr. Cantrell. There it was again, in all its glory. There was no chance now of ever falling to sleep.

"BUT WAIT AGAIN!" his voice would pitch to a shriek. "It was not until Joseph F. Glidden of DeKalb, Illinois, attended a county fair where he observed a demonstration of a wooden rail with sharp nails protruding along its side, that the world began to change," he would triumphantly declare. "Mr. Glidden went home and sat down and fashioned barbs on an improvised coffee bean grinder, and placed them at intervals along smooth wire, and twisted another around the first to hold the barbs in a fixed position."

Catching his breath, he would conclude, "And yes, today, Mr. Glidden's placement of those barbs, his twisting motion and his fastening of the smooth wire to hold them intact, is fully automated with one of the finest machines every created by man. Aren't you children proud of your families for being a part of history forever being made?"

We were wide-awake now. It was all too much, really.

If I walked down to the end of my street and stood on my tiptoes, I could see Mr. Glidden's marvelous invention, spikes and all, snaking out in endless, threatening strings from the twister section at the mill. The guy on the roller line's job is to roll the wire into twelve-foot-high bales, big as the hay bales you can see lying in the fields outside of La Junta, sixty miles to the south and east of town.

Sometimes at night when I would work myself up thinking of the roller mill, and imagining myself walking each morning through those gates to begin my shift, every day for the rest of my miserable life, I would actually throw up. Often when I did puke, I thought that I might be a coward, or worse, queer, since my brother once told me that the two queers who had opened a flower shop on the west end of Fourth Street had refused to work at the mill. I picked up a corsage there once for a girl named Rosalina, my date to the Central High School prom, in my senior year, 1942. The prom was in May, just five-and-a-half months after President Roosevelt's speech to Congress declaring war, and two months before I first set eyes on Camp Claiborne on that muggy Louisiana night with the temperature hovering around ninety. Those two nice, queer florists were in business for 40 years, and retired to a grand estate in Boca Raton.

Chapter 6
That First Taste of Scotch and Scuffed Brown Shoes

Carlo marked his second year at the mill by tasting his first shot of scotch whiskey. He said it was so strong he nearly choked on the first swallow. He was with his buddies from the mill in Central Park on a warm evening in early spring when he took that first big chug. He said they didn't even notice his gasp and watery eyes from the sting in his throat. But he was able to control the stuff going down. Carlo was disciplined. That's the way he lived his life. He had not missed a day at the mill since he started. He still sauntered off each morning, and returned home each night to assume his role as head of household. But as he neared the end of his fourteenth year, a change was in the offering.

It first began when one Saturday evening in 1933. That night he was conspicuously absent from his position at the head of the table.

"*Dove e' Carlo?* Where's Carlo?" Sophia asked our mother. Angelina just shrugged her shoulders. I also wondered about my brother, with mild alarm.

"*Ice ghiaccio tale storia.* I think he's taking a bath," speculated Helena. I listened. Now I could hear the rare sound of my brother sloshing in the tub in the bathroom down the hall. Through the paper-thin walls, the sound was easy to identify, especially since our dining room was only a short ten paces from the bathroom door. I hadn't even heard Carlo heating the water on the stove.

One thing about Mr. Rockefeller's houses was the running water and indoor plumbing. Since so much water was needed to service the mill, it was easy for them to tap into the huge main water lines that ran into the mill to supply the cooling baths as well as other workstations. So when our house was built, along with most others in Bessemer, they hooked onto those lines to supply us as well. We were lucky. In most areas of town at that time, indoor plumbing wasn't even heard of.

After that, Carlo began to bathe more often, much to my delight, and no doubt that of the rest of the family. We began to notice that when Carlo's shifts ended on Mondays, Wednesdays and Saturdays, he begged off most boxing matches (unless he really disliked his bojon opponent) and came home to take a bath and change clothes before catching the bus at the corner of Goodnight Street and Fourth; headed for places unknown.

I was dying to know what was going on. He had told me a couple of Wednesdays before that on his lunch break earlier that day, he had finally been invited to join Tony's Cronies. Anthony Spinuzzi worked the coveted day shift on the roller lines along with Carlo and fifty other mill men. His special group who Carlo had told me about and we had dubbed his "Cronies" met each day at lunch. Tony was an older guy, probably in his early twenties. He was tall for a Sicilian, maybe as tall as six-feet-one or -two inches and weighed around two hundred pounds. Like Carlo, me and most of our cousins, the normal stature for fully-grown Sicilian men was about five-feet-six or seven and around one hundred fifty pounds. Tony's size and his big mouth commanded him attention, and from many, reluctant respect.

As Carlo explained it, Tony's lunch break meetings were events many working the day shift longed to attend, and Carlo's pride was profound when Tony invited him to join one such gathering that Wednesday at noon. The topic that day, and most every day to follow, was booze. But only after the group had thoroughly analyzed all the relevant body parts of the new secretary in the administration typing pool.

Even when I was as young as maybe twelve, I would hear stories that before the end of Prohibition there were at least three places in town where, if you were clever, and if you had connections, you could get inside and with twenty five cents, order a single shot of Canadian brown nectar. It was fairly good stuff, too, they said, not the clear, noxious, and occasionally poisonous brew you could get for two dollars a gallon from the toothless moonshiner lurking inside a well-hidden lean-to in the woods just outside Fruita.

This stuff was a light chestnut color, sweet and smooth and easygoing down. It was straight from Canada, terrific scotch whiskey, and it came down through Montana and Wyoming, sloshing around inside fifty-gallon oak barrels for fine aging and easy transport. Occasionally, if you really looked, you could detect the "Four Roses" label still legible on some of the barrels, despite efforts to rub out the lettering and obscure the distiller's origin.

"Four Roses" whiskey, promoted by its founder Uncle Joe, flowed west and south across the borders and into Colorado as freely and predictably as the Colorado River meanders south to Arizona and carves out the Grand Canyon. Uncle Joe named his label after his lovely Massachusetts bride, and it quickly became the standard bearer for the market.

41

You see, the Italians and Sicilians were not known for getting along very well with the Irish, particularly the Irish immigrants who crowded the slums of New York and Boston. But there were a few (a very few) Irishmen who moved out of the slums and figured out how to make peace with the Italians and Sicilians. In making peace, they also figured out how to make money. A lot of money.

The Irishman who became a master at both was Joe Kennedy, and Uncle Joe's booze and his "Four Roses" label made him immensely wealthy.

But the source of the booze, even with him being Irish and all, didn't matter as long as it made its way south to meet the everlasting demand. Carlo had his first sip of whiskey near the end of one of the most divisive periods in American history, and it took the repeal of the 18th Amendment to the U.S. Constitution to stop the bickering and bring back the booze bottle; this time, legal and pure. Prohibition was a law scoffed at and ridiculed from its inception, evidenced by the fact that even a young boy like me knew all there was to know about booze and how it found its way to the local taverns. And my somewhat street-wise sense was no exception. It was common knowledge in the neighborhood, and Carlo knew many of the details of the operation long before Tony's invitation came that day to join his lunchtime meeting. Carlo knew that there were a select few at the roller mill and at the cooling baths who drove the '32 Chryslers, who bathed regularly and who wore suits to places other than Mass.

It was all because of the booze, and just a little innocent bootlegging. No harm to anyone. Just fulfilling the thirsty need of those willing to pay the price. These few hoped and prayed Prohibition would never end. Uncle Joe was probably among them. But even when it did end late that year with the ratification of the 21st Amendment, bootleggers continued to illegally ship their product to the United States, allowing Tony and his cronies to keep buying those expensive suits and big, brand-new cars. They sure weren't doing it on steelworker's pay.

Prohibition was the law throughout my early grade school years, but that didn't matter. What mattered was that bootlegging flourished and helped make my town wealthier. I don't remember a whole lot about those days other than what I learned through Carlo and a few others. He told me how our town, and in fact the entire country, went from Prohibition to poverty almost overnight with the onset of the Great Depression. I remember the Depression more vividly because I was older and I do remember after booze became legal, it was easy to find out how Tony and his cronies continued to make good.

You see, Prohibition ended because it was a highly unpopular law, an unenforceable law, and when the Depression came, the country needed the tax money from booze to help pay its mounting bills, including the huge costs of funding President Roosevelt's New Deal. Income taxes collected by the federal government in the 1930s had declined steadily by as much as 15 percent less than what was budgeted, so "sin taxes," primarily including those on liquor, became popular new sources of revenue both for Uncle Sam and the States. After Roosevelt was elected in 1932, his supporters looked back at the revenue lost for the past fourteen years and moaned in agony. In 1929 alone, despite the best efforts of organized crime and a few adventurous moonshiners like the old man outside Fruita, the government had confiscated and destroyed nearly four-point-five million gallons of illegal booze. The Feds, we were told, once raided and smashed up the Fruita man's still, but he was back in business in less than three weeks. The lost revenue, fully taxed at the rates put into effect in 1935 with

43

federal and state liquor stamps, was well over two hundred million dollars. That amount would have paid for more than a few of Roosevelt's ambitious social programs.

But the veteran bootleggers weren't about to pay the taxes, so the flow of booze from Canada still came in the barrels, but bypassed the legal bottling plants where the taxes were paid and the tax stamps applied. The booze shipped in the barrels was still bottled in great quantities, but minus the tax stamps, and absent the taxes. Profits often grew beyond those during Prohibition Days, as the supply increased and the illegal distribution system broadened. At the center of it all were the veterans at the game, the nasty crooks of La Cosa Nostra.

Some of the cops in my town joined forces with the Mafia to become the most flagrant offenders of the fourteen-year ban on booze. And when Prohibition ended, they certainly didn't mind looking the other way when tax stamps were mysteriously missing from bottles appearing on the shelves of the local taverns. The cops enforced the law when it suited them and ignored it when it didn't. The law was their leverage, and occasionally they enforced it when a bojon cop was in a beef with a wop cop and the wop cop's cousin was the doorman at one of those taverns. So you had to be careful and somewhat discreet if you wanted that tasty, throat-stinging shot, and pay no tax on it.

However Tony's group, with Carlo about to be right smack in the middle of it, could relax just a little more than the rest of the town folks out on a Saturday night trying to quench their thirsts. Being in Tony's group meant you just might earn enough on the side to buy plenty of shots, and even maybe experience the gratification from one of those look-alikes from the magazines hidden in Carlo's shed.

Everyone knew about those special girls from Trinidad who passed around their pleasures and were every bit as fine as any of the models smiling and shimmering from the pages of Carlo's stash.

Chapter 7
Don't Spill a Drop

Carlo

Carlo's first assignment after becoming a Tony Crony came one Saturday while working an overtime shift. The order had gone out for the mill to step up production of new and sturdier rail tracks, critical to keeping pace with an expanding and modernizing national rail system. Overtime shifts meant six dollars a day in the pay envelope. When Tony told Carlo to meet his man Jake at Sixth Street and Beulah Avenue at seven that night, Carlo became a man with mission.

"Carlo, you're still a fucking little punk, but I think you have potential, and I think you can handle riding shotgun for Jake," Tony said. "Jake's a surly bastard, so don't cross him and don't talk back even if he calls your mother his punching bag. Just keep your mouth shut and do as he says. Watch his back and make sure no one spills a drop. If you don't, I'll do your mother myself," Tony warned.

Like a stupid little kid handed a lollipop, Carlo grinned back at him and nodded. Then he turned and shook his head, somehow knowing that Tony's words were meant for his protection, and the part about his mother was the tough guy routine for everyone else's benefit. Mothers and sisters were sacred in American Sicilian society, and all good men protected them, regardless of kinship or not. Angelina was as safe in her neighborhood as a nun in a walled convent.

Even though his gut churned inside for the rest of his shift and his hand shook in the murky water of the bath he took instead of sitting for dinner that night, Carlo knew things had changed for him, maybe for good. Maybe he was ready for it; he wasn't sure. At six-thirty he walked past his family sitting at the dinner table and out the door without a word, and at five to seven, he stepped off the bus at the corner where Jake was waiting to greet him, but not with a handshake. Jake was no more than a year or two older than Carlo, the same height but forty pounds heavier with a belly that swayed as he waddled. He growled at Carlo, "The car's over there and you're goddamn lucky you're on time."

Jake drove south, not uttering another sound. The sun still blazed over the mountain peaks to the west, temperature still in the high nineties and, of course, the wind still blowing. At times the dust settled so thick on the windshield, Jake had to use the hand-cranked wipers on the '31 Dodge four-door to wipe them clean. Carlo sat in silence, his shirt and brown pinstriped three-piece suit soaked with sweat. The bootlegging uniform was suit and tie, polished shoes and Fedora, regardless of the weather. Jake was in grey, and his suit was just as wet.

Carlo expected the silence, but it didn't make it any easier. Nervous did not describe what he was feeling, but neither did scared. Just anxious, and excited maybe, but sweating all the same. He didn't know it at the time but this was only Jake's third run. Carlo was sure envious how Jake seemed outwardly rigid, even stoic, during the drive. The only thing he noticed was the slight twitch in Jake's right cheek as his eyes stared straight ahead, locked on the winding road. The twitch made him look like he was trying to wink.

Maybe he's nervous after all, Carlo thought.

Tony had told Carlo to keep his mouth shut and only take orders but damn it, it was becoming very frustrating not knowing what those orders were, so he finally broke the silence.

"Jake, what am I supposed to do?" he asked, probably too meekly, and with a slight quiver in his voice.

"Kid, no one asked you to speak. No one is going to ask you to speak. You keep your shit eating mouth shut until I tell you otherwise. Understand?" Jake barked back, his eyes still riveted on the road. The ash from a half burned cigarette dangling from his lip dropped on his pant leg as the Dodge bumped over another rut in the road.

Jake brushed the ash from his leg and the cab was silent for the next hour.

This was supposed to be a simple run for simple people in a simple business. That's why Carlo supposed rookies were qualified to participate. If all went well, they were to load the fifty gallons of coveted liquid through a siphon hose from the disguised water tank in the back of the flatbed '36 Ford truck which Tony had told them to look for as they approached the exchange point. The Dodge had a fifty-gallon steel tank made to fit snugly beneath the back seat by a couple of real craftsmen on Tony's crew, and they were to deliver the haul to the back door of the White Goose Tavern, where they would be met by the owner, Mr. Maranzano. His place was at 10th and Elm, next door to the Elks Club.

Upon delivery, they were to be given five hundred dollars, of which they would give four hundred and seventy five to Tony. Jake would get fifteen and Carlo would get ten, a little less than two day's pay for four hour's work. And if they were really lucky, Maranzano would invite them in for a shot or two and the chance to watch one of the elderly patrons explore under the skirts of a girl who came up from Trinidad for two-day, eight-hour shifts. A buck fifty was the cost for each journey beneath the white clinging lace just above the thigh. The adventure could last no more than five minutes, and venturing inside the undergarments was prohibited at those rates. Going further, gaining passage behind one of the Tavern's two-second floor private room doors, would cost the old geezers ten dollars per visit. Mr. Romeo, from up North, was supplying a steady stream of fresh young talent for Maranzano's clients.

Sure, Carlo had heard about what went on inside the White Goose, but he didn't know how the night might unfold. He could only hope. He figured Jake knew, but he was sure keeping it to himself. Carlo watched the road along with Jake and speculated what was running through the mind of the punk behind the wheel.

No need to tell this little bastard anything. I know I can make this run alone. I don't need Tony's little shit heel sitting there looking stupid and thinking he's part of us. Besides, he gets my ten bucks. Fuck him. You have to earn your way in, and this kid has big dues yet to pay. Maybe Tony felt sorry for him because his old man's head nearly got knocked off, and his mother has seven kids to feed. But who cares, everyone should play by the same rules. Anyway, I'll get this over with, and maybe I'll get to touch under that Mexican's skirt tonight; that one from Trinidad with the long black hair and the enormous tits.

Carlo suppressed a smile.

As the Dodge bounced along, his attention alternately shifted from the heat, the choking dust from the road and the .38 Special lying beside Jake on the threadbare

49

upholstery. Carlo had actually expected to see a gun, but as they drove on, he chose to try and forget it was there.

Jake had turned off the two-lane black top a mile or two before onto a wide dirt road and was whizzing past the barren, rocky landscape, sprinkled by a few green patches of alfalfa and cornfields. As they rounded a corner, the barrel of the revolver caught the rays of the setting sun shining just right through the Dodge's smeared windshield. Carlo's eyes blinked at the flash just as they did the night before when he gazed upon the town's newest and brightest neon sign announcing the grand opening of the Village Five & Dime, which was just two blocks from the White Goose Tavern. The sign seemed to light up the whole block. Carlo looked away from the shocking glare from the gun as his gut once again twisted in spasm. He fought to control the flicker of fear and once more tried to make conversation.

"Look Jake, I know you don't like me, and I know you don't want me here, but I will back you up. Just tell me how this goes down," he pleaded.

Jake turned to him and seemed to soften his scowl momentarily before he caught himself. "Watch the side roads for cops, bojons or other wops, don't matter. That's all I want you to do," he said, looking away.

Just then Jake cranked the wheel hard and turned straight onto what looked like a cattle path winding its way into a freshly cut hay field. The sun blinded both of them for an instant as Jake slowed the four-door and the rutted path bounced them forward. The Dodge soon began to climb a hill with a crest just high enough so anyone driving on the main road could not see beyond its peak. As they came over to the other side, Carlo stifled a gasp.

There in the clearing stood their welcoming party, three of them, each with a long double-barrel 20-gauge shotgun pointed straight at them as they approached the flatbed Ford.

Jake hit the brakes and skidded to a stop, sending a great cloud of dust billowing from beneath the tires.

"Out of the car, you little bastard, you're thirty minutes late," one of them yelled over the clattering engine of the Dodge. All three were dressed in uniform, suit coats still intact, and all three were stained in sweat in equal measure to Jake and Carlo. Apparently they'd been waiting for a little while, but Jake looked at his watch to confirm they were on time.

Jake killed the engine and grabbed the door handle to exit. Carlo quickly followed, nearly tripping on the floorboard as he scrambled out of the front passenger seat.

"Evenin' boys; how was the drive down?" asked another member of the greeting party. This one seemed like the leader of the group. He was bigger, and stood a step in front of the others. Carlo could see a gap between his two front teeth wide enough to slip your little finger between. With each word, the big one whistled through the gap. "Jake. Looks like you brought along your bodyguard. He looks like a real tough customer. Jake, you don't need no protection from us as long as you're a good boy and you brought the money. But tell the kid next time to buy a suit that fits. I can't stand sloppy clothes; makes him look like a midget pimp." The third one laughed.

Jake stiffened, threw his head back with some measure of defiance and tried to boldly declare, "I got the money, and the stuff better be good. Last time, Tony's customers said it tasted like somebody pissed in the bottom of the barrel."

"Kid, you tell that guinea cocksucker Spinuzzi he can kiss my ass; there ain't nothin' better than our stuff, and if he's got any further beef he can take it up with Mr. Carlino," hissed the one in charge.

Jake glared back at them for an instant before a slight grin began to turn up the corners of his mouth. He stepped forward and extended his hand to the big one, and they embraced and swapped kisses on each cheek. Then he shook hands and embraced the others. The shotguns were placed to rest against a nearby tree trunk. Carlo stood there, half-conscience that his mouth was hanging agape. Jake turned to him and announced, "This punk here is Carlo; works with Tony at the mill. I'm breaking him in tonight. He's here to hold my cock. He won't say a word. He'll just stand there with his thumb up his ass, holdin' my cock, because that's all he good for. Right, Carlo?"

All four of them hee-hawed like rabid hyenas as Carlo kicked the dirt with his new, and admittedly two-sizes-too-big, brown pointed-toe wingtips.

Jake and the welcoming party broke into a jabbering, rapid-fire Sicilian, finger-in-the-chest exchange that concluded with Jake ordering Carlo to move the sedan up along side the Ford. Carlo silently breathed a quick Hail Mary, thanking Her that he knew how to drive, and with a smooth easing on the clutch, he moved the old sedan into position. Jake opened the rear door and lifted the back seat to expose the shiny steel tank. Soon the siphon hose was in place, and the gurgling sound of the ninety-five proof brown nectar flowing rapidly from one tank to the other was like a fine symphony to Carlo's ears. The smell stung his nostrils at first, but soon brought a sweet odor to the air almost as intoxicating as Angelina's red tomatoes sautéing in olive oil, ready for the scallions. The whole process took no more than twenty minutes. Jake pulled seven fifty-dollar bills from his inside vest pocket and placed them in the hand of the big one, who smiled broadly, exposing his cavernous gap.

"Grothee," he spat.

Again, the four embraced, kissed each other on both cheeks, and soon the Ford flatbed was bouncing along the cow path in the opposite direction of the sedan. The sky was nearly dark by then as the sun passed behind the southern branch of the great Rockies. Jake eased the grimy, dusty Dodge back out onto the main road and steered north for maybe a minute at the most. Then he suddenly slammed on the brakes, swung open the driver's side door and threw up in the road.

Carlo watched the wrenching with amazement, and some amusement. But he didn't say anything, just waited for Jake to finish and get back behind the wheel. When he did, Jake looked very pale, and Carlo could see he was trying to regain his composure as he ground the gears and pushed the gas pedal to the floor. The sedan was loaded with at least five hundred pounds of liquid cargo, and the engine coughed and sputtered to gain speed under the load.

For most of the way back to town Carlo grappled with the scene he had just witnessed on the cow path, and as both of them stared ahead in silence, he tried hard to piece it all together. He thought he had just observed Jake and the three suppliers demonstrate an open sense of trust, respect, and above all, common business interest.

But if all of these guys were friends, what made Jake just puke his guts out?

Damn, that's strange, Carlo thought. Was Jake actually petrified like Carlo had been throughout the night? Or maybe it was just a bad case of bad marinara sauce?

The thoughts rolled through Carlo's brain for a few more minutes before he shoved them away and began concentrating on the ten bucks that awaited him at the end of the evening. He had the unsettled feeling that something wasn't quite right with these guys and he wondered, just who Mr. Carlino was.

The ride back to town took longer than the ride out with the load under the backseat limiting the Dodge's speed to about 45 miles an hour. They saw no bojons, unfriendly wops or cops along the route, and pulled into the alley behind the White Goose Tavern at eleven o'clock.

Jake finally spoke. "Get out and watch both ends of the alley. If anyone comes, you stall them any way you can. Don't let anyone near the car. Understand?"

Carlo did as told, and found each street perpendicular to the alley empty. He turned to watch Jake knock at the back door. Unaware of Carlo's attention, Jake stood at the threshold. An eye jutted from the peephole and a gruff voice sounded   from   within. Jake announced, "We're here, Mr. Maranzano."

Carlo could hear the unintended waver in his voice. Maranzano, his huge apron swaddled belly encrusted with streaks of dried red sauce, emerged. "Make this quick, you little bastard." The proprietor opened the door wider to allow his helpers to exit toward the car. His docking crew consisted of three burly, shirtless, overall clad gentlemen who kept their heads down and concentrated intently on the payload. Carlo thought all three looked familiar, having perhaps spotted them at one time or another on the roller lines or near the blast furnace.

At his post at the alley entrance Carlo watched for the next few minutes as Maranzano's crew emptied the rear tank. They used a device fashioned with a valve mechanism and flexible hose that created a strong, uninterrupted vacuum in the tank and a steady stream of siphoned whiskey into one-gallon glass jars. As soon as each jar was filled, it was carefully whisked inside by Maranzano's men, who then vanished down the cellar stairs.

With the tank empty and the glass jars presumably safely stored in the cellar down below, Jake turned to Maranzano with his hand out. A slight smile crept on the proprietor's thick lips, and without further prompting; he counted out ten fifty-dollar bills. Within the last four hours, Carlo had seen more money in one spot than he had seen in his entire lifetime. Jake stuck the bills in his inside suit vest pocket, and then boldly asked Maranzano if he and Carlo could come inside. The tavern owner looked both of them up and down and replied with a chuckle, "Not tonight boys. Time to go home to your mothers." Jake started to object, but before he could launch his protest, their customer had stepped back inside the rear door and slammed it shut. Jake muttered, "Fucker, mother fucker," and turned and motioned for Carlo to get in the car. They again drove in silence for the six blocks to Carlo's bus stop, with Carlo wondering wildly if he was to see his split before the night was over.

Jake came to a stop just as the final bus of the night was arriving to collect the last small batch of lingering passengers for the trip across town. He turned to Carlo and said, "Don't worry kid, Tony will make the cut Monday at work. By the way, you did good."

As he turned to climb onto the bus, Carlo's disappointment waned and was replaced by a swelling sense of achievement. He'd done good, and tomorrow everyone would know it. He'd wait for the money. Jake's comment was reward enough for tonight.

Chapter 8
Let the Weather Break Before You Go

I knew my brother had arrived home late that night because when he got into bed he thrashed around and kept me awake. I may have slept about three hours, and I know that's all he slept too. We both rose wearily with the regular six o'clock alarm, and as usual, I was downstairs before him, always the quicker one when it came to getting ready for breakfast. However the next morning, he passed through the kitchen without breakfast after kissing our mother goodbye, and as he moved toward the back door, he patted me on the head. I was startled and thought for a moment the pat would be followed by a swat, but instead, Carlo called over his shoulder as he stepped outside, "Have a good day, my brother."

As Carlo would soon reveal, his short-lived stint as a Tony Crony was filled with alternating moments of big man puffery – strutting around with his chest stuck out, his hat cocked to one side with money jingling in his pocket and a swagger of self-confidence – followed by times of despair, paranoia, and downright humiliation having caught the blunt and brutal rebuke from those he thought respected his presence. Mules are beasts of burden, fed well and pampered one minute then often brutalized with unbearable loads the next. That's all he was, a mule, but he didn't know it at the time. So the day after Carlo's first night on the job, he entered a new, un-chartered world through which he had no clue how to navigate. All he could do was ride the swirling waves.

My curiosity about his newfound manner was gnawing at me like a hound dog with a soup bone. Every time we were alone, I would nag him about his late-night ventures. He would clam up and tell me to shut up and mind my own business. When he finally came clean with the details it became all too clear why his emotions at the time were very similar to the wild ride we took on the rickety old roller coaster that was the featured attraction at the carnival that came through town each August. He eventually described his anxious saga in vivid detail as if he was talking about a stranger, detached, foreign without identity. He'd go on about the events as if looking through a pair of binoculars turned backwards.

Our mother had enjoyed Carlo's presence for supper every night for the past month, but when I saw him late that afternoon filling the bathtub with hot water boiling on the stove, I knew there would be an empty seat at her dinner table.

I was in our room reading when Angelina discovered the oversized brown pinstriped suit tucked behind Carlo's work clothes in our bedroom closet. She did not smother her gasp or mask her horrified expression at the sight, and I heard her utter the word "Mafia."

After the day my mother found the suit, I couldn't stop thinking about what was going on with Carlo, and what my mother knew that I didn't.

So off to the library I went. It had to be in a book somewhere I rationalized.

The Bessemer Library (why name it anything else?) was a small blonde brick building near our school. My task was to find something to give me a better idea of the dark world from which my mother had escaped, but the library had no books on the Mafia; I couldn't even find the word referenced anywhere. So I asked Miss Murphy, who all of us kids who had any notion of the meaning of books, loved with a blind passion for the infectious hunger for knowledge she shed each time a question was thrown her way. Although she wore round-rimmed spectacles, had grey, mousy hair always tied neatly in a bun and a sweet smile that made you feel like you were cuddling up with your mother to read a book around a roaring fireplace on a cold winter night, Miss Murphy knew about the Mafia. Darn right she did. It's funny too, she wasn't Italian or Sicilian, yet she proved to be a walking encyclopedia on the topic and I got everything out of her I could. Miss Murphy was Irish and her family was from Hartford Connecticut. She'd grown up in the rough part of town where the Irish mob, she said, controlled the rackets. See, she even taught me the lingo, real quick. Anyway, she was taught to hate the Italians and to loathe their brand of the Mafia. She went to college, she told me, and in college she studied all she could on the subject, and in my opinion, became an expert. I must have driven her to drink (she occasionally had that sour stench to her breath) with all my questions, so finally she told me I could meet her on Tuesdays and Thursdays after five o'clock when her day ended and the part-time staff came on to finish the day. She would take me to a small desk in the rear near the Natural History section and she would talk away. I was beyond fascinated.

The way she told it, the Mafia goes all the way back to Roman society, during the chaos and strife surrounding the assassination of Julius Caesar, and the temporary rise to power of his nemesis, Mark Antony. She said that in the absence of a centralized government at that time, as Antony chased Cleopatra around Egypt, his loyalists remained in Rome and formed "protection" rings, established gambling parlors, ran whore houses, and generally strong-armed the masses into submission.

With the Roman legions divided in their loyalty, their allegiance swinging wildly from Antony, to Cicero, to Claudius or others, this power void was filled by Mark Antony's band of gangsters, who seized control through intimidation and murder. A centuries-long tradition of corruption and murder was born, and nowhere in the world did this horrific system find more fertile ground than in societies like modern-day Italy and Sicily where governments change as often as one changes the sheets on their beds and power vacuums are created. So my ancestors, according to Miss Murphy, practiced their craft with the greatest of skill and permanently infected their countries with their disease. Now, that virus has spread to America, carried on board the ships from Palermo, Rome, and Naples to the fertile harbors and teeming tenements of Manhattan and the Back Bay of Boston. And now with the movement of our people west in search of better lives, lives free of this hideous harness, they sense the creeping infestation once again. God, Miss Murphy could carry on about this. I remember how she seemed almost poetic as she described her feelings and laid before me the knowledge she had long ago stowed away. I was entranced with it all. She didn't just pound away at the Italians or Sicilians as the sole founders of corruption however. She also was quick with her stories of the Irish mob, those from Dublin, or Belfast, many of whom were as crooked, in her opinion, as any of those from the Eastern Mediterranean.

She said that crime syndicates are part of every society, in every nation, and most of those who become members of crime families, regardless of their heritage, come from a long two-thousand-year tradition of criminality having faithfully studied their lessons from the ancient criminal textbooks written by the Roman thugs living at the time of Christ.

Undoubtedly from Roman times to today, parents have pleaded with their children to reject the allure of joining the mob, and the irreversible journey one takes when membership is confirmed. They still speak in hushed tones about the murders, and how each quickly becomes justified for the good of all. One's livelihood and the advancement in society often depend on that membership and the loyalty that must prevail, Miss Murphy told me sternly.

So it was easy to conclude from her private lectures that neither my mother's family nor Nick's was immune to La Cosa Nostra's influence in Palermo, and some members of both families probably took part; some likely in prominent positions. Miss Murphy wanted me aware that the fingers of the Black Hand spread into every household and touched every life in Sicily during that time.

Angelina and Nick and generations before them had coexisted with those in Palermo who professed blind loyalty to these menacing knots of sinister scum. The cruel sheer power that La Cosa Nostraheld over Angelina's people stretched from border to border and enveloped the entire population. She would tell us as a child, she remembered the warnings and stern instructions uttered to her to help her chances of survival in that threatening environment which dominated her daily life. It must have been a hell of a way to grow up.

But that was life when you lived in the clutches of a society infiltrated by the Mafia. It was then I realized that Carlo's suit symbolized a certain kind of evil for Angelina. Now, it seemed she'd be challenged to confront those kinds of people again, but this time she was all alone, without

Nick. And this time it involved her son. Miss Murphy confirmed what I had suspected that Angelina must have known upon arrival in America – affirmed dramatically during her time with Nick in the Manhattan slum awaiting fare out West – that Omerta ruled in her new homeland as well.

I tried to imagine the horror for Nick and Angelina when they discovered that this sacred silence, and the strict rule of saying "nothin' to nobody," was as prevalent in the New York slums of Little Italy as they were in the ghettos of Palermo.

"Mafia," Miss Murphy cautioned, was a word never used, there or here, even though its history is crudely stitched into the fabric of Sicilian culture. Mafia means "refuge" and is affixed in an ancient Arabic dialect.

It's no secret, she said, that a secret society was reborn in earnest in Sicily during my great-great grandfather's early life in the mid 1700s by patriots who sought refuge from Arab and Norman invaders in the mountains of the island. Men armed with primitive weapons fought off the invaders and offered protection for their neighbors, all for a price. Again, they filled a power vacuum just like their Roman ancestors did. The Black Hand became the symbol for those who offered that protection. Those who didn't pay or who violated Omerta could expect kidnappings, bombings and murder. Few didn't pay, and even fewer spoke out in protest.

Poor Angelina. I knew my mother's strong will, and how she had probably hoped and prayed with all her might that when she boarded the ship for the West, that part of her life would wither and die under the blazing Colorado sun.

Now I understood the horror that struck her face as she stared at Carlo's suit hanging behind his overalls. I'm sure her mind was racing back to the time with her husband in New York and their realization that they had failed to rid themselves of the scourge of the mob, and their only hope by moving West to bring them the peace they richly deserved had vanished.

~

Carlo

After he left the house that morning, Carlo worked hard as usual until the lunch break whistle. He stepped off the line and quickly made his way over to where Tony and the boys had gathered. Tony noticed him approaching and moved away from the group. He extended his hand, which Carlo took, and immediately Carlo felt the bill in his palm. He hoped it was a ten.

"Jake tells me you were less of a pain in the ass than he thought you'd be. That's good. I'll have something else for you soon, but go eat your lunch somewhere else. We got some business to take care of here," the oversized Sicilian had declared before turning and strolling back to the group.

Carlo stood there dumbstruck, but soon gathered his composure and found a seat by himself on a nearby bench.

Several days passed without even an acknowledgement from Tony, Jake or anyone else in the group. Carlo hadn't spent a dime of the ten-spot he'd earned, keeping it in a tobacco chew tin embedded in a coil spring under his bed. Then on a day in early September, when a freak early fall snowstorm had struck and the white stuff was quickly piling up in two-foot drifts and the temperature outside had fallen to twenty five degrees, Tony approached the bench where Carlo was eating alone and plunked down beside him.

"As soon as the weather breaks and the roads are cleared you are to meet Jake, same time, same place, for another run. I will let you know when," Tony said, "and come join us for lunch."

Three days later, when the temperature was back into the low sixties, the snow almost gone, and the roads a red-brown quagmire, Tony gave Carlo a nod when passing him along the line, and uttered a single word,

"Tonight."

Chapter 9
Old Miss Murphy and Crates
Filled with Cantaloupe

It took nearly one hundred and fifty years after my great-great grandfather's time for the first man to rule as a true Mafia "Godfather." Miss Murphy said his name was Rafael Palizzolo, and he was a shrewd, quick-witted, relentless man without conscience. Palizzolo quickly became a national symbol of defiance and strength, and turned intimidation into votes, becoming the first, and to anyone's knowledge, the last, Mafia chieftain to hold public office. He and his hand-selected Prime Minister Don Crispi took control of the Sicilian government, and after exiling the rebels, infected their corrupt principles into the muscle, bone and fiber of their constituents.

When Nick and Angelina disembarked at Ellis Island, a man by the name of Don Vito, (Vito Cascio Ferro was his christened name), had already established his grip on New York crime operations. Vito was the acknowledged Capo de Tutti Capi of the Sicilian Mafia in the U.S.

When the century turned, his band of criminals fled Sicily and found refuge in New Orleans and New York. Soon however, they discovered the Manhattan Isle offered much more fertile ground for their prostitution rings, extortion rackets, protection schemes and gambling operations. More money was to be made in the Big Apple than at the mouth of the Mississippi, and power was soon shifted out of the corridors of the French Quarter and onto the streets of Little Italy.

Don Vito was old and tired by the time Nick and Angelina temporarily settled in their one room flat in New York City. The Mafia chief had all but relinquished his self-proclaimed throne to younger, more ambitious types who roamed the streets and spread their vice. The sidewalks where Nick looked for day jobs were filled with many of these young thugs who, during Prohibition, became household names, idolized by a yellow press and romanticized by a public hungry for vicarious adventure.

One of those was who found short-lived fame and fortune was Giosue "Don Gesuele," also known as "The King" Gallucci. Carlo told me later that Nick passed him in the street once. Each day, clad in his signature white suit, bowtie, handlebar moustache and red boutonnière, The King would swagger down the sidewalks with a hooker on each arm. Sometimes he would offer his girls to the people of his city, as he'd pass them by. But, Carlo said, our father wasn't offered the services of Gallucci's working girls the day they rubbed shoulders in the afternoon crowd. I guess The King could tell by my father's attire that too few coins jingled in his pockets. The price was only a buck-twenty-five, yet The King and Nick passed without speaking. Gallucci was an old man, forty-four at the time. This would be the last year he breathed. He would die of bullet wounds that spilled his blood and ruined one of his five hundred dollar suits.

According to Miss Murphy, the story goes that Gallucci, an Italian whose rackets were mainly confined to Harlem and who was a rival to the Sicilian Black Hand, thought he answered only to himself. Like many who followed, he saw himself as a modern day Julius Caesar, invincible, above reproach. The King met his fate just six months after Nick and Angelina left for the West. He and his son were gunned down while enjoying an afternoon espresso at their coffeehouse on East 109th Street. There were no eyewitnesses. The Morello family succeeded The King and re-established the Sicilian dominance that would rule New York's neighborhoods for seven years. Nicholas Morello was actually the first to emerge as the family head, or Boss. He fought for control with Neapolitan, Irish and Jewish gangs, and was winning when he was ambushed along with his bodyguard and died of too many gunshot wounds to count. Their remains lay outside a Navy Street café covered in newspapers and trash for nearly a month until the hot sun of the late September summer finally attracted too many stray cats.

Even after the slaying, power remained with the Morello family, concentrated in the hands of Sicilian interests, when Guiseppe "Joe the Boss" Messeria took the helm to shepherd operations. Nine years later, he too paid the price when he trusted one corrupt Sicilian too many. While dining on Coney Island with the up-and-coming Sicilian prostitution ringleader Salvatore Charlie "Lucky" Luciano, Joe took two in the throat and one between the eyes. Word around town was that the assassination was a collaboration between Lucky and the young, enterprising Vito Genovese.

Vito and Lucky still had work to do and dues to pay before rising to the top. Later, FBI records (which Miss Murphy said she would scour through each time they were made public) would show that Joe's successor, Guiseppe "Peter the Clutch Hand" Morello held sway only temporarily. Less than a year after taking office, he met his maker at the hands of an accomplished young Capo with a garrote that nearly took his head off.

You see, those in the Mafia learn from experience that often one has to kill those within close quarters at either a sign of weakness or the need to establish new leadership at the top. Selective, controlled murder was the acceptable way to remove the one on the throne of power. Homicide is the method of choice, dating all the way back to the days in ancient Rome. Killing has always been considered by mob as a peaceful, democratic changing of the guard.

After five successive assassinations of New York crime bosses, a new generation of criminals operating under the crest of the Genovese family gained power. Absolute control stayed put in New York, although branches were springing up in other major cities like Newark, Chicago and Detroit.

Lucky Luciano didn't take long to pay his dues and rise to the top. He was born and bred for his job as mob boss. He took over the New York prostitution rings in the early twenties. During that time, Lucky was still collecting two hundred dollars a day from his whores, at two dollars a session, on average. But the Boss was struggling to make ends meet with inflation a problem, even for him and his hookers. Labor costs had been hurting Lucky's bottom line. So, he had no choice but to impose an increase for services over the traditional "two bucks a fuck" pricing scheme. Those fee increases (and keeping his ladies in line) earned Lucky a solid reputation among the criminal elite, and helped pave his way up the line of succession.

Scrupulous use of time, money and human flesh launched Lucky's career, but it was murder that put him at the top of the heap. Bosses don't become bosses if they hesitate pulling the trigger. Murder was the true test of one's commitment to the cause, and Lucky was a master at mayhem. He survived an ice pick attack in 1929, all the while steadily climbing the criminal corporate ladder. In 1931, he gained control of the Genovese family, the one I told you about before, with Vito waiting in the wings, still wet behind the ears, to become the largest, wealthiest, and most dominate of the New York criminal empires.

Lucky Luciano, who had on-hand remnants of Murder Incorporated, his private band of assassins made famous for many high-profile mob hits, quickly became the epitome of a crime boss. Tall, handsome, and ruthless, he centralized power, consolidated the operational branches and planned for a bright and prosperous future. Lucky, soon after taking office, sensed the end of Prohibition, so with bootlegging still the number one enterprise, the Boss stepped up the shipments from Canada, garnering, they say, nearly fifty million dollars in two short years prior to the law's repeal in December 1933. This windfall helped bankroll his expansion plans in the West.

Among many other things, Lucky also was particularly adept at criminal franchising, which is what brought him to my town. Lucky was constantly on the lookout to either establish or improve branch operations in cities where there existed a soft, fat, hungry underbelly seeking vice and corruption served up by the plateful. A large, vulnerable Sicilian and Italian working class added to the appeal of my town. Language and cultural integration were easy to achieve. The crooks fit in well with the general population, making them harder to detect and root out.

So it was that my town grew to become Lucky's largest and most important western branch. Even after Lucky arrived and reorganized organized crime in Pueblo, steel still dominated the economic and social landscape, but after the mob moved in, in force under Lucky and his handpicked minions, my town soon realized it had another major business enterprise. It was not long before the whole town found itself caught in the clutch of the Mafia. Even kids like me always knew there was some mysterious influence out there beyond that of our parents and teachers. Something that made those who guided and protected us weary, less than self-assured, not ever completely confident they could control the direction we would take.

Steel had made my town famous and legitimate. The mob, with Lucky Luciano pulling the strings from New York, would soon make it infamous and illegitimate. I learned from Miss Murphy that by no means had Pueblo been a haven for the pure and unspoiled before Lucky took charge. A man named Pete Carlino and his brother Sam had been in charge of a madcap band of malcontent mobsters in Pueblo for about eight years before Lucky flexed his muscles. As the story goes, the brothers arrived on the noon train at Union Depot one blistering hot, miserable day in July; two twenty-something, fat, balding refugees from Messina.

At the time of the Carlino brothers' arrival, command still rested with the New York Morello family under a loose knit network of crooks scattered across the country. In our part of the world, the Carlinos were assigned to look after Pueblo by a cadre of bums based in Denver. Most of their duties were simple. Run the easy rackets; don't make waves, send the big money up north to Denver, and oh, by the way, help wrestle control away from the Irish dominated Klu Klux Klan.

The Klan was prominent in parts of Colorado, and it was widely and openly supported by a number of social, political and Anglo ethnic groups. With the help of Denver's Irish cops, who provided the muscle behind their rackets, the Klan had all but run the Sicilians and Italians out of

Denver, and they were moving south to grab the meager spoils in my town as well.

Gambling, prostitution and bootlegging were fruitful endeavors, and to some it was unacceptable that enterprising Sicilians were not in control. The Klan and the Mafia were not on friendly terms. They hated the sight of each other. The Klan ruled for racial and business reasons; the mob was all about business. So, when the Carlino brothers arrived, they needed to tip the balance of power back in favor of their own kind. To the utter amazement of everyone who was paying attention at the time, the Carlinos proved their worth and then some.

Through a series of coordinated attacks, Pete and Sam soon killed so many of the white hooded scoundrels that the Klan gave up their exploits in the southern part of the state and returned to the safety and security of Colorado's capital city. The New York families, especially the Morellos, professed gratitude and devotion to the brothers for their help in eliminating the white racist scourge. As a result the Carlinos were firmly re-implanted as the criminal caretakers of my nice, little out-of-the-way town in southern Colorado, about which few knew and fewer cared.

Yes, my town was back on the Mafia's map, even though for now, it was only a dot on that map. But it didn't stay that size for long.

After the carnage, the Carlinos took up shop in a second-hand clothing store on Union Avenue. Pete worked in the front; Sam stayed in the back counting money and moving goods and services. Later it became apparent that their master strategy was to use my town as an obscure, corrupt base of operations to coordinate, under their management – not New York's – all the bootlegging, whoring, gambling, protection and extortion that our region of the country had to offer.

And Pueblo was a perfect spot for that kind of strategy. It had all of the necessary components: isolation, but decent roads to move inanimate and human cargo north and south to Denver and Phoenix, and from there, points west to California and selected stops in between. Heading east, the vast open plains could swallow you up, if need be. To the west, remote mountain passes were natural safe houses. The Carlinos had also taken advantage of our susceptible and corruptible police force and local government. Once the Klan was gone and the select Sicilians were back in charge, my town became wide-open territory for them to operate.

My town was not chosen by mere chance as the western crime capital, but it was to become a hub for the experimentation and exportation of many sophisticated criminal enterprises. It didn't take a genius to realize that big money flowed through my town from numerous sources. The very existence of the steel mill meant an almost guaranteed stream of millions of dollars, keeping steel workers' pockets reasonably full, local businesses flourishing, and the cops and politicians stocked with plenty of cash, either in return for their ignorance or their participation in all sorts of illegal activity. It was up to them if they reaped what was there for the taking. All they had to do was look the other way and hold out their hands. There was no other place like my town out West. It was special, I guess.

By the time Lucky took charge of my town, Pueblo was a recognized oasis of prosperity in a nation diving headlong into the shallow bottom of the Depression. The onslaught of the Depression left no town unscathed, yet my town was economically insulated, to a degree, and geographically isolated, making it a highly attractive, easily vulnerable enclave.

Soon after President Roosevelt took to the podium to calm the nation against its own fears, Pueblo gained recognition as the wealthiest of any city between St. Louis and Los Angeles. Eight years of peace and tranquility had replaced the deadly squabbles among Colorado's organized criminals. Pete and Sam had done their jobs well. They had become rich and content amidst the tranquility.

When things started going bad for the Carlinos, Pete's hand-me-down shop was turning a nice profit selling ladies hats, some still stained with sweat on the inside rims, for fifty cents. He took a twenty percent mark-up on consignment, too. He had many lovely customers. They all paid cash.

The backroom of their shop was furnished with counting tables fully staffed with two eight-hour shifts. Twenty thousand in small bills were shipped back East each month on trucks in crates filled with cantaloupe, watermelons, and lettuce, all packed in ice. The money came mostly from bootlegging, and a little gambling. Harmless endeavors, really, and no one got hurt.

Not long after they moved to town, the Carlinos had decided they didn't like the protection rackets, or the whores, or the new business of narcotics peddling. Too messy. Not their style. And they were confident their weekly cash shipments back East – courtesy of the numbers racket, loan sharking, and a little bootlegging – would keep the boys, even the new boys in charge, happy and off their backs. To a greater extent, they cherished their positions in society. Pete was president of the Knights of Columbus. They were model citizens. Pete and Sam were immune. No one could touch them. They slept well each night.

But when Lucky took charge, the bosses in New York noticed that the Carlino brothers were raking in too much off the top. As soon as Lucky and the Genovese family became undisputed kingpins, Pete and Sam could no longer escape scrutiny. Lucky became dissatisfied with the brothers and what he saw going on out West. Lucky wanted a western crime capital, not a remote outpost producing a measly twenty thousand a month.

As the Depression set in, Lucky scanned the horizon of his adopted country and, like most enterprising business executives; he was challenged to counteract the effects of a crumbling national economy. He was in charge, and needed to create a business plan for the mob's survival and long-term prosperity, and needed the best people and the best places on the map to carry out his plan. He needed young, vigorous, loyal lieutenants, all functioning in tandem in strategic locations to assure each enterprise prospered, even as the economy stagnated in the throes of America's worst economic crisis ever.

Lucky's attention was quickly riveted on my town. He recognized its potential, and was not pleased that this dynamite little community, sitting serenely along the spine of the Rockies, was now under the control of lazy, second-tier, tired, old, worn-out gangsters. Pete Carlino and his brother were not Lucky's kind of mobsters, which made them very unlucky.

The possibilities Lucky envisioned for my town were great. In his mind, under proper leadership, Pueblo could become a bustling center for the second biggest business for fifteen hundred miles in any direction. Lucky was an astute businessman. He was realistic in thinking that his plans for the town might be too ambitious to overtake the profit margins of the steel mill. But this is America – anything was possible.

It didn't take Lucky long to carry out his plan and leave his lasting imprint. Two months after his blood oath inaugural as undisputed Capo de Capo, Pete's riddled body was found in a ditch along a road outside Canon City, west of Pueblo. The very next day, Sam's headless body was found floating in the Bessemer Ditch. Sam's head was spotted that night atop a lamppost only a block from their clothing stand.

Some in my town thought the murders were the Klan's way of retaliating for their ousting. Most knew better. The Carlinos' store burned down the night after the grisly discoveries, and an insurance claim was filed the day after that. Word on the street was that the insurance company paid off the following month with a check for twelve hundred dollars. The money went to Pete's widow. Each month thereafter, she received an anonymous cash payment of one hundred dollars delivered to her post office box on South Main Street. She and her five fatherless children lived well off that money. Two went to college. Sam's only family was Pete. Lucky's conscious and his record remained unscathed. His minions had done well. The double homicide investigation was over in a week. No eyewitnesses; no suspects. By the time the bodies were found, the contract executioners were already on the train back to Chicago.

Last I heard, the Carlino cases remain unsolved.

What I didn't know was that the same day Sam's head came down from the lamppost, Angelina's neighborhood gathered in her living room, keenly aware of what had taken place. Up until then things had been calm. Under the Carlinos, there hadn't been a murder in town for two years, and all in the neighborhood had been content. The hand-me-down shop had become an integral part of the neighborhood's relatively comfortable life. No one got hurt by the Carlinos or their businesses activities, and things were run clean, nice and tidy.

But all that had changed.

At morning Mass at Sacred Heart Cathedral, Angelina said a special Hail Mary thanking her Blessed Mother that Nick had been spared witnessing the horror of Lucky Luciano's arrival, and the first of his many brutal acts.

Chapter 10
What's Under Her Apron?

My mother coped with bad events in her life by cooking. She shielded her emotions and expelled her grief, anger, frustration, and fear and yes, sometimes joys, by concocting the finest, most delectable southern Mediterranean dishes imaginable. Her reputation became renowned not long after she and Nick moved into town. Without question, if there had been organized cooking contests in my town, she would have carried off the prize, uninterrupted, for several decades. She would definitely be the undisputed champion.

It was rare that a Sicilian, known for their red sauces, could create a masterpiece white cream sauce crafted to perfection for dripping over fettuccini. Generally white sauces are the strict fare of the Neapolitans and their cousins in Northern Italy. The red sauces were usually confined to the skillful chefs to the south, especially from Angelina's homeland island. Angelina, with mouthwatering wisdom acquired from her grandmother, bridged this culinary gap with proficiency both northerners and southerners found irresistible and incomparable. My great-grandmother was a rare product of a mixed marriage of a Neapolitan father and Sicilian mother seldom seen in those times, or even now.

Few ever questioned Angelina in the kitchen, and most had the utmost respect for her prowess as she prepped and stirred over the low flame of her blackened, well worn, wood-fired cook stove.

Because her reputation in the neighborhood was so distinguished, on many occasions she was asked to violate one of the most sacred of the marriage covenants in Italian and Sicilian society. She would provide, for a small fee, of course, not only the sauces, but often the entire meals for the neighborhoods' mamas, who would declare to their families that the delicacies were their own. If anyone had known at the time, oh, what scandal it would have caused. But the secret was well hidden for many years, during which my town grew to learn a lot more about the secrets of La Cosa Nostra than it did about Angelina's clandestine cooking.

Proposals for her pastas usually came in the afternoon, no later than one o'clock, and in my mother's native tongue. They usually went something like this:

"My dearest Angelina. My Giovanti is due home in two hours. I was sooooo busy today with sooooo many other things. Washing, cleaning, shopping. Baby Corrine was sooooo sick. Please help me. Giovanti's heart is set on a fine Agro Dolce sauce. I have two, nice, thick venison steaks from his hunting trip last winter. Please, I want to please him so. He works sooooo hard at the roller mill."

Angelina would smile, hug her neighbor and nod while extending her hand for payment. Usually, if her customer brought her own ingredients, the price was two dollars for the feast. Without ingredients, the price was three dollars. She would make enough for one dinner that fed four, and leftovers for at least one noon meal. With dollars in hand she would dismiss the customer and set to work, but not before telling them to return at three o'clock sharp.

All of her recipes came from memory. For the Agro Dolce Sauce, she took two tablespoons of sugar (either brown or white, it didn't matter) and added one-half cup of currants, a quarter of a bar of grated chocolate, one tablespoon of chopped candied orange, one lemon peel, one tablespoon of capers, and one cup of vinegar. She mixed the ingredients well and let the mixture soak for ninety minutes. Angelina was particularly sensitive to timing with her cooking. It was vitally important that her requests were received by early afternoon so she had time to prepare the meals and send her furtive customers on their way home well in advance of their beloved spouses return from work. If her neighbors' lovely (but irresponsible) wives were to be caught laying false claim to the prize on the dinner table that night, the uproar would have been heard blocks away, and marriages may be even compromised. So Angelina worked within a two to three hour window of time from receiving requests to handing over her captivating creations. With strict instructions to let the sauce soak for another thirty minutes, my mother would call out to that particular day's deceitful mate as she crossed the walk, "Simmer ten minutes before gently pouring over the meat."

I remember one of Angelina's regular customers vividly. Her name was Lola. She was Guiliano's wife from two blocks down and I can see her now, waddling furiously up to Angelina's doorstep one cold Wednesday afternoon. I was home from school with a nasty cold and was lounging in my mother's warm, cozy kitchen waiting for her wonderful hot chocolate to finish heating on the stove when Lola barged through the back door. She didn't bother with a hug for my mother or even a hello for me, not having time, since she arrived at quarter until two. She handed over three dollars and fifty cents for Angelina's services, admitting that she hadn't even shopped for the meat. Angelina told me after Lola left that this was a regular occurrence. She wanted meat sauce over penne pasta, and she needed it by five that afternoon. Guiliano was bringing his crew chief home for dinner.

"My God, how could he do this to me?" Lola wailed as Angelina stuffed the bills and quarters into her apron pocket.

After Lola quickly exited, Angelina found her favorite saucepan. She placed two pounds of large beef chunks and one-half of a finely chopped onion with three ounces of cooking lard inside the pan and sprinkled in parsley, salt and pepper, one clove and a very small slice of ham. I watched as she fried these ingredients over a hot fire for a few moments, moving the meat continuously with the wooden spatula in her tiny hand. When the onion was browned she added four tablespoons of red wine and four tablespoons of tomato sauce as sweet as honey, then waited for the sauce to sputter before adding more, little by little, to the boiling water. She let me taste the sauce from my seat at the kitchen table and I was in awe as she scurried about her favorite domain, her hands and arms moving graciously to attend to her creation like a maestro conducting a full symphony.

She tested the meat for tenderness and poked it gently to allow the juices to escape. When she noticed that the sauce had turned a golden color, and she had sufficient quantity to cover the meat, she covered the saucepan and pushed it to the back of the stove to simmer, continuously cooking the meat. When it was succulently brown, she removed the beef, slicing it in smaller cubes while checking on the status of the pasta softening in the boiling water on the other burner. She gave me one tiny bite of the meat and it melted in my mouth.

When the pasta was tender and moist, she scattered and mixed in the meat while pouring in the sauce, gently stirring it all together. Finally she topped it off with butter and grated cheese to await Guiliano's wife's return.

As Lola, her exceptionally large behind demonstrating an uncanny ability to elevate and drop to resemble a teeter-totter in full use by two four-year-olds, shuffled off with her full bowl of that night's supper tightly tucked under her arm, Angelina and I knew she would be back for more, probably within a month.

Angelina's recipes were as secret as her application of their contents. Asked, even begged, repeatedly for a description of the contents and techniques she employed, her answer always was, "*Tu fare non simile mio modo trovare qualche uno trimenti.* You don't like my way, find someone else."

But they never did. Her customers always returned to her back door, knocking politely for entrance into her sacred sanctum. All except Lola. With the money Angelina earned, she was able to surprise me, or Katrina, Sophia, Nicole or the others, with a new pair of shoes, a dress, a winter coat, socks, hats or gloves. Once she even bought Carlo a new dress shirt and tie. She equally dispersed these special gifts, and all of her children knew not one was being singled out over the others as her favorite.

To me, the best part of Angelina's cooking business was that she always held a little something back for her own family. On most days, the air drifting out of her kitchen windows filled the sky with the fragrance of her current delightful endeavor. We knew a special treat was in store when the aroma wafting from the kitchen was especially pungent with the robust scent of olive oil, garlic, onion, and sweet, sweet plum tomatoes (grown in a patch in our backyard near Angelina's clothesline) simmering in her sauté pan. Those basic ingredients served as a foundation for a number of delicious dishes, depending on what was stored on her shelf and her mood that day. Most times, there wasn't much in the pantry, so supper would go something like this: slow cooking a dozen or so of the succulent tomatoes for several hours (she never added sugar to cut the residual bitterness; slow cooking was preferred for that remedy), then serving the sauce over freshly made, hand molded and cut ravioli, filled with ground veal from the leftover veal shanks prepared two nights before.

Making ravioli, or tortellini, or anolini, or dumplings, or lasagna, or fettuccini, or simply spaghetti became a delightful undertaking for Angelina and my sisters. Carlo and I were not allowed to participate in this fare. Angelina would announce her intentions that morning exclusively to her girls, gathering them around the breakfast table. Squeals of joy would follow, and we boys were dismissed to pursue our own priorities, realizing the process would take most of the afternoon. We were clearly not tolerated at home during this entire time. The pasta-making extravaganza usually occurred on Saturdays. I didn't let my mother or Carlo or any of my sisters ever know, but I was envious of the tradition in which only my sisters were given the rare privilege.

At Christmas the year before Nick's accident, he had saved the eight dollars needed to buy Angelina a new, hand cranked pasta machine. It immediately became her favorite kitchen utensil and it held a prominent place on a shelf above her stove.

From this wonderful machine rolled out such incredible table delights as Lasagna Verdi alla Napoletana (lasagna noodles with their ribbed edges usually layered between ricotta cheese); Timballo di Mezzelune (half-moon pasta, succulent and sensual, again with ricotta and stuffed with cooked eggplant); Spaghetti (in all circumferences depending on the number of passes through the fine tuned rollers, often seasoned alla Sangiovannino (cherry tomatoes were in abundant supply at the local farmers' markets, but took seven days to sun-dry); Anolini al Ragu di Prosciutto (prosciutto could be purchased in ample quantity from the pig farmers down the road, but it didn't keep well in the dry, hot climate, so when my mother purchased a bundle wrapped tightly with string, it found its way into several dishes served throughout the span of a week).

Even though I never thought so, Angelina always said something was missing from the dishes she prepared. The quantities of fresh fish, lobster and shrimp abundant in Sicily were delicacies my town couldn't offer. Pueblo had lots of lakes and streams to the West toward the mountains, but only trout and fresh water bass and occasionally pike thrived there, which had to substitute for the tons of snapper, octopus, squid, cuttlefish, scallops, sole, sardines, anchovies, and sea bass that could be purchased each day at the docks along the Mediterranean shore.

My mother used to tell us while our forks twirled the pasta that these fresh catches would be taken inland and packed in ice, ready to anchor the main course at many Sicilian tables each evening. Pesce alle Erbe, Pesce al Forno con Carciofi, or Sogliole in saor (Venetian style), or Canestrelli di Chioggia (scallops served in their shells) were among her favorites, and I considered her a master of adaptation, watching her make do with Pueblo's meager fish supply.

Sunday afternoons after Mass were usually times for leisure, and Carlo and I could generally be found at our favorite fishing hole on those days. Small brown or rainbow trout were available for those who were patient and skillful with their lines and hooks. If our good fortune held we would come home with a full, heavy string of fish. Angelina would smile. She then had her substitute for sea bass or red snapper, and she made the best of it.

After Carlo cleaned the trout (heads were kept on), she would soak the fish in cold water for about one half-hour with a little coarse grain salt. Meanwhile, she would preheat her wood-stoked oven to just the right temperature, which she could feel without the use of a thermometer. After the half-hour was up she would drain the fish and pat them dry. She used parchment to wrap the fish before placing them in the pan after receiving a slight sprinkling of salt and pepper. She'd bake the fish for about thirty minutes, turning them over once during that time. She would then unwrap the fish and transfer them to a larger serving platter, wringing out the juice from the parchment, collecting it in the baking dish, and pouring it over the fish on the platter. Then came her herbs, mostly supplied by her backyard garden. In went fifteen sprigs of parsley, one bunch of fresh dill, ten fresh sage leaves, two sprigs of fresh rosemary, five sprigs of fresh mint, five large bay leaves, five large basil leaves and one-half cup of light bay rum. Ahh, the rum. I always savored the taste of it, warmed over low heat and poured over the mounds of herbs. She would light the finished dish with a match, flaming it just high enough.

My brother and sisters and I would be waiting in the darkened dining room, and when she appeared, we would cheer in earnest at the expectation of the feast to come.

Now that I look back, I can see that, at this time in our lives, Angelina was terribly sad without Nick. She mourned every day, and gracefully moved about her kitchen wearing only black. But I hope she knew how her cooking brightened the lives of her children and her neighbors with an unmatched skill neither Nick's death, nor the Depression, nor the oppressive presence of the thugs among us, could dampen. When she cooked, she was singing inside, and occasionally a few bars of her sweet soprano hum would escape her lips.

Chapter 11
A Warning Unheeded

Carlo

It wasn't long after Angelina had purchased the dress shirt and tie for Carlo with her secret culinary earnings that he donned them under his brown pinstriped suit for the first time. It was a Saturday evening, and he was hurrying on his way out the door to catch the bus, determined, once again, to prove himself to his chosen peers despite the terror he knew was swelling in his mother's heart. Angelina hadn't questioned him about finding the suit in his closet, and Carlo hadn't mentioned it either. I had told Carlo about our mother's discovery, and that she knew what the clothes meant.

At the mill that day, working another overtime shift to help meet increasing rail supply demands for America's industrial expansion, Carlo was sitting with the lunch crowd when, in hushed tones, Tony made it clear that a new man, a big man, had been put in charge of bootlegging operations in town.

"He's been sent down from Denver," Tony sneered. "We think he's just a capo given a promotion. Those assholes up North have no idea that down here is where the power is." As the lunch break ended, Tony brought Jake and Carlo aside.

"A shipment is ready for us tonight, but this time we go west, near Florence. I don't know why the change in location, its just another fuck up by this new guy Blanco. He's the new boss, we're told. He and his Denver crowd are ignoring our system, our way of doing business here. The rotten bastards," Tony ranted.

Tony explained that, despite resistance in the ranks in Pueblo, the boys back East, well, one boy in particular, Mr. Lucky Luciano himself, had decided that for the time being, Denver would still call the shots over activities down South. So Joe Romeo, a smalltime hood who had apparently carried out some special assignments for the top Mafia echelon, had been given temporary criminal custody of the western region, including Pueblo. And in turn, Romeo had chosen one of his henchmen to run the show in Pueblo. His name was Charlie Blanco.

"He's the one they're blamin' the Danna killings on?" Carlo asked, fearing what Tony's answer would be.

"'Fraid so," was Tony's response.

"Oh, shit," was all Carlo could say. His stomach wasn't feeling so good.

Charlie Blanco was a nobody gangster who no one had ever heard of before but suddenly appeared on the scene wrapped in bluster and bound to show his muscle at the first opportunity. And that he did. Pueblo was still reeling from the shock and anger over the slaughter rumored to be his responsibility. Even those in Pueblo who had grown accustomed to the Mafia's violent way of handling its internal disputes could not accept this pointless act. Killing innocent members of a non-connected family was not tolerated. Around town, Blanco's name had already been trampled in the mud and he had barely taken office.

Even little Johnny and his friends had heard about the Danna killings, and Charlie Blanco too. It was all around school and was once even brought up at the supper by Nadine. Angelina refused to talk about it. They'd never heard the word before, but she exclaimed "Omerta!" and that was the end of the discussion.

Yes, the whole town knew about the Danna family; that was no secret. But Carlo came to know more than most; sooner than most. And the reason he had such a bad feeling right now is that he had discovered how the family had fought desperately to stay alive and safe in the face of fierce, overwhelming odds. The details of their struggle, ending in their deaths, were recorded in a diary kept by the oldest son, Tommy Junior.

The diary had been found by a sheriff's deputy who stumbled onto it while inspecting the crime scene in the boy's upstairs bedroom of the Danna farmhouse. The son of the deputy, a fellow line worker, had somehow gotten hold of it and brought it to work, waving it around during lunch break, claiming to have the key to the mystery that had shrouded the town in anguish. Carlo had snatched it from him, appalled at how this poor family was being treated after their deaths.

In spite of his morals and his best instinct, Carlo's curiosity had gotten the best of him, and he had sat down that day at lunch, away from the crowd to read the diary. Tommy Danna had been a proud family man living about 20 miles outside town, to the East. His six-hundred-forty-acre dirt farm situated on the dry plains was the prettiest around. Every building, every fence, even the flagpole in the courtyard, were freshly painted; not a broken shingle or splintered fence rail to be found. His winter wheat crop was planted in parallel and perpendicular rows precisely the right distance apart. The pigpen was raked every day, and even the cows looked clean. He and his wife of twenty years were raising six children. The oldest, Tommy Junior, was seventeen and working in the fields with his father. All the children were in school. All were at Mass every Sunday. They scraped by, but life had been good since Tommy's parents had left the farm to him to run when they moved to an old folks home in town. Tommy was an honest man, but he was a stubborn man. As the story goes, his pride is what got him and his family killed.

The coroner's inquest ruled it a murder-suicide, but the town knew it was far from that. Besides, the coroner owed his elected job to those in the rackets. Everyone knew he wasn't able to practice legitimate medicine due to a temporary suspension of his license by the State Medical Exam Board. He experienced never-ending bouts with alcoholism, and more than a few malpractice allegations had been leveled against him. So, covering up murders for the mob was the coroner's specialty, and one of the most reliable sources of his livelihood.

As the story goes on, the sheriff, acting on an anonymous tip, found the seven bodies at the Danna household; two on the front porch, one on the couch in the front parlor, two in their beds and two in the kitchen, some dead of wounds from gunshots fired at point-blank range. Their horrible deaths and the devastation they brought to the town all started on a Friday night when Tommy confronted two strangers who had driven their short bed cattle truck into his driveway.

Saturday, April 16, 1932

"Tonight was a night I will never forget as long as I live. I can't sleep. I am really scared so I'm writing this down so I remember all the details. Right after dinner, my

mother and sisters were in the kitchen doing dishes. I was out feeding the hogs in their pen by the barn, when this truck pulled into our yard. My Dad was in the living room reading the newspaper and listening to the radio. We all heard the rumble of the engine as the strange truck pulled into our driveway. My Dad knew something wasn't right when the passenger who jumped from the cab with a friendly smile and handshake was dressed in a blue pinstriped suit, white shirt and tie. Dad was informed by the stranger that he and his friend needed to park their truck loaded with its mysterious cargo in our barn for the night. I knew what was in there. I could smell it when I walked up to the truck as my Dad talked to this man in his suit in our front yard.

"We'll be back for it in the morning, but we want you to make damn sure nobody touches anything," the well-dressed, easy-to-spot bootlegger told my Dad. I know what a bootlegger is. All of us do. Some of the kids in my school say they'd like to be one. Not for me. No sir.

My Dad refused the thug's order, and, instead, ordered the pair off our property. In response, he was sternly warned to cooperate, and after several moments of heated exchange, and only at the point of the truck driver's gun, did Dad step aside to allow the driver to carefully maneuver the truck into the barn and close the door.

The argument continued between Dad and the trespasser, more severe than before, and the threats against him and our family intensified. But Dad wouldn't back down. He was knocked to the ground. Sorry to say I joined him there when, right after I ran out and tackled the driver and was getting the best of him, a sharp blow from what I think was a nightstick smacked me on the back of the head. A second vehicle, it looked to me like a black Cadillac sedan, rolled into the driveway, and the pair of thugs, still *screaming obscenities and threats, climbed in and drove off. The last thing they heard was my Dad yelling as he struggled to get to his feet a warning that he would, "burn down the barn and everything in it before I'll let you bastards take charge!"*

After my mother tended to me and my Dad's minor head wounds, Dad sent all of us to bed. He remained outside, leaning against the barn door to ponder his next move. He couldn't sleep either. I watched him from my upstairs bedroom window. I knew him well. I knew what he was thinking. I knew he had decided to fight. I was frightened beyond belief. But I was with him. I could just imagine what he saying to himself. I heard him say it many times before. "They might run this town, but they don't run me."

It was just before dawn as I watched my Dad open the shop door next to the barn and retrieve a five-gallon can of kerosene. I knew he had just filled it the day before. He herded our animals to an adjacent holding pen. I wanted to help him, but I knew he would be angry with me if he knew I was awake and spying on him. He had the perimeter of the barn soaked with the highly flammable liquid in less than a minute. The sturdy hardboard structure that he and his father and a few generous neighbors lovingly built one summer when he was just fourteen ignited with a giant whoosh, and, along with the short-bed truck and three hundred gallons of prime whiskey was reduced to ashes in less than thirty minutes. I watched the building burn from my upstairs bedroom window. I didn't realize my mother and sisters did the same. Dad then loaded his double-barrel 20-gauge Remington shotgun that he and I used for duck hunting, his .22 single shot that we used for rabbit and raccoon hunting, and his father's antique .45 caliber revolver that he used for our protection, and finally went to bed. *I snuck into my parent's room after he fell asleep. He had the shotgun next to his nightstand.*

Friday, April 22, 1932

> *The rubble and ashes of the barn are still smoldering.*

Thursday, May 19, 1932

> *We've begun clearing the charred remains of the barn and its contents. A month has passed. No one has returned to confront us. Nonetheless, my Dad and I continue to take turns staying awake each night with the shotgun in our laps, swaying in the dark on a swing on our front porch.*

Friday, May 20, 1932

> *It is the 35th night of our vigil, and earlier Dad was startled from dozing at his post on the front porch by the sound of a chugging engine of a car moving slowly up our dirt driveway. I also came alert immediately, my senses acute. Dad watched the night-shrouded vehicle creep toward the farmhouse as he moved from the swing into a defensive position on his belly slightly under the porch and behind a fairly thick row of fully leaved-out hedges that ringed the perimeter. I crept to my pre-assigned post from my temporary bed on the couch in the front parlor. I heard his shotgun cock, and I caught my breath and listened. Something was familiar about the sound of that out-of-tune motor. It belonged to a pickup. The driver's side door squeaked open, and from the dim interior light I caught a glimpse of the round, ruddy face of our neighbor, Louie*

Salardino. *Dad released the double lever on the Remington. My fear was replaced by a muted sigh of relief.*

"Papa, is that Mr. Salardino?" I whispered from my station behind the white pillar of the porch. I had my .22 single shot expertly aimed and continued to track the truck's lone occupant as Louie cautiously inched his way toward the house.

"Yes, son, it's Mr. Salardino," Dad said. "Lower your rifle, but I want you to stay on the porch while I talk with him. Sit over there in the swing. Keep your rifle ready," he instructed. Louie came forward. Dad met him at the bottom of the front porch steps. They moved together back toward the truck, its headlights still burning.

"Louie, what the hell are you doing out here at this time of night? You're too damn old to be chasing possum," Dad said with smile and extended hand. "Besides I thought you gave up eating those rodents some time ago." I had crawled further to the edge of the porch and could just barely hear the conversation. "You scared the holy dickens out of me," Dad added.

"Tommy, my dear friend, so much to say." Louie said, shaking his head slowly and sadly.

"Come out with it, Louie," Dad demanded. "Why, why did you burn the truck? Why couldn't you just let it go? You have so much here. You take this place from a ruin to a farm of greatness. Me and all of your neighbors watch you over the years doing so much good. We are so proud to be your neighbors. Your wife, your children. This home of yours. Why do you throw it all away?" Louie stammered with the questions.

"Louie, please," Dad pleaded. "Tell me what you know. Is there something you've heard? What is it?"

"These men are bigger than you. They are stronger. They are vicious. They have no conscience. They will have

revenge," Louie said, continuing to stumble over his words." I cannot let them come on my land and walk over me. Push my face in the mud. They will not win. Tell me Louie. You must," Dad insisted. "They are coming for you tomorrow. Two of them are arriving on the train from Denver. They have come from Detroit. They will strike like rattlers. You will not see them," Louie responded.

"Where did you get this, Louie?" Dad erupted as he grabbed his friend by the lapels of his jacket and pulled him close, nose to nose. "Tell me. Is it true? I have to know!"

"Tommy, I come to you tonight at the risk of my own life. The lives of my family. My words are true. I can say no more. They arrive at noon, tomorrow, at Union Depot. The conductor will approach them. You will know which ones they are. The conductor will signal. God bless you my dear, dear friend," Louie said as he gently removed Tommy's grasp and slowly walked back to his truck.

As his friend drove off into the night Dad called after him, "Louie, you are a gift from God. I will never forget what you've done." I watched Dad turn back towards the house.

"Papa, is everything all right?" I asked when he stepped back upon the porch. "Son, everything is okay. Mr. Salardino just needed some advice on tuning that old truck of his. He admitted he was out hunting possum," my father lied calmly. "An old pastime for him. Said he couldn't sleep. Worried about his corn crop. He did tell me they're starting up a new farmer's market in Rocky Ford tomorrow morning, so tell your mother that I'm going down there to check out the prices, costs of setting up the stands, you know, like we do in Canon City. Will be nice to find new customers. Maybe we will alternate every Saturday. Break up the routine. Rocky Ford, then Canon City. Now, you get back to bed, Tommy. It's too late for me to sleep any more.

I'm going to do some work in the shop and I'll be gone before you wake. The old guy did scare me though. Glad it wasn't anything important."

"Me, too," I said. "Sure woke me up fast when I heard you jump up from the swing. I was asleep on the couch in the living room where you told me to be. Should I stay on the porch for the rest of the night?" I asked. "No son, go onto bed upstairs. We still need to be careful. We make a great team. Don't we? I'll watch things for the rest of the night. Get to bed. Like always, you keep that .22 close to you when you get up to do the chores. Keep those extra shells in your pocket," Dad told me. "Will do, Papa."

My Dad hugged me to his chest while opening the screen door for me to pass inside. I cannot shake the fear. I did not go to bed as ordered, rather I laid back down on the couch in the living room, vowing to remain awake through the night and insist on accompanying him wherever he was going in the morning. I tried hard to stay awake as I listened to the muffled noise of my father rummaging through his tools in the workshop.

I know my father has a very special possession that he keeps hidden away somewhere in the shop. He has shown it to me only once, saying on my eighteenth birthday, it will be mine. I will be eighteen in just two months. It was a gift to his father from his grandfather who had purchased it with some of the extra profit from an abundant alfalfa crop in 1912. A sleek, beautifully carved, walnut-butted and gripped antique Swiss Peabody Martin 9.3, rimmed, with a long lens scope for targets well over three hundred yards. My grandfather intended it for big horn sheep hunting in the Rockies above the old mining camps West of Leadville, but the second anticipated bumper crop that next year withered from a seven-month drought. My grandmother wanted the rifle sold for cash for much needed sugar and flour, but my grandfather refused, firmly believing the next year would rekindle his dreams of a trophy sheep for the wall of his living room.

The second bumper crop never came, and the rifle remained packed away in its red velvet-lined, leather case until it was given to my father prior to my grandparents moving into town. So far, Dad hasn't fulfilled his father's dream for the trophy big horn, but once a year, he cleans the magnificent weapon and shoots twenty rounds at distant targets located deep in the streambed West of our property line. Twenty rounds are all he can shoot. The shells are way too expensive to fire any more. Even with as little practice as he has, Dad seldom misses his targets.

Saturday, May 21, 1932

My Dad told me what happened next. Last night I fell asleep and didn't help him take care of the men who were coming to hurt us. I was ashamed for failing him and told him so, so he told me what he did. He wasn't ashamed and neither was I. I was proud of him but he wasn't looking for praise. He never did. He kept good things, great things he did, to himself. And this was a great thing he did. I'm glad he told me. He trusted me. I'm glad.

In the early morning mist, Dad found the rifle easily, cleaned it, loaded it, and departed before the sun rose. We were all asleep and not stirring when he fired the motor of his Dodge long bed truck with its high railings for hog hauling and eased down the driveway and out onto the road.

Later that morning, less than six hours after his wrenching conversation with Louie and when the sun was two hours into its trek across the southern Colorado sky, my Dad was napping behind the X made by two strategically chosen cross beams about eight feet beneath Pueblo's two-lane roadway. I'm not sure why my Dad added this part, but he thought it was important. He said in 1921, after months of bitter negotiations, the steel company and the Santa Fe Railroad finally reached agreement to share, equally, the cost of building the East-West Fourth Street bridge to span the rail yards and connect the two wings of the town. The town fathers had argued for a four-lane bridge to accommodate increasing traffic flow from the ever-growing number of Model Ts and recently redesigned Buicks and Chevrolets, but only two-lanes ended up being built, suspended by the steel, cross-hatched super structure on which Dad was perched. It cost nearly one hundred thousand dollars to build, about half of the city's entire yearly budget. The only relief was that the steel for the bridge was made at the mill about twenty blocks away; otherwise the cost would have doubled. It's strange that he wanted me to know this part. I think it might be that he's always been interested in how things were built and he follows local events closely, so I suppose when he used the bridge like he did he wanted me to know a little of the history. He always wanted me to learn all that I could.

For routine maintenance and painting, the bridge's engineers had designed an eighteen-inch footpath at the lower level, just wide enough for Dad to sit and lay back to rest. Very little traffic sputtered in the two lanes overhead. The wind was calm, the sky a deep grey. Tiny raindrops fell sporadically. A fog had rolled in off the Arkansas River, which runs parallel to the eight sets of tracks in the rail yard. Soon it began to lift. From Dad's position on the bridge, his view of the cargo and passenger platforms of Union Depot was completely unobstructed.

His back ached and his legs were stiff. He estimated that the distance from his position to the passenger platform was at least three hundred yards. He knew the muzzle power of the massive long barrel could reach that far, but his confidence in his own accuracy, even with the magnifying capacity of the scope, waned as the minutes ticked by toward noon. Each time he looked with a naked eye at the platform, it seemed to move farther away, yet when he brought the scope to his squint, his confidence returned.

At the shrill of the noon train whistle announcing the arrival of the *Santa Fe Express*, Dad bolted upright, banging his head on the steel beam above. The throbbing was excruciating, and he saw stars for a moment. The stark ray of sun that had pierced the clouds was shining directly in his face, adding to his momentary blindness. It took an instant for his brain to reconnect its temporarily disjointed signals, and though a trickle of blood ran down his forehead to his brow, he was able to re-focus on the task at hand.

Two minutes passed. Then three. Dad watched as the steady stream of men, mostly in the presence of women and children, stepped off the train and onto the platform. None of those men were not his targets. He knew that. They didn't look the part. Dad even recognized two of our neighbors as they carried their belongings across the platform into the depot lobby. Then the expanse was empty. Only two Negro conductors were left in view, chatting amiably, having already assisted the passengers with their suitcases and duffel bags. Departure was scheduled for no later than 12:15. The conductors parted, moving slowly toward their respective rail passenger cars. They signaled with the familiar wave of their arms as a warning to any who wanted to board or disembark that the time was near.

Then they appeared – two who were out of place. They didn't belong with the rest of the passengers. One was very tall and lanky. Dad observed him through the scope.

The other was short and stocky. Both were in traditional garb. Suits, coats, ties and Fedoras. Dad silently questioned them from his lair. Why be so obvious? Why not come in disguise? You arrogant bastards. You think you're untouchable. Above all the rest of us. More powerful than any. Can't be any other answer, he thought as he watched his prey standing in the grayness below. Each lit a cigarette. One of the conductors approached and said something. The short one waved him away with a grimace, and a look of disgust. Two satchels, one long like the lanky one, the other short like the stocky one, lay at their feet. They smoked and looked around, but not up toward the bridge. Dad waited. The conductor took a step back from the pair, pointed toward the sky and nodded, maybe at him, maybe at no one, Dad didn't know. He pulled back the rifle bolt to lock the first bullet in place.

The short one died first, a shot through his left eye and out his rear cranium. There was a splatter on his friend's cashmere black overcoat. Dad had aimed between his eyes. The lanky one, stunned to see his friend's brains out of their container, instinctively crouched to reduce his exposure. His friend was on his back, one eye staring into the shrouded sun. Dad hit the lanky one in the middle of the hat perched on the top of his head as he was attempting to roll in a ball for better protection. He slumped forward, his hat falling aside to expose what was left of a sculpted Sicilian profile. A third shot severed his spinal cord, just to be sure.

At 12:15 sharp, the Express, bound for Albuquerque, moved out of the Depot, its conductors both in place, waving to the engineer to proceed. The two corpses lay motionless in massive pools of blood staining the empty platform. Dad rested for a moment before dismantling the hot-barreled Martin, gathering his things and climbing to the roadway above. Few cars passed him by as he walked slowly toward his truck, parked a quarter-mile away.

That night Dad told Mom and the rest of us that we would definitely be traveling to Rocky Ford next Saturday for the new farmer's market. He told her, before they went up to bed, "We should make good money there. They particularly like beans and squash."

~

Carlo couldn't believe his eyes as he scanned the words of the boy, written in perfect penmanship on bright yellow parchment, bound in red leather, his initials embossed in gold lettering on the front cover. TMD, Jr. It had to be a loving gift from a loving family member, Carlo thought. He nearly wept and was late in returning to his shift. He decided he would turn the book over to the sheriff after work that day. The truth about the tragedy might come out if only the cops would investigate what the diary told.

Tommy Junior's eloquently written account contained other trivial entries leading up to the killings, but they stopped abruptly – three days shy of the four-month anniversary of Tommy return home from his sniper's perch. But Carlo already knew the rest. The heartbreaking end to the story had been made public by official reports from the investigators. Other parts of the story came from people who didn't ever talk to the cops. Anyway, the authorities said Tommy Junior died from a single shot to the side of his head, delivered by a sniper, maybe as good as Tommy, using a Mauser 7X57 Custom. Tommy Junior was sleeping soundly in the front porch swing just before dawn and never woke up. The .22 was still in his lap. The deadly shot rang out as the sun was peaking over the horizon. As the story goes, as Tommy burst through the front door and raced to his dying son, he took the next shot through the heart and was dead before he hit the floor of the freshly painted front porch.

Tommy's shotgun was used on the rest of his family, all except for one.

Tommy's wife was apparently the last to die. Those who were in the know suspected that she was forced to witness the deaths of all her children, and was shown the bodies of her husband and son before being placed on the front parlor couch and blasted with both barrels. Only her youngest, three-year-old Margaret (they called her Maggie), survived. Her mother had laid her in the bottom of her bedroom wardrobe and covered her with clothing as the shooting began. Maggie stayed exactly where her mother had instructed her to, until, after four days, she grew so hungry and dehydrated she began to whimper uncontrollably. A deputy heard her while inspecting the crime scene, and she was rushed to the hospital, only to spend two nights there before being placed in Saint Bernadette's home for orphans.

Before Maggie's hospital stay was complete, the assassins were surely long gone, probably, Carlo assumed, on the morning train back to Detroit. When mob killings occurred it was commonly assumed the triggermen came from Detroit. Carlo didn't know for sure, but he suspected their blood money had arrived by mail pouch on one of the Super Eagle Express trains from Denver, the same way other hired killers were always paid for their deeds. One time, Carlo heard, the payment pouches were stolen by one of the black conductors (maybe the same one who signaled Tommy) after an assassination of a wayward dope peddler who had tried to move into the territory from Pittsburgh. The conductor disappeared. Rumor had it he made his way down south to Mississippi where he was protected by friends and family who shared in his good fortune by buying out his sharecropper uncle's leased farm.

Anyway, it didn't surprise anyone when murder-suicide was the ruling following the inquest into the Danna family massacre. Carlo heard the town coroner got so drunk the night after the inquest ended that he had to be driven home from the Blast Furnace Tavern, passed out in the back seat of a black Cadillac that sounded eerily similar to the car Tommy Junior described in his diary hauling away the two bootleggers who had stored their ill-fated cargo in the Danna family barn. The diary's contents were kept under wraps for some time but eventually the *Chieftain Journal* newspaper printed excerpts. The town speculated that the sheriff tried to sell it himself but failed, and rumors about its existence brought enterprising local reporters to his office demanding release. He finally relinquished the contents and the *Chieftain Journal* sold more newspapers that week than it ever had before.

For a long time Carlo thought about Tommy Junior speaking to him from his grave in such captivating verse. Carlo prayed nothing like the Danna killings would ever occur again in his town. He couldn't believe mass murders like that were ever carried out with such brutality anywhere else in the country.

Anyway, that's why Charlie Blanco became an instant monster in my town. Responsibility for the killings was placed at his doorstep. Those gutless pukes pulling the triggers that night were all known to be acting on strict orders only given by the man in charge. But instead of his revenge bringing on an unsettling order to the town, it prompted open rebellion, and that was the message Carlo hoped was finding its way back to Lucky Luciano sitting behind his seven-foot mahogany desk in his East Harlem penthouse. Revolt among the people was bad for business and Carlo knew from Tony that Lucky was all about business. No one would stand in his way to expand the Genovese family fortune and influence, and if Pueblo was rebelling he would find out why.

Now Carlo snapped his attention back to Tony. "We've never connected at Florence before, and the guys making the delivery are also new, so be real careful," Tony told them. "Make the transfer quick and get back here. You're expected at the Minnequa Club by ten. Mr. Florenzia will be at the back door."

He turned and walked back to the roller line. Jake followed after a quick glance at Carlo, almost to say he was glad he was coming along.

Chapter 12
Meeting the Family

It was important to know in those days how the mob came to entangle my town like a butterfly trapped in the web of a spider. How did those who planted themselves in the center of that web and waited patiently for their victims to be ensnared in the sticky spindles of the intricate deadly domicile known as their territory? Miss Murphy, the best librarian known to man in my opinion, was my master mentor at the teachings the Mafia's secrets. Not only did she know the ancient history of La Cosa Nostra, she constantly updated her private criminal encyclopedia to modern times. Apparently she had many sources of information, some probably shady, but she had the facts, and that's all that mattered. She was an eager instructor, and I wanted to know all I could about the one responsible for the Danna murders.

Turns out that Blanco came to power in Pueblo through a long association with numerous mobsters, including Romeo. He was not a rookie at his craft, and the mobster had spun his snare around Pueblo very quickly and expertly. The most important thing to a mobster (besides his own personal income and safety) was his image. To succeed in the underworld, crooks like Blanco had to project themselves as larger than life, fearless and cunning, intellectually brilliant (even thought they were mostly brainless), and above all, unchallengeable in their leadership role. So, when a new boss came to Pueblo or any mob haven for that matter, he was preceded by a well-orchestrated public relations campaign to bolster his public persona.

Even though Blanco was on the throne in Pueblo for a short time his impact was great, and the truth about him eventually came out. Miss Murphy knew the truth better than most, and she loved to share it with me.

Far from the dashing Hollywood screen image that Lucky Luciano and his cohorts were known for, Blanco was a short, fat man with thick black hair slick with grease and combed straight, front to back. His bushy, black eyebrows bounced up and down as he spoke. A black cigar always hung from the corner of his mouth, and his impeccable suits and gold watches were always accented by a diamond pinky ring on his little finger and a gold front tooth. Blanco more or less fit the "Al Capone" likeness of a mobster, at least with his outward appearance. But Miss Murphy described Blanco as a coward's coward, using front men his entire career to carry out the nasty deeds one needs to demonstrate to move up through the Mafia hierarchy. He liked to throw his weight around, (figuratively; he was far too fat to move anywhere quickly) when it was convenient and safe, and few were in a position to challenge his authority.

Blanco came to power answering; he was told to Joe Romeo and no one else. Miss Murphy explained that Romeo was stepping in to fill the temporary void left while Lucky was busy with his own problems in the East. With Lucky occupied, Romeo had taken credit for eliminating the Carlino brothers; that is, when talking to everyone except those in power in New York. It was Lucky who appointed Romeo to enter the post-Carlino era while he tended to a gang war in Havana. Lucky had few choices at the time. Colorado and the West were still in the developmental stages of sophisticated organized criminal activity, and there was no clear definition as to where power was to be centered. Rumor had it, my librarian said, that Lucky actually picked Romeo's name out of a hat after surveying the landscape and coming up with only a few others more or less qualified to take the post. The Smaldoni family of Denver, another bunch of small-time hoods, offered up candidates, but they proved to be even worse. Miss Murphy pegged the hapless Smaldonis on the mark early on. When given the nod by Lucky as the lesser of numerous evils, Romeo moved with great haste to solidify his independent position before New York stepped in to mingle in his madness. On the day he took office Romeo was determined to wean himself from the mother's milk of New York long before his infancy grew to adolescence. Once given power, Romeo was not one to share it, even with his New York benefactors. According to Miss Murphy, Blanco was an underling who had found favor in Denver, but he hadn't even made it to capo status when he had the Pueblo assignment dumped in his huge lap. He had been plucked from the lower ranks by the new Denver mob boss without much executive experience. The era of Carlino mismanagement and diffused power was to be corrected and never allowed to happen again, according to Lucky, Miss Murphy explained. Romeo's answer was Charlie Blanco. That is, if the guy could keep his head on straight. Blanco was to run it all, according to Miss Murphy, feed everything to Denver; all the money and all the information, so in time, no question would remain as to the lines of authority, and they led straight to Joe Romeo.

Not long after things appeared to settle down, even though Lucky had lost sight of the West for a while, it became clear that Joe Romeo was not cooperating. It didn't take a genius to notice the hangover of lingering disharmony. In the Mafia, dissent, a break in the line of authority, is not tolerated under any circumstances, and my town was becoming far too valuable as the mob's western hub to allow discontent to rise into open insurgence over the Danna murders, among other miscues. Lucky knew the Danna murders had already tipped the scales in the wrong direction. For long-term success, the Mafia depends on acceptance from not only the authorities in a particular location, but to a great extent, the general population as well. Any crime capital must either openly support the culture or allow it to be swept under the rug. This environment enables law enforcement to function more openly in harmony, usually permitting, sometimes even supporting certain corrupt enterprises. However, if the town folks become angry and rebel, business becomes difficult, positions are jeopardized, money is lost, and even some key bosses hit the penitentiary.

Lucky had thought that by having Romeo at the helm, but on a short leash, he could quell any persistent discontent. But he was wrong. It was soon apparent that Romeo brought too much attention to himself; partly due to his selection of personnel, partly due to his business tactics, and mostly due to his own self-declared importance. He liked to call himself "Little Caesar," and he just didn't get along well with most people. He was nasty and mean, Miss Murphy said. He was selfish, a loner, bad in social settings, always brooding, but when drunk, boisterous and blundering. He didn't know the word "generous," either with his time or his money, and mob bosses always needed to be generous with both. And they needed to act sincere, even if they weren't, and interested in others, their families, and their well-being. There were many people to pay off, and if you got stingy, that was tantamount to inviting a deadly bite from the spider truly in charge.

Romeo's only rivals were the disjointed Smaldoni family. Miss Murphy described them as a bunch of keystone cop-types who were long-time Denver hoods. They were headed by brothers "Checkers" and "Flip Flop," and known for being more comical than criminal. Soon after Romeo's appointment, and after choosing Blanco, he did another dumb thing. Miss Murphy told me he made peace with the Smaldonis by buying them off with simple tasks and token posts. But within a month after the deal, on orders to complete a simple truck hijacking of table radios on the road between Cheyenne and Denver, the Smaldoni thugs accidentally killed the driver and touched off a major statewide manhunt for those responsible. The investigation, eventually stymied through a series of expensive payoffs, got way too close to Romeo's front door. From there, things went from bad to worse. A botched extortion scheme which ended up bilking little old ladies out of pension money for fixing non-leaking roofs by Smaldoni-controlled shyster contractors; a blundered check kiting scheme that brought the Feds down their necks and wire taps to their phones; and the first of its kind stolen car chop shop that was raided after they sold the Frankenstein version of a '41 Ford to the police commissioner's third wife all added to Lucky's mounting dismay. Romeo, Blanco and now the Smaldonis'. A mess is what Lucky deemed it. Mobster misfits, he declared. Shameful; an utter disgrace, Miss Murphy said in a fit of giggles. She was really enjoying herself. So was I.

Chapter 13
Overcoats in the Summertime

Eventually Romeo and Blanco crossed Lucky one too many times. Everybody knew that if you fell out of favor with Lucky for any reason, or simply performed blatant acts of sheer stupidity, you were in deep trouble. And Romeo had created disharmony with more than his share of idiotic adventures. Lucky hated disharmony, and he hated those who were responsible for it.

So the night my brother left the house for his appointment with Jake to embark on their latest assignment no one knew, especially Carlo, that the hours ahead of him were to present a razor sharp turning point in his life. It sure started out different for him than the way it ended up. I could tell when I watched him step outside. He had a swagger to his step like no other. He looked like he was on top of the world. Yeah, as he told me later, he thought a little about what Tony had said earlier in the day about Charlie Blanco and his new hold on Pueblo, but that didn't affect him. He was just a runner, a mule hauling the goods. They were paying him good. He had things going his way now, and Tony and the boys respected him. Jake was the top driver, and Carlo was his top wingman. Okay, so they had to follow Blanco's new rules. Meet at a new place. So what my brother thought. They were good. They could adapt easy. Just keep the booze flowing and they'd catch it, bottle it and get it down the thirsty throats of their worthy customers. Be damned if it was illegal. My brother thought he was part of a good thing.

But he was wrong.

The night before Jake's funeral, Carlo reluctantly spilled his guts to me about the bootlegging run that changed his life. Once I got him talking, he retold the story in great depth, as if he was reliving every second. And when he finished, he said he would never tell it again; not to me, not to anyone, so I made sure to remember every detail. For him, it was like lifting a thousand-pound anvil off his back. This was the way he told it.

~

My brother stepped off the bus at exactly seven that evening, walked over to the Dodge, and slid in on the passenger's side. To his surprise Jake actually nodded at him, as if to say hello.

Carlo thought this was going to be a great night. It was his seventh time riding with Jake, and he had grown accustomed to Jake ignoring him. Seven times, and Jake was finally getting comfortable with him. He could feel it. This would be their first trip up to Florence, but Carlo convinced himself that it was "gonna be easy." Didn't matter if it was a new drop point. They could handle it. They were good. Now, as always, beside Jake lay the .38 Special. Somehow, knowing it was there comforted Carlo this time and he relaxed a little in the passenger front seat. They hit the road, heading west out of town on Route 50, the newly paved two-lane back top. Top speed, forty-five miles per hour.

109

Surprisingly Jake was the first to speak. "This one won't take long, maybe only an hour to get there and an hour back," he announced.

"Where are we meeting them?" Carlo asked.

"Off Route 50, north of the town and a little West, but this side of Canon City," Jake responded.

When I was much older, rocking in my rocking chair on my front porch one evening, I read an article about the meeting place Jake was describing to Carlo that night. That exact spot had been chosen as the site of Super Max, the new maximum-security federal penitentiary. The land on which the Feds decided they would build their escape-proof and impenetrable compound was the ugliest most barren scrub-filled piece of dry, flat terrain one could imagine. The Mohave Desert is prettier than this place. But it was perfect for the most secure joint in the Federal Prison System. It would house the most violent and notorious of America's criminals including terrorists, mad bombers, and spies. I remember thinking at the time that Super Max made Al Capone's Alcatraz look like a country club.

As the years passed, Super Max became somewhat of an ironic symbol for a new Pueblo and its surrounding neighbors. It ended up being a rare boom to the local economy; the crime and corruption that plagued our region for nearly a century had been replaced by a monument to law enforcement, but we still saw few, if any, of the sons of our old mob adversaries join the prison population there. Instead, the real bad asses hell-bent on terrorizing our country and killing randomly for the sake of a religious or political cause were the ones who occupied the solitary confinement cells. Such acts against America would never cross the minds of the boys of Lucky's generation, or even the inheritors of his regime. These men loved America. They wanted their adopted country to thrive. Her prosperity and security meant just a little could rub off on them, assuming they worked hard at their craft, and remained disciplined and diligent. Mobsters just want to be left alone to run their businesses. No harm, no foul; bygones be bygones. And unless you knowingly and willingly ventured into the world of the mob, and you made a stink, your chances of being whacked by a gangster were worse than winning a million dollar jackpot at the slots in Las Vegas.

All I know is that if any of the old boys of Lucky's generation were given access to the cells in today's Super Max, there wouldn't be a terrorist, mad bomber or spy enjoying the custody and care of the federal government and American taxpayer for very long. Lucky's boys would be standing in line, and would take real patriotic pleasure, extending no mercy, in eliminating the whole lot of them, saving our government a lot of time, trouble and money for their lifetime welfare.

Anyway, as my brother and Jake passed the same spot that is now the razor-wire-covered outer perimeter entrance to Super Max, they were riding in silence, lost in their own thoughts. It was a clear, cool evening, and the wind was calm for a change. Even though in Carlo's mind, the two were growing comfortable in each other's company, until the transfer was made, neither of them could even remotely relax. As they neared their destination, Carlo remembered his nerves becoming sharper. So far, his runs with Jake had been uneventful. They usually involved the same three Fedora-topped howling hyenas with Jake playing his part and Carlo taking the brunt of the jokes. With every job done, my brother would tuck another ten bucks in the coil spring under his mattress and imagine a growing sense of belonging and accomplishment. I found his wad of cash once while searching for a lost shoe under his bed. I counted out over two hundred dollars before placing it back in the tobacco tin, my hands shaking for fear he'd catch me.

Carlo admitted the night he spilled it all to me, that his bootlegging days were troubling, to say the least, for our mother. And he knew that she knew what he was up to. No, he didn't want her to worry, but he knew she did. And he rationalized everything by telling himself that it was our mother's role to worry, and that it was the role of every mother, especially when their husbands and sons were willing (sometimes grateful) participants in these types of activities. She would just have to live with it, he had concluded. When he told me that, I could have smacked him for putting Angelina through all this, but I didn't want to interrupt. As he went on, I grew tenser. Yet, he remained real calm.

As the two-lane blacktop road turned to gravel, Carlo sensed that they were almost there. Jake made the turn, again onto a winding, narrow dirt cow path leading away from the hard pack asphalt and up over a rise, out of sight of any travelers passing by. As they crested the hill and bounced down the other side, a different flatbed truck surrounded by a different team, awaited them. These guys were total strangers. My brother and Jake glanced at each other. Jake's jaw stiffened. Carlo's throat felt tight. After pulling to a stop, Jake stepped out of the Dodge first, with Carlo close behind. The .38 remained on the seat. Carlo found himself praying they wouldn't need it. He wondered if Jake was doing the same.

"Evening gentlemen," Jake said. "Nice night, wind's not blowing."

"No shit," a real skinny one, whose suit hung on him like one of those clowns in a circus, responded without a hint of frivolity or friendliness. His wide purple-striped tie clashed in spectacular fashion with a green pinstriped suit.

112

Clowns choose their wardrobes for laughs. Carlo didn't think the skinny one knew any better.

"Move the car up and let's get this done," ordered another punk, oddly wearing a long black overcoat and standing near the truck.

Even though it was close to dusk, the temperature still had to be over ninety. Last week it was spitting snow; now it was a very strange Indian summer dry. This guy must have missed the weather report, Carlo concluded. Having practiced this maneuver many times, Carlo got back in the Dodge and adeptly steered it into position for the transfer.

Soon the pungent fragrance of the freshly distilled liquor filled the air as the illegal spirits flowed smoothly from tank to tank. No one spoke; they all just stared warily at each other. Carlo kept his eyes trained on the one in the overcoat. Sweat was dripping from Mr. Overcoat's forehead. He scowled and fidgeted with the sleeves and lapels of his outer garment, dying to rip it off, Carlo was sure, and throw it aside, but something held him back. The heat was not enough to prompt Mr. Overcoat to strip.

It was not until the tank in the Dodge was topped off that the third one in the group, the tallest and ugliest of them all, took his turn to speak. "Okay, just so you know, from now on this will be the transfer point. We will be your contacts, and you tell Spinuzzi we will need at least a week's notice before any further shipments."

Carlo could tell Jake was stunned. "Wait a minute," Jake fumed. "Three days' notice is the most we've had to give. Our buyers don't want supply stackin' up in their basements temptin' raids. Besides, most ain't got the money set aside, and we ain't either, to stake them for a week."

"Too fuckin' bad," Mr. Overcoat shot back. "This here's the way it is. You pricks down here have had it your way for too long. You're playin' by our rules now. Denver talks. You listen. Mr. Blanco is no one to fuck with and neither are we." He paused. "Final thing, price is four hundred."

"Not gonna happen," Jake shot back. "You're supplyin' the same rot gut shit you've always given us, so we ain't payin' a dime more than three-fifty as always. Go fuck yourselves. I'll pour this shit on the ground before you're gettin' four hundred," he raged. A cold chill ran up Carlo's spine as he watched Jake move toward the back door of the Dodge. Carlo selfishly saw his twenty-five bucks (he had been promised that much for this job) slip away. He eyed Jake's hand grasp the door handle. In slow motion, it seemed, my brother saw the tall one closest to him slide a tire iron down the sleeve of his suit coat and into the grasp of his hand to use it to smash Jake's knuckles. Jake screamed in agony as the skinny one caught him on the side of the head with a blackjack, which came from the suit pocket of his oversized green get-up. Jake hit the ground hard. Carlo, by sheer instinct, moved around to the front of the Dodge to assist his fallen friend, but was stopped short with a double-barrel shotgun swiftly swept from beneath a black overcoat.

Mr. Overcoat planted both barrels firmly against Carlo's chest. My brother tingled in fear, but anger rose inside that he couldn't control. He looked down the double barrel and up into the face of Mr. Overcoat and shouted, "Put down the gun you motherfucker and I'll rip your head off!"

Mr. Overcoat laughed so hard Carlo thought he would drop the weapon or accidentally fire it through his chest. "Stand very still kid and you might not get hurt," he chuckled as he poked the barrels deeper into Carlo's flesh.

Carlo interrupted the story then to open his shirt to show me the faint, round bruises remaining from the imprint of the gun barrels. They hurt me just to see them. He closed his shirt and went on.

Carlo looked over to see Jake rising out of the dirt almost as quickly as he had gone down into it. He came up swinging, biting and kicking, taking an earlobe off skinny and catching the tall one square in the balls. Carlo, on guard with the shotgun held firmly to his chest, watched Jake fight like a madman, but he was finally subdued by Mr. Overcoat's wounded partners who managed to pin Jake to the side of the truck bed.

Jake received another blow from the tire iron that rendered him unconscious. Carlo had never seen anyone fight like Jake, and Carlo had seen plenty of fights, in fact, he had been in more than he could count, both inside and outside the ring. Jake had his opponents bloody and battered. With him finally down, Mr. Overcoat, very relieved, lowered the double barrel and pushed Carlo with his free hand against the hood of the Dodge, saying with a smile, "If you move, I will blow you in half."

As he sprawled across the hood of the Dodge, Carlo felt the heat from the motor beneath him. He turned his head just enough to see that Jake's chin had flopped forward to his chest, one eye already swollen shut and a deep gash running across his hairline. The shoulder pad of his new blue pin stripe was torn and the knee was out of his pants. He groaned as skinny grabbed his hair and jerked back his blood stained face. The tall one was rubbing his swollen crotch as he stood by, watching.

Skinny whispered, "I told you not to fuck with us. Now you've got to learn a simple lesson."

"Move him away from the truck," Mr. Overcoat ordered.

My brother had no way of knowing what was about to happen, but he guessed, whatever it was, it was not good for Jake or him. Again it seemed like they were moving Jake away in slow motion. Carlo observed both skinny and the tall one were in almost as much pain as Jake. God, he thought, I just can't *stand* here.

What followed was the reason my brother made the Central High School baseball team at age fourteen. He could throw a fastball; a good curve and even a slider by then and the coach started him on the mound the first game. Carlo struck out seven, walked only two, and won the game two to one. It was his first and last game. He had to quit baseball after that and go to work at the mill. Makes me sick to think about it.

Anyway, the second all three of those goons had their backs to Carlo, he rose from the hood of the car to look around. Down his eyes went to spot an oval rock luckily about the size of a baseball that lay at his feet. As the other two dragged Jake away from the flatbed, and Mr. Overcoat shuffled along behind, my brother stooped, picked up the rock and hurled his best fast ball into the back of the head of the tall one with the extremely sore testicles. The last thing he remembered before a sharp pain to his skull sent him into a blackness blacker than Mr. Overcoat's overcoat was hearing a terrible thud and seeing blood spray from the top of the tall one's pointed skull as the rock bounced off to the side. Strike one.

To this day Carlo has no idea how long he was unconscious. What woke him was a strange growl and yapping sound. When he opened his eyes, he was staring into the snarling, frothing jowls of a wild red-eyed coyote. The canine licked its smiling lips and caressed its teeth with his long, drooling tongue. It inched forward to sniff at my brother. As his senses finally began to return, Carlo got to his knees and growled and barked at the approaching menace. The coyote stopped and backtracked slightly, and probably figuring my brother was not as easy a meal as it had originally thought, turned to join a mate happily lapping up something from the dirt beneath a lonely nearby pine.

Carlo's head throbbed like a base drum and blood had caked on the collar of his new white dress shirt. As he rose to his feet he saw the twisted heap of a new, blue pin stripe in the distance. The heap lay on the ground in an odd configuration, devoid of substance, it seemed. One shoe was attached to an appendage of the heap; the other lay a couple of inches away. Carlo was too wobbly to walk so he dropped back down to crawl toward the tree as the coyotes turned and snarled at him, both bearing their bloody fangs. It was way past dusk by then, and the wind had picked up. He retrieved another rock, but this time, he was too weak and disoriented to throw it hard or straight. Instead he tossed it in the direction of the canines, and thankfully, not willing to fight for their meal, they scampered off with a whimper as the rock splashed in a puddle from which one of them had been slurping. When Carlo finally reached the tree, he did not recognize what was left inside the blue pinstripe. It appeared Jake had been blown in half, and most of his jaw and the right side of his head were missing from a second, or maybe third blast.

Carlo somehow managed to avoid vomiting. Instead, he looked away and fought to regain at bit of self-control. His eyes, now filled with tears, scanned the surroundings. It was hard for him to admit that he had cried, I'll tell you that. Tire tracks were all that remained to provide evidence of the murdering bunch that had just left their ruthless remnants. Carlo wiped his tears and looked back toward the Dodge. Both of its passenger side doors were open. A lake of brown liquid lay beneath the car from where the backseat tank had been punctured by yet another shotgun blast.

As calmly as he could, Carlo grabbed what was intact of Jake's head, torso and legs and carefully, reverently, carried his shredded carcass to the car, laying him gently in the back seat. It took two trips to retrieve everything that remained. He removed his own suit coat, now soaked in Jake's blood, and placed it over the body. With great effort he reached inside Jake's suit coat for the money Carlo knew he carried in his inside pocket, but all he pulled out were his own bloodstained fingers. Not a cent remained.

My brother got in on the driver's side, started the engine, turned the wheel and inched his way back to the gravel road and eventually out onto the two-lane asphalt toward town. The .38 was gone from the seat beside him. The tears came back in torrents as he drove.

Over the chugging sound of the Dodge's motor, he spoke to Jake. "Man, I'm sorry. I didn't do my job. I let you down. I let everyone down. I didn't watch your back. I tried, I really did, but I failed and now you're dead. I'm sorry, please forgive me." He couldn't manage to say anything else for the rest of the dreadful drive back to town.

For some time Carlo had known where Tony lived, even though he'd never been to his house. It was outside our neighborhood in a part of town mostly inhabited by line supervisors and mill administrative types, accountants and the sort. Jefferson Street. It was named for the president. My brother weaved his way through Central Park and easily found Tony's street. He drove two houses past Tony's house, parked, and walked back to the expansive front red brick porch and freshly painted white pillars supporting the peaked portico. Picture windows graced either side of the stained heavy walnut door. Lamps were lit behind the drawn curtains.

A shiny brass doorknocker mimicking a canine's head with pointed ears, narrow-set eyes and long, pointed snout, glared back at him. A ring hung from the canine's clamped-shut jaw. For a moment Carlo couldn't touch it. Its eyes seemed to blink, and its mouth dropped open to snap at his hand. He flinched from his warped hallucination. The sky was dark by then, and a few of the neighborhood dogs were barking; the sound reminding him of the snarling coyotes as he stood fixated on the terrifying figure in front of him. He blinked and the crazed carnivore returned to its permanent place fixed to the door with brass screws. The barking from afar stopped. He wasn't sure he would ever like dogs again.

He grabbed the ring in the fox's snout and tapped it lightly against Tony's front door. It was Saturday night, and he desperately hoped someone was home. Almost immediately Tony appeared, peering through the curtains to the right. He switched on the porch light to illuminate the scene. As he swung open the door Carlo looked Tony in the eye and unconsciously tried to wipe the dirt from his filthy face and make the blood caked on his soiled shirt from the deep gash in his scalp disappear. Spinuzzi, his leader, stepped outside onto the porch.

"I was afraid this might happen. I was afraid," Tony said, more to himself than to Carlo.

How could he know what had happened? Carlo hadn't said a word. He didn't have to.

Tony reached out to take Carlo by the arm, steadying him as they turned to descend the front porch steps. They walked to the Dodge parked two houses away. Two streetlights illuminated the corners of the block, but the Dodge was parked in the middle so little light shed upon the grisly scene Carlo was about to present.

As they approached the car, Tony asked, "Is he dead?" Carlo still couldn't speak. It seemed just then that his jaw was wired shut.

"You did the right thing, coming here. You did right," Tony said. "Did anyone follow you?" he asked. Carlo shook his head.

"You did right. I was afraid this might happen," Tony repeated.

Tony drove and Carlo rode quietly beside him, the remains of their friend scattered in the backseat, to the rear entrance of Balducci's funeral home on Ninth Street. It was only two miles from Tony's house. The stench was overpowering. Tony rang the bell, awakening Mr. Balducci. Tony whispered instructions to mortuary owner and the body parts were gently removed from the car. Tony drove my brother home. I awoke then they arrived and watched from the window as Carlo got out and walked up the path to our front door. I knew something was wrong. Tony drove the Dodge away. None of us ever saw it again.

I didn't say anything to my brother when he entered the bedroom. I pretended to be asleep. He lay back on his bed and I think he fell asleep immediately. I couldn't sleep the rest of the night. As I lay there wondering what had happened a creeping fear came over me. Unexplained but real terror. On one hand I was glad Carlo told me the whole story the next day. On the other I wished I'd never known. Replaying, reliving through him the events he described. That experience. That horror. That cold-blooded murder. Finding the bloody mass. And the fact he somehow had been spared, certainly not out of compassion or caring. Those bastards killed for kicks. How easily they could have, probably should have for their sake, turned the double-barrel on my brother. Why didn't they? Did something spook them off? Maybe the coyotes? Or God? Or was Carlo spared for other reasons? Did he have another assignment he was meant to carry out? Something worthwhile? A mission? I chose to think so. I chose to think my brother might have escaped death for a reason. What I do know is that what happened to my brother that night brought him to his knees. And it took him a long while to get up.

Carlo let me come with him to Jake's funeral. There was no open casket for obvious reasons. The wake and funeral were spectacular. High Mass – lasting two hours. It was hot, the Indian summer hanging on to torture us. There were hundreds of flowers and wreaths, dozens of wailing women and several drunken men. The bishop said the funeral Mass. The cathedral was filled with standing room only. There must have been three hundred people who attended the service. The funeral procession stretched for ten city blocks out to Rosemont Cemetery for a gravesite service attended by most of those originally at Mass.

Tony paid Carlo thirty dollars for the run on that horrible night, even though, Carlo said, the goods had quickly soaked into the ground after the Dodge's hidden tank was peppered with several shotgun blasts. I couldn't help thinking that maybe one or more of the blasts had been intended for my brother.

My mother and sisters didn't attend the services. Carlo literally forbade it. Later, he explained that he didn't want to have our whole family seen as mourners. I know my mother cooked for Jake's mother a few times, and they were friends. But that didn't matter. Carlo wanted to keep our family as far away from the death and its consequences as possible. Miss Murphy attended the funeral. I saw her in the back corner pew, all alone. She winked at me as we took our seats, two pews away. The next week I went to see her. She had the latest scoop. She was amazing.

She said word passed around a few days before that Tony had placed a call to New York the day after the funeral. To judge from the events that followed, he apparently got someone's attention. Miss Murphy couldn't predict what happened next, but she did say, "Blanco won't last long." She didn't suspect that Lucky had any idea who Tony was but she concluded that there was outrage in New York over the details of the killing that Tony had likely relayed to the young Vito Genovese, the mob boss' third in command. Vito was known to take those types of calls for Lucky, and Miss Murphy was right, it later became all too real that Tony got their attention.

Just one year after being given his post, Charlie Blanco was snuffed out. His murder was all over the newspapers. When the end came he was asleep with his mistress at a motor inn near Fountain, about twenty miles north of town. He and his companion each took a single shot to the head, and one to their spines. Few knew about Charlie's unlucky lover. As a good will gesture, and to preserve the reputation of his wife and family, Charlie's mistress was taken to the reservoir to provide a fresh meal for the trout and bass that someday might be wrapped in Angelina's parchment and cooked together with her fresh pasta.

Around the same time, Little Caesar – or Mr. Romeo – called a meeting of his business council. At the meeting in classical theatrics his most trusted allies turned on him and stabbed him to death. That was in the newspapers too. What the press didn't realize but Miss Murphy knew took place was a gruesome mob ritual surrounded the death. Shakespearean in its reenactment, Romeo's associates stabbed him twenty seven times, she said, somewhat like the Roman Senators did to the real Caesar, twice each with the last three thrusts into the abdomen coming, Miss Murphy thinks, from Romeo's successor, who already had been hand-picked by Lucky.

Now the slate had been wiped clean. The Smaldonis were relegated to bit-part players, too insignificant to kill or worry about any further, and I'm sure they were too afraid to make any more noise. Miss Murphy predicted that Lucky would make it clear that if the Smaldoni brothers wanted long, happy, prosperous lives, they would shut up, take orders and stay out of the way.

From then on, Pueblo, not Denver, was the syndicate's central headquarters in the West. All activities from St. Louis to Los Angeles were to be run through our town. All answered to the Genovese family and Lucky Luciano. The Genovese clan was now the single, dominant Mafia power throughout the country. Lucky's dream of himself as regent and his family as a monarchy had come true. Even Giuseppe "Joe Bananas" Bonnano Senior, a rising star within the cadre and whom Miss Murphy believed was first in line for the top Mafia post in the West, was sent off to Phoenix, and told he too would answer to the new boss coming to our town. Romeo was gone.
Blanco was gone. And Lucky had
found his man.

By then a middle-aged capo, bred, born and nurtured into maturity in the underworld's fine art of criminality, Jimmy "Black Jim" Clemente was Lucky's choice. With this guy this time Lucky demanded low-profile leadership. To finally fulfill his vision of centralized control for the region, he needed a man who stayed out of the spotlight, was not flashy, operated discreetly but effectively, and above all, was ruthless. Black Jim was soon dispatched to Pueblo to take charge. Miss Murphy said she was surprised at the choice, and worried. And that frightened me more than anything.

Chapter 14
Can't Put Out The Fire

The night after Jake's funeral, I was awake when Carlo came home very late. He'd dropped me off at home after the services and drove off in a car I didn't recognize. I asked him if the car was his, but he didn't answer me. When he entered our room he reeked of alcohol and cigarette smoke. He leaned down close to me, and I again pretended to be asleep. I did a lot of that lately. He rose and circled the room, his shadow tracing on the walls as he walked in short strides. He didn't say anything. With one eye open, I watched him undress in the moonlight shining through our only window and pile his dress shirt and the brown pinstripe, the only suit he had, in a bundle in the center of the floor.

His actions were particularly strange. Usually when Carlo got home from being out during one of his mysterious nights, he would neatly hang his suit and brush it down, carefully removing every speck of dirt before placing it in the back of the closet. Then he would polish his shoes (which were usually very dusty) before placing them in their original box and sliding them to the back of the closet. This was his ritual. He had never varied from it before tonight. Before I pulled the facts out of him about his excursions, I always wondered why Carlo's shoes were always dusty, and occasionally caked with mud, when I figured getting dressed up like he did meant he was going to some fancy place to either work, or drink, or better yet, to meet girls.

Carlo always seemed to come home dirty, and it finally made sense once I learned it all. It had been disappointing, and frightening to know that his exquisite suit and ties and shiny shoes were not for pursuits of pleasure, rather dangerous escapades into a bleak, empty, no-reward world offering no means of escape.

I watched as Carlo, now in his long johns, put on his work boots and overalls. But it was Sunday and three o'clock in the morning, and I knew Carlo didn't have to work today. I just lay still and watched my brother move about the room, illuminated only by the moon rays streaking in. Before long, Carlo gathered his suit and shoes and quietly exited the room. I waited for a few moments, keeping very still. I heard him open and shut the back door. I slipped out of bed and crawled over to the window. Peering out into the darkness, I saw Carlo emerge from the shadows and walk into the backyard.

I watched, bewildered, as my brother dropped his clothes onto the ground and scan around in every direction apparently to see if anyone was watching. Carlo stood over his stack of clothing for a moment, and then suddenly disappeared, back into the night. I knew he hadn't seen me, since in my spying spot under the windowsill I too was shrouded in darkness. I looked left to right in the yard, desperately trying to locate my brother as the clouds passed in front of the moon to momentarily drape, and then brighten the scene. Then I saw him move out of the blackness and into the dim light. He stood over his clothes and began to splash what I could clearly see was gasoline from the red can we kept stored under the back porch. He lit a match and tossed it onto the pile. The blaze was intense,

125

but only for a moment. Then the bright light from the flames flashed a beam on Carlo's face long enough for me to see the tears streaming down his cheeks.

It was the first time I ever saw my brother cry.

~

The next morning I couldn't wake him. In fact, he wouldn't get out of bed at all that day. He skipped Mass. Our mother was furious. The next day he returned to work, as always right on time, as if nothing happened or nothing else mattered.

That morning after Carlo had left for the mill, my mother asked me if I knew anything about Carlo's head wound. I said I didn't. I don't think she ever asked Carlo about it. The next week, Angelina told me she noticed Carlo's suit was missing from the closet. She asked me about that too. I didn't lie this time. I just didn't tell her anything. It wasn't my place. One month later, after work on a Monday, Carlo opened up to me again. He told me that Tony had caught up with him as he was coming off the lunch break. He hadn't been invited to join Tony and the others. He had eaten alone.

"Kid," Tony said. "I know that was tough. I know you never expected it, but those things happen in this world, so you'd better get used to it and take it like a man. If you have any doubts about returning to the job, and you'd better not, I need to know right now. You have until the end of the day to tell me when you're ready to take another run." Tony poked his finger in Carlo's chest and rambled on. "Remember, you little shit, I never got your delivery from the other night, and I still gave you your money, more than you deserved, so suck it up and get back to work." Tony started to turn away, then looked back. "Oh, by the way, we caught those three sons-a-bitches, trying to cross the divide up by Gunnison. That truck of theirs broke down and they were just sittin' there by the side of the road, waitin' for somebody to come along and give them a lift. Well, lifted them we did. Right off their feet with about twenty rounds each from a Thompson. God damn if they weren't splattered all over that ditch by the time we was through," Tony chuckled and grinned.

Carlo said there was absolutely no way he could respond to that, so he turned and just shuffled off to rejoin the line and complete his shift. He hurt inside, he told me. His head ached. He was scared. He was confused, but he knew he had to somehow get over the shock and gore. His mind raced through it all out loud while I sat and tried to be a friend, and not a judgmental brother. He had made the mistake of thinking Tony would understand, give him a break and let him off the hook. He thought Jake's murder would make everyone realize how dangerous this whole business was, and maybe they would stop. God, how stupid was that, he asked me. Jake was just a driver, and Carlo was just a mule, easily replaced by other eager mill worker fools just like them, looking for the extra dough and a little excitement. All Tony had to do was put the word out. They'd line up at attention. Both Jake and Carlo had been stooges. Nobody cared about anybody.

Carlo was scouring for answers. He said it was hard for him to concentrate on the work lines that afternoon. I was worried — a lack of concentration on the lines could get you killed. He had to snap out of it. Jake gave his life defending these guys and their operation. Carlo had seen it with his own eyes. He had had his blood and brains on his hands, and under his fingernails. Carlo had said Jake had fought back hard. He wouldn't let those bastards jack up their prices and still provide cheap, watered down booze. That's all it was. Was that worth dying for? But he got himself killed, and Carlo couldn't help him, and he damn near got himself killed too by standing up to those guys. And now all Tony could say was forget it; take it like a man. What was Carlo even thinking about? He said Tony told him he had until the end of his shift to decide if he was going to take Jake's place.

"I can't do it! I've got to get out," I was relieved to hear my brother say. "But how? They might kill me. I know a lot about a lot of things, and knowing too much is dangerous. How do I get out?" He wasn't really asking me this time, more himself. But then he turned and looked me straight in the eye. "That could have been you instead of Jake. Next time, it might be me or you, unless I get out, turn away right now. But how?" Carlo looked at me as he choked out the words with such desperation I had to turn away.

Maybe I was too young for this. Right then, I wished to God I was still just a kid walking to Central Park with my older brother holding his hand, carefree, worrying only about keeping up, matching his stride. But no, this was real. This was life, and not one any one of us wanted. And for the first time Miss Murphy's private lectures, abstract before, far away, involving someone else I didn't know or could give a good shit about, had become all too real, all too close, and all too sinister. I didn't want to learn any more. I wanted it all to go away.

Chapter 15
Angels in Their Cocoons

Julia Gail DiAlanicio's house was exactly midway between our home and Bessemer's only real commercial district. The small, family-owned businesses were all clustered together on a single block and consisted of Stefano's Corner Grocery and Fresh Meat Market, Tiny's Auto Repair and Towing Shop, Lucas's Pharmacy, Castellano's Dry Cleaning and Laundry Service, and Renaldi's Barber and Beauty Shop. Everyone in Bessemer shopped at Stefano's, got their cars repaired by Tiny (he weighed in at three twenty five at last count) sent their suits and winter coats for cleaning once every six months to Castellano's, bought their aspirin and castor oil at Lucas's, and got their hair cut and permanents done at Renaldi's. Each business kept a tab if you didn't have the money to pay right then. You never skipped out. You paid when you could. For sure, you paid when you could.

Carlo and I knew the inside of these establishments as well as the interior of our own bedroom. And for sure Carlo knew how to get there even if he was blindfolded. He just had to walk past Julia Gail DiAlanicio's house. And when he did that, his heart skipped a beat – or at least that's what he told me – every time. Carlo was deeply and forever in love with Julia Gail DiAlanicio. He had felt that way as long as I could remember, probably since the first time he saw her which was at Mass on some Sunday morning long ago, when he was about eight and she was probably seven. Yes, Carlo could have no other than Julia Gail. He and just about every other boy in our neighborhood.

Julia Gail was a gorgeous child. Angelic, graceful. Walked like a ballerina. She had coal black hair that hung down her back to the bottom of her spine; always adorned with a different ribbon. Her smile was like a beacon through the fog. She sparkled. I always wondered if she knew how she was worshipped from afar by the boys in her class. When she spoke to Carlo, he would just about melt on the spot. Plus she was the best speller in class, always winning the Friday afternoon spelling bees, once spelling the word "hypoallergenic" correctly when she was in the third grade. Just for an excuse to pass by her palace Carlo would look for excuses to run errands for Angelina to the pharmacy or market. She was his queen.

And then she got sick. And nobody knew it until she missed Mass on the day of her confirmation. In fact she was so sick for so long, she was seventeen by the time her ceremony was held, and seventeen was very late in life for a young female Catholic Italian to be confirmed by the church. This sacred act generally occurred in pre-teen years, and certainly no later than fifteen.

You see, on the Sunday after Julia Gail's twelfth birthday, she was to be confirmed along with twelve other boys and girls, including Carlo. But she didn't show up. Father Murray went ahead and confirmed the seven boys and five girls that Sunday morning. My mother, sisters and I were in attendance, and we were all wondering why Julia Gail was missing, but probably none more than my brother. We knew it wasn't a matter of her questioning her faith. She was an ardent student of the Catholic teachings. There had to be another reason.

She had disappeared. She missed school, was nowhere to be found. My brother couldn't believe it. His days back then were made whole, fulfilled with just the sight of her. Now she was gone. Rumors spread as they always do in neighborhoods like Bessemer. Julia Gail was missing. Why? Did she die? Was she shipped off to boarding school? And then as mysteriously as when she left, she returned, but certainly not like before.

Turns out that Julia Gail, like millions of strong, vigorous Americans, young and old at that time, had been struck down by polio. Quickly, her stately legs bent, her strength was sapped, and the simple task of breathing became so hard I heard she wept in fear of suffocating.

On a Tuesday afternoon, two weeks and two days after Carlo was confirmed, a white-paneled truck pulled into the driveway of the DiAlanicio house. A kid in our neighborhood, Ronaldo Uliberri, came running up to Carlo and me as we were walking to the market and yelled out that something strange was going on at Julia Gail's house. Carlo took off in a sprint, with me following close behind. We stopped two or three houses away from hers so we didn't look like we were spying. We watched Julia Gail's father, Thomas, emerge from the passenger front seat of the van and move to the rear and open the double tailgate doors. He offered his hand to help Julia Gail's mother, Theresa exit. As she stepped out, we saw her plunging some sort of handle up and down into a strange looking box. He had a steady rhythm to her motion. A tube was connected from the box to something inside the truck. With the help of the driver, Thomas reached in and pulled out the strange contraption. It looked like something from outer space – a long, metal tube. I heard Carlo gasp. Julia Gail, by evidence of her head exposed from one end, was inside. The metal cylinder was on wheels. They gently rolled it up the sidewalk to the front steps of the house. We could see her angelic face was ashen, her black hair cut short. The family disappeared inside with the driver, who came out a few minutes later and drove off.

My brother just stood there, mouth gaping open. He was dumbstruck, and finally turned to me to say, "Julia Gail was inside that thing but she is alive; that's all that matters," he said breathlessly.

Neither of us had any idea what "that thing" was. Funny enough, the next day, the *Chieftain Journal* ran a story about the invention of the "thing" Julia Gail was now confined in. It was a hideous looking life-giving sanctuary called the iron lung.

And so it was that Julia Gail, Carlo's post-pubescent dream, was sheltered away, lying encapsulated in sheet metal from her shoulders down and breathing only with the help of the relentless clang and swoosh of that ingenious apparatus. The family's living room became her hospital suite.

Angelina was among the first of our neighbors to call on Julia Gail and her mother and father during the early months following their acceptance that the town princess would be confined, perhaps indefinitely, to that tubular cocoon. My mother brought food, some of her best dishes. She never charged them, although they always offered to pay. When she returned from her visits, Carlo would beseech her for information. But Angelina was discreet. She told him as much as she considered appropriate, leaving out things she didn't feel were necessary for his understanding.

Our mother learned from Theresa that Julia Gail had been born on the ship coming over from Naples. It had been a hard delivery – very hard. Theresa was in labor for thirty-seven hours before Julia Gail was born, frail, but demonstrating a boundless will to survive. Theresa told Angelina she knew at that point she could never bear children again. Even at birth, Julia Gail was a beautiful child in so many ways. Her parents told my mother she had translucent olive skin and stared up at them with deep, cobalt blue eyes that blinked slowly as they took turns holding her the first night of her life.

As she grew, they said, Julia Gail fell victim to more than her share of childhood diseases, victimized by an immune system that left her vulnerable to infections. Yet as she blossomed early into womanhood, her parents were well aware she was gaining the attention and affection of nearly every boy who roamed or lived in the Bessemer neighborhood. Even after the scourge of her polio, the attention paid her by Carlo and her other neighborhood friends did not wane. Each day, including Sunday, I could spot a Bessemer boy or girl standing on the dirt road just outside Julia Gail's front yard, looking toward her house. Through her front window all they could see were her lovely face and now shoulder-length black hair leisurely flowing from the end of the iron lung as it pumped life into her.

Her parents kept the curtains open to let the sunlight in on most days, and at night, the living room was lighted, allowing her to read one of her favorite novels, with the words on the pages reflecting from the mirror above her head. She expertly flipped through the pages with the eraser end of a pencil tightly wedged between her teeth. Angelina told us that Julia Gail's parents were never ashamed of where or how their daughter was currently living her life, or the condition she was in. Rather, they were extremely proud of her courage, her acceptance of her plight, and her unbending will and optimism for recovery.

"Daddy, I will get out of here someday soon, and take a walk with you around the block," she would say.

Of course, Carlo was one of those boys who took turns (probably far in excess of that due him) watching Julia Gail from a designated post outside, helping keep the vigil, and while never speaking to her or anyone in her family directly, he and the others, including me, silently encouraged her to flourish.

Chapter 16
Roosevelt's Lesson

Carlo

One day nearly two years to the day after Julia Gail was stricken, Carlo told me he was slowly walking by her house when the girl stopped her reading, slowly turned her head toward him, and smiled through the living room window. For a moment he thought his heart might have stopped. He was stricken, embarrassed; she had caught him staring, like some perverted voyeur. So he was surprised when, a moment later, her father appeared at the door, motioning for him to come closer. Mr. DiAlanicio met him halfway down the front walk.

"Your name is Carlo, right?" he asked. "You're Nick's son? Nick was my friend. He helped me in the early days, to get started, to earn my way up. I pray for his soul. A fine man. You should be proud. Your mother is a fine woman, too. Loyal. Good mother, good neighbor. She helps others. She is strong raising seven on her own. You take care of her, right?" he asked again.

"Yes sir. I do, sir. I take care of my mother. I am sorry for bothering you. I didn't mean..." Carlo stammered.

"Son, you don't worry. Call me Thomas. My daughter would like to talk with you. She wants you to come in. Do you want to come in?"

"Are you sure?" Now it was Carlo's turn to question.

By then Thomas had already turned toward the front door and was walking that way. "Come, sit with her awhile," he commanded over his shoulder.

Carlo cautiously stepped through the doorway into the living room and was immediately confronted by the clamor of the breathing device as it sucked air from the room and into Julia Gail's ravaged lungs. Yet he was struck as he saw the reflection of her face in the mirror and the broad grin that crossed her lips.

"Hello, Carlo," she said between the up and down movement of the bellows beneath her.

Carlo steadied himself and moved to the side so she could see him without strain. "Hello, Julia Gail." His knees were shaking.

"I've seen you standing out in the street many times. I think it's nice that you come by to see me," she said. "I just wanted to thank you for thinking about me."

Finally he gathered his strength, and as her father left the room, said, "I hope I'm not bothering you. I know many of the other guys also come by. We all want to make sure you're alright."

"Carlo, you know, I'm going to get out of here real soon. I'm going to walk again and I'm going to run again, and when I do, I hope you will go for a walk with me," she said confidently.

"Sure. I will come and walk with you, but I don't run very fast so you might have to wait for me," he responded with a soft smile.

But she did not smile, instead a tear formed in the corner of her eye. "I know I will; walk again, and run again. So, I will wait for you to catch up."

They talked for a while longer until Carlo noticed she was wearing down as each breath now came with more difficulty. Before he left, he promised to come back, and the next time, he said, he would bring a book for her to read, hopefully one of her favorite books.

He would find out her favorite books, he promised himself. As he stepped through the front door, the nerve-shattering sound of the iron lung that before had drilled into his skull was no longer there. In fact, he didn't hear it at all. All he heard was her say, "Bye Carlo. See you soon," as he closed the door behind him.

From then on, almost every Wednesday, Carlo visited Julia Gail and read to her. The other boys in the neighborhood gave him hell for having that privilege; no one else was ever invited inside the DiAlanicio home. Carlo became the envy of his friends and some of his enemies, and soon, the others just passed by Julia Gail's window without stopping, without looking, accepting Carlo's lofty position without further challenge.

Carlo was not much for reading, other than a few periodicals, detective novels and an occasional newspaper. But when Julia Gail allowed him inside her sanctum for such an intimate view of her struggle for life, he set out to learn everything he could about the hideous tin monster that was keeping her with him.

It didn't take him long to become an expert. The *Chieftain Journal* article only gave him a hint. Johnny introduced him to the library, and the reference books there filled in the blanks. He discovered that the iron lung was invented in the late 1920s, just a few years before. It was designed to aid victims of polio in the first days or months of their affliction. They were very expensive and hard to acquire. In fact, there was only one other machine in Pueblo, and that was at St. Mary of the Divine Hospital. To have one in your home for private use was unheard of, particularly for a steel mill worker. Carlo knew the presence of the machine had prompted several in the neighborhood to question how Thomas had provided it for his ailing daughter.

The iron lung was not meant as a permanent means of sustaining life, although several articles Carlo read said that there were predictions of polio victims living long, fruitful lives with the aid of the mechanical cradle. At first glance, some viewed the monstrosity as de-humanizing, but those relying on the metal cocoon, and their loved ones, saw it as the only way to become human again. Suffocating was the alternative. The device worked well in many cases by allowing the body to breathe effortlessly and to rest and repair itself from the ravages of the disease. But more often than not, Carlo read with dismay, when one emerged from the tube with enough strength restored to breathe and partially function on their own, they lived their remaining days confined to a wheelchair.

Later that year, after his election, President Franklin Roosevelt would become that living example when the world finally found out about his affliction with polio and his confinement to a wheelchair. Roosevelt was rarely photographed in his chair, yet bring crippled only added to his appeal. And when Carlo, Julia Gail and the rest of America saw Roosevelt's strength displayed in ways other than with his legs, the wheelchair became his mighty vehicle from which to maneuver the country through the Depression and lead America in war.

Rare as it was that picture published in the *Chieftain Journal* of the president in his wheelchair was inspiration

Julia Gail needed to venture out of her pulsating tube for the first time. Carlo wasn't with her when she did it. Actually no one was home at the time. Her hands and arms had been steadily gaining strength each day, and on this day, she was strong enough to turn off the pumps, unhook the latches and slowly wiggle out.

When Carlo arrived that Wednesday, she described the experience to him as being born again, not in the evangelical sense, but literally likening it to a journey down a cold, hard metal birth canal. Recalling her first moments of freedom, she said that when her mother returned home and found her sitting on the platform which usually supported her neck and head, she gasped in terror before breaking down in sobs and then laughing with her daughter in joy.

Another Wednesday, Carlo experienced a similar sensation when he walked up the sidewalk to Julia Gail's and failed to see her black hair dangling and her big smile waiting. His knees buckled in fear. For a moment he couldn't muster the strength to knock on the door. For a moment, he thought she had died. But when he heard that deep throated, sweet twang he knew so well, say, "You don't have to knock, Carlo, just come in," he nearly broke the door handle getting it open.

From then on, each Wednesday, Carlo knew Julia Gail would be outside her machine, waiting for him, remaining inside the artificial lung until just a few minutes before he was due to arrive. He was never late; he knew she could stay outside the contraption for only up to a half-hour. But as each day passed, her "fresh air" time became longer, and Carlo's job changed from reader of favorite novels (she liked Louisa May Alcott) to deputy assistant amateur physical therapist.

The articles that Carlo had read said in rare occurrences, when it was possible, a polio victim's next step to a temporary or permanent recovery was regaining strength and stamina in their legs and arms. But Julia Gail's case was unusual because the disease had first attacked her lower extremities and then moved up through her torso to rip into her lungs. When she freed herself from the iron lung, her lower legs from the knees down were twisted and bent so severely that her feet were nearly at right angles from her ankles. When Carlo saw them for the first time, it took all his strength not to turn away and gasp. But almost from the moment she first sat on that platform outside the contraption, she began to regain some movement and began to swing her legs back and forth from her knees. She had good circulation to her feet too, even though her leg muscles had atrophied to shrink to encapsulate not much more than the diameter of her bones. She seemed to be healing in reverse, Carlo thought.

One afternoon Carlo asked Thomas as politely as he could, out of earshot of Julia Gail, if there was any type of therapy or rehabilitation program for those suffering from polio. Carlo thought he might find something at the library, but he hadn't; very little had been written on the subject of rehabilitation in the early 1930s, and doctors, including Doctor Stein, were still generally convinced that full disability, with the legs of victims straightened and strengthened with heavy metal braces, was the only future awaiting polio's population.

Doctor Albert Stein was a kind (although pessimistic), short, stocky Jew, part of one of ten Jewish families in Pueblo. Their synagogue was in a converted three-bedroom bungalow in Pueblo's only so-called upper class neighborhood about five miles from Bessemer. Doctor Stein's shaggy white hair grew in a mane well over his collar, and his spectacles were constantly slipping off his nose. Once he came to call on Julia Gail while Carlo was there. Carlo had to wait outside for forty-five minutes while Doctor Stein examined her. When he was done, Carlo had only fifteen minutes left before he had to go to work that night. He was working the swing shift and he was angry the whole night that his time with Julia Gail had been cut short.

That same week, Theresa told Angelina that during the house call Doctor Stein had made it clear that Julia Gail would be no exception to the commonly held belief that permanent disability would be her fate. She would remain a cripple, the doctor maintained, and he told her parents she would be barren as well. Carlo was surprised that Angelina had decided to tell him all of this, including the most private part of Julia Gail's life. Our mother gave him the details for a reason. She now saw him in a different light after these past months, watching him care the way he did for Julia Gail. Her candor further intensified his commitment to help the girl he loved and to prove the doctor wrong.

Nobody told Julia Gail about her pre-disposed destiny. So with blind faith and a steadfast determination she created her own self-designed and self-administered recovery program. Instinctively, she instructed her parents (and Carlo on Wednesdays) on assisting her with her exercises. Gently, at first, they massaged her ankles and feet, and then began moving to reposition them, ever so slowly, back to their natural place. Most of the time the pain was unbearable. Drugs were unavailable. Only her will dulled the agony. But in less than a month they all noticed some restorative movement. Carlo was amazed. Her feet and ankles appeared less distorted, more to the proper position. Her legs, too, showed signs of heft as each day she rotated them in a bicycle-pedaling fashion with the help of her mother and father.

It was improper in those days for Carlo to give aid to her as she rode her imaginary bicycle since a boy should not be touching a girl there, even under those circumstances. Rather, when visiting, Carlo was assigned the task of strengthening her arms, wrists and hands, rotating them to stimulate the circulation, muscle tone and nerve sensitivity. He was ashamed the first few times while holding her hand of that familiar tingle in his crouch. It served to divert his attention from his assigned task.

There were dreadful days when she was too exhausted to escape the cocoon, and some of those days were Wednesdays, so Carlo was turned away at the door. And there were times when she tried and failed to turn the non-existent bicycle pedals just once, or she would push Carlo away, breaking his grasp of her hand, and tell him to leave. It was just too hard, she cried. She wanted to quit. But Carlo always returned the next week. In fact, it was all he could think about during the days in between.

Yet slowly, ever so slowly, she improved. Days and weeks turned into months. After six of them, she resumed some of her school lessons. Every Wednesday, Carlo brought her the assignments for the week, and returned her work to school when she finished. More time out of her tin can, more time exercising, and then her first steps. And this time, Carlo was there to witness the miracle. Although he knew it wasn't a miracle – she had worked so hard. She was spent after three faltering steps, but they were steps nonetheless. Julia Gail described those steps as if she had just run the women's high hurdles and placed second behind Babe Didrikson in the 1932 Olympics in Los Angeles. Carlo didn't know who Babe Didrikson was, but Julia Gail sure did. She was her favorite athlete of all time.

Then, a few days later, for the first time, she slept outside the tube. All night, and did not return until the next morning, and only then for an hour. She told Carlo about her night in her own bed; the first outside her confinement in more than three years. She hugged him that day with strength he hadn't felt before, and he thought he detected a brush of her lips on his cheek. After that more progress and another encouraging event. Doctor Stein couldn't explain it. She had her first menstrual cycle. With her honesty and openness, she could not resist sharing the news with Carlo. He was uncomfortable, but could not help but share in her joy.

Barren, my ass, he thought.

He told our mother that night and she paused to say a Hail Mary.

Julia Gail would venture outside in a wheelchair at first, but rolling about was unacceptable for her. That depressed her more than anything since she was determined to skip that part of her recovery and go directly to braces and crutches. She was fitted for those "god-awful leg braces," as she called them, but they further helped strengthen and straighten her legs. Soon, she was taking more steps with the crutches only, abandoning the braces as often as possible. She ignored the wheelchair whenever she could. She smiled more, and the month before her sixteenth birthday, she turned to Carlo one day, this time with her leg braces shoring up her balance, grabbed his neck and kissed him square on the mouth. Her tongue parted his lips. It was such a surprise; a shock really, that he didn't have time to react.

"Carlo, I couldn't have done this without you. You mean so much to me. I'm trying so hard to be pretty again, just for you. Please give me time. I will be pretty again. I won't have these ugly things around me, I promise," she gasped.

Carlo was dumbfounded, caught his breath, stammered something unintelligible, but realized he didn't want to talk for fear of dissolving the taste of her lips from his. So he just stood there for a moment before bringing her back to him and kissing her again, this time until the tingle in his crotch became almost unbearable.

Chapter 17
Craps, Cue balls, and Spittoons

As I grew older, people used to say that I was one of those kids who could "stare down a rattlesnake," or "patiently count the straw in a haystack." I'm not sure what all that meant, but I do think I could concentrate on tiny things most other people would ignore, or on events that might completely pass others by. For instance, I could sit for hours watching ants build their anthills. I was fascinated by the teamwork, skill and unbelievable strength of the little creatures as they went about constructing their new home with each pebble carefully put in place to form the growing mound.

Once I read a book on the Egyptians building the pyramids. It reminded me of the ants and building their homes. I was completely drawn into how the slaves carved and placed each block of stone and the higher they went up the pyramid, the tougher their jobs became; just like the ants. Some people thought I was crazy for talking about the ants and the Egyptians, especially my sisters.

Another thing I had, what one doctor told me, was almost super-human eyesight. I could read a roadside sign nearly a quarter of a mile away. I could read newsprint from across the breakfast table. I could spot a cockroach in a corner at thirty paces. And best of all, I could tell the color of

145

a pretty girl's eyes from way down the hallway at school. When Carlo took me hunting for rabbits in the fields outside Blende, I usually bagged enough bunnies in thirty minutes for at least two weeks of good rabbit stew. My specialty was head shots at thirty yards with a bolt action .22 rifle tracking a rabbit at a dead run, bobbing and weaving. I was always careful not to destroy any of the meat.

My eyesight and my ability to pay close attention to immediate tasks made me a pretty good student, yet I was easily bored with mundane classroom exercises. But I got good grades and usually placed near the top of my class. I really didn't have to study that hard to excel, allowing me time to examine the people and the world around me with a keen interest.

Sometimes when I was paying close attention to someone, Carlo used to tell me I was just "plain goddamn nosey," and to mind my own business.

"Go watch the ants, kid," Carlo used to say. But that didn't bother me much.

I liked to predict what people were feeling. Happy, sad, anxious, content, scared, shy, or just obnoxious, my goal was to figure them out and try to do something to make things better. Occasionally I made things worse with things I said or did, but I kept trying. My biggest challenge was always my mother. Reading her was tougher than reading perfect Latin to the nuns. Angelina seldom showed her emotions outwardly, and my sisters and brother always seemed to come to me to ask how she was doing on any particular day. Sometimes I got it right, other times she would baffle me, but when I correctly found her feeling low, probably thinking about Nick, it was my job to tell the others and we set out to cheer her up.

All of us speaking in particularly good Italian usually brought from her at least a slight grin and acknowledgement of our efforts. I took some pride in applying my people-prying talents with perfect strangers. Sensing their state of mind, I would do my best to say or do something to change or improve their moods. I was pretty good at telling jokes, and I liked to act out the scenes with gestures and facial expressions that solicited an extra hearty laugh from an audience, even if that audience was only one. Sometimes my jokes fell flat, and sometimes my acting brought scorn, but I guess as I watched and learned from the behavior of other people, this helped me get a better grip on my own personality.

My efforts to accurately judge a person's state of mind at an exacting moment eventually ended up being put to some practical use. I gradually became a fairly decent gambler. I especially liked poker. My skills served me well when I went overseas, and probably saved my life more than once. And my concentration at the poker table, over time learning to count cards with some precision, helped win more than a few pots.

I also used my hunger for detail to figure out how to fix almost anything. I loved to take things apart and reassemble them, often rendering them more improved than their original state. For these projects I relied on my long attention span, plus my fingers moving rapidly and skillfully. Thinking of myself as a surgeon, I went about examining, probing, twisting and turning, screwing and unscrewing until the object was perfect to my standards.

From about the time I was twelve to maybe sixteen years old, I worked real hard to gain the lofty status as a neighborhood fix-it man, the go-to guy when the car wouldn't run, the radio went out, or those damn, new-fangled bread toasters would spark and blow out all the fuses in the house. The extra money I earned helped out at home a lot, and Angelina would let me keep half of what I made.

Over time, I saved more than a hundred dollars, and like Carlo, I kept it wrapped tightly in a bundle and stuffed between the coil springs below my mattress. Finally, right before I turned twelve, from just a month of secret cooking around the holidays, when the demand was higher and the pay better, our mother had saved enough to buy us twin beds. But we still shared the same room. Two of our younger sisters, Helena and Priscilla, still slept in my mother's room, and when Katrina moved out, Sophia and Helena got their own rooms. It was long about 1936, I think, and Katrina had married the year before and lived to the west of Bessemer, closer to downtown, on Cherry Street. Sophia planned to marry the coming summer. She would move to a house on Spruce Street. Even though my town didn't have many (streets or trees), they named some of the streets in my town for trees, and some after our dead presidents.

Anyway, I was easily bored with the games most kids played in the schoolyard, what I deemed childish pastimes after school. Games of skill and chance; now those I loved. Before real gambling and before I started making money fixing things, marbles were my favorite. This is when I started getting into trouble sometimes when I paid too close attention to some people and the things they were doing. Carlo could have been right. Maybe sometimes I appeared too nosey and my nose, once or twice, suffered for it. But when I was observing a contest, I couldn't help it, I would concentrate real hard and I'd get real close to the action, too close sometimes. More than once, I took a shot to the nose and showed up at home bloodied. Like the time Timmy Costello was shooting the eyes out of the marbles in a play circle with a great long-range skill shot using his favorite purple agate, and I happened to be bending over too far, lost my balance, and fell into the circle, scattering all the marbles in twenty different directions. Boy was Timmy and the rest of them mad. I got a black eye out of that one, along with a bloody nose. But I couldn't help it. I had to figure out his game, so I could beat him when they finally decided to let me play.

By the time I was twelve I had collected more than five hundred marbles: agates, clear, and clouded cat-eyes, shooters, and peas of the broadest array of colors around. I eventually sold most of them back to the kids around the neighborhood off which I'd won them, for up to twenty five cents apiece for the best agates, usually the onyx ones. When I turned twelve, the bigger boys, those about Carlo's age who were close to graduating, finally invited me to play craps.

Craps had been my real objective all along. Marbles was just a warm-up. By the time I got into the games, I had been fixing things for a little while and had a few bucks on me most of the time to get me in the game and keep me going. After a few games, most of the guys I knew wished they hadn't let me meet the stakes.

I got pretty good at craps. Real good actually. Before I got into a game, my habit was to take the time to size up my opponents. If I sensed real strong competition, backed by the confidence of a wad of cash and a hot hand, I might get in and out quickly, or not get in at all. If I sensed weakness, little cash, fewer brains and wild betting, I would play hard, taking slightly more risk, and usually I'd come out ahead. My craps system worked even better for me at poker, when there was more time and a calmer environment, allowing me to really focus on my opponents and their playing tactics. Like I said, I also developed a fairly good method for counting cards, giving me quite an advantage.

Not long after I started playing, after getting caught by Principal Carl at school once too often, we permanently moved the games behind Joe's place, but even there, we still had to sneak into the action for fear Joe would catch us and run us off. I was one who, if Joe was spotted coming at us to break up the game, I would hightail it fast. I didn't want Joe mad at me, ever. Not that I liked Joe all that much at first, but it was his marvelous establishment that housed the game of all games. Joe's had snooker.

From the time I was old enough and tall enough to peek into the windows of Joe's pool palace, I longed to be on the other side. Inside was the stench of cigar smoke and stale beer, the shine of the mahogany railings ringing the tables, the lush-to-the-touch green felt cushions, the sound of the cue ball crashing into the rack and the yelps of the crowd as the final numbered ball rolled into the side pocket and the cash hit the center of the table. This was paradise, and I could not wait to enter. Joe was a stern gatekeeper of his kingdom, and if he didn't like you, and thought you were a troublemaker, you might not ever get in. It was a rarified privilege to be a regular, and my brother, only a few short years my senior, was one of those who held that honor. Carlo was a decent pool player, and a not-so-good snooker player – his eyes failed him. He lacked good depth perception. Not a problem I had inherited, I later discovered, but my goal in the meantime was to stay on Joe's good side so that when I got old enough, the invitation to enter snooker heaven might be forthcoming.

Joe Massina's House of Billiards was what he called it. But the term billiards is the not-too-accurate catchall description of both of the games of pool and snooker. Actually, billiards is the ancient game invented by kings and queens in Europe, and the tables have no pockets. Technically Joe didn't have a billiards parlor; he had a pool parlor, because all his tables had pockets like they should have, but no one cared about the name he chose. We all adored the place just the same. It was located at the east end of our Bessemer neighborhood, on Poplar Street, only about eight blocks from my house.

From my child window-peeking vantage point, I couldn't see all of the features that graced the interior of Joe's parlor, but when I turned about twelve-and-a-half, I got the word one day from Carlo that if I kept my mouth shut and stood along the wall out of everyone's way, I could come along with him that night. He was playing nine-ball against Freddie Marconi. I was beyond happy. My world had just been made complete. After he gave me the news, I turned my back on my brother and made the sign of the cross in thanks to my heavenly Father. Two agonizingly long hours later, when I stepped over that hallowed threshold, I was not disappointed. Inside, out of my line of vision from the window for all those years, was a magnificent solid oak single-plank bar with a white inlaid marble top that ran its entire twenty-seven-foot length. The heavily carved, ornate mahogany framed mirror that hung over the back of the bar ran twenty of the twenty seven feet, and on each side were stunning oil paintings of love-seat-reclining nudes painted by the local artist Carlos Mendoza, a Mexican national, who later became a citizen and moved to New York to illustrate for the *New Yorker Magazine*.

I found out that night from an old man shooting eight ball that for decades there was wild speculation around town as to the true identity of the models. The mystery was finally solved after Joe's death in 1985. Turns out the pair over his bar were two of his cousins from Fort Garland, which lies west of Trinidad.

Anyway, under Joe's once whitewashed, now smoke-tarnished, grey ceiling stood four regulation-size pool tables in a neat row a good distance from the bar. I would later discover that sometimes, in taverns, they place the pool tables too close to the bar, resulting in crowding and disturbance of the players. But those aren't real pool halls. Those are joints. Joe's was the real deal.

The regulation tables were for the nine-ball and eight ball games. But in the back of Joe's establishment you found the prizes. Two exceptionally lovely deep-red cherry wood snooker tables stood just before the double doors to the storage room. Light gambling occurred at the pool tables in the front – those less skilled at the geometric and physical intricacies of the game.

Those more accomplished players who could read the angles, the slices, banks, spins, forward and back "English," and could stop a cue ball on a dime by handling a cue as skillfully as my mother handled her spatula, played snooker. Joe allowed the top twenty players in town to permanently store their personal cues in two locked wall racks on the side of the room. Some cues had mother-of-pearl grips.

From that first night watching Carlo take a buck-fifty from Freddie at the nine-ball rack, I knew I needed more out of the game. Snooker had to be it, so over the next nine months I taught myself the game and practiced until the blisters on my fingers bled. Joe would let me in after school to practice if I swept up, polished the bar, dusted the felt on each table and occasionally cleaned the toilets. I didn't mind. It was worth it.

Part of mastering the game was becoming familiar with its history, so again, off to the library I went. Snooker found its origins from pocket less billiards, also played by royalty in England. Maybe Joe was half-right after all with the name of his palace. History doesn't record when the bright idea occurred to someone to put pockets in the corners and sides of the tables. But someone did, and the modern version of the game was born.

You see, snooker is played on a six- by twelve-foot table, a table one foot wider and two feet longer than a regulation-size pocket pool table. Instead of fifteen numbered balls and the cue ball on the table, like in the eight ball game, snooker has fifteen solid red balls and six numbered balls, plus the cue ball. A triangle rack with the red balls goes at one end of the table with the numbered six ball at the front point of the rack, and the numbered seven ball centered behind the rack at the base of the triangle. The five ball is placed in the center of the table and the two, three, and four balls are placed on the cue line at the opposite end. The four ball is in the center of the line, lined up the length of the table precisely with the five, six and seven balls. The cue line is called the Baulk, and must not have a radius any greater than eleven-and-one-half inches. The cue ball is placed in a semi-circle drawn from the lined-up two and three balls, and that's the only position after a scratch occurs that cue ball is place d to start play again.

Just like eight ball, snooker play begins with breaking the rack. To score, a player must sink a red ball, scoring one point. Then he (or she) takes a turn at a numbered ball. There were three women who were good enough to be allowed to store their cues at Joe's place, but they were only permitted to play Sunday afternoons after Mass and on Wednesdays. The theory was that the men would be mellow and more gentlemanly on Sundays after Mass and on Wednesdays in the middle of a workweek when they hadn't already started gearing themselves up for the weekend.

If a numbered ball is sunk, points are scored to coincide with that number, and that player keeps their turn, shooting again at a red ball, then numbered ball, continuing to alternate between the two. When all of the red balls are

153

sunk and off the table, the numbered balls are played in sequence until the table is cleared.

Snooker balls are two and one-sixteenth of an inch in diameter, and the pockets are much smaller than those in pocket billiards tables. Across that twelve-foot span, with a cue ball at one end and the object ball at the other, the pocket sizes look like pin heads. But I like I said, I had good eyes and good depth perception. Looking from my end of the table to the opposite end, I could pick out a speck of debris obstructing a smooth path to the corner pocket. That eagle-eye gift gave me a definite advantage in this game. Both gifts (that's what I refer to them as) paid big dividends in close matches.

So, like I said, I practiced in the afternoons (when I wasn't fixing something for someone), and at night, when Carlo let me come with him. I observed, absorbed and mentally honed my skills. I just stood around and watched the other guys. It didn't take me long to realize that I could strike my target with deadly accuracy and apply backspin, topspin, or right or left "English" to land the ball exactly where I wanted it, setting up my next shot either off the side or end cushions. They may have called the skill of cue-ball-maneuvering "English" since England was the place where the term "billiards" began, but I don't know for sure. Probably the Brits or some king of the Brits wanted the credit, who knows?

Anyway, just like in craps and poker, I also loved to play to my opponent's state of mind in. Wearing down his confidence, I would alternate from defense to offense as the mood of those I challenged changed with the ebb and flow of the game. In snooker, a player can deliberately place the cue ball in a position that blocks their opponent from a first strike at either a red or numbered ball. If successful, the opponent "table scratches" and it costs him four points. A player can do this as many times as he wants, deducting points and playing defense as shots and scoring opportunities are manipulated along the way. Snooker is to pool as chess is to checkers. That's why I made snooker my game of games.

I was finally allowed to challenge the players after Joe watched me run a table with only five missed shots. He set high standards for the contestants at his precious parlor, so when I got Joe's nod I went for the man on the top, and that was Raymond Castillo. My favorite of Joe's many decorations were the two gold-plated spittoons on the floor at either end of the bar. Only Raymond Castillo used them, however. If he was in the middle of a game, you only got near Raymond or the spittoons once if you were wise. His splatter was awful, and the stain wouldn't come out no matter how hard your mother tried.

Raymond was seventy-two and could still consistently run a snooker table in one turn, stopping only to aim and shoot his juicy wad at the shiny bowls lying ten feet away. Carlo told me I was a fool to take him on, but I couldn't resist. I lost four dollars to old Raymond that night, at five cents a point. It had taken me nearly a month to earn that four dollars and it took me seven attempts to finally beat old Raymond in a marathon match that took three hours. And I still only won a dollar and fifteen cents. It was a close match. Most of the other guys I beat regularly, but I think when old Raymond died I was into him for more than fifty bucks.

Joe did not serve liquor during Prohibition, over the bar anyway, and his place was not one of the taverns supplied by Tony's operation. Nonetheless, it was one of the most popular places in town. When Prohibition was repealed, Joe decided only to serve beer. He said his place was a place for games, not a place at which to get drunk.

Drunks were not tolerated in Joe's place, ever. There was just too much money on the line at each of the six tables, and drunks disturbed one's concentration.

The **Coors** beer distributor had provided the colorful glass shades for the lamps over the tables. "Pure Rocky Mountain Spring Water" was the motto in script decorating each side of the rectangular shades. A heavy cloud of smoke constantly hung at ceiling level throughout business hours, and the smoke curled lazily around the low hanging table lights centered above each green felt surface. Joe mostly served **Coors**, but you also could get a **Black Label** or a **Miller High Life**. Joe wouldn't let me have a beer until I was sixteen.

Angelina didn't like Joe's place very much. She objected to both Carlo and me being regular customers, but she sure didn't mind the extra money I brought in from the parlor. Her protests became less severe as the years passed until she finally gave up. Between my neighborhood jobs and occasional schoolwork, I played snooker as often as I could; only laying off in the fall during football season. And that was only later in my junior and senior years of high school.

Soon, recognizing my ability, Carlo assumed the role of my protector and agent, booking my snooker games in advance, setting the stakes, and discouraging those who might protest too loudly when his little brother counted his coins at the end of the contest. Carlo's reputation as an accomplished boxer helped in that department.

Everyone wanted their shot at the thirteen-year-old snooker whiz kid. Our schedules outside of work and school became so complicated that we had to arrange games a week or two in advance. I might have a car repair job on Tuesday. Carlo's Wednesdays were exclusively devoted to Julia Gail. Mondays and Thursdays worked for both of us, but Fridays and the weekends were difficult since it seemed many of my neighborhood tasks came about on those days. It seemed as if more things seemed to break on those days, or at least that's when the people decided they needed to have them fixed.

Chapter 18
Slightly Better than Elmer Fudd

One of my first and eventually my most frequent fix-it customers was a woman named Nadine Montlero. I was around fifteen at the time. Nadine was married to Julius, an administrative clerk in the accounting division at the mill. They didn't have any children, and Julius worked regular eight-hour shifts and very seldom worked overtime, so his schedule was very predictable. Nadine became a good customer mostly because her husband didn't know which end of a screwdriver to use. And he could barely change a light bulb, at least that's the way Nadine described him the first time I arrived to repair her leaking faucet.

It was a Wednesday and she had stopped me as I was walking to Joe's after school. She said she had heard that I was pretty good with tools and wondered if I could look under her sink since water was dripping there non-stop. So, somewhat disappointed with missing a potential match, I told her I would try to help. Her house was nice on the inside. Actually it was spotless. Nothing was out of place, it seemed. The furniture shined like new pennies, and the smell of furniture polish was so thick it was almost nauseating. She had two electric, rotating fans going in each room, but it was still sweltering inside. She pointed me to the kitchen. While I was under the sink, (unwinding a towel

158

I think Julius had tied around the pipe to stop the leak) Nadine talked non-stop. She went on and on about Julius – his no-good brothers and sister, the lack of recognition for his loyalty and hard work at the mill, the heat, the cold, the wind, the dust; nothing seemed right for her. At the time, most of what she was saying was beyond my comprehension, both by choice and the fact that I was trying to concentrate on the task at hand. I fixed the faucet in less than fifteen minutes. She paid me fifty cents, but it was strange, she didn't seem to want me to go. She was still talking after I said goodbye and closed the door behind me.

One week later, Nadine was on her front porch again as I passed by her house returning home from school. I wasn't planning on going to Joe's that day so it was easier to accept her plea for help. She told me a floor lamp in her living room was broken. This time, as I followed her into the house, I noticed Nadine was quite full-figured, as they described some ladies – a nice way of saying she carried a few extra pounds on her five-foot six-inch frame. Yet she was striking, with high cheekbones, deep-set green eyes, auburn hair, and freckles that gave her a perpetual look of youth. Her legs were shapely and her calves narrowed to delicate feet, with toenails that were painted a bright red. I also noticed her long fingers, and could imagine them easily dancing across the piano keys of the upright that stood in the corner of her living room.

Her hair was coiffed gracefully on her head in the current style, with long rolls on each side and a straight-back flow down the middle from her forehead to her neck, then wrapped in banana curls to the middle of her shoulder blades.

As we entered the living room, the light seeping through the windows revealed her bright print cotton housedress, tied with a belt at the waist, oval cut at the neck, sleeveless, and very lightweight. No stockings, bare legs, and white sandals. I couldn't help but notice the outline of her white slip through the sheerness of the dress, and she was careless with her bra straps, allowing both to be exposed as she pointed at the lamp and took a seat on the couch opposite me.

Then the chatter began. This time, the job was a little easier and I paid more attention as Nadine gave me the details of her days; how she didn't see many people, read a lot of magazines, and when Julius came home promptly each night at six, he was often asleep in his favorite chair no later than eight. She told me she loved to play two-handed Canasta, even if it was often by herself. Her voice was melodic, soothing, and mesmerizing, even though it was none of my business what she was saying about the intimate details of her mundane life. I soon found myself very distracted by her words, and having difficulty concentrating on the simple wire connections I was inspecting. I even crossed the hot wire with the ground wire on the lamp, and just barely discovered my error before switching them back and reattaching the brass cover.

While I fiddled with the lamp, I was sitting on the floor of the living room with my back turned to Nadine. She remained seated on the couch opposite me, still talking but now with a lower voice, almost a whisper. As I finished reattaching the brass plate, I turned toward her – and found myself staring straight into her wide-open crotch. Her most private parts were shielded only by the pure white "v" of her panties exactly centered between her spread legs. I know I had that deer in the headlights look, but I didn't look away. I couldn't.

I could detect the black wiriness of her pubic hair sneaking out each side of the elastic panty bands pressed against her exposed thighs. I could feel every nerve in my body at that precise moment. My ears even burned. I didn't move. She didn't move either, for what seemed like the longest time. Finally, she slowly closed her legs and crossed them. She had stopped speaking. She was not smiling. She just stared at me.

I composed myself, which was difficult, to say the least, and rose to my feet. "Mrs. Montlero, the lamp should work now. The wire was broken. I had enough slack in the wire to re-strip it and reattach it. If you have a bulb, we could test it." I tried to keep my voice from quivering as I spoke. I probably sounded like Elmer Fudd.

"Certainly," she said, and rose from the couch to walk to the kitchen.

She returned with a bulb, placed it in my hand and stood close by me, so close I could feel her breath on my neck. It seemed I was just a little shorter than she was so I rose on my tiptoes so I was eye-level with her. I swam inside her eyes for that brief instant, and it was luxurious. She still didn't smile, so neither did I. We just stared at each other, me doing the backstroke in the pools of those gorgeous green pupils. The scent of her rosewater blocked all my other senses, but I finally broke the spell and screwed in the bulb, plugged in the lamp cord and twisted the switch. The light from the lamp illuminated her face. But she resisted my awkward attempt to lure her back to our mutual fixation and moved away toward the door. Terribly disappointed, but getting the hint, I followed behind like a scolded puppy.

"Now Mr. Montlero will have his reading light for tonight when he returns home; that is if he doesn't fall asleep the minute he hits this chair," Nadine said. "Would you like some iced tea, Johnny?"

"No thank you, Mrs. Montlero. I need to get home," I squeaked, swallowing. My mouth and throat were very dry. To this day I can't understand why I acted so stupid.

"Very, well then, here's your money and thank you for your help," she replied, but with a distinguishable edge to her voice. I took my fifty cents and was out the door.

That evening, it was impossible for me to make any sense of what had happened. I barely spoke at dinner. Angelina was very curious about my daze and the blank look I'm sure I had in my eyes. I was not known to daydream, but the events of the afternoon were definitely far more intriguing than the dinner table conversation. Carlo was absent that night and not expected home until much later. He was at Julia Gail's having dinner. That was good. The last thing I needed right then was to deal with him. I just wanted to get lost in my own thoughts. The clatter from my sisters, each practicing her Italian for the benefit of our mother, was a din in the background. The only vision before my eyes was those white panties, occasionally interrupted by those green eyes.

Later, in my bed, I replayed the living room scene with Mrs. Montlero over in my head many times until I finally drifted off to a fitful sleep, swirled with confused dreams of crooked wires, tangled white sheets flapping in the breeze and a rosewater-scented perfume bottle spilled on a nightstand with smoke rising from it, scalding to the touch.

I knew a little about sex but not much. Carlo's stowaway magazines from the backyard shed were easily accessible. I'd found them when I was around ten and had gawked at the pictures probably a hundred times. Conversations at school and bad jokes at Joe's place constantly brought the topic to the forefront, yet the actual act, and the process leading up to it, remained a dark mystery. I had never seen anything like what Nadine had shown me nor had felt the emotions she boiled up inside me. Too bad my brother hadn't bothered to share anything helpful with me, now that I needed his advice, or thought I did anyway.

Several times, I had accidentally caught sight of one or more of my sisters as they scampered naked from the bathroom, down the hallway, and into their bedrooms, their bodies glistening, and so different. But seeing Mrs. Montlero's open legs and her deliberate and calculating slow motion in bringing them together, leaving ample time for my blatant gawking, stirred my flesh and scrambled my brains.

So off to the library I went. The *Human Nature* books, as they called them, were way in the back at the bottom of a single rack, out of sight but well used. I spent a wondrous, joyful afternoon that weekend, reading the texts and studying the crude pencil drawn illustrations, and in the end, I came away with a pretty good idea of things about human nature.

Each day for the rest of the following week and the next, I would adjust my route to and from school or from Joe's or from my jobs at other houses in the neighborhood to walk by Mrs. Montlero's. Not once during that time did I see her. I kept questioning myself why these daily walk-bys were so important, but down in my gut I knew. Regularly I saw Mr. Montlero, always clad in his neat navy blue suit, white shirt and red bowtie, coming and going from his house to his job at the mill's administration building. Once, as I meandered by, he was arriving home and stopped his two-tone blue Packard before entering the driveway.

He rolled down his window. "Son, thank you for lending a hand with the lamp and plumbing. Mrs. Montlero likes having her things working, and finding someone to fix things is a big help to me as well. I'm not very good with tools. Keeps her happy having someone else do it. Keeps me out of trouble, too," he chuckled.

"It's okay, sir, glad to do it," I replied.

"You're a good boy. We will find you when something else breaks," he smiled. I tipped my baseball cap to him and kept on walking, twice looking back over my shoulder for a glimpse of her, but she was not there.

That next Wednesday afternoon, when I knew Carlo was with Julia Gail and I didn't have a snooker match or any neighborhood jobs, I went to Nadine's house and knocked on her front door. God, I was petrified. I nervously looked around to see if anyone was watching, and knocked again. Still no answer. As I stepped from the porch to leave, the door creaked open, but no one was there.

"Come in," I heard from inside. "I didn't call you. What do you want?" She was in the kitchen, her back to me.

"Could I have that iced tea now?" I asked. She still didn't turn around, but I noticed she was again dressed in a thin cotton housedress, this time light pale blue in color. Her hair was parted in the middle and hung straight, almost to her waist. She was barefoot.

"I will have to brew some, and I don't have much ice. No matter, have a seat in the living room. The lamp is working, plenty of light," she added.

I sat gingerly in Mr. Montlero's favorite chair. The floor lamp was burning brightly as the only source of light in the room. The curtains were drawn. For some reason my throat was dry again and my palms clammy. I thought I might be sick.

She didn't speak again until I heard the teakettle whistling, and then she asked, "Lemon, sugar, or both?"

"Both," I said. "Thank you." I hated iced tea. I was a soda drinker. Loyal and faithful. Occasionally lemonade, but never iced tea. What was I doing?

Seconds later, she entered the living room and placed a tray balancing two glasses of iced tea on a table in the center of the room. I rose to retrieve my glass. She sat on the couch, her knees touching tightly, her dress pulled down to cover her legs to mid-calf and a napkin in her lap.

"I was trying to think if I had any jobs for you today, but I don't. Things around here seem to be in good working order," she declared, and then asked sharply, "Why did you come here?"

I couldn't think. My normally pinpoint-sharp thought process was in shambles. My normally rock-steady hand shook a little as I raised my glass to my lips. "I-I thought maybe you might need me," I stammered. "I didn't have any other jobs today." It was all I could produce.

"That's not the reason," she proclaimed. "You've been thinking about me. Do you want to play Canasta?"

"Yeah, sure," I replied. Canasta was a silly game, but why not? Wait a minute, what did she just say? Me, thinking about her? How does she know? On second thought, how couldn't she know? She's no dummy. A few days ago she let me have a peek at her most private parts, and she's got to know that affected me, like a punch in the stomach. But what did I know? I had no idea what I was doing.

"Good, come with me," she ordered. "Bring your tea."

I followed her into the kitchen and she motioned for me to sit at the kitchen table. She went to the drawer beside the stove and pulled out a deck of cards. Sitting opposite me, she shuffled the deck, rather expertly, I noticed. Maybe she played poker. I didn't ask.

"I know how to play Canasta," I volunteered. "I play with my sisters, usually after Mass on Sunday afternoons."

"That's sweet," she responded. "I like to win. I always like to win. Do you think you can beat me?" she asked.

"I don't know," I replied, as I gazed around the kitchen. Suddenly, I wanted to run. I felt trapped. I saw the back door on the other side of the kitchen and started to get up from my chair. I panicked. Time to go. Don't look back. She seemed to sense it. Her card shuffling stopped. She gently placed her hand over mine and whispered the same way she did from her seat on the living room couch two weeks before. "Take it easy, Mr. Fix-it man. Everything's okay. Just relax," she purred. I settled back down in my chair; her hand now caressing mine in short gentle strokes. After a moment, she pulled it away to deal the cards.

Time passed in silence as we played several hands. She kept score on a note pad with a pencil beside her on the table. I did relax a little as she had ordered, and actually began concentrating on the game, my instincts for getting the best of my opponent taking over.

Then after several hands with her ahead by twenty points, she said, "We have to think of something you've fixed for me this afternoon. Julius will be home soon. The neighbors probably saw you come in. You've been here for over an hour, and it usually takes you much less time to fix things."

I looked around the room again, trying to imagine a plausible task. "What about the sink again? Faucet working?" I asked.

"Yes, it's worked fine since the first time you were here. We need to be creative," she stressed. At that moment my nerves gripped me again, I felt a sense of desperation, panic creeping up again. My anxiety infiltrated the room. My head spun. I was short of breath.

"I know," she said finally. "The waffle iron. Sometimes it burns Julius' waffles in the morning, and he gets very upset. That's it." She rose from her seat at the table, brought the waffle iron from under the counter, and handed it to me. Ten minutes later I had it apart and was examining the control switch.

"I think the problem is here," I announced, pointing to the loose wire. "This connection doesn't seem to be touching the temperature gauge inside, so when you turn it on, it automatically goes to full heat. I can fix that," I proclaimed rather proudly. As she strolled the around the kitchen, thumbing through a stack of magazines she had retrieved from a side table by the refrigerator, I worked feverishly. We didn't speak, but as she walked by where I was sitting, after she took off my baseball cap, chastising me for wearing it in the house, she would run her long, slender fingers through my unruly hair. It was very hard to concentrate each time I felt the scalp message, but I managed to keep going. Fifteen minutes later, I had Julius' favorite cooking device back together again and in proper working order. With the waffle iron nicely repaired and sitting perfectly in the center of the kitchen table, I waited, hoping for more of her caresses, something.

Touch me again! I silently yelled.

Instead she said, "It's time for you to leave now. Here's your money." She grasped my idle hand rather hard, placing a silver dollar in it. I looked at the coin and up at her, but by then she was on her way through the living room toward the front door. I sheepishly got up from the table and followed. But as I went for the doorknob, she grabbed my other hand with both of hers and placed it on her left breast. She took her hands away and there was my hand, all alone, there on one of her privates.

I thought my heart would stop. I really didn't know what to do. I just kept my hand there. Cupped. If I squeezed, it might hurt her. But I wanted to, not hurt, just squeeze. It was soft and warm. I could feel the lace she wore hidden under her dress, covering her flesh. I was startled. I knew what a nipple was. Was it getting hard, emerging between my fingers? I read about that happening in one of the books at the library.

She brought her hand back up to mine, thankfully giving it company, and ever so delicately, she led my hand to depress her soft flesh. I felt the firmness of her nipple with the tip of my middle finger. Then she stepped aside and put my hand back on the doorknob.

"Be patient, my little fix-it man. Now go," she commanded.

I obeyed without hesitation, confused and bewildered. But as I strolled home that late afternoon, my confidence was soaring and soon the clouds in my brain cleared. I smiled to myself, and felt even better than when Carlo would find me a snooker player mark at Joe's at a dime a point. I reached in my pocket and caressed the coin she had given me the way I hoped I could learn to caress her breast.

Later in bed that night, I tried to think it through. Was I right in just leaving my hand there like a dead stump? Or should I have moved it around? Up and down? Side to side? Around in a circle? I didn't know. I had no practice at this. But man, did it feel good, certainly for me, but probably not too good for her. Maybe Carlo would know how nipples get hard. Hell, he probably wouldn't tell me if he knew.

Chapter 19
Assassins Can Be Your Friends Too

Carlo

It was not long after Jake's murder that Prohibition ended. Bootlegging was still all the rage, but since drinking booze was now legal, the problem of clandestine transport of the elixir was no longer an issue for the mob. It was now how best to create a scheme to evade the new high taxes on liquor imposed the Feds.

Black Jim Clemente was deeply entrenched in power by this time. He was at the forefront of dodging the new taxes on his alcoholic imports and his customers throughout the region couldn't be happier. But other than that, under his command, mob activity in the region had mellowed somewhat, and after the series of bloody Mafia power shifts, the underworld seemed to drift along more serenely, with the criminals riding merrily and somewhat quietly along through the waning days of the Depression.

On the afternoon Carlo was ordered by Tony to make his decision to replace Jake, Carlo had evaded the confrontation by working a late double shift and slinking home in the pitch black of night. Tony saw him the next day, but said not a word, just pointed in his direction and grinned. This went on every day for months, but nothing more. Had the organization and operation changed under the Clemente regime? Carlo didn't know. He prayed it had. And he prayed for Tony's menacing points gestures and grins, and nothing more, to continue.

As the days, weeks and months rolled by, Carlo prayed and held his breath. He worked, organized my snooker matches, and fell even more deeply in love with Julia Gail. He slipped into a comfortable routine of work and family, although the danger of his situation, for both him and those he cared about, never escaped his mind.

Although he missed the extra money he earned from Tony, he certainly didn't complain about being ignored. When Tony did speak to Carlo, he was even cordial at times, until one day, just about two years later, Tony caught up to Carlo at the beginning of his Monday morning shift. It was the day after Carlo had attended Julia Gail's confirmation.

"You still owe us you little son-of-a-bitch," Tony whispered in his ear.

"What are you talking about?" Carlo replied.

"Once you're in, you're always in. You don't question me or anyone. We've laid off you for the last couple of years, but now the business is reorganized. Now we need your help. We need collectors, not drivers, and you're gonna be one of them," Tony hissed. "You'll get your orders this afternoon." He walked off, leaving Carlo stunned, shocked and mad as hell.

Carlo stomped to his workstation, thinking wildly about what Tony had said. *A collector? This can't be happening.*

Collectors were protection enforcers, insurance agents, the lowlife scum who muscled people, mostly legitimate business people, into forking over exorbitant unwanted payments for protection or "insurance" for unexpected but deliberate catastrophes, like mysterious muggings, fires, lost inventories and even an occasional rape.

Upon hearing Tony's new label for him, Carlo immediately recalled the recent unexplained fire at Tiny's Auto Repair Shop. The blaze had destroyed Tiny's work bay and most of his inventory. He had been out of business now for six months, and word around town was that he may never start up again.

"They've destroyed me, the dirty bastards!" Tiny had cried one afternoon when Carlo was walking past his still-charred shop on the way to a haircut at Renaldo's. "I wouldn't pay at all at first, and then when I started with their blood money, they always wanted more. I'm through!" he had moaned, his meaty hands covering his grease-smudged face.

Carlo couldn't do anything but say, "I'm sorry, man," and walk next door to climb in the barber's chair. Yet he couldn't get Tiny out of his mind. And now he was seeing himself as one of those sub-humans that went around ruining people's lives.

Collectors were despised. And because their tasks were so disgusting, the townspeople they serviced quickly identified them, and if the victims banded together (which was often the case) collectors soon had bull's eye targets on their backs wherever they went. Consequently, the sidewalk enforcers, those collectors out in the open, didn't work locally. They moved from town to town quickly to avoid being victims of their own evil deeds. The bosses never got close to the enforcers or collectors. Too grubby, too despicable. Yet the money was fantastic.

Christ! Carlo thought. *This is crazy. I can't do it. I won't do it. Never!*

Carlo could not concentrate after Tony's announcement, even thought he knew how dangerous that could be. His mind drifted from Tiny to Tony to his family to Julia Gail, and more than once he had to snap back to attention to avoid the hot sparks and boiling steam that could instantly bore into his skin, leaving third degree burns in their wake.

When his shift was finally over, without hesitation he moved into the crowd of workmen making their way to the plant exits and out into the yards toward the gates. He kept his head down, trying to avoid eye contact or connection in any way with Tony or any of his henchmen, all who would undoubtedly be looking for him. Maneuvering himself into the core of the scurrying horde of dirty, smelly men, Carlo avoided detection, and soon was out a side gate and on his way home. He knew avoiding Tony was dangerous, and he knew that stalling a decision might be worse than facing Tony straight on. But he needed advice, someone to turn to whom he could trust.

Julia Gail's recovery had not been swift, but it had been steady. Since their first wonderful kiss, she had steadily regained her stamina, balance and her poise. Eight weeks ago, she had shed the braces, and four weeks ago she had taken her first walk around the block, not with Carlo, but with her father as she had promised. That time she walked with the crutches, but the crutches were gone when she took her second walk with Carlo. The process was slow and halting, but they made their first journey together in less than an hour, and it was a joyous hour for both of them. They giggled and joked, with Carlo, much to his delight, being allowed to place his arm around her waist for most of the time. Once, Julia Gail broke loose of his grasp and turned to him with arms open for a discreet embrace.

The iron lung had been dormant for more than six weeks, and the only time Julia Gail seemed to have trouble catching her breath was when Carlo held their kisses too long. Or when Carlo's hands began to move to places he knew she secretly welcomed, but had to resist. She had told him it just wasn't proper. He would have to wait. Besides, most of this groping happened in her living room with her parents talking quietly in the kitchen. It would be awful if they got caught.

The intolerable Doctor Stein still could not believe her progress, and he consistently predicted a relapse. Her family made sure their daughter didn't hear any of his predictions, though, and they were ecstatic to pay his last bill and send him away.

Just one week ago, Julia Gail had marked her seventeenth birthday with cakes, presents, songs and later, before the evening ended, in the quiet of her living room with her parents asleep, Carlo's hand caressing her left breast, on top of her sweater.

Now Carlo, at a rapid pace, passed by his own house and headed straight for the DiAlanicio's house. When Julia Gail greeted him at the door, he knew his expression gave away to the problems swirling through his brain. He could tell she was hurt when he seemed to brush by her and ask, "Can I speak with your father?"

"Sure. What's the matter?" she asked.

"Please, I need to talk with him. It has nothing to do with us. It's just a problem at work and he's the only one I know who can help me," Carlo responded, grasping her shoulders and attempting a smile that appeared more like a grimace.

Just then Thomas came through the back door of the house. "Can I speak with you, sir?" Carlo approached the man he had grown to admire without reservation.

173

Over the months and years of Julia Gail's recovery, Thomas and Theresa's trust in Carlo had evolved and their fondness for him flourished. They still addressed each other formally, and there was that persistent wariness that parents of girls had for boys and their testosterone in abundance, yet they remained ready to help him in his adolescent trials and adult challenges. Carlo had much affection for Julia Gail's parents, especially her father, but always maintained the proper and reserved protocol as was expected. Carlo had often thought. If anyone in Carlo's life could ever come close to substituting for Nick, it was Thomas. But never before had there ever been a moment like this or a situation in which Carlo needed a marble pillar to lean on.

Carlo knew his near desperation was transparent, and without a word, Thomas motioned to him to move outside. They climbed into Thomas' year-old Buick sedan, parked in the driveway. Carlo felt somewhat comfortable, temporarily sheltered from Tony's pursuit, but his nerves were primed, and anxiety welled as Thomas turned to him. "Boy, you look like shit. Come clean with me now. I know somethin's not right with you."

It was the first time Thomas had spoken to Carlo that way, like a man, man to man. Carlo fought to capture his calm, but before he could speak, Thomas said, "Look, there ain't no secrets here, especially in this town, specially among us guineas."

Now totally bewildered, Carlo tried to speak, but was cut off. "Look, you've been good to my girl. You've been someone maybe I can trust with her. Someday you might marry her if you ask me proper. Because you been good to her and since I think I can trust you I'm gonna tell you a story. Nobody knows this story, not Theresa, not Julia Gail, nobody, but I know what you been up to, and I know you maybe don't like what you been doin' and maybe some of this is you thinkin' about your future, so let me tell you about some things and maybe it will help you make up your mind," Thomas began. "If you say a word to anybody about what I'm gonna tell you, not only will you never marry my daughter, the next time she dresses up won't be for her wedding; it might be for your funeral."

Carlo sat silent. His eyes locked on Thomas as the closest thing he had to a father spoke in a slow deliberate manner, measuring his words like Carlo had never heard before.

"Spinuzzi is a shit punk. He's a bagman, no more important than a ground hog out there stickin' his head out his hole. Yet he's been movin' up, so you've still got to be careful of him," Thomas paused, waiting for a reaction.

How the hell does he know? Carlo thought.

Thomas picked up on his expression. "Like I said, there ain't no secrets, so listen. The runs you were makin' with Jake were tests. You did good, especially the night they blew him apart. But things changed with Prohibition ending and Clemente coming to town. The business took on new things, different things to pick up the slack. Like everyone else, Tony laid low until things got reorganized. It took a while, but now their movin' ahead and they need new, fresh blood. Tony's still convinced you have promise, and he's tryin real hard to build up his team of bagmen to impress Jimmy and the boys who make the decisions. Jake gets himself killed and you handle the situation real well. No cops, no investigation. The body's buried and it's forgotten. Real good. Now, who's Jake's replacement? Naturally, you are, but you're not sure, and that goes against Tony's plan. He don't like static. He don't like back talk, so he's pissed off," Thomas continued.

Then abruptly he questioned, "You want out?"

"Yes," Carlo nodded.

"Okay. Now, here's the story. You remember this well. The old boss is gone. A new boss is in town. Before Clemente, Blanco did pretty well in the early days but fell out of favor quick. He got lazy, and he got stupid. Killin' the Danna's; that was real stupid. Allowing his rogue bootleggers to get away with killing Jake, that was stupid. Answerin' only to Romeo, that was stupid. He pushed way too many people around, and once he got himself all involved in business outside the business, with his dick, he was as good as dead. It took someone to make that happen when the final decision came down. How do you think my Julia Gail got her machine?" Thomas asked.

"Jesus," murmured Carlo, just audible enough for Thomas to hear.

"I don't deal with Spinuzzi. He makes no decisions. Word came to me from New York, not Denver," Thomas went on. "I took the job on one condition. It would be my last, and they owed me two favors in return. The first one I collected," he paused again. "The second one, I haven't asked for."

There was even a longer pause. Thomas looked away, staring out the side window of the Buick, his mind appearing to drift. Carlo stared at his profile, still sorting through the shocking details of what he just heard.

My God, he thought. *This man is an accomplished assassin yet he has to be the kindest, gentlest man I know. And he's revealing a secret to me that could get him killed and probably his family as well.*

Thomas turned back to him then, his gaze drilling into Carlo's skull. "Those three who killed Jake probably were just young recruits. Hotheads who wanted to be big shots to impress somebody, when, in the long run, all they did was get their boss killed. Jake was a nobody's nobody, workin' for Tony like he did, but that don't matter here.

176

Those little pricks probably acted on their own, and in their position you don't wipe your ass without permission," he noted with a slight half-smile.

"Blanco's biggest mistake was not takin' control. He let those scum run around without somebody watchin' over them. Charlie was more concerned about beddin' down some skank whore than watchin' the store. It got him killed. New York had to remove Blanco to make way for someone they could trust. That's Jimmy. Black Jim, they call him, cause his skin's so dark. He could almost pass for a colored, especially in the summertime. You won't hear a lot about him and you may never see him in your whole life, but by God, you'll know he's here. The whole country will know he's here; at least the mob and the honest cops trying to catch him. This place is way too important to them as a base of operations for Charlie's type to be in charge."

He took a breath. "Now you're in a pickle, your ass in a sling, but getting you out of it comes down to you and me. I can remove the knife at your throat, and I can make sure Tony leaves you alone and finds someone else for collection services. You can get out but only through me. Understand? You can't do it on your own. They will bury you and maybe a few members of your family if you try to walk out on your own. You're in too deep, and like they say, once you're in, you're in for life. Maybe you ain't taken a blood oath yet, but that don't matter. You know too much. Omerta, you know what that means?" He paused again, much longer this time. Soak it up Carlo, was Thomas' clear message.

Before Carlo was ready for more, Thomas grew impatient. "If I do this for you, and get you out, and you change your mind and go back in, that scene you saw in the newspapers with Charlie's brains splashed all over his bed will look like Sunday communion services compared to what you'll look like when I'm done with you," Thomas carefully and slowly explained. "No matter how much my daughter cares for you."

Dead silence again. Thomas turned back to the side window. Carlo knew he was finished. He wanted to ask him dozens of questions, but he wasn't that stupid. He knew better. He sat there awhile longer before he spoke.

"Sir, I do want out. Early on, I thought it was the life for me, my way of becoming important. And my only way to make some money on the side. I don't mind the mill. It was good enough for my father so it's good enough for me. I just needed something else. Shit, I only made two hundred bucks for all the time I spent," Carlo lamented, and then hoped he didn't sound like he was looking for sympathy. He knew he wouldn't get any here.

"Watch your language," Thomas scolded.

"Sorry. I'm gonna be eighteen years old soon. I've got a good job. The union's helped me move up, probably because of my father, but I work hard. It's a good life here, and my life is so much better now that Julia Gail's in it. She's the one who made me realize I could be something without dependin' on Tony. And, shit, I know bootleggin' is only the beginning. I know it leads to other things," he caught his language. "Sorry, I didn't mean it." He tried to be as clear with Thomas as possible. "But me collectin' protection money? I can't do it. No way."

Out of the corner of Carlo's eye he saw Julia Gail. He turned. She was gazing at him out the living room window. There was a deep, troubled frown on her face, her eyes riveted on the scene in front seat of the Buick. He smiled back at her, watching the tension in her face appear to fade. He knew that she was the one who'd make this right. Without knowing a thing, she would make it right. But this gentleman, this man who now had Carlo's very life in his hands; the one sitting next to him, if he chose to do so, would set things into motion.

"Sir, I promise you. I swear to you, if you help me, I won't change my mind. I'll stay out. They can kill me before I'll go back. Maybe they'll kill me anyway, but at least you and Julia Gail will know I tried," was Carlo's final plea.

Thomas turned back to him. "Julia Gail won't know a thing, even it they string you up by your balls. She must never know. No one can know. You will die if she ever finds out," he whispered to Carlo through his teeth.

And for the first time, Thomas's anger overtook his control. Carlo watched the veins in his neck swell and bulge as he gritted his teeth and gripped the Buick's steering wheel with an intensity that prompted Carlo to think he might even snap it in half.

But a moment later Thomas relaxed, calm returning to his voice. "I've protected my family from what I've had to do," he was speaking to no one in particular now, staring out the window. "And I can't let anyone or anything ever change that. I've chosen to live a simple life. I know I could go right back there any time I want, and they would be happy. I'm very good at what I do. Or used to do. I have no remorse since all of them had it comin'."

God, there's been more than one. Carlo kept his mouth shut.

"This conversation is over," Thomas declared, turning back to Carlo. "You get out of here and go home, and stay home. I'll tell Julia Gail you'll come around tomorrow. She'll be all right. We will never talk about this again. If I decide to let you into my family, you will take the things we talked about here to your grave. Remember everything I said. Be careful at work, at least for a few days. Don't put yourself in a corner. Go straight home every night except if you come here. You'll be okay." His tone softened ever so slightly. And with that, he motioned for Carlo to get out of the car.

As Carlo walked briskly away, the Buick backed out of the driveway, and sped away in the opposite direction. Carlo knew Julia Gail was watching as her father drove off, and she turned to see him wave, ever so quickly, as he stepped around the corner toward home.

Chapter 20
Where's Babe Ruth When We Need Him?

One afternoon after school I was sitting at home with nothing to do. I hated homework so I always tried to get it done during the one free work period we had at school. On this particular day, I didn't have any chores or homework, so I was lying on my bed, reading Huckleberry Finn and trying to understand the dynamic relationship between old Huck and Injun Joe when I heard Carlo run in through the back door and straight into the bathroom. The sound coming through the paper-thin walls of our Bessemer bungalow was like someone had dropped a small stick of dynamite down the bowl of the john. Wham! Swoosh! Splash! Ahhh. When Carlo emerged and entered the bedroom he was white as a sheet.

"You alright?" I inquired, thinking it was the rest of the family I should have been worried about since, I'm sure, serious danger now lurked behind the crapper door.

He didn't answer, just lay down on his bed and breathed deeply. A man's private bathroom habits are his and his alone, so I just rolled off my bed and opened the window as wide as it would go.

You see, when there is but one bathroom in a tiny house which at one time had five girls, one woman and two boys residing there, activities therein are somewhat common knowledge among family residents since your own routines must be scheduled around, intermingled with, and sandwiched in-between those of the others.

So I always assumed Carlo to be a mid-day, at-work person. He hardly ever went at home – even on Sundays. I never heard or smelled it in all of those years; that is, until today. Even though you would think females were much more discreet and secretive about their habits than males, I always had a hunch when my sisters partook in the luxury of our indoor plumbing. And you could set your watch by me, never fail, always at 6:45 a.m. Bank on it. But Carlo was a different story. He partook elsewhere and since he went to work almost every day, I assumed the mill was his place of choice, or a place of simple necessity.

Then, just two days later, it happened again. And then again. *Okay*, I thought, *what's going on?* This guy is a creature of habit. His routines were textbook. He never wavered except during his bootlegging days, but even then, after a short while, he just created a new routine. Came home from work, took a bath, dressed in his suit, left the house, came back late at night with dirty shoes and mostly acted like a jerk. Now that he wasn't engaged in that illegal part of his life, or so I assumed, he had gone back to the work routine at the mill. But this part of it had become different. Not only was he out of sorts with his offerings to the public sewer system; he was off-center with just about every other part of his daily activities.

What was it now? I began to probe. "You okay? Everything alright at work?" I would ask. "You seem a bigger prick than normal." Anything to get him to loosen up. But every time I asked he went deeper down into his hole. Even after he'd come home from Julia Gail's (God, I hope he wasn't doing his duty there. One time and she'd break up with him for sure.), he'd seem farther in the crapper.

Figuratively, I mean. One day I saw him walking toward the house and he kept looking over his shoulder. Literally, every few steps. Glancing behind him, as if someone were following. He was jumpy, nervous. Talked in his sleep. He was short with everyone, even our mother. He just wasn't the same guy.

"Tell me what's going on. What is your problem? You aren't much fun to be around," I dug for answers.

What I was afraid of was seeing my brother transform from a big kid with a chip on his shoulder and a strut in his walk to a guy who was totally unsure of himself. A guy who was scared. Wary of everything. I suppose he saw himself differently after cleaning Jake's brains from under his fingernails. I suppose anyone would try to change after that, but sometimes, as I observed him from my little kid vantage point, I would think I liked him better the other way; a bad ass, you know. I didn't know how long this new horribly meek phase would last, but I had no choice but to ride along and watch it happen, only occasionally getting in his face for information he always blocked with a blank stare and a forefinger wave in my face.

Finally, one night when I least expected it, when we were both in our beds and I was just drifting off to sleep, he said, "Man I am so tired of it all. I can't take it any longer." He sounded totally frazzled.

I sat up. "What's going on Carlo?" I asked, as kindly as I could.

With that, he finally opened up. He told me he had made the decision to resign as gracefully as he could from the employ of Tony Spinuzzi and his Cronies. So he *was* trying to get out, I thought. He had made up his mind. No wonder the poor bastard was acting like a monk hiding a bottle of booze under his cloak.

At first I thought he was just being paranoid. Here was a guy who, in the past, would gladly break your nose if you crossed him, and now he was craning his neck, tiptoeing through life with every step. At the mill, he said he was avoiding all of the dozens of dark corners in hallways, along catwalks, in tool rooms, storage lockers and coal bins. He told me when he had to use the bathroom; he would wait until a number of workers, other than members of Tony's circle, were heading in that direction as well. He went about his business quickly. That explained the new evening routine. Not a chance would he be caught with his pants down in one of those stench-filled cubicles.

I felt for the guy. I really did. The mill was his life, his only option at a decent livelihood. Every single day he had to go to work with this hanging over his head, thinking he may not even live through the day. Often, he said he would spot Tony at a distance, but neither he nor any one of the Cronies made a move. Day after day the same paranoid thoughts went through my brother's head. Would this be the day they took him down?

But after his confessional that night as the days went by, my brother stayed safe. There were no incidents. I'm not really sure if Carlo had just resigned himself to taking what came at him or he had come up with a plan to rid himself of this black cloud hovering above his head. All I knew was I started seeing him more at ease. A few more weeks passed, and Carlo seemed close to being his old self again. I couldn't help but think that maybe my brother had cut a deal, sold his soul to the Devil. He'd already met the Devil once, I thought, and now had he offered his head on a platter to him again? Would he be buying a new suit to replace the one now in ashes? These thoughts made me crazy.

But as Carlo bounced off the ceiling less and less, it was great to have him around. Now that he had finally relaxed, and he wasn't marching off in his suit to those mysterious destinations, it seemed like we were getting along better. He was less quick to slap me upside the head for a comment he found annoying, and he was including me more often in his activities. I liked that part of it a lot. We even began to listen to the baseball games on the radio together at night, even though neither of us were big baseball fans other than when Babe Ruth was playing. Our interest in baseball had sort of waned after Carlo's short but distinguished stint on the hill for Central High and his aim at the head of the goon who killed Jake.

Best of all, now I was more often than not invited to accompany him to Joe's place again. I was constantly hounding him to arrange a snooker match for me – it had been almost two months. Our rule was that I was not allowed to accept a match on my own. Carlo was the only one who negotiated over the terms of my play, the stakes, winning point scores, and of course, he chose my opponents. I was always anxious to play, but let Carlo control my games from every angle except the shooting. Finally, he came home one afternoon and announced that I had a match the day after tomorrow, on Thursday.

"Carlo, I'm out of match play practice. I haven't had a game in six weeks. You haven't let me play in a real match for all this time. Yeah, I've been practicing at Joe's when I can, but you say this guy's no easy mark. You think I can handle him?"

"Sure you can. It won't be a piece of cake, but you'll be okay. Stakes are a dime a point for the first to five hundred, and then a quarter a point to a thousand. Let him move out ahead past five hundred and take him in the final series of racks," Carlo instructed.

"Carlo, you ever felt a tit?" I abruptly interjected.

Stunned, Carlo replied, "None of your goddamn business. What's wrong with you anyway?"

"Nothin', nothin' at all," I quickly retreated.

I could tell Carlo sensed an issue with his little brother, but I also could tell by his reaction that maybe tits were a real sore point for Carlo at this very moment. Was Julia Gail being stingy with her feels?

I suspected Carlo had been granted limited access to Julia Gail's wonderful endowments and I would bet only on the outside of her blouse. Anyone could tell she had the loveliest mounds ever bestowed on womankind. Well, maybe next to Mrs. Montlero's. A clothing-encapsulated feel; that was all he could get; nothing more, and sometimes less, I was sure. I had once walked in on them going at it (well, the kissing part anyway) – I'm talkin' tongues, teeth, earlobes, necks. They were in our living room and I came in the back door and had removed my boots since they were muddy. I guess I was pretty quiet because they apparently didn't hear me for all heavy breathing going on, so I probably should have stomped my feet so they could, but they still might not have heard.

Anyway I stood there for longer than I should've and just watched. Carlo's hands were moving over her as quickly as his boxing jabs, but she was just as quick to move them off her chest and back down to their proper position around her waist. Before they saw me I quietly tiptoed down the hall and into our bedroom, giggling to myself, but also felling kind of sorry for him.

Carlo had told me that Julia Gail's parents were very strict with her. They still seemed to view her as a fragile flower, needing to be shielded from the harshness and threats of the outside world. Even though they embraced Carlo outwardly – in their presence, he had said he felt a sense of family – they still severely restricted their daughter's time alone with him, and the places they went together. Julia Gail accepted her parent's conditions without objection, meaning that true intimacy was off the table for my brother for now. He either had to accept it or move on, and the latter never seriously crossed his mind. I knew that for a fact. He would never leave her, no matter what. Yet I was guessing that in spite of the infrequent but intense necking, my brother was getting bored, and probably extremely frustrated. And here was his just barely fifteen-year-old brother, whom he probably thought barely knew how to whack off, and I'm asking him about tits as if I need some instructions. Carlo was fit to be tied. He was about ready to smack me.

Mustering his self-control, he asked me, "Okay kid, what do you want to know?"

"Well, see, I had this girl," I began. "No, never mind," I abruptly tried to end the conversation.

"What do you mean you 'had this girl'? Did you screw somebody? Tell me!" Carlo commanded.

"No, no I didn't screw anybody. Never mind, I can't talk about it. Shouldn't have brought it up," I said.

"Alright. I know you been sneakin' peaks at my magazines. That's okay. I've read them so many times myself all the pictures are faded away anyway." I couldn't help but crack a grin when my bother admitted that. He stammered for a second, failing to control a quick smile at his unintended confession. It seemed to break the ice. "You can look all you want, but make sure mother doesn't find them," Carlo told me.

I knew he could relate to my inquisitiveness. I knew in his mind, over years of intense scrutiny of those enticing pages, he had had every one of those girls, many times over. I took a deep breath, knowing I'd come close to making a real mess of things by telling Carlo about Nadine. Nothing had really happened anyway. No big deal. Maybe someday I would tell Carlo, and either it would make him real mad or real proud. But right now, I didn't know which way it would go so it was best to drop the subject. In my own mind, however, the subject never faded for a moment.

That Thursday my snooker match was cancelled. Someone Carlo didn't know well, name was Frankie or something, was arranging the match. Carlo told me he had seen Frankie several times at Joe's recently, not playing, just standing at the bar sipping a beer. Frankie had told my brother that afternoon, while still working his shift at the mill, that the match was postponed, rescheduled for Saturday night. Apparently Carlo agreed and never thought any more about it, until I was waiting for him at home that afternoon.

"After dinner we'll walk over to Joe's, right?"

"No, cancelled until Saturday. Go read a book," Carlo instructed.

Damn, I thought, I was ready; had myself all prepared. Oh well. No big deal. So I waited until that Saturday evening. We left our house at seven thirty. It was cool outside. The sun had disappeared early behind a cloudbank over the distant mountains. A slight breeze blew refreshing, compared with the normal stiff wind, and a light rain that afternoon had temporarily settled the dust.

It was a perfect night for a walk and on nights like these Carlo normally would have been walking with Julia Gail. I wondered if he was with me tonight heading toward Joe's somewhat out of protest. He had told me he'd told her earlier that he wouldn't be coming around tonight, and he'd said, sure, she was disappointed, but she understood and would see him after Sunday Mass. I looked at him as we walked toward Joe's thinking that maybe he felt satisfied, for once, perhaps denying her a little of him as she continued to deny so much of her.

Joe's was nearly filled to capacity when we arrived, and there were a few in the crowd who were unfamiliar to Carlo and me as we made our way to the back tables. News of one of my matches seemed to bring out regulars and strangers alike, and all of this made Joe very happy as the beer flowed freely. I was to play Danny Ventimiglia who had recently arrived from Detroit having been laid off from the Packard plant. He was probably in his twenties and came with a sharpshooter's reputation. He had been warming up on the table for thirty minutes or so when we arrived. By the time Carlo and I approached, the betting was running in Danny's favor about three to one. The crowd was watching him practice, and he wasn't missing many shots, no matter the degree of difficulty.

In big games I always made a habit of ignoring my opponents until I got them into the match, so I disregarded Danny as I took a few practice shots myself. I would wait to size him up through the first rack.

I shook hands with Danny and turned away from the confident sneer on his big mouth. Both cue ball lags rested inside the semi-circle, but Danny's was closer to the line by about a quarter of an inch. He broke first, knocking a red ball at the corner of the rack far enough away to deny me a decent shot. I missed the first shot, the cue ball scattering the rack only slightly. Forty-five minutes later, the first rack was done. Danny was ahead by twenty points, up two dollars, at sixty eight to forty eight. With his first win, Danny's supporters began taking odds. It took only twenty minutes to play the second rack. Danny remained ahead, but this time by only ten points. Down to a dollar. And so on it went, for four straight hours, back and forth, with the lead changing hands dozens of times. The final score was one thousand to nine hundred and seventy seven. Carlo placed five dollars and seventy-five cents on the table for Danny to retrieve. When we shook hands again Danny's sneer was gone, replaced by a look of respect.

"You're a hell of a player kid," he told me.

"Thanks, so are you. Let's do it again," I replied.

There was light applause with the betters on me paying off to Danny's supporters. Most of the crowd was either gone or asleep by then, with two regulars curled up in chairs ringing the perimeter of the room. It was approaching one o'clock in the morning. Joe started to shake them awake as Carlo and I, after packing away my cue, headed for the door. But before we could get there, four of the strangers we had noticed earlier emerged from the shadows outside to block the doorway. They stepped inside and one took a pool cue from the wall rack and slid it between the door handles to temporarily close off any escape.

"What the fuck do you think you're doin' Frankie?" Carlo snapped at one of them. Oh, so that was Frankie. What the fuck? I thought frantically.

Another one of Frankie's pals appeared at the doorway at the back of the pool parlor, grabbing another cue from the rack. Joe moved behind the bar. The two regulars were already back to sleep.

"Get the fuck out of my place!" Joe yelled.

"Shut up old man, and you won't get hurt, and we might not break up this shithole," Frankie shouted back.

Okay, this was serious. We were in trouble. Big trouble. We were gonna have to fight our way out of this and my only hope for survival was my brother's boxer punch and his guts. I hoped and prayed (both of which I did real quick) that I could help. But then I got mad, and with my anger my fear subsided and a confidence rose.

Then all hell broke loose. Out of the corner of my eye I saw my brother issue a well-executed uppercut into Frankie's chin, and seeing this jerk reeling toward me, I instinctively raised my leg just right to place a boot square in his balls. I had always been told by my brother that when your opponent is bigger than you, or you're outnumbered, always hit first and try to hit the hardest. Frankie went to the floor with a groan not knowing whether to rub his chin or grab his nuts. I don't think the other three expected us to throw down first, and I saw them hesitate, just for a second. But then they were on us both. I ducked under the first swing of Frankie's friend's cue, but the second swipe caught me across the shoulders. I went to my knees momentarily and looked up to see the other two whaling away on Carlo. I noticed with pleasure that they were both bleeding heavily from what I suspected were broken noses. I could just imagine the swift, blinding-speed jabs that Carlo had landed to send their body fluids flying in all directions. By this time, Frankie was up off the floor. He caught me again to my neck, back and legs with cracks from his cue. Now I was hurting and felt myself growing weaker, thinking all I wanted to do was roll up in a ball and wait for them to stop. Soon I realized, as I brought my knees to my chest and covered my head with my arms, that my brother was there beside me. He wasn't moving other than when one or two of them kicked him in the ribcage.

Even with both of us down and offering no resistance, the beatings still didn't stop despite my pleadings to Jesus for some relief. I blacked out, wondering if the old guy up there was too busy that night to hear my prayers. Carlo told me later that before he slipped into blackness, he was startled by the sound of a nearby explosion.

191

~

Some weeks after the attack, Joe explained what happened next. Apparently as I lay crumpled on the floor with deep facial cuts, kidney bruises, and blood running out both of my ears from a heavy concussion, Frankie and company were getting ready to break both of my hands by stomping them into the wood floor. The explosion Carlo heard was Joe pulling a shotgun from under the bar and blowing a hole in his own roof. Thank God.

After damaging his precious palace, he told us proudly he had the shotgun leveled at Frankie's chest, receiving the undivided attention of our attackers. Apparently, Joe had told the thugs very calmly, "I think I know who you guys work for. But I don't care. I'm telling you to leave and I'm telling you if you ever come back, I'll take your heads off."

It became clear Frankie and his friends had not been sent to kill us. That would have been going too far. It had not been sanctioned. And the one they answered to was taking a chance with his order for the attack, so all four took Joe at his word and quietly walked out. The two regulars had been rudely awakened by the sound of the shotgun blast and ran for the door at the back of the bar in panic.

Joe told us he grabbed towels from the bar racks, wetted them down, and went to Carlo and me to wipe off the blood. Both of us remained unconscious, but Joe said he found we were breathing regularly. He actually admitted that when he turned us over and saw both our faces so badly swollen and already turning bright red and purple, he started to cry. I was amazed that a man like Joe, with his shiny bald head and white, neatly trimmed goatee sitting atop his six-foot-four-inch, two-hundred-fifty-pound frame, could be reduced to tears by two punks I thought he could care less about. Then, Joe said, his towel dripping with Carlo's blood and mine, rose, went to the telephone, and called Doctor Stein.

Chapter 21
Doctor Stein's Wrong Again

I awoke a day-and-a-half after my beating to the tear-streamed face of Julia Gail (although she looked awfully like Mrs. Montlero) peering down at Carlo from her seat on the edge of his bed. I tried to smile, but my jaw was too sore. Carlo lay in his bed close by, still asleep. I was still groggy, disoriented and disappointed that Mrs. Montlero had mistaken my brother for me. How could she be sitting there right next to me holding his hand and giving him her warm, passionate touch while I was trying to rest in the very next bed, yearning for her gentleness? I fell back asleep, feeling sad and very jealous.

Doctor Stein had declared that although we might experience a hallucination here and there, neither my brother nor I, despite my broken nose and Carlo's three cracked ribs, had sustained permanent injuries, and in two weeks' time, we would both be fit enough to return to work and school. I wasn't so sure. Everything hurt, down to the tips of my toes. And Carlo moaned and groaned while awake and even in his sleep. He kept it up. All the time, except when Julia Gail came to visit. Then he was brave. They were quiet and they whispered to each other things I couldn't hear. One time she even lay down beside him and cradled his head in her arms. God, I felt sorry for myself.

Why couldn't someone do that for me? Our mother and sisters were in and out of our room quite often to offer their sympathies and bring a never-ending supply of chicken soup, but that didn't phase my self-pity.

Late one afternoon while both of us lay in our beds and Carlo had begun his routine groans right after Julia Gail had left; I turned my still very tender frame toward my brother. "All right; time to come clean. Did getting our asses whipped mean you re-joined the mob, and was that a new sort of ritual initiation? Or did they nearly kill us because you think you found your way out, and that was just a taste of greater things to come? You know I watched you burn your suit that night. Now if you're back in, I'll bet they make you buy a new one. That would be expensive," I said with as much sarcasm as I could muster.

"How'd you know about that?" Carlo snapped. "You're just a goddamn snoop, you little bastard. Don't you ever spy on me again. Leave it alone." He paused for what seemed like an hour; then said, "I can't talk about it."

"Hey buddy, just in case you missed it, I'm in this with you up to my ass and I don't like it. Remember, I'm just a kid. I'd like to live awhile longer so I have a right to know everything. Okay, you tell me little bits here and there but keep most of it all to yourself. One minute you're sad and pissed off at the world, and the next minute, when Julia Gail's around, you're jolly like some goddamn Santa Claus. Okay, Jake was killed. You saw it all. You had to gather up his body parts and bring them home. I can understand how that might make you crazy. It sure would make me nuts, but you seem to have gotten over it; at least for a while. Then you go through another phase, where your thinkin' someone's out to get you. So that goes on some more and then something happens and you relax again. Then we go to Joe's and they beat the shit out of us, and I know it wasn't

195

revenge for me beating somebody on the snooker table. Hell, I lost that night!" I had sternness to my voice that surprised even me. I wanted an explanation, and I wasn't going to let this go on any longer.

I gathered the strength to raise my head off the pillow and rest on my elbow, wincing. "Tell me goddamn it! I'm old enough to know!"

Carlo had his back to me, but I could tell he sensed my anger. He let out a major moan, rolled toward me and spoke heavily. "Look little brother, I'm sorry you had to get mixed up in this. I never meant for anyone, especially you, to take a fall for me. I need to take care of my own problems, so don't ask me any more questions, 'cause I won't answer them."

"Bullshit, Carlo. Come on," I came back at him hard. I even swung my legs around and for the first time in a week, sitting up with my feet to touch the bedroom floor. My head spun like a right English hit cue ball. "Do you think I'm an idiot? What are you doing, going back again to be their mule? I think maybe you wanted to quit, and maybe for a time you figured that they were gonna let you quit, but then those bastards changed their minds, so they sent those goons after us. And now either you're selling out to them or you've figured out a way to get out. Either way we got our whippin'; so now what's your next move, genius?"

With that, I would have bet my last dollar he would have punched my lights out for mouthing off to him like that. Instead he just sat there. I think he was shocked to say the least. His eyes dropped their glare and he looked resigned. He turned his head to stare at the ceiling and gave a deep sigh, grimacing from the lingering pain of his slowly healing ribs. I waited. I knew he knew he had no place else to go.

"Okay, okay. I couldn't do it any more," he admitted. "I told them I wanted out and they couldn't handle that. I thought I had it taken care of. I got careless. It was stupid for us to be there at Joe's that late at night. I'm sorry."

I softened my tone just a little, sensing his anguish. "Why did you think you could take care of it? How? By yourself? Or was someone helping you, us, I should say?"

"I had some help, yeah, but maybe it wasn't enough. I don't know. I can't wait to get out of here and find out," Carlo admitted.

"Yeah, man me too, get up and go find out. Who was helping you? Anyone I know?"

With that Carlo's expression stiffened and he stared me down. "That's it little brother. No more. That's all you can ever know. So stop right there."

So I did, I stopped right there. I was no dummy. I knew I had pushed him too far just then. There was someone who he had counted on, who maybe he trusted, who said he could help, but then failed him, us, and that was too much for my brother to handle. But I couldn't resist another question.

"Do you think it was just a warning? Will they come after us again? Just show me a few more jabs and crosses, and next time they'll wish they never got close to us," I tried to joke, to bring him around just a little.

Carlo brought his eyes down from the ceiling and looked at his little brother, and for the first time in his life, I think he saw me as an equal, or nearly one anyway. Or maybe at least a trusted partner. A man I hoped he felt he could depend on. Someone who would fight with him, side-by- side, for what was right. My heart sank as the seriousness of Carlo's position sunk in even deeper. I was still this kid next to him, for whom he had always protected, but I had gained respect in his eyes, I knew, with one good kick to Frankie's balls. We had gone down together, and thankfully, unless someone decided otherwise, had come up together.

"Kid, you have to understand," Carlo volunteered, speaking from his gut. "I can't tell you everything. In some cases, the less you know the better off you are; actually the safer you are, so you have to trust me on this one. Our mother and sisters must never know even as much as you do. Let me get through this my way. Soon, I hope I will know more if it's over, if they are coming after us again, the whole story. And we will work out a plan together. I won't keep you in the dark; that's a promise. Take it to the bank." He waited for my response.

I sucked in Carlo's words, accepting them as the truth. Even though the danger still might be out there, waiting to strike again, I was comforted knowing he had taken me in, trusted me, and thought me capable of sharing the burden and working in harmony to protect ourselves and our mother and sisters. I think he knew that I got his message and accepted him again without a doubt. All I could say was, "Yeah, brother, next time let me take the front, and you watch my back."

I lay down and rolled over for another healing nap. "Let's get out of here soon, so we can go help Joe fix his roof."

Just as I suspected, Doctor Stein's two-week prediction of our return to work and school didn't hold up. When he checked us that Sunday before permitting our release, he realized Carlo's ribs needed another week to mend and I was still passing a little blood in my piss. So he sent both of us back to bed for another seven-day stay.

That next Sunday, after that grueling, boring time had crept by and the piss was clear and Carlo could raise both arms over his head without a piercing pain in his side, we were finally allowed our freedom.

~

Carlo

Carlo's first visit to Julia Gail's house after the night at Joe's was interrupted with Thomas's summons for a walk. He had struggled through his first day back at work, ribs still taped, and the deep cut above his eyebrow still bandaged. By the time his shift was over he was nearly crawling in exhaustion through the front mill gates. He staggered unsteadily toward his lady's front door. Before Carlo could step inside, Thomas was there with his arm around Carlo's shoulders, escorting him back down the sidewalk.

"You look like you've been through a meat grinder, but you're tough," he began. "They won't touch you or your brother again and your sisters and mother won't be bothered."

"You had to take that beating to settle the score. I couldn't stop it. They went too far when they started to break your brother's hands, but Joe took care of that with the shotgun. He really likes that shotgun. He was real happy when we told him he could keep it."

Carlo anger grew in his throat. "You mean that was all staged? We walked into a trap, and Joe was in on it?"

"Son, it's over. You have to forget about it. You're damn lucky as it is. Most guys end up in a shallow grave somewhere, and a family member waking up with a hand or eye missing," Thomas replied. "Just stay away from Tony. Mind your own business. Be a good boy and be extra nice to Julia Gail."

Carlo lowered his head and his walk weaved a little until Thomas stiffened his arm around his shoulders to straighten out his gait. He sighed heavily. "But why my little brother? Why did he have to suffer? Why do they have to involve everyone's family? I'm the one who made the dumb decisions."

"I'm not going to say anymore. They sent their message and it runs right through you to the ones you love. That's how they drive home the point. That ain't ever gonna change in this business. You get involved; your family gets involved. Them's the rules, dear lad," Thomas's voice was still calm and instructive, but contained more than a hint of compassion.

Carlo finally had had enough. He was so tired of it all, yet still full of fear. But with Thomas' words came a certain relief rising up through his soul. He could trust this man. He knew it. This man who had seen the evil, and Carlo guessed had probably spread some himself, had made his pact with the Devil, and part of that pact was protection, a shield for his family. Thomas's deal, sealed by his past deeds, meant Carlo, Johnny and the rest of those dearest to him would be okay. They could go on with their lives. But Carlo didn't know if he would ever stop being cautious and wary, but he would play it smart this time. He was convinced Thomas was telling him the truth. He just might be free.

Chapter 22
Pea Traps and Rosewater

I ventured out of our homebound recovery room about the same time Carlo did. Limping a little and displaying a nose still twice its normal size; I returned to school and resumed my odd jobs in the neighborhood. I avoided returning to Joe's, for the time being. Joe's roof already had been repaired, and besides, the thought of a snooker match held no appeal for me at the moment.

What I did find appealing was the idea of returning to Mrs. Montlero's. But that didn't happen for another two weeks. Not for a lack of trying, however. I was desperate to see her, but she wasn't there. I went by her house every day, sometimes two or three times a day, but each time, the door was shut and the curtains drawn tight, keeping me out and maybe telling me to stay away. Something told me that I couldn't just knock on her door again and demand to be let in. She had to be there, one of these days, to invite me in. Much to my delight that invitation came a few weeks shy of my sixteenth birthday.

Early on a glorious afternoon, detouring as I had done so often to purposefully pass by her house on my way home from school, there she was, standing on her front porch. I stopped dead in my tracks when I saw her. She didn't see me at first. I could tell she was looking around for something, or maybe someone. Finally her eyes swept in my direction. She saw me, I could tell. I waited. She seemed frozen for the longest time. Then slowly turned to go back inside. My heart sank. But then she hesitated, and at last, I saw her right hand, now clasped in the left behind her back, curl with just the slightest motion to ever so discreetly beckon me. She continued on inside the house as I moved forward, and left the door open for me to enter.

I stepped inside, my heart now racing. From the kitchen, I heard, "Young man, I'm having a problem with the sink in the bathroom. Please see to it. I think my husband clogged the drain with all the hair falling out of his head."

I noticed her rosewater scent as I diverted my path from the kitchen to the bathroom, which was off the living room and next to her bedroom. Okay, I thought, this really stinks, but it's okay. She's not going any further. What was I expecting anyway? She had her fun, her little experiment with me, so now I would just go back to work, earn my fifty cents or dollar and be on my way. Sure I was disappointed, and a little hurt, but come on; this was just a fantasy, so I repeated to myself what Carlo says to me all the time, "Grow up!"

But let me tell you, if growing up was going through these kinds of disappointments, I wanted no part of it. Besides I just got my ass kicked royally and that was more than a disappointment, and now this; again feeling sorry for myself.

I think I'll charge her a dollar, maybe more, just for putting me through this.

I stood there in the bathroom for a moment and shook my head, sighed heavily, and crawled under the sink. I had disconnected the pea trap under the sink when I heard the door to the bathroom swing shut. It startled me. I was still a little jumpy and besides, being in her house like this again made me nervous as hell. But why was I nervous? I had nothing to be nervous about. My little escapade into the erotic was over. If her husband came home right now and found me like this, he would be happy knowing I was there doing what I was supposed to be doing. I dismissed the slamming door to the wind from the open bathroom window.

God, she's right, I thought, as I gathered the glob of slimy balled up hair from the pea trap's curved section. The nasty wad was black in color, not auburn like hers, so Julian's expanding baldness was the culprit, all right. I cleaned out the pipe and reattached it without difficulty.

"No problem here, Mrs. Montlero. Real easy fix," I announced as I opened the bathroom door to make my way out.

There was no response. I started out, but was caught by an image in the mirror that hung on the bathroom door. The reflective vision was blurry at first, so it took a moment for my eyes to focus and my brain to connect to realize what I was seeing.

Just another fantasy. I was hallucinating again. But, no, not this time. There she was, in the mirror, lying on her bed, wrapped in a pale blue shiny robe. I rotated slowly away from the mirror and stood to gaze upon her directly. Her eyes were closed and her lips were parted. The robe moved up and down ever so slightly with her shallow breathing. She was before me, an incredible, indescribable creature. The rays of the sun streaked through the window to sparkle the brownish redness of her hair spread across the pillow where she rested her head. Her ankles were crossed, and her arms to her sides. Her ten picture-perfect toes were again painted that vivid red.

I stood there, like a marble statue. I couldn't move except to utter, "Are you okay, Mrs. Montlero?" She did not move a muscle except to open her eyes.

"I'm glad you weren't hurt too badly, my little fix-it man. I don't know what I would do if you couldn't fix things for me." She brought her hands from her sides, untied the robe at her waist and slowly pulled it open to reveal her naked body. "Please come here and fix ME," she commanded.

Okay, now what was I supposed to do? Without having much of an idea how things like this were supposed to go, even though I had dreamt about this moment for weeks and studied at the library, I couldn't think of what came next. I was a rookie at this, but that was no excuse. My mind was scattered but for the wonderful sight before me.

"Don't be afraid, I won't bite you. I'll be gentle," she said, stirring something inside me to move, and that I did with no more hesitation.

What came next will forever live vibrantly deep inside me. And when I choose, I can relive the hour or so with her at will; just give me a second, and it all comes back. It's my secret, and no one can share it. I suppose it's like that for all other human beings when they experience their first time. For me, it was grand; for her, I'm not so sure. What I remember from that afternoon in her bed− clutching her breasts, feeling her wetness, hearing her gasps and sharing each other so completely − was I wish everyone in their most private moments could relive it with such true, delightful intensity.

The details are stark. The colors, the smells, the sounds, the movements. Her skills, my awkwardness. Her instructions; gentle, kind, coaxing, understanding. My complete surrender. And then, once we reached the third round, I took over. She accepted, welcoming me again with legs open, enticing, willing, wanting more.

Exhausted then, although not wanting to be, we had no choice but to stop. It was time to go. I now needed to cover her. She shivered. The steaming sweat from our bodies cooling. I reached for the robe that lay across the foot of the bed. I had never felt anything like it. I asked her what it was made of. The answer was silk, "you silly." I had never felt a silk garment before. At least Julius was doing something right. I rose from the bed to dress, and there on the nightstand, neatly folded in a square, was a pair of white panties.

"They're for you," she cooed. "Take them. Remember me," she noticed the question on the tip of my tongue, "Yes, they are the ones," She assured me.

I stood in the doorway of her bedroom for what seemed like hours, but in reality it was only for a moment or two, drinking her in again. She lay exactly as she had an hour so or before; dressed only in the robe, legs crossed, hands at her side, eyes shut. Not talking, only breathing ever so slightly, her hair again spread like the wings of a mammoth butterfly across the pillows. Just like nothing had happened. Had it been a dream? Another trip into the pages of Carlo's tattered and torn magazines? No. She was there. Her scent still covered my skin. This was real. I knew it.

As I wandered home through the neighborhood late that afternoon, I reached in my pocket instinctively and found nothing except the folded-up panties. She hadn't paid me. *Damn*, I thought. "Oh well," I said out loud. And then, in a moment of blatant arrogance, I reasoned, okay, well today didn't cost Julius anything. But did it? Had I stolen from him? Had I violated what was purely precious to him? I must have. It wasn't right. He didn't deserve it, no matter how big his ball of fallen hair became.

Damn, I thought, trying to push the thoughts out of my head. Why can't I enjoy the moment for what it was? Yes, I had robbed him of something, his and his alone, but could he possess her if he didn't give enough back? Wasn't she allowed to find more? Now I was really confused. I shuffled the rest of the way home, alternately feeling miserable, elated as I kneaded her panties inside my pocket, and very tired. I didn't talk much at dinner that night and went to bed early, re-living that afternoon again and again. My dreams only occasionally interrupted by Julius' extended hand and good wishes.

I had tucked her underwear inside my tobacco can among the coins and bills riding in the coil springs beneath my mattress. Eventually I convinced myself that what had happened between us wasn't completely right, nor was it completely wrong. I felt deep in my heart that I did fix Mrs. Montlero that afternoon, and week after week thereafter, until I departed for Camp Claiborne on that blistering summer day two years later.

Chapter 23
Praying Helps Sometimes

Angelina

My mother was alone in her bedroom, sitting at her vanity, staring into the mirror. Her hands were clasped in front of her as if praying. But I knew she wasn't praying. She couldn't pray. Her mind was running in every direction, emotions from sheer joy to deep sadness, each replacing the other. All in a flash. It was Nicole's wedding day, but Angelina was locked away from her daughter, from me and the world, for just a time, until she could once more understand and forgive.

I knew what she was thinking. She needed God to help her do both. She would tell me later the many thoughts that ran through her mind. I am guessing at the rest. The joy came when her thoughts were on Nicole. She was to marry Silvio Bustamonte.

He's from a good family. He's smart, he's handsome, he'll make a good husband and father. A good provider. I am glad for her. She did well. Her life will be good, she smiled to herself. *Joy for her.* But then, *God in heaven, this is hard, so hard to do again without my Nick.* Sorrow, bitterness. *God forgive me.*

It was on days like this, special days that were family days, days for parents and children to be together, that she felt she had been denied. He'd been taken away. Snatched from her forever.

Why is God punishing me, and why does He keep on punishing? She thought angrily. She was angry at herself for nearly dreading this day, just like the days before, the wedding days for her daughters Katrina and Sophia. Again, she would celebrate and mourn. It wasn't fair.

Nick, I curse you for leaving. I can't do it again. But she knew she had to. She rose from the vanity bench and walked to her closet. Today, as was her tradition, she would shed her long black dress, this time for the pale blue one she had purchased with money from her secret cooking account. The other two mother-of-the-bride wedding dresses hung before her in the closet, and as she glanced over them, she prided herself on now having three. Most of her friends in the neighborhood could afford only one such dress, no matter how many daughters and how many weddings took place in their families. For her good fortune she was joyful. For the longest time, she would offer to lend her dresses to the other Bessemer women. But they never accepted her offer. Yes, they accepted her cooking. They were willing to hide and sneak her steaming dishes home under their aprons to present them as their own. But to wear one of her dresses in public at their own daughter's weddings, well that was out of the question. Too much pride. She finally gave up offering her dresses, but she kept on cooking. That was her joy.

She placed the pale blue dress across her bed and turned back to view herself in the mirror. Her ankle-length slipcovered what she still considered a handsome frame. Her figure was round, and after all these years, she remained shapely. Her hips were womanly, mature, with little evidence of the seven children she had birthed. Her once-coal-black hair hung to the small of her back. Even though it was now streaked with grey, it glistened in the artificial light from the vanity lamp. She had drawn the curtains tight and the door to her bedroom remained locked. She remained safe and alone in her world – for now. She was not ready to perform, alone, once again, just yet.

I curse you Nick.

She found herself running her fingertips over her breasts, still finding them sensitive to the touch. They were large but firm. Her body was bountiful, still fertile, despite her age. Many of her friends complained of their dryness, wistfully longing to sustain their womanhood just a while longer. But her remaining youth was all wasted. Her sensuality wilting. Yet her desires remained.

I have no one.

There were many nights when she lay awake, alone, with nothing beside her except the cold sheets of her empty bed. She coveted Nick's touch. Any touch other than her own would have been welcome. She felt ashamed having these thoughts. The Devil brought them to her. She must deprive herself of another man.

I curse you Nick. Must I continue my self-imposed celibacy?

It was agony, especially when the widowers after Mass sought her company. But she continued to deny them, and herself. She must live through her children. Take pleasure in their pleasure; live with the knowledge of their joy. Find happiness there, not from within; never selfish, never conceited. She knew she must not be bitter, must not direct her anger at the blessings Nick and her God had given her; the ones she loved the most. She despised her anger toward her daughters, even the jealousy she felt as she witnessed their time with their men, and now Carlo's time with his woman.

It is theirs alone, not to be shared. I curse you Nick.

She turned away from the mirror, back toward the simple, elegant garment awaiting her on the bed. She slipped it over her head as she heard the knock at her door.

"Can I help you mother?" came Sophia's voice. "We have one hour before we must go, and Nicole is asking for you. Can you come?"

Angelina went to the door to welcome her daughter. She pivoted as Sophia entered. "Please button me up," my mother said, "I am ready."

As Angelina embraced Sophia before going to the bride, her will power struggled to hold her emotions deeply in check. Mixed with her tangle of elation and melancholy, she could detect the hard edge of fear. She was now confronting the reality of her adopted country at war, and that very war had become her personal plight when I made my announcement the night before.

"Momma, I'm going to join the Army," I had declared to her softly. We were seated at the dining room table. The families of the bride and groom had gathered for the traditional pre-wedding night rehearsal. The occasion had been festive.

Angelina had prepared a most delightful Tagliatelle con Dadi di Proscuitto preceded by Fettunta o Bruschetta al Pomodoro as appetizers and Pomodoro con Porri as the soup course. The guests had been too consumed by the aromas and tastes of her latest delicacies to hear my words.

As soon as Angelina was sure she had registered those words, her eyes rose slowly from her plate. She looked into her youngest son's eyes and found on his face a concoction of concern and sympathy. Since Pearl Harbor and America's entry into the war, she had been terrified this day would come. She knew my attitude and ambition.

She stared at me, not responding. Carlo was seated across from me. I don't believe he heard my statement but caught our mother's reaction and knew something was amiss. I knew Angelina wondered, after everything she had been through, why she couldn't, like so many other mothers in the neighborhood, watch her son march off to the mill instead of marching into battle. But apparently, God was taking her son on a difference course.

I will face this too alone, she thought. *Nick, where are you? Give me strength.*

She then turned away from me and sat very still, unable to move. She could sense that I was rigid as well, waiting for her to speak, to do something, to react. She must compose herself and move. She did not want her guests to see her come apart.

More pasta, that was it. She looked across at Carlo. His eyes were dancing from hers to his brother's. Everyone else at the table was oblivious to what was happening between the boys and their mother. They just continued to eat and jabber. More pasta. She noticed my full plate. I wasn't eating, and neither was Carlo.

Finally, she put down her fork and crossed herself. She pushed back from the table with the out-loud excuse to those who were listening of the need to fetch more pasta from the kitchen. She walked slowly toward the closed kitchen door. Both of her sons rose to follow her.

Carlo lit into me the second the swinging door to the kitchen had closed behind them. "Why the hell can't you just accept the line job? You are good at just about anything you try. You could be a mechanic, maybe even a technician, one of those guys who monitors the calibration and tonsure strength of the rails. You don't have to do this!" he was almost pleading.

Angelina stood with her back to us at the kitchen sink. *You must do this right,* she told herself. *You must make sure they both understand.*

From the instant she knew that her husband had been killed at the mill, she had put her faith in her sons to grow up without a father. And they had both done fairly well despite a few setbacks. She loved them equally, no matter what they chose to do. She had made it her motto to always build them up, never tear them down. Support them with all her strength. She knew God would give her that.

She turned to face her sons, both shouting in the lowest voices they could manage, in Italian, for her benefit, she knew, out of respect. Carlo continued his tirade, his finger trying to poke a hole in his little brother's chest. She listened. Waited. Their words were harsh, but she knew they must be released. She waited a moment longer, and then spoke.

"Yes, why can't you hear your brother? Why are you so stubborn? Your family needs you more than the Army," she declared − in English. She knew using her sons' native language might be her last chance to change my mind. She had to take it. Her sons didn't know she practiced her English when no one was around. Now she used that language to speak her heart.

Carlo stopped his poking. His mouth dropped open, and both of us stared at her in disbelief. "Mama," I stammered, "What did you say?"

"Shut up and listen to me and to your brother." She had our attention now. "Hear my words. I say them to you in English so there is no mistake," her voice was even more forceful than before. Deep inside, she knew she would lose, and so would Carlo. I *was* stubborn, willful, yet as my mother, she had to try.

We were still stunned. For me was the first time in my life I had heard my mother utter a word of English. Angelina moved away from the sink towards us, stepping between Carlo's withdrawn finger and my chest. She waited for a response. She saw me hesitate, but only for a moment. She could see me mustering up my strength.

"Momma, I have to go," I put my hand on her arm. "I don't want to work at the mill. Carlo knows that. I've told him before. I want to fight. I'm not afraid."

Carlo interrupted, spewing with rage. "You little bastard, are you accusing me of being a coward? Afraid to take on the Nazis or the Japs? Who do you think you are? If mother wasn't here I'd take you out back and beat your ass."

"I didn't mean you!" I was quick to correct. "I know you're not afraid. I just need to do this for my own good. I need to see if I can." I was pleading for understanding.

Angelina looked at Carlo. "Your brother would never disrespect you. No one in this family is a coward. Never use those words again. Now, more than ever, we need each other. There will be no words to divide us. Our time together is short."

She remained between us, and as the room fell silent, she reached out and pulled us to her. Her short stature only allowed her to grasp us by our waists, but her strength was impossible to resist. Her embrace calmed the tension.

"*Miei ragazzi.* My boys," she said, squeezing us. "*Miei bei ragazzi.* My beautiful boys," She took a breath. "*Voi siete coraggiosi. Vostra madre e' orgogliosa. Vostra padre e' orgoglioso. Lui vi guarda da lassu'e vi da la sua forza. La sua mano ferma con il suo soffice tocco, lui sara'con voi dovunque andiate. Portatelo con voi. Lasciate che vi guidi.* You are brave. Your mother is proud. Your father is proud. He looks down on you, and gives you his strength. His firm hand with its gentle touch. He will be with you wherever you go. Take him with you. Let him guide you." Her boys remained quiet.

"Carlo, *tu vai al tuo lavoro e fai le cosec he sconfiggeranno quelle persone che stanno distruggendo il mio vecchio paese. E tu, mio Johnny, vai a combattere se devi. Fai la tua parte.* Carlo, you

213

go to your work and make the things that will beat those people who are destroying our country. And you, my Johnny, you go, if you must, to fight. You do your part." She released us, lifted the reserve pasta bowl from the kitchen countertop and marched through the kitchen door, swinging it widely to return to the dining room. But not before glancing over her shoulder to see tears welling up in both her boys' eyes.

~

It had become her eldest son's job on this day and the wedding days of her other daughters in the past to act as his father's stand-in. His role only added to Angelina's sadness as he escorted each sister down the aisle. As he would bring them to their mother in her lonely front row pew, her performance would begin. She would stiffen up, straightening her body into a perfect posture, and maintain that position and a painted-on smile throughout the ceremony. Through all the hugs and kisses and good will, the heartfelt gestures of congratulations that would come from the hundreds in attendance those days. To those watching, she would appear stoic, yet stunning.

In her bedroom, just hours from the third wedding of her children, Angelina's dress felt snug as Sophia buttoned the final top button. She turned to see herself in the mirror. The dress fit perfectly to accentuate her shape. She dabbed on a hint of makeup, and took one last look. Her daughter stared back at her in the mirror. They smiled at one another, reflected in the glass, and then went together to attend to the bride. She would celebrate her third daughter's wedding with genuine joy temporarily replacing her sadness and fear. She would find her voice again that day, singing quietly in the ear of the bride as she helped her dress and coif her hair. It was the first time Angelina had sung in many months. She thought of Carlo and the lovely Julia Gail. They would marry later in the summer, but I already would be gone, on my way to fight. The song she chose to sing this day, although not one of happiness was bursting with hope.

Part II

Chapter 24
The Wrong Prom Date

Like millions of other American men in the summer of 1941, my journey into World War II began with a duffel bag over my shoulder and a tearful scene at the train station. As I stood there awaiting the three o'clock Union Pacific to arrive from Denver, my sisters and my mother surrounded me. The men in the family, Carlo and the three brothers-in-law, stood to the side awaiting a goodbye handshake. Rosalie Giancano, my date for the high school prom only two weeks before, stood even further apart from the group. She would get the last hug, and perhaps a kiss on the cheek. Mrs. Montlero was nowhere to be found. I had told her when I was leaving and why I needed to go. She had wept, slapped me across the face and ordered me out of her house. I think I understood why she reacted that way, but it was no less difficult to leave on the day I told her.

The next day, when walking by her house, I saw her on her porch and she waved me over. Things went back to normal for us that last afternoon, but in the end, she cried again. I was sad for her and asked her to come see me off. She said she wouldn't do that, but I still wished she would. Between the embraces from my sisters, I scanned the area, hoping she had changed her mind. But she hadn't, so other than those from my family, and Rosalie, the platform was empty.

Apparently there were no other volunteers or draftees leaving from Pueblo on that particular summer afternoon. I was a volunteer, not a draftee. Being not quite eighteen years old, Carlo had helped me add a year to my age and forge our mother's signature to the parent waiver to convince the Army recruiter of my legal capability to serve. Both of us felt justified in making that frequently seen and mostly ignored alteration of my true age to my enlistment papers. We became forgers after receiving Angelina's blessing the night before Nicole's wedding. After our confrontation in my mother's kitchen that night, Carlo seemed to accept my decision to enter the service. He never really said any more about it, but the fact he was there to see me off, and had actually helped me pack my duffel bag (even if it had been in total silence), was enough for me to realize his blessing and his encouragement.

As we expected, the Army recruiter who had set up shop in the downtown Pueblo post office literally two weeks after Pearl Harbor, didn't look too closely at the crudely altered document, so the next day, exactly six weeks before I stood on the platform waiting to leave for good, I had made the trip to Denver for my Army physical. I had looked forward to the six-hour train ride covering the two hundred mile round trip. It was my first ride on a passenger train as a legitimate paying customer, sitting in a regular, comfortable seat.

I had ridden the rails many times before, but only as a temporary stowaway. In my younger years, a few of my friends and I would hop aboard the boxcars and coal haulers as they crept through the mill's rail yards to ride as hobos south until the excitement faded to boredom. Then we would catch a train heading back north before it became too dark and we risked falling victim to vicious wanderers looking for easy, young prey. You had to be very careful of the vagabonds because if they caught you, they'd likely take all the money you had, strip you of all your clothes and throw you off the moving trains, at times traveling as fast as thirty miles an hour.

There also were stories of some kids being raped by these scoundrels, so we played it extra safe hiding from them as well as the railroad police who patrolled regularly. When I look back on that train ride to Denver, I recall just about all twenty of us would-be recruits were cutting up and cracking jokes non-stop from our plush seats in the Pullman. We had a great day overall (although there were some parts not so fun), but all of us were punks with wild-eyed confidence and naïve optimism. I easily passed the rather superficial physical exam designed by the Army to screen its soldiers. The only setback came when I became terribly nauseous during the routine group examination for hemorrhoids. (That was the not-so-fun part.) In a circle of one hundred and fifty fresh-faced teenagers, at the order of the five trained medics, we each simultaneously turned, dropped our trousers, bent and spread our butt cheeks for a close-up view. The room, the size of a high school basketball arena, immediately took on the fragrance of the Denver stockyards, maybe even the Chicago stockyards. The medics wore surgical masks. The recruits did not, and nobody offered us any. Five of the boys in the circle fainted dead away, but were revived and passed the exam anyway. I just held my breath for as long as he could. I sure did get woozy though.

After the butt cheek spreading and a little fresh air for everyone, I guess about one hundred and thirty other recruits and I were offered hearty congratulations for being fit for duty by the twenty-one-year-old lieutenant in charge. We knew he was twenty-one because he told us so, plus he told us he had just graduated from West Point. At the time I didn't know what West Point was, but I went to the library when I got home and read up on it. Man, what a history that place has, and the people who went to school there. Pretty impressive, I thought, but it was a world far away. The other nineteen in our group were sent home with flat feet, chronic asthma, less than twenty-sixty eyesight in both eyes, or too many missing fingers or toes. One in our group who failed the exam had a foot wound and two absent toes. It looked like the accident had occurred very recently, and his two neatly severed digits were enough to give him a pass from the war and a ticket home.

I had taken my written exams before going to Denver and had done pretty well on all of the recruiter's tests. Well enough, in fact, that they told me I could qualify for training at any number of different posts. I could be a radio technician, if I wanted, a medical corpsman, or even enlist in the engineering brigades. But those weren't for me. I wanted to be in the infantry. In fact, I had pretty much made up my mind that I wanted to be a paratrooper. I can't tell you why. The recruiter had given me some information on the potential formation of a special corps of soldiers who would be taught to jump out of airplanes and land on the ground to fight.

Since I wasn't really fond of boats at the time, or long rides in a truck, I thought getting into the fight from the air would be quicker and easier. And I figured being a paratrooper offered a special challenge, and with it, maybe special recognition. I'd never been in an airplane. The highest I'd ever been off the ground was three feet eleven inches in an intramural track meet in high school. I didn't even come close to making the varsity team.

As I stood there on that platform, my childish mind couldn't grasp the war and the vastness of it; its complexity, and what it meant to fight and kill the Japanese and Germans. Country against country, how big was that? It was hard for me to understand what the newsreels were describing that spring when I would go to the downtown Ute theatre for the matinee showing. What was a Nazi anyway? They looked like us. They couldn't be all bad. Were they really committing atrocities? I didn't know what an atrocity was. And the Japanese; they looked different, a little meaner maybe, but we were out to annihilate them? Not for a minute could I grasp the idea that armies over there were massacring people by the thousands, maybe millions, and that our country, so far away, was being threatened. All I knew was we had to defend ourselves and go help out our friends, especially the Brits and the French, but to imagine that Hitler and Tojo were as big of badasses as they said they were was darn near impossible for me to accept. At first, that is.

My mother's view about that prick Mussolini and him destroying Italy and Sicily helped me understand a little better, but I still had no idea what I was getting myself into. I knew America was really pissed off, especially after what the Japs did in Hawaii, so I was pissed off too, and I wanted to fight along with everyone else, and I knew we had to win. So I was okay with combat. And I didn't care where they sent me. I kind of liked the idea of going directly to Italy, for instance, to fight Mussolini. Maybe my command of the language might make me even more valuable as an interpreter, maybe one that extracted combat intelligence from Italian prisoners who, the newsreels were saying, were already surrendering to the Brits in droves.

At the platform, I gently broke from the circle of my sisters to shake the hands of their husbands. I didn't know these guys very well, so that didn't take long. Then I stepped up to Carlo. As always with me and my brother, encounters like this (goodbyes and hellos) were stiff and stoic. We were in the habit of holding in any emotions at the risk of appearing too soft and giving up our manhood. But when I dropped Carlo's extended hand to grasp him by his shoulders, Carlo seemed to give in, let loose, and for once, he openly returned the embrace, short-lived as it was.

Before we separated, however, I did have the chance to whisper to my brother, "I love you." As we faced each other, all my brother could do was nod in agreement. I could tell that if he had tried to speak to me just then, the risk of breaking down into the same tearful state as my sisters and mother would have been too much. So he didn't speak, nor did he cry, and neither did I.

As the huge, black, smoke-bellowing iron locomotive chugged to a stop and its airbrakes hissed at a piercing pitch, I politely pecked Rosalie on the cheek and turned to board the passenger car. She had told me she would write every day until my return, but I didn't believe a word of it, and frankly, I wouldn't have been all that disappointed if not a single letter ever came from her. Prom night had not been the least bit exciting. Rosalie was home before midnight, and I went to find a bottle of Jim Beam to drown my sorrows for not having invited that cute little Danna girl named Maggie who had been eyeing me for the last month or so in math class. She really was a knockout, and there was something about her that lingered on in the back of my mind. More than her figure, I might add. She never seemed to miss even the hardest of questions, and was always first to solve the algebra equations the stogy old Miss Lofgren would post on the blackboard.

At the prom, I had seen Maggie dancing with her date, and had been tempted to abandon Rosalie right there on the dance floor and grab Maggie away from the jerk she was with, but I didn't. So I missed that chance and I also missed one last opportunity with Mrs. Montlero. Julius had been home that day with the flu. Afterwards, for two whole days, my head hurt and I wallowed in my sorrow and self-pity.

As I settled in my seat for the long, hot trip south through New Mexico, across Texas and into Louisiana, I looked around the passenger car and saw that it was half-filled with boys just like me. At every stop – in Trinidad, Roswell, New Mexico, onto Amarillo, into Shreveport, all along the way south and eventually east, more recruits boarded to fill up the car. Some looked older, some looked younger, but they all looked resigned to take what would come their way. I swelled with a sense of invulnerability as the train chugged toward my future. I was on my way to Camp Claiborne, Louisiana.

Chapter 25
Louisiana in the Summertime

"Goddamn it's hot," said the red-haired kid from Montana sitting across the aisle from me in the Pullman passenger car.

I awoke, startled by the strange, loud voice, and opened my eyes to the sun blazing through the window. It temporarily blinded me. I had been dreaming of Mrs. Montlero, and when the light and sound blasted into my brain to shake me to consciousness, I became oh-too-aware that I was not in her bed.

We had been traveling for three solid days. The floor of the fancy Pullman looked as dirty as Joe's place after a full house on a Saturday night and smelled worse than the gym during the hemorrhoid exam. There had been no time or opportunity for showers. There weren't any on board and the stops along the way only gave us ten minutes to stretch our legs. Decent sleep was out of the question, with the noisy poker and craps games and all the whiskey that had been smuggled on board. I won eighty-five dollars in a five-card stud game the first night and lost all but ten the second night, and so I had to quit and tried to sleep, but with little success. Even a few shots of Canadian Club didn't seem to help.

The next sound I heard was the bellowing from a guy about my size in height but he must have weighed two hundred and twenty pounds. I looked up. He stood at the front of the Pullman, erect as a lamppost. His hands were on his hips and he was thankfully silent for the moment, displaying a Cheshire cat grin. He had no neck, I remember. His enormous head balanced square on his shoulders. He screamed again in a voice that I swear penetrated my soul. Then, this red-faced, square-jawed, steel-grey-eyed man whose Popeye arms proudly protruded from his rolled-up shirt sleeves displaying three stripes on each lowered his voice to the most sinister whisper I've ever heard.

"Get up you lousy little shits," he quietly ordered. "This is Camp Claiborne, in the grand and glorious state of Louisiana." And then the drill sergeant yelled, "For the next two months I am the devil and you are in hell!"

16 July, 1942

Dear Carlo,

The Army says I can now write a letter home. I have been in Louisiana at a place called Camp Claiborne for two months. This is what they call boot camp. It's the hardest thing I've ever tried to do. We get up in the morning at five. We go to bed at night at nine. In between they work us like dogs.

We run all the time, every place we go. We crawl on our bellies through mud pits strung with barbed wire just above our heads. (Just thought of this ... it's probably barbed wire made at the mill.) Anyway, we do five hundred push-ups a day, now with our thirty-pound backpacks on our backs. Before, we didn't have the packs. Tomorrow they say one of our buddies will be sitting on our backs as we do them. It's kind of what I expected, really, since I know that we've got to be in good shape to go fight the Krauts. I won't be going to fight the Japs, but I can't say anymore than that because there are people who read our letters to make sure the enemy doesn't find something valuable in them. They think there might be spies running around.

Anyway, this is the infantry. In the next few days they are going to teach us how to shoot the M-1 rifle. I think I will shoot pretty good with that gun, since I could shoot those rabbits with the .22. Thanks for teaching me to shoot. If you want to write me back you can. I think from now on I will write my letters to you and you can pass the news on to mother and all the rest of what's going on with me here. I hope that's okay with you. In between the push-ups tomorrow, they tell us we are going on a 20-mile hike with our backpacks and our M-1s, but we don't get to shoot them. We started out with 24 guys in my squad. Tonight there are 19 left. Our commander is General William Lee. Maybe you've read about him.

Your brother,
Johnny, Grunt Recruit

Soon after I wrote Carlo about my first weeks in boot camp and mentioned General Lee, an article came out in the *Stars and Stripes* newspaper about him. In the military journals it was common for high-profile generals like Bill Lee to see glowing articles about themselves published regularly. General Lee had a full platoon of Army press agents whose sole job was to get their boss the best press possible, and because General Lee had a reputation for bucking the boys upstairs (his superior generals), he needed all the favorable newspaper ink he could get to support his programs. And I'm glad he got it. If it hadn't been for Bill

Lee's persistence and good press there may not have been a paratrooper division at all.

I picked up a copy of the paper and read the article the same evening before lights-out in our barracks. The bit in Lee's General Order Number 5 (which by the way, was posted on our barracks bulletin board), about a "rendezvous with destiny" got me to thinking what he really meant by that. Was he saying if we failed our country would be destined to life under Hitler, but if we succeeded, our country would return to normal? God that was a mighty big load to carry, but I was reminded how the mental part of the military game is as important as the physical part, and no equipment, no matter how advanced, was worth a damn unless some grunts like my buddies and me decide when and where and how to use it most effectively.

As I came to find out, that was Bill Lee for you. Always pressing us for more. Always playing with our heads to make us think we were better than the enemy. Now it was time to prove it, and I guess General Lee thought we were ready. Anyway, the article gave me some good insight into our commander and it served to boost my confidence a little that my buddies and I were in pretty good hands.

Dateline: 19 August, 1942
By Ernie Pyle

After months of internal wrangling within the Army hierarchy, Major General William C. Lee, a 49-year-old Army careerist who served in World War I, has succeeded in convincing the top brass to gain formal recognition of the airborne combat soldier. General Lee has finally been given approval to create his new command. President Roosevelt had supported the General's request over the objections of Lee's superiors and formalized creation of the unit. A division of approximately ten thousand fresh recruits from the Army infantry in boot camp at Camp Claiborne, Louisiana, have been placed under Lee's skillful wing. Thousands of other ambitious determined young recruits will soon gather under that wing, and surely their love for their new commander will grow with an unbridled passion.

General Lee is a real history buff that likes the moniker of another General Lee since in his mind; his assignment has placed him in a class quite near his hero Robert E. The modern General Lee is a serious student of the Confederate general. He is from the south, a little town called Dunn, North Carolina. He graduated from NC State, and formed his first parachute group at Fort Benning, Georgia. He has studied Robert E.'s tactics; his ability to out-maneuver superior strength forces, his uncanny skill to capitalize on surprise, and the art of outflanking to divide and quite often conquer his enemies. He also has carefully researched his namesake's psychological profile and tried to duplicate General Robert E. Lee's outwardly stoic strength of confidence and fortitude in the face of frequently insurmountable odds. This Army's newest General Lee is no less of a soldier than Robert E. and he intends to prove it with his paratroopers at his side.

Early on in his research of his idol, General Lee noted the prolific, poetic pen. Among so many other attributes, Robert E. Lee was a masterful writer. His letters are among the nation's most prized historical prose. He never wasted words, and his persuasive arguments, set to almost musical cadence, will live forever in America's archives. Not to be outdone, William C. penned his "General Order Number Five," marking the birth of the

101ˢᵗ Airborne Division, the Screaming Eagles, with these words of inspiration:

General Order Number Five

The 101ˢᵗ Airborne Division, activated at Camp Claiborne, Louisiana, has no history, but it has a rendezvous with destiny. Like the early American pioneers whose invincible courage was the foundation stone of this nation, we have broken with the past and its traditions in order to establish our claim to the future.

Due to the nature of our armament, and the tactics in which we shall perfect ourselves, we shall be called upon to carry out operations of far-reaching military importance, and we shall habitually go into action when the need is immediate and extreme.

Let me call your attention to the fact that our badge is the great American eagle. This is a fitting emblem for a division that will crush its enemies by falling upon them like a thunderbolt from the skies.

The history we shall make, the record of high achievement we hope to write in the annals of the American Army and the American people, depends wholly and completely on the men of this division. Each individual, each officer and each enlisted man, must therefore regard himself as a necessary part of a complex and powerful instrument for the overcoming of the enemies of the nation. Each, in his own job, must realize that he is not only a means, but an indispensable means for obtaining the glory of victory. It is, therefore, not too much to say that the future itself, in whose molding we expect to have our

share, is in the hands of the soldiers of the 101ˢᵗ Airborne Division.

Major General William C. Lee

General Bill, as he likes to be called, will surely quickly turn his recruits into incomparable fighting units.

I can only say that General Lee became the second hero in my life, next only to my brother. Even though I more or less worshiped Lee from a distance, he was the kind of guy who you felt you could really get next to. Yeah, I guess, he was a father figure. He was everyone's Papa, but you better not cross him and you better do what he said. He commanded us, as a commander should, with skill and discipline. His insistence on perfection saved many of our lives. We might not have appreciated it at the time when we were crawling through the mud and pouring blood out of our boots from the ruptured blisters, but we know it now.

However a cruel twist of fate denied him the pleasure of seeing his men in action. Just prior to D-Day June 6, 1944, Bill was permanently sidelined with either a heart attack or a stroke, and was forced to return to the States for the duration of the war. God, we hurt when he had to go home. It was like a death in the family. He retired from service in August 1944. He followed his men from Normandy to Bastogne, and into Hitler's Eagles Nest, but had to do so through the newsreels and newspapers like all of his homebound countrymen. But we would always remember him for his vision, his leadership and the love of his men.

General Maxwell Taylor assumed command of the 101ˢᵗ after Bill was sidelined. He was a very visible personality among his peers in the war. Not on the scale or in the same league as Patton, Bradley, McArthur,

Montgomery or certainly Ike, yet he parlayed his command of the 101st Airborne, created by his predecessor, onto a vertical stepping stone to the top.

During his long, illustrious career, General Taylor would become superintendent of West Point; Army Chief of Staff during the war in Korea; Chairman of the Joint Chiefs of Staff under President Kennedy (he became a vocal critic of President Eisenhower's military policies during the 1960 presidential campaign); and Ambassador to South Vietnam after vocally supporting the troop buildup there for both Kennedy and President Johnson.

I'm not so sure why I didn't feel the same way about General Taylor as I did General Lee. After Bill Lee left us, I saw General Taylor many times during my training days in England, and once on the ground in France on June 7, 1944, the day after the Allied invasion. General Taylor was the first American general to step foot in France during World War II, we found out later. And he did so despite fierce warnings and lectures from the top Army command. He parachuted behind enemy lines along with us, and from a command post, he led the 101st through its European campaign. He was back in England, however, when the battle raged at Bastogne, later declaring that missing that fight was the greatest disappointment of his military career.

That's what the newspapers said, anyway. But to this day, Bill Lee is still my man, and I know for a fact he rested that way in the hearts of most of the soldiers I served with. Sure, we respected General Taylor's larger-than-life presence, and him being with us on the ground in Europe, but I still don't think he quite filled the shoes of Bill Lee when it was all said and done.

I can tell you that the guy who rivaled Bill Lee, maybe even stood above him, if that's possible, was the big guy himself, Dwight David Eisenhower. Now, there's a general, and I'll never forget him for what he did for me.

Chapter 26
Learning the Lingo

The letter Carlo received from his little brother while I was training in Louisiana was the first of thirty-four letters Carlo would receive from me during my four-and-a-half years as an Army paratrooper. I found out later that Carlo kept every one of them. He told me he would tell our mother, and our sisters, when they were present, that a letter from me had arrived, and he would insist on reading it to them. That way he could select the parts he wanted them to hear and leave out the parts that he didn't want them to hear.

For me, by writing these letters, I realized I could understand things that happened to me with much more clarity and depth. For some reason my letters helped me remember, and they helped me forget. I could get the bad things off my chest to discard from memory, and I could place the good things in safekeeping to recall at will. I never thought for a moment that Carlo would give them all back to me one day.

30 August, 1942
Camp Claiborne, Louisiana

Dear Carlo,

Please let mother and the sisters know that I am well. We're real close to being done with boot camp. I don't know if I told you or not, but I have volunteered for paratrooper training. About a week or two ago, our commanding general Bill Lee had a big parade in the training field. We all stood in formation and he told us that a new division had been formed to fight the Krauts by parachuting out of airplanes. There are about 10,000 men in a division. It's called the 101st Airborne Division, and I was the thirtieth guy in line to volunteer after the formation broke and we stood down from attention. They are going to call us the Screaming Eagles and give each of us a patch of the head of an eagle to wear on our sleeves. Other groups they call regiments will join to make up the division. A regiment is about 2,000 men. I have to learn all of this stuff. Army lingo.

I get that patch if I make it through another four months of training. Can you imagine jumping out of an airplane? I've never even been in an airplane, and I'm sure the first time I will be scared to death. But I think if they told me to run twenty miles I could do it. A guy in my platoon said the other day that he guessed in the last two months we might have done 40,000 push ups.

My platoon now has about 50 guys, about half of them new because the other half couldn't make it through boot camp. I don't know if they went home or to some other outfit of the Army. It may sound strange but I don't want to come home. I want to make it through paratrooper training and get that patch on my sleeve. I like what I'm doing and I want to do it better.

How is work at the mill? I hope you don't mind me talking on and on about stuff happening with me. It's not that I don't care about things you are doing, or mother or our sisters. It's just by writing these things down I somehow feel better. Does that sound girly? Anyway, I'm supposed to hear in the next day or so whether I stay here in Louisiana or go somewhere else for paratrooper school. I will let you know, but I might not be able to tell you exactly where I am because of all the spies. You can write me back if you want, but I don't know if I will get it since I might be shipping out soon.

Your brother,
PFC

PS. I expect I will get a promotion when I finish boot camp. Private First Class, and I will get another $15 per month.

August 31, 1942

Dear Johnny,

I'm glad you made it through boot camp, and I'm glad you are going to do what you want to do in the Army. I've told mother and our sisters about the things you are doing and that you are well. I am writing this letter back to you on the same day it arrived here so that if you move around it stands a better chance of getting to you sooner. Your mother and sisters send their love. Me, too.

Your brother,
Carlo

When I had arrived at Camp Claiborne (before Bill Lee's creation of his Screaming Eagles), all recruits had been assigned to the 82nd Infantry Division. When President Roosevelt intervened to put the seal of approval on Bill Lee's idea, the 82nd was split in two to form the 82nd and the 101st airborne divisions. In the fall of 1942, both divisions were deployed to Fort Bragg to begin paratrooper training. I eventually became part of the 506th Parachute Infantry Regiment of the 101st.

22 November, 1942
Fort Bragg North Carolina

Dear Carlo,

I think the last time I wrote, I was about to ship out. Well, I did. I am still in the U.S. at a new camp; no, this is a fort, a lot bigger than Camp Claiborne. It's called Fort Bragg. The place is huge. I can't tell you any more about this place other than its size, and there are a lot of soldiers and grunts like me running around. They tell us we're still grunts, not soldiers just yet, that's why I still call myself that. I get the feeling from some of the classes we're taking, the things we might be ordered to do — that is if they ever let us get into the war — could be secret, and with all the spies around, they might find out about this fort and what kind of training we're having, and tip off the Krauts or the Japs.

Anyway, I hope you and mother and the sisters are well. I seem to forget about their husbands. I know there's Tom, and Paul, but I don't remember the name of Nicole's husband. I must be getting old. Ha ha. Have any of our sisters had babies yet? Do you ever run across Mr. and Mrs. Montlero? You know I used to work for them off and on, fixing things in their house. Mr. Montlero was all thumbs. I don't think he could screw in a light bulb if he had to. Anyway, just curious. They used to pay me pretty well. To fix things, that is.

You won't believe this, but I jumped out of an airplane for the first time yesterday. And you're darn right I was scared. I've been here about three months, I guess, and most of the time we still run everywhere we go. But now we are learning things that will help us fight better. I've shot the M-1 rifle. Boy, is that a good gun. It has a clip of bullets so you don't have to reload all the time. On the target range I scored high even at 250 yards. I also shot a .45 caliber pistol. That thing will jerk your arm off if you don't hold it right. They say most guys will carry one in a holster on their belts when in combat, kind of like the Old West. I'm better with the rifle than the pistol, but most guys are. Speaking of weapons, after thinking about the ones I want to carry, I almost forgot that I also shot a bazooka. Darn near made me deaf, but I only missed the wooden target of a Kraut tank by a few feet.

Anyway, after thinking about it, I'm going to ask to train with a machine gun. A big one, ground-mounted on a tripod. They are .30 calibers, and when you fire them you can rip a two-foot tree trunk in half in about 20 seconds. Amazing. They also taught us how to shoot off mortars. I don't like them much because you kind of have to shoot blind. You're not sure where your target is so you shoot this round in the air and hope it lands beside the enemy. It's like artillery, which I also don't like. It takes too much time to move it around. I know it is important, but paratroopers won't be using much artillery if we get into the fight.

Oops, I hope if they open this letter to read it they don't throw it away because I'm telling you about some of *the stuff we're training with. But talking about the weapons we have doesn't sound too bad to me. I thought you might be interested since we used to shoot at them rabbits together. If you see either Mr. or Mrs. Montlero tell them I am fine.*

Your brother,
The Paratrooper

December 23, 1942

Dear Little Brother,

Your letter got through, but the envelope was open and taped back shut. And I guess it took a month to get here. You are an uncle, actually twice over. Katrina has a son and Sophia has a daughter. Both are about a year old. And soon, you will be an uncle a third time. Julia Gail should have the baby long about January. Mother is fine. All the rest are fine, too. I'm glad you'll be shooting a machine gun because you will need one by the time you get home to kill just one rabbit. You never were a very good shot. The boys miss you at Joe's. Nobody can beat that old bastard Raymond so they want you back in one piece to finish him off. Me, too. I saw Mrs. Montlero in her yard the other day and I told her that you said hello. When I said that, she just turned her back on me and ran into the house. She's a strange old bag.

Take care of yourself. By the way, Merry Christmas. Don't forget to go to Mass. Mother wanted me to say that. Write when you can.

Your brother,
The Messenger

Chapter 27
A Red Scarf for Christmas

I celebrated Christmas in 1942 along with my buddies huddled in our barracks playing craps and poker around a two-foot Christmas tree. A bad, freak winter snowstorm had struck to blanket the area with eight inches of snow drifted by a howling wind.

We paratroopers were happy, nonetheless. Our platoon sergeant had given us the day off and let us sleep in until 0700 the next morning. Plus he let us skip a planned, forced ten-mile hike with fifty-pound backpacks, a hundred rounds of ammunition and the M-1 strapped on. I missed Mass on Sunday, but won forty-five dollars in a poker game and took the money to buy my mother a present at the PX – a red wool scarf. They had a black one there, but I didn't want that one. The bright red one was better because it would make her not look as sad as she does in her old black winter coat, over her old black dresses. I hoped my mother would wear it since it came from me. Yeah, she might look happy wearing the red scarf, and it only cost three dollars. I didn't buy anything for anyone else that year, and felt kind of bad. Instead, I took the forty-two dollars left from my craps winnings, played poker the next night, and lost all but seven.

3 February, 1943

Dear Carlo,

I'm sorry I haven't written to you sooner. We are very busy here. I hope everyone had a Merry Christmas and Happy New Year. Did mother get the scarf? The training never stops, and right now it seems like we are just doing the same thing over and over. I think the word is monotonous. I looked it up in the dictionary and it seemed right for what's going on here. They keep telling us we will be in the fight soon, but nobody knows when. I can't believe how cold it's been. I thought Colorado was cold in the winter, but here they say when it gets cold it seems colder because of the humidity. All I know is when the wind blows it's like being on top of Monarch Pass.

We heard the other day that a Kraut submarine had hit one of our ships off the East Coast and sunk it. They tell us when we go to the fight we will cross the ocean on a big troop transport ship. I hope they get those Kraut subs before we have to go.

We still run, crawl on our bellies, jump over creeks, swing over rivers on a rope and all that stuff. They shoot live machine gun rounds over the tops of our heads when we're crawling through the mud. One guy raised his head a little too far the other day and took one right between the eyes. Died on the spot. They hauled his body away and ten minutes later we were back on our bellies in the mud. That was a good warning for everyone. The only good part is sitting in the classroom where it's warm and learning about tactics, maneuvers, flanking and outflanking. Still, that stuff is sometimes hard to understand because you have to think about a whole bunch of guys doing the same thing at the same time, kind of like a bunch of ants building an ant hill, and the enemy being in one spot and letting all these guys outflank them, or surround them and shoot them down.

Seems kind of stupid to me that they think those Krauts or Japs are going to just sit there and let us do that. Anyway, that's what we talk about in class. I hope nobody busts me for saying our classes are stupid if they open this letter, but sometimes, that's the way I feel.

I really have fun taking apart my M-1 and putting it back together again. I can do it now in 45 seconds. I want to get it down to 30 seconds. Next I will be taught how to dismantle and reassemble (they taught us to use those words) my machine gun, but right now I'm learning how they make them and how it works by reading the manual. Boy, what a gun! It's a .30 caliber and air-cooled. Bigger machine guns are water-cooled, but they are too heavy to carry around, and they jam too often. These are fully automatic, recoil operated. We wear a 250-round belt and carry several cases of belts while out on maneuvers. It weighs only 41 pounds and can fire 400 to 550 rounds per minute with a range of 1,100 yards. Wow. The barrel stays cool, they say, because of a metal jacket with holes in it, but the other day I burned my hand real bad grabbing the barrel instead of the handle. Won't do that again.

Okay. Enough about me. Wow, a nephew and a niece, and I guess another one if Julia Gail has your baby. Tell the guys at Joe's not to worry, I'll take on old Raymond when I get back, but I will need a couple of days' practice. Mrs. Montlero is a little weird, but she's nice and treated me real good.

Your PFC Paratrooper,
Johnny

April 17, 1943

Dear Brother,

> *Your latest letter arrived today. Glad you are well. Interesting thing — I could tell the envelope had been opened, and the second, third and fourth lines of the third paragraph were blacked out. Also it looks like someone started to black out the part you wrote about the Kraut submarine in the second paragraph but then didn't. Someday you will have to tell me what you wrote about that they didn't want me to read.*

> *Maybe a better word for you is just bored. Julia Gail had a girl. We named her Julie. She is healthy, but her mother had a real tough time, and the doctor doesn't know if she will be able to have anymore. That's all right with me. I will be fine with that, but it would be nice to have a boy too. We'll just have to wait and see. Mother is fine. She did wear the scarf you sent her, just once around Christmastime that I know of. But I don't see her that much anymore. We moved out of the house and into our own, about four blocks away on East 7th Street. It's almost the same house as ours but the kitchen is a little bigger.*

> *Every day we read about the war. I wonder if they let you have the newspapers and the radio, because some of the news is not so good. When you read about how many islands Tojo has captured, and how Hitler is beating the crap out of the Russians and bombing the hell out of London, sometimes you wonder if they won't be marching down 4th Street soon. Before that would happen though, I bet they would have to kill every one of us at the mill. Sometimes I wish I had gone with you, and sometimes I talk about it at work. When I do that the union guys get real pissed off because they say we are doing our part to*

help fight the war, but I just don't know. I stopped talking about it at home because Julia Gail gets afraid that someday I might run off and join up. You don't sound like you have any regrets about joining. You might be happier than me.

I saw Mr. Montlero the other day and boy, he's as strange as his wife. For no reason he told me never to talk to his wife again. I couldn't believe it. I never did anything to those people. Did you? Keep your head down, brother.

You are my best friend ad your brother,
Carlo

I kept as many of Carlo's letters as I could for as long as I could, but lost most of them, along with some of my gear, when my stuff got mixed up in a storage compartment on the transport ship across the Atlantic.

2 August, 1943

Dear Carlo,

They keep telling us to be ready to go any day now so I hope you don't mind if I write more often because it seems to help me pass the down time and say things I wouldn't say to the guys in the barracks. I'm glad to hear about your daughter. I just hope she looks like Julia Gail and not you. I'm glad mother wore the scarf and I'd like to think she wore it more than one time. We do get some newspapers and magazines sometimes, and once in a while we get to listen to the radio, but mostly it's the comedy shows or the westerns. Not much war news. I guess they don't want us thinking about all the stuff going on, rather have us only think about the training. And that's pretty much all we do.

I'll bet I've shot 10,000 rounds of ammunition through the machine gun and I've walked and ran 1,000 miles and crawled 100 miles on my belly, but they still want us doing more of it. And still lots of classroom training. What did you say? Boring? Yeah, I think all of us are going to die here of boredom. There are so many fights in the barracks that the sergeants got together and decided we should build a boxing ring beside the parade grounds. Now when we go at it, they break it up and put us in the ring with gloves and everything. That way you can't bite or kick the guy, but you can beat on him until he goes down. Besides teaching me to shoot (and I will kill a herd of rabbits with one shot for each of them when I get home), thanks for teaching me to box.

I got into it with a guy about 6 feet tall and bigger than me by 30 pounds at least, and like all the rest, they broke it up and put us in the ring. I looked at the guy when the sergeant made us shake hands, and I kind of got scared for a minute. He tried real hard to look mean but I had already hit him real good with a right cross before they broke us up, so I think he might've been a little worried like me. It all started when he called me a guinea bastard and knocked my dinner tray out of my hand. Somebody said he was from Buffalo, New York. Why would they name a town in New York Buffalo? I don't think they have any buffalo there; they're all in Wyoming and Colorado, aren't they? Anyway, they break us after the hand shaking and he swings at my head, but I duck and give him one in the ribs and I think it knocks the wind out of him, but then he gets in a lucky punch and knocks me down. Damn, that made me mad. I get up, he swings again, I duck and hit him three times, with a short jab to the nose, a left and right cross, and I think I break his nose, because he's bleeding pretty bad by then.

Then I get another one to his ribs and he's had enough, I think, so I let down my guard, and, wham, he gets me right in the jaw and it feels like he hit me with a hammer. I see stars for a second and then he comes at me with wild punches, but I'm able to block most of them. Before they ring the bell, I catch him in the nose again with a left jab, and boy, the blood shoots out all over the place. So, the sergeant sits us down in each corner and goes back to the center of the ring to wave us out after a minute rest. I'm so happy when the guy from Buffalo puts up his hands to quit first. Then I do the same thing, real fast after that. The fight's over, and they say I won but I don't know.

It's funny, but they gave us a pass to town last Saturday night. It was the first time they let us off the post. So I see the guy from Buffalo and he's still got tape on his nose, but he comes up to me and sticks out his hand to shake mine. Yeah, I shake his hand quick, and you won't believe it, but we go into this bar together, like brothers, and he buys me some real good whiskey. I drank three of them and I bought one for him before curfew. I see the guy from Buffalo all the time now, but I don't call him my brother. You're my only brother. His name is Mike.

I didn't do anything to Mr. or Mrs. Montlero other than fix their lamp and sink and a few other things. They are kind of strange.

Your half-assed boxer brother,
Johnny, PFC

245

Chapter 28
Joe Louis Punches Pretty Hard

There were many important things about the war that I told my brother in my letters and later when I got home, and some important things that I didn't bother to tell him. At the time, some of my experiences didn't seem important enough for me to write about. One of those things was the work my superiors, all the way up to my commanding officers, did on our heads, I mean the training we got for our brains. I didn't see it or truly understand then how some of the mental parts of our training were just as important as the physical parts. My buddies and I didn't realize it at the time, but the military brass were constantly driving home the point that we, their men, were the best at everything, and one way of doing that was to set out to set military records. Striving to set records was a good way to hone skills, create comradeship and forge a keen sense of belonging. No, we didn't have to love each other, in fact, I despised a few of the guys around me, but I did learn to belong and I did become convinced that the brass was right about a lot of things, including this old idea of competition.

When the officers think their men are the best, and the men think they are the best, I suppose it just has to sink in to the point where we would try to act that way on the battlefield. One thing we did know is that America and the world desperately needed that attitude to dig deeply into the souls of its fighting men being readied for what one snot-nosed lieutenant said at the time was a "monumental crusade." We all thought this guy was a jerk, especially talking to us like he was some Bible preacher, but one time, on the radio one night, I heard Winston Churchill say just about the same thing, so I guess this guy wasn't too far out in left field.

Like I said before, I became a member of the 506th Regiment of the 101st Airborne Division. It was formed under the command of Colonel Robert Sink, a pretty good guy and all-around square shooter, at Camp Toombs in Georgia. That was my first stop after leaving Louisiana and before moving on to Fort Bragg. Back then, in the minds of the soldiers in training, whether you were in Georgia, Alabama, North Carolina or anywhere, it really didn't matter. Before I left for boot camp, I hadn't been outside of Colorado my whole life, so you'd think it might be exciting or interesting to visit Georgia or Alabama, North Carolina or Louisiana. Well, it was exciting all right, and interesting, but we never saw the sights, as they say. All we saw were the swamps and the fields that were made to look like the fields of France or Germany. Visiting New Orleans or Atlanta or someplace like that was out of the question.

In Georgia, my regiment trained, and trained some more, in preparation for jump school. Jump school took place at Fort Benning, about one hundred and forty miles away from Camp Toombs. But before the 101st went there, our commanders told us there was this little business of running to the top of a mountain. That gets back to the goals they set for us as a group, and the mental stuff that was to make us stronger in the head. The mountain was called Currahee, named after some Indian chief, I guess. They told us it would be a leisurely trek up that mountain, and that everyone had done it time and again. Sure, maybe a Colorado mountain goat could do it all the time but a dumbass GI carrying a hundred pounds on his back; different story, let me tell you. Mount Currahee became one of the most grueling training courses ever. Yet the way our commanders gave it to us, it became our mission to get up that damn mountain in faster and faster times. See, that was the competition among ourselves, in our own heads, which one of us could do it faster each time? So, as we climbed and climbed up that slope day after day, its steepness and treachery got less and less until it almost seemed flat to us. Currahee became a symbol of my regiment, a symbol of challenge, courage, and conquer. So important and symbolic was this mountain to us we adopted its image on our shoulder patches before we later traded that image in for the patch of our beloved eagle.

We conquered that mountain and as soon as we did, our commanders looked for another challenge. One day, Colonel Sink had us all together on the parade grounds and told us that the Japanese Imperial Army had, by either truth or legend, claimed the world's forced march distance record. Well, let me tell you, that's all it took. In telling that story Colonel Sink knew exactly what he was doing. No Jap was ever going to claim any record like that, not in our lifetimes, that is. Sink's men were dismissed from our formation hell-bent on breaking that record. The idea was to march from Camp Toombs to Fort Benning to begin jump school. The distance was about one hundred and twenty three miles, and most of us covered it in a little more than three days, breaking only for periodic one-hour rests along the way. We broke the Japanese record, legend or no legend, by far.

There was one regiment whose orders got screwed up and they didn't march, instead rode to Benning in trucks. Those poor bastards never lived it down. They had "pussy" stamped on their backs for the rest of jump school even though it wasn't their fault. Some clerk no one could identify was really to blame.

It wasn't long after the 506th Regiment began training at Fort Benning that our brother regiment, the 509th, shipped out for North Africa. Eventually the 509th, after serving in North Africa, was deployed to England and absorbed into the 506th along with other regiments for last minute reinforcements for the Normandy invasion. By the time many of the battle-hardened veterans of the 509th reached England, they had had enough war experience to fill many lifetimes. Fighting the renowned German General Rommel was no picnic. And they didn't know it at the time, but nearly two years of the fight remained in front of them. I had the pleasure of meeting t a few of these veteran soldiers and immediately became a great admirer of most of them, particularly those who didn't think their shit didn't stink and who would take the time to help the rookies through the shakes as the invasion approached.

So we trained at Fort Benning and then moved onto Fort Bragg. We were getting closer and closer to the Atlantic Ocean which meant, of course, closer and closer to heading east to Europe, at least that's what we all speculated. None of us knew for sure that somebody up the chain of command wouldn't change their mind at the last minute and send us back west to California to head out to the Pacific, so we waited and trained and waited some more. Finally we got word that the transports were at dock and we were heading east.

August 22, 1943

Dear Little Brother,

All right, what's going on? First, I'm getting letters from you left and right and then you stop writing. I hear nothing. You tell me you're shipping out soon and then I don't hear a thing. Have you left the U.S.? We're hearing news reports that seem to hint about an Allied build-up in England, but we also hear that there are some land battles beginning in the Pacific. Are you heading east or west? I hope you're not in the Pacific already. I'd rather think you are on your way to England, still in training. But you'd probably rather be in the fight, and there's nothing any of us can do about that.

Speaking of fights, who do you think you are, Joe Louis? I can't believe you couldn't knock out the guy from Buffalo. I looked it up on a map, and Buffalo is way up north in New York State, and no, they don't have no buffalo up there. You're right about that. And to boot, you make friends with the guy later. What's up with you? All is fine here. Keep writing as many letters as you want. Your mother and sisters are really happy when they come. Me, too.

Your brother,
Carlo, Your Trainer

I did head east across the Atlantic on the SS Samaria troop carrier to become a part of the ever-expanding 506th that swelled the population by the thousands around Uppottery, England, the 101st's eventual European base camp between September 1943 and June 1944.

I found out later that some of Carlo's letters never caught up with me since we departed for England on September 5. It was a real rough crossing because our ship and the two others carrying the rest of the 101st zigzagged in rolling seas most of the way to avoid the German U-Boats. Just about everyone on board, including me, were seasick a good deal of the way. When we finally got our feet on dry land and began training again, it was a big relief. And although practice jumps in the rolling-hilled countryside around Uppottery were thrilling to us at first, like all other exercises in preparation for battle, this too became mundane. We were crammed in close quarters. There were few passes, and security was so tight we were warned that if you got drunk from the clandestine scotch brought into camp and wandered toward the fence line after dark, you would likely be shot and questions answered much later. Down time was card playing, letter writing, growing anticipation, and for many, mounting fear.

It would be another nine months before the 101st got into the fight, and it was to become the biggest and most important fight in American history. Waiting for the Longest Day nearly drove me and the rest of the Screaming Eagles mad.

I wrote this letter the night before our jump into history. My fellow paratroopers and I had stood on the tarmac at the Uppottery airfield for three hours in full gear waiting for the order to board, and then we were sent back to barracks. Clouds, fog, wind, you name it, had scrubbed the mission yet another time.

5 June, 1944

Dear Carlo,

I think, by the time you read this, I should be in France or somewhere like that. Can you imagine a kid like me from Colorado going to France? I remember mother sometimes talking about Italy and Sicily when she and our father lived there.

I like the way she described the trees and the forests and the vineyards, and, I think, the peaceful lives she and our father had before they had to leave. The way she talked, it seemed like it was a beautiful place. Since I've been here and with all the spare time we've had, I've read some stuff about Italy and Sicily, and I'll bet she's right. They are beautiful places. That is if the Nazis haven't blown them up. I hope not. I want to see these places and be able to tell mother when I get back that she was right, and that if she is ever able to go back for a visit, that they will be peaceful places. England is nice. There are a lot of trees and forests, but it rains all the time. I wish the sun would come out like it does at home and dry up this place for a few days. It's June here and I don't think it ever gets warmer than about 60 degrees. Back home it's probably already 100 degrees, right?

Last night they finally gave us some details about what we are supposed to do when we jump over there. They think we will probably be in a pretty big fight, right off the bat, but maybe with enough of us on the ground we will surprise them and get in a lucky punch or two. I am pretty nervous right now. It's like in school when some kid wants to fight you after school and you have to wait through all the classes before you start. You get nervous, right? You don't know if the kid's going to be real tough, and you don't know if he's fast, or slow, or likes to dance or stand still and slug it out. So you wonder about that all day long. Me, I'd just as soon start punching right there and not wait. I don't know how you do it when you have a boxing match after work. Wouldn't you rather start swinging right then, rather than wait all day? Anyway, I doubt if I will get much sleep tonight. There are a lot of guys around me talking, some in their sleep, and some guys crying. Those guys are really nervous, but it's strange, instead of making fun of them, for crying that is, even the sergeants try to help them stop. They tell them a joke, or get them talking about their girlfriends and if they ever got a feel, or about their cars back home, or their favorite dinner that their mother fixes. I don't want a guy crying around me when we drop, but right now, I think it's alright to help these guys who are crying, because we need all the men we can get.

I don't think I will cry, at least I hope not.

I think I will be carrying my machine gun strapped to my back. I will break it down but it will still weigh about 40 pounds. When I jump I will probably get to the ground first with all the extra weight bringing me down quicker than the other guys. If that happens I will just have to make sure there aren't any Krauts around to hurt the other guys still up in the air. On the ground, I'll need to mount my machine gun and put it on the tripod, so I will have to remember how to assemble it in the dark, because I think they are going to have us jump at night. Darn, how stupid is that? But I guess they want us jumping at night so the Krauts can't see us.

I hope everyone at home is fine. I think about home a lot these days, but I still know this is the best thing for me to do. You know there are guys who have brothers working at home like you and all of us say the same thing. We need

253

you guys there, doing what you do, to help us do what we have to do. Making steel is important, and you know how to do that better than anybody. And I tell these guys that. Most of them agree, but there was a fight the other night when this guy said his brother was home on their farm, and decided not to join, and another guy called him a pussy. They went at it pretty good, but later, they agreed that the good farmers even making those darn C-Rations are helping us out. We need them too.

Wow, the sergeant, his name is Tim Kelly, he's an Irishman from New Jersey, just yelled out that we have 15 minutes to pack up. This letter has taken me all night to write. I didn't sleep at all but I'm not really tired either.

Tell everyone that I am fine and that I will be home soon. It won't take us more than a couple of months to get the job done here. I hope I get to see Hitler when they arrest him, or maybe his body after they kill him. That would make me happy. Anyway, I love everyone very much. I hope that doesn't sound girly, but I do.

Your brother, just a Little Scared,
Johnny

Carlo told me later my letter didn't arrive in Colorado until August, and by then, so much history had been written. I had a buddy in the postal unit tell me that the night before the invasion the Army post at Uppottery processed more than one hundred and fifty thousand letters for shipment back across the Atlantic, so it took a little time for each to find its intended destination.

Chapter 29
This Time, for Real, Solider

I found out my next series of letters to Carlo weren't received until nearly five months after D-Day. Like always, I would tell him about things I wanted to remember and leave out things I wanted to forget. There are many stories, hundreds, if not thousands in fact, about those first few hours after the beginning of Operation Overlord. Some of my stories could neatly fit in the well-known chronicles of the exploits of the elite America's troops of which I was privileged to be part. Others weren't so common.

One thing I couldn't manage to put into words at the time were descriptions of events surrounding two men who helped me more than any in those early hours of the war. One man was famous to the world; the other would become famous only to me. It's weird how sometimes in life, the littlest things become the biggest, and no matter how big the person is, it's the message you get that has the biggest impact.

It was a cloudy, cool, afternoon, typical of that time of year along the southern coast of England; our base camp was located within spitting distance of the English Channel and a thirty-minute aerial hop into hell. It was June 6, 1944, and as always, Sergeant Kelly was yelling at us. But this time, there was a certain edge to his voice when he brought us to attention. And suddenly his shrill turned mellow, almost hard to hear for those like me standing erect at the other end of the barracks from where he stood. It was easy to tell that he was out of breath, but he calmed himself before he said, almost in a whisper, "We got the order to go."

"For real this time, Sergeant?" someone in our ranks asked just as quietly.

"For real soldier," Sergeant replied.

I think it was about four or five o'clock in the afternoon and since we knew we would have to wait until nightfall to fly, some of us couldn't figure out why he was there to tell us so early. We had the packing and deployment drill down pat. It would take us only twenty minutes to hit the airstrip tarmac from our barracks with full gear. One GI groaned, "Now we're gonna have to stand out there for hours. Bet they'll send us back in again. Weather's too crappy to fly in anyway."

"That's enough, Sergeant Kelly barked, "No bullshit out of you. Fifteen minutes to our assigned spot on the airfield." There was no doubt he was as nervous as we were.

So, in orderly chaos we moved quickly to gather our gear and hurried to get into formation to march to the airfield. Our barracks, which were temporary at that time, were only about two hundred yards from the tarmac of the airfield, so it didn't take us long to get there and line up. In fact we made it, this time, in thirteen minutes, flat.

I also thought to myself that this would be another dry run. By the time we were in formation it had started to rain a little bit and the wind had picked up. We were at ease, and had probably been that way for thirty or forty five minutes, just standing around, trying to act calm and cracking a few jokes, when all of a sudden, it got real quiet. Well you remember me talking about the big guy, the grand honcho of them all, General Eisenhower, well I was looking down to make sure I still had my canteen hooked to my belt, and when I looked up, I'll be goddamn if Ike's wasn't standing right in front of me, smiling. I nearly shit my pants.

I jumped to attention, and he said, "At ease, soldier."

"Yes sir," I said, but I was so shook up just then that I didn't go at ease, so he said it again.

"At ease, soldier," and finally I did.

"What's your name soldier?" he asked. I tried to speak, but I couldn't. All I could see were those five stars on his shoulders, and that grin on his face. Finally I told him who I was.

"Where are you from soldier?" he asked. So I told him. And goddamn, then he gets this funny look on his face, and says, "Do you know that Mrs. Eisenhower is from your hometown? She lived there for a time when she was a little girl."

I didn't know that, so all I could say was, "I didn't know that," and then, "I mean, I didn't know that, sir!"

"I hear it's a nice town," he said, and I said, "Yes sir, it's a nice town."

And then he said, "How do you feel soldier?"

I looked at him, and the grin was gone from his face, and it took me a minute to think about what I should say, but finally I said, "I'm scared."

And you know what he said? Goddamn if he didn't say, "I'm scared too, soldier, but we'll be alright."

Then he said, "God bless you son."

And I said "God bless you, sir."

And he said, "Thanks."

Can you imagine him saying thanks to me? Well he did, and then he walked down the line, but turned his head around and looked back at me and kind of winked and got that grin back on his face. Swear to God.

257

All the guys around me were looking at me like I was some kind of a freak, but then some guy patted me on the back and the others started pushing me around and laughing and joking so for a minute or two there, we were all kind of relaxed.

There are many famous photographs of Ike talking with his soldiers, standing at ease on that tarmac at Uppottery in the late afternoon and early evening of June 6, 1944. Several are in museums, including the D-Day museum in New Orleans. The most famous, the ones most recognized in the museums, capture exchanges like the one Ike had that day with me. They will forever be a part of the fabric of America, and speak directly to the reasons why Ike and his soldiers did what they did, and the fact that Ike became beloved to them, and them to him.

The other story that hit me hard involved the pilot of the C-47 Skytrain twin-engine troop transport plane which fourteen other paratroopers and me boarded about two hours after my encounter with Ike. Operation Overlord, as it was codenamed, was then the largest seaborne assault in history. It involved seven thousand ships, and landed one hundred and fifty thousand troops on the beaches of Normandy. The airborne assault delivered fifteen thousand paratroopers in one thousand planes and gliders. I never got the name of that pilot, but I remember him vividly, and liked to talk about him just about as much as I liked to talk about Ike.

You had to enter the transports through a small door in the side of the plane because they kept the jump doors sealed so the rip lines wouldn't get tangled. A tangled rip line meant you either fell two thousand feet and became a puddle on the ground or you looked like the best Italian sausage ever, coming out the other end of the plane's propeller. Take your pick. So you didn't get your lines crossed. No matter what.

Anyway, I was carrying so much crap on my back that I got stuck in the door, and two guys had to push me through. We finally got settled on the benches along each side of the fuselage. It took another two hours or so after I boarded the Skytrain before it was positioned in line for takeoff, so there was plenty of time for strained conversation to take place on board. It wasn't long before this guy, the pilot, came back from the cockpit, and damn if he wasn't so tall he almost had to stoop in half to get back where we were.

He might have been better off crawling on his knees. Anyway, it was pretty quiet after we got settled, and I began to wonder if he wasn't a chaplain or a priest, because he was coming up to each of us and asking us if we wanted to pray with him. Plus he was a Limey. You never expected that from a pilot, much less a Limey. That is, him acting like a priest. On all of our training missions, the pilots usually were the biggest assholes going. Most of them acted like it was their job to take over from the drill sergeants and treat us like cattle being herded in and out of a pen. The crew chiefs were usually a little better. It was the pilots who thought they were kings or something. But this guy, even though he was a Limey, was with each guy going down the line, talking real low but directly at each one, really sincere. There were a few guys who didn't want him to do that, but most did.

When he got to me, he said how proud he was to be on this mission with us, and how grateful he was that we had come over here to save his country. Before he said that, I never thought of us coming to England and saving them. But it's true, because Hitler had just about bombed every standing building and was set to invade when we got there.

259

I did say a prayer with him, but not the one this guy sitting next to me said. That one, you know, "The Lord is my Shepherd, I shall not want, in the hour of my death," and so forth. No sir, I wasn't saying that one. No way.

Anyway, the pilot helped me say mine and it went something like this: "Lord God, two good soldiers come before you tonight. Each of us has a job to do tonight, and we ask you to help us do our jobs well. We ask you to bless our mission, and help us find success. We really believe that we are doing the right thing, and our enemy needs to be defeated. There will be some soldiers on the other side who believe in you, like we do, and believe that they are doing the right thing too. Their leaders are the bad ones, though, and our hope is for the soldiers who believe in you, that you will accept them in heaven, after we put all of them up there for you to welcome. Lord, with your help, our job won't take too long, and we'll be home soon."

The Limey pilot thought that was a pretty good prayer. He especially liked the part about putting as many Krauts in heaven as we could. He really helped most of the guys on the plane that night. He calmed us down. After he talked to each of us by ourselves he said he promised he would get us over there safely, and to a good drop zone. Just then his co-pilot hit the switch and the engines started up. He saluted, and climbed back in his seat in the cockpit, almost crawling on his knees to get there.

I never saw him again. I know he didn't make it back. The German flak was so heavy near the drop zone of St. Mere Eglise he had to veer us off course. I think our drop zone was about ten miles away from where it should have been. But it wasn't his fault. He did the best he could. Anyway, since I carried the machine gun, I was one of the first out the door that night. Maybe the third or fourth. My line didn't get tangled and I was floating down without a problem when our plane took a direct hit. There had to be some guys still in the plane when it was hit. The concussion collapsed my chute for a second and threw me into a nosedive. I came back out of it about tree-height so I was okay. The plane banked right, real hard, then banked left, and then blew to pieces.

Sometimes, I wish I had found out his name, and sometimes I just think about him and how good he made most of us feel. You didn't expect that of a pilot. The movies never talked about those guys, and how they flew those planes and gliders, unarmed, right into all that flak. They were sitting ducks. They flew so slow, they were very easy targets. More of them, the pilots and the crew chiefs, should be recognized for what they did. They were heroes. They were a big part of the mission, and many of them died that night getting us to a safe drop. Our Limey pilot was one of them heroes, for sure.

Photos

Sicilian Immigrants at Ellis Island

Catoctin Furnace

Sir Henry Bessemer

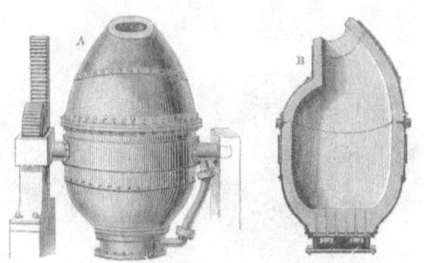

Bessemer Converter

Ludlow Monument

Ludlow Death Car

Rockefeller is seated in the middle

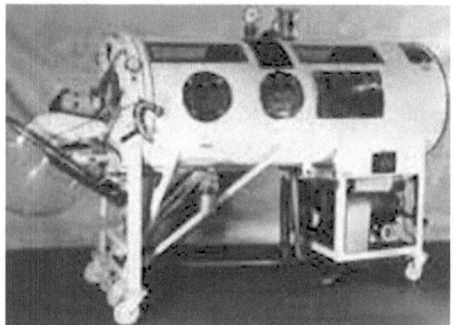

Before the vaccine

Not giving up

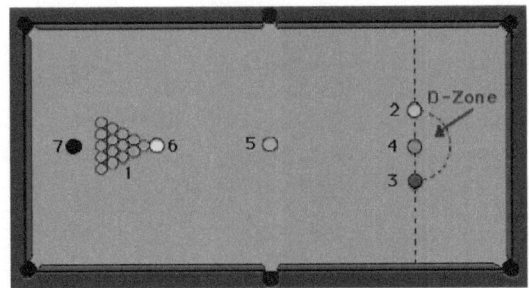

Snooker

Major General William Lee

Eisenhower on the Tarmac

America's finest

Machine Gun Nest

Appalachin Meeting House

Battle of the Bulge

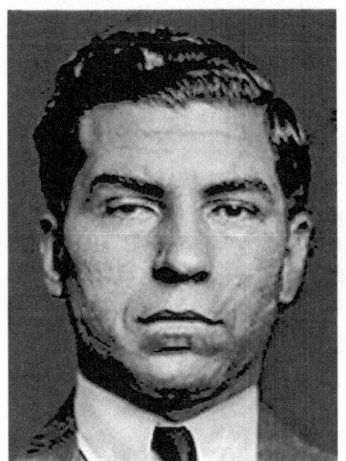

Charles "Lucky" Luciano

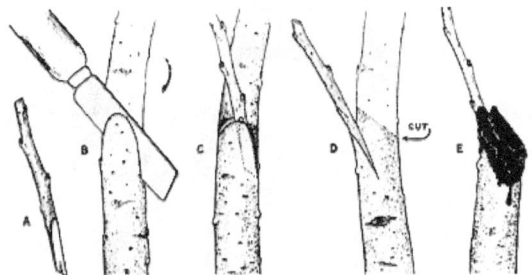

Expert Grafting

Vito Genovese

Peter Lawford

Dan Rowan at his Prime

Chapter 30
Longing for Mama's Cooking

Some people say I'm a pretty good storyteller when I'm in the mood, but with the exception of the story about my conversation with Ike and the prayer with the British pilot on D-Day, I always prefer to tell stories about what is happening in my life in the present instead of what happened to me during the war. The war was yesterday. Today is today. I want live here, not dwell on the past. So seldom does a day go by that I don't talk freely about the strange customers who frequent our restaurant, or about an obnoxious county health inspector who harasses us about a speck of dirt on the floor of Angelina's kitchen, or about some cowboy who yours truly has to throw out of the joint after he picks a fight with a GI who's out on his last date with his girlfriend before leaving for Vietnam.

The fights would occur after Carlo and I built the ritzy nightclub on the back of the restaurant that featured live music on Friday and Saturday nights along with delicious meals, plenty of pistachios and women who didn't pay the cover charge. I like to describe how the GI would gladly place the heel of his combat boot down the cowboy's throat if I didn't intervene to break it up. And then, after the cowboy leaves against his will, but still with his teeth in his mouth, I buy the GI and his girlfriend a drink and pat him on the back, unless he is too drunk, and then I make sure his buddies get him back to base on time.

Or, better than anything, you will hear me brag about my kids, or my wife, or gripe about my wife's dozens of sisters, brothers, aunts, uncles and cousins, many of whom think our restaurant is an easy mark for a free plate of spaghetti, or at least one at a reduced price. No one disputes that our Italian food is the best in town, perhaps the best in the state. Neither Carlo nor I ever refuse a free plate for any of our next of kin, by blood or marriage, ever, even though we constantly bitch about doing so. Actually, truth be told, we are somewhat proud that our extended families will drive across town for our food.

Yes, I live in the present, not the past, and it may take hours of prodding to get me to even think past two weeks ago, let alone thirty years back, to that incredible day. But occasionally I will loosen up. I know this story pretty well.

D-Day, the Longest Day, is a day in American history told in countless articles, books, documentaries and feature films. As for my involvement, the mission of the 101st on D-Day was daring, even reckless, in the minds of many war historians, but no one ever disagreed that if the paratroopers hadn't succeeded, the one hundred and fifty thousand troops storming ashore at Normandy and Utah Beaches likely would have been beaten back.

General Taylor's sky fighters had been assigned three missions. But first, after hitting the ground, we had to find each other in the pitch black of night while engaging in firefights with hundreds of scurrying German panzers trying to regroup from the surprise behind-the-lines assault. With literally moments to spare, we were able to secure causeways leading from Utah Beach for the troops charging ashore from the barges that would be landing at dawn.

Our forces also destroyed a number of bridges leading into the key road and rail communication center in the town of Carentan and, patched together as the first Allied fighting force in Europe, we encircled and captured the town of Pouppeville, a key point blocking the causeway leading from Utah Beach. Rather easily, with little resistance, the cobbled-together group of high-ranking officers, MPs, artillerymen, clerks, signalmen, even cooks, took the town and secured the route inland. The paratroopers, although few in number, led the charge to overtake the tiny French hamlet. The local citizens cheered when we arrived.

Frankly, I don't remember much about Pouppeville; it was a blur since my squad charged through while it was still pitch black outside, but I certainly remember getting to Carentan. And it wasn't easy. That I know for sure. I described the events of that night in a letter to Carlo.

20 June, 1944

Dear Carlo,

I'm back in England now. We've been given a short leave, and we really needed it. When we finally got here, I slept for almost two days. So did most of the guys. They left us alone so we could sleep. And since we've been here we've had the best food since being in the Army.

They tell us that folks back home are reading and hearing a lot about the invasion, and our fighting in France. Brother, let me tell you it was a fight, the biggest fight ever. Now that that part is over, I guess they won't mind me telling you a little about it, since every German in the world, including the spies, must know we're here, and we are kicking their butts. But it hasn't been easy, let me tell you.

271

Before I tell you some of what happened, do me a favor and don't show this letter to mother or our sisters. They might get upset and that wouldn't be right. I want them to think that I'm okay, and that I always will be okay, but you know and I know that that might not always be the case. I'm darn lucky I made it through the last two weeks while we were on the ground in France. Of the 40 guys in my platoon, 18 of them made it back to England with me. It's best our mother and sisters just keep thinking that I will be home soon and not worry.

I think what I'm doing in telling you these things is maybe by putting them in a letter, I can forget about them. Maybe I won't forget, but if I write it down, it might help. I did have a few nightmares sleeping those two days, and I hope after I write it all down it will get better.

Okay, here goes. Even though it was night when we landed, there were flares all around, so for quick flashes we could see other guys land and go over to them and join up. Also sometimes you could see for more than a quick time from the fires burning from the transport planes and gliders that had hit the ground from the flak. Anyway, it was all pretty confusing. There were no officers, at least commanding officers, so for the first few hours on the ground all of us kind of took command of ourselves. As best we could figure we were a few miles from our assigned drop point of this little town called St. Mere Eglise, so we needed to hurry back there as quick as we could.

We were pretty good at getting organized in the dark and moving in the right direction from the training we'd had, so that part was easy. About 50 of us got together and started back east toward the town, which is about the size of Fountain. Anyway it was easygoing for a time, until we ran onto a German patrol. No telling how many there were, but they had probably spotted us first, so they hit us first with rifle and machine gun fire and mortars. I had been carrying my machine gun for about five miles, so the funny thing about it was, when they hit us; I was almost relieved to get the darn thing off my back and onto the tripod. You know, I think I told you that I had probably shot 10,000 rounds through that type of gun, but that first time, firing away at those Krauts, was real different.

Before, no one was firing back and I wasn't really trying to kill anybody. It was so loud you couldn't hear a thing, but soon some of our guys fanned out in two directions and we were able to outflank them. Now I know why they trained us so hard about flanking and outflanking the enemy. Our guys flushed them out of their position behind one of them hedgerows about 50 yards away.

I remember Mr. and Mrs. Montlero had hedges in their front yard. They were always trimmed real nice, the same height, all green, even in the wintertime. I think Mrs. Montlero did the trimming. If she let her husband do it, he would have probably cut off his hand, he was so clumsy. But theirs were about three feet tall. These over here are 10, 15, 20 feet tall, so it's real easy to hide behind them but real hard to shoot through them because they're so thick.

So, our guys flush out the Krauts, and guess what? They run directly toward me. I had stopped firing and was loading up another belt when somebody yelled at me to open up. I didn't have time to think, just snapped the cover and opened up. They went down, three or four at a time. I could see because of the flares. It was easier than shooting them rabbits, by far. I just kept firing and they just kept falling. Then it was over. I stopped. They stopped coming. A couple of guys around me got up and walked into the clearing. You could hear the Germans moaning and crying, one or two for their mothers. Nobody laughed though. I just laid there on my belly with my finger still on the trigger. I watched our guys walk up to those still moving or moaning or crying. They kind of looked around, talked to each other for a minute, and then, one by one, with their .45s, shot them. Soon there was no noise, just a couple of our guys moaning and crying as they were being treated by the medics. I threw up. But nobody laughed at me, either.

One of the nightmares I had was about rabbits running away from me and then turning back all of a sudden and running towards me, hundreds of them, jumping and flying at me, and I had run out of bullets. Then I woke up.

Maybe by writing this down, the rabbits will go away.

I am taking care of myself as best I can. Sometimes, I feel happy, other times I feel sad. I think most of the guys are trying not to make too many friends, at least good friends. My two friends, and I wouldn't even call them best friends, just friends, didn't come back to England with me.

We might get a short leave off base, and the rumor is we might even get to go into London. We'll see. You know, I already feel better. Please send my love to everyone at home, including yourself.

Your brother, Still Damn Tired
Johnny

PS. I might start writing more cuss words in my letters since I hear so many all the time, and cuss more myself. That might make me feel even better too, especially when I cuss the enemy. All the more reason not to show these letters to mother.

Chapter 31
A Shiny New Machete

When I finally got stateside in 1945, I found that the military censors during the early days after D-Day had lifted some restrictions on the press when it came to reporting on the details about Normandy and the overall success of the Allied invasion.

Every time I wrote Carlo, I always wondered what the censors would do with my letters, but honestly I really didn't care. Like I said before, all I wanted to do in writing to Carlo was get stuff off my chest. I couldn't stand to have it bottled up inside me so I let loose with my pencil. One thing I know the censors didn't allow was accurate body counts to be reported. That was real clear in the newspapers we read while on leave from the battlefront. But we always had a pretty good idea of how many we'd lost. Word on the numbers of GIs killed always filtered down to us survivors even though the brass tried their best to keep that information secret. They were quick to count the Kraut corpses for us but the true casualty numbers of the Allies never made it into the official reports posted around our barracks the newspapers.

The reports always did stress our achievements over our setbacks, to rally support and boost morale at home and on the frontlines. So years later when I read the letters I'd written about many of the events making headlines in those days, I discovered most made it through screening without so much as a smudge on the contents.

The morning after the slaughter of the German patrol, my contingent joined the disjointed forces of the 506th Regiment under Colonel Robert Sink's command. We moved southward, in force and with precision. We took the town of Vierville after crushing German resistance, but not without fierce fighting. The air-cooled barrel of my machine gun got so hot during one point in the battle that it glowed red. We pushed the enemy back to St.-Come-du-Mont, another small town, strategic to the vital need of keeping the causeways open from Utah Beach for the thousands of foot soldiers coming ashore by landing craft.

By noon the next day our ramshackle regiment had overtaken Angoville-au-Plain and swept quickly to the outskirts of St.-Come-du-Mont. There, the Germans were dug in and well fortified. Another intense, prolonged firefight ensued. The 506th, largely intact and supported by reinforcements of the 501st Regiment and the 81st Airborne, laid siege. Close combat followed, hedgerow to hedgerow, through field after field until the streets of St.-Come-du-Mont were occupied with soldiers in hand-to-hand, house-to-house, street-to-street fighting. For the first time, but not the last, members of the 101st took on the German 6th Parachute Regiment, touted as the Krauts' counterpunching force to the Screaming Eagles. They were strong opponents, for sure; quick and agile like us, and equally dedicated. Every time we came up against these guys we had our work cut out for us. We had had the opportunity in France and again in Holland a few months later, and it was no picnic either time. Eventually, however, we got the best of them.

By June 7, resistance among all of the occupying Nazi forces in France diminished. The Germans fell back again, and the 101st moved on to secure Carentan, our main objective. Capturing and holding Carentan was critical to allowing the Allies to link forces landing at both Omaha and Utah beaches for their inland assault. Literally encircled by waterways, canals, swamplands and the Douve River, Carentan was a natural fortress easily guarded by well-placed German encampments.

My second letter to Carlo after D-Day was written two days after the first while my regiment was on temporary leave, stationed at our base camp in England.

22 June, 1944

Dear Carlo,

They're still giving us more time off than we usually have, but today we had to do some light work and go back to class for briefings. There were quite a few mistakes on the first landing, and the instructors are trying to teach us how to do better so our guys can land closer together and form up for assignment once we hit the ground. We don't know where our next jump will be, but we really don't care. Some of the guys say they want to get back in the fight soon, others are quiet about it. No one says they don't want to go back at all, but I'm sure if given a choice, which we won' t be, there are more than a few who would stay right here through the rest of the war. I wouldn't mind staying, but I don't mind going either.

When you're fighting you really don't have time to think about what you're doing. You just do it. If an order is given, you do it. If there is no one around to give orders, you have to try to make the right decisions on your own. You think about trying to stay out of the line of fire, stay clear of the artillery and mortar fire, and especially run like hell if a tank tries to corner you. After that first night on the ground in the dark, and until we finally captured Carentan the next day, we all saw plenty of each of those things.

When the sun finally came up on June 7, we were able to find a good number of our guys from the 506th early that next morning near St.-Come-du-Mont. And by then we had reinforcements that had either jumped or come ashore. We had walked all night and didn't scrap any more with the Krauts, but all night we heard fire all around us. I think we might have slept about an hour after we got to the town, but we were up shortly after dawn. It really surprised me how much backup we had. I mean the cooks were cooking up a storm, the latrines were there, and we were taken care of pretty well. Had a good breakfast that morning, believe it or not. But we were on our way in about 30 minutes after we woke up it seemed. A big push, let me tell you. Since I was carrying the machine gun, I didn't have point patrol and stayed mostly with the main body marching on the causeways. The first town we got to was Angoville-au-Plain. There was little resistance. I think about 30 Krauts surrendered without putting up much of a fight, probably because they saw how outnumbered they were. So our squads moved out fast after securing the town and headed toward St.-Come-du-Mont. I carry a little pencil and notepad in my pocket, and each time I see one of the signs for the towns I write it down. That's how I can remember them and spell the names right for you. Maybe this way you can see where I've been on a map, maybe at the library.

Anyway, the patrols soon came back to the main group where I was and told us we were about two miles out of town, and they think there's a pretty big force of Germans on the outskirts of town, along the canals, and guarding the main bridges across this river. I didn't ever get the name of the river, but it might have been as wide as the Arkansas in some spots.

We begin to spread out and, as the officers say, 'deploy our forces' to approach the town from different places. I'm with a group of about 30 guys led by a captain and a lieutenant. I hear them tell each other they went to West Point so they thought they were both pretty hot shit. Good officers, though, as much as I could tell. So we're moving fast at a trot along this causeway when I hear this whistle overhead. It's hard to describe what it's like, bigger and louder than a roman candle. I hear it coming, but it's too late. A round hits somewhere around me.

The next thing I know I'm sitting against the trunk of a tree, maybe 20 yards from where I was running a second before. I look down and there's the head of the lieutenant at my feet. His eyes are open and his mouth is open and it's like he's about ready to speak to me, maybe give me an order, but his head is all there is. I try to move away from him, but for a second my legs are numb and I can't move. I look at my feet again and see that the heels of both my boots are gone and one sole is gone, and my sock is ripped, but there's no blood. Damn, I'm mad. My boots are messed up real bad. For a second I don't think about the lieutenant's head, only my boots.

Finally I get to my feet and look around. There's several guys laid out on the ground, all their parts in place but you could tell they were dead. And there were severed parts of guys all around as well, some of them still jerking and twitching. Then another whistle. This time I dive behind the tree but it hits some distance away. Then I hear the captain and I see him waving at everyone to come toward him with one of his arms, but his hand is gone. Strange though, I'm again thinking about my boots. So I crawl over to a guy who is more or less in two pieces, and I take off his boots and put them on. I also took his socks since one of mine was ripped. I kept the other sock, so now I have three.

We had to leave all the dead guys, but we were able to help the wounded ones, including the captain. Someone put a tourniquet around his arm to stop the bleeding. His hand was lying on the ground but he just turned and walked away from it. Soon the medics were there and an ambulance or two. And soon after that we joined another couple of squads and started moving again toward the river. I think there were about 20 guys we left behind. I'll tell you the rest tomorrow. I'm real tired now. I think I can go to sleep.

Your brother,
Johnny, PFC

PS: I got a brand-new pair of boots when I got back to England. And some new socks.

I didn't write the next letter for a few days after that, and Carlo told me when I got home he thought I had written this one in a real hurry. And I remember it that way, too. It was like my time was short and I needed to get it all down on paper to get it out of my head.

27 June, 1944

Dear Carlo,

Before I get into this, I keep forgetting to ask about mother and our sisters, and all the stuff about you, Julia Gail, and all the babies. How is everyone doing? And since

I don't much feel like telling a priest this, I am going to make a confession to you. You better throw this letter away after you read it.

The reason I keep asking you about Mrs. Montlero is because, as the guys say around here, she was my first lay.

God, this is not easy to write, and I am not bragging or anything, it's just you're my brother, and for some reason I want you to understand that she's not crazy. In fact, she's a great lady and someone who made me very happy when I was with her. It all started one afternoon after I fixed the sink in her bathroom. I had been over to her house several times before, fixing things like her lamp in the living room and such, but from the very first time I was there, it seemed like she was lonesome, maybe afraid, and really may not have cared much for her husband.

I know this was a sin, and the next time when an artillery shell hits, I'll probably end up in two pieces myself, but I tell you it didn't feel like a sin. It wasn't dirty. She is a beautiful woman inside and out, and I miss her a lot. I know if I ever get back, I won't be able to see her again, but it was worth it while it lasted. I won't give you all the details because I'm a gentleman and she is a lady. Just try to understand that she needed me as much as I needed her, and I do think about her at times, and it helps me get through some of the bad stuff.

So there, you know the truth, so if you see her again, in her front yard, trimming her hedges, think nice thoughts about her. She was very good to your brother.

Okay, enough of that, back to today.

We formed up for the march toward the bridges again, but had to cross several canals before getting into position to make the assault. Just about the time a company strong of us were moving off the causeways into the fields, we came under fire again; this time real heavy, bullets flying everywhere. Mortar fire as well. Before long, the firestorm was too great. We were firing back and not hitting anything at all, and soon came to realize we were pinned down. But damn, we were in this swamp. There were swamps in Louisiana, but these seemed worse, maybe because you were getting shot at every time you poked up your head. So we just had to lay there, all wet and stiff, and had to hold our heads up to keep them out of the water. I swear I could have drowned, but maybe that would have been better than taking one between the eyes.

Anyway, I found out later that this colonel, Robert Cole was his name, got real pissed off at us having to just lay there and let them shoot at us, so he jumps up and yells something like, 'Bayonet attack!'

In training we would do this. They would pin us down with machine gun fire, and we would crawl around for a while, and then someone would yell at you to fix bayonets, and it meant just that. Fix them and get your ass up and charge like hell straight at the enemy.

So I look over at this guy next to me and both of us kind of shake our heads and I'm thinking, man, this is it. Well, I can't charge very well with a bayonet and a 40-pound machine gun on my back and two belts of shells, so I strip them off. I grab the bayonet off my belt and fix it to the M-1 and wait. Pretty soon, sure enough, it's charged, and up we got, running in that mud, slipping and sliding and whooping and hollering. I had to leave my .30 caliber in the mud. That made me real mad. We kept taking a lot of fire but I think us coming at them might have shocked or scared the Krauts, because some of them, particularly those around the bridge, started running in the other direction. Some didn't run though. They wanted to fight it out. And that we did. It took us forever, at least it seemed that way at the time, but maybe it was only about 30 seconds and we were on them. Guys were jumping directly into the German trenches and foxholes, and into their blinds, and some even made it to some of their tents, which were behind the lines.

I kept with a group and we went from one trench to another, but didn't get close enough to use the bayonets. We just kept shooting and reloading and shooting some more. Both sides were taking direct hits and a lot of guys were going down, but like I said before, in that situation you just keep going. They call it adrenalin that's pumping through your body. So, at some point I look around and every one of my guys is gone. I'm alone and I'm now really thinking this is it, but I keep running, I don't know where, just running until I come up to this foxhole. I think I'm just going to jump in and take a little rest, so I do and damn if I don't jump right on the back of this Kraut who's stayed behind for some reason, either scared like me or wanting to fight it out. I don't know. Man did we go at it. Slugging, biting, kicking; everything we could. He had somehow managed to knock my rifle out of my hands so I didn't have that, and I couldn't get to my pistol either. So we just wrestled and slugged it out.

Once he got his hands around my throat, he was choking me real hard but I managed to hit him beside the head in the ear, and he let loose. They taught us that in school, to hit them in the ear with your open hand. Then I was able to grab his machete (it had a pointed tip), which he had in the foxhole with him, and I got him, stuck it through his gut.

When I stuck him, he looked at me straight in the eyes and mumbled something I couldn't understand. So I leaned closer into him, knowing that he was dying, and then he said it again, and this time I heard it. He said,

283

'Good fight American.' But then he said, 'Fuck you,' in the best English you ever heard. And then he closed his eyes.

I sat there a minute, and before I knew it some of my guys were shouting down at me to get out of there. So I grabbed the M-1 and then I grabbed the machete, not that most machetes are good for anything, I think, but cutting grapefruit, but for some reason this one had a pointed tip and I wanted to keep it, so I took it. I guess when I think about machetes, at least the ones with pointed tips; they are good for killing after all.

From that point we seemed to have the Krauts on a run. I really didn't think anymore about the soldier in the foxhole, but right now, when I think about him, I respect him. It was like when you are about to start one of your boxing matches, you shake hands even though you probably hate the guy. It's out of respect, and when you beat him, you do the same thing. Shake his hand. Out of respect. Even though he said, 'Fuck you' to me, I think he respected me by what he said before. Anyway I respected him. He was probably a good soldier.

Soon, we were in the center of town at Carentan. Everybody's cheering, and there are even some French girls coming out of their houses to kiss a few guys as we went by. It seems I haven't seen a woman in months so that was real nice, and some of them were really pretty. None of them kissed me though. Then I see this guy carrying around a big German Nazi flag, so I go over to him, and there are a bunch of guys also gathered around. Then a bunch of these Army photographers come up to us, one with a big box camera and one, I think, with a movie camera, and they line us up and take our picture, this guy with the flag, and me with the machete and a whole bunch of other guys standing around. All I know is I'm happy I wiped the blood off it before they took the picture.

Otherwise, brother, I am well as can be. I think we are shipping out, or should I say, flying out, again soon. Give all my best, and be nice to Mrs. Montlero if you see her.

Your best friend,
PFC Johnny

The ironic thing about the events and images I described in that letter to Carlo is that they have been written and rewritten hundreds of times by hundreds of learned scholars, and the images capturing those events have been printed thousands of times in periodicals, history books, broadcasted on television and even filmed for the movies.

I am still amazed when I look at it. The picture, that is. Is that really me? It couldn't be. But, yeah, I was there, looking smart and cocky, having helped kicked so many German asses just then. We all look like we think we're invincible. Actually, we were scared shitless and thinking any minute we'd turn a corner in that town and come face-to-face with a seven-foot-tall Panzer with metal teeth and a .50 caliber stuck up our nose.

They say that photograph is a very special one that portrays the confidence, cockiness, even arrogance of America's fighting youth during those desperate times. As for me, I still don't know quite how I feel when I look at it. Maybe it haunts me, maybe it pleases me, maybe it saddens me. Whatever it does, I can't say for sure. Like I said, once I told Carlo about the events leading up to the photograph in my letter to him, I wanted to be finished with the whole thing. In a matter of two days, I'd seen guys blown to bits and several wounded buddies hauled off to who knows where, screaming in agony. I'd seen fiery buildings tumble down like falling Tinker Toys; bloated, dead cattle rotting in the fields; women exposing their private parts and offering sex to us, their so-called liberators, and I was just this punk nineteen-year-old kid from Colorado trying like hell to follow orders, to keep going, keep shooting and trying to survive. All I know is when the picture was being taken, that it felt good just to be alive, at that very moment, not knowing if I'd be alive the next.

Chapter 32
All Noisy on the Western Front

Carlo

Life in Pueblo during my four-and-a-half-year tour of duty was quite different than life in most other towns in America during the war. After the Japanese attack and Hitler's ongoing reign of terror, like all of the rest of America's cities and towns at the time, Pueblo had its recruiting offices, its draft boards and its tearful farewells at the train station – but its role in the war effort was unique. There were fewer men from Pueblo marching off to Europe and sailing in the South Pacific than from most other American communities.

The steel mill, as it had in every other aspect of life in town, dominated the course of local events. Carlo was one of the men who continued to march off to the front gates of the mill instead of off to the front lines. He was proud to say the steel mill had rightfully become a vital cog in America's war machinery. And the men, and a small number of women, who worked there became critical sources of skill to keep those war-making wheels turning. Carlo loved to use those sorts of words to make all of the people around him swell with pride. America needed steel and plenty of it, he would declare.

Life in Pueblo during the war years was vibrant. Work went on twenty-four hours a day, seven days a week. The steel mill ran at a torrid pace, operating around the clock with three shifts of workers at their stations. Because of his seniority, Carlo usually worked the day shift. The town's economy hummed along, actually roared ahead, making it richer by the day. Stores remained open night and day to supply the workers and their families. Merchants got rich. Bars and restaurants thrived. Everybody was making money. The Depression was definitely over.

Labor and management got along well; no strikes, no slowdowns, only a single purpose in mind – to produce as much steel for the war machine as possible, and then produce some more. Exceed all quotas. Keep going. Don't ever stop. Millions of tons of the stuff were needed for armor plating, for nuts and bolts and washers and springs, gun barrels, billions of replacement parts and, of course, barbed wire and railroad tracks. Products from the mill, as Carlo made clear to the men he supervised, had to be of the finest quality and production, the most reliable and predictable, with all the goods delivered on time. Every one of the steel products they made, he told them, was vital in crushing the Fascists, and must continue to roll out of the mill to support the all-out effort.

As a production supervisor, Carlo was legitimately declared by the local draft board to be an "essential person" – one of the hundreds whose training, experience, and tenure on the steel production crews made him irreplaceable. Carlo was one of millions of essential persons serving honorably at their posts during the war. Sure, some were working in safer places than others, and a steel mill was certainly a safer place to be than in a foxhole fighting off hordes of Nazi storm troopers, but most mill workers served honorably just the same.

Honor, that's what it was all about. Carlo knew his family's pride in him was a mountain high and a mile deep, and they believed in the honor of his work, but he just wasn't sure he believed in it. Something still gnawed at Carlo every day as he agonized over his decision to remain behind, allowing his brother, as he saw it, to be over there in his place. So Carlo worked harder than he ever had before; at least believing what he and his team were producing at the mill was helping those like me who were so far away win the war. But not everyone shared his views.

There were those who made Carlo so mad it took every ounce of his will power not to smash the faces of every one of them. They were easy to spot and to him were disgusting to think about. He refused to talk about them. Most other Bessemer neighbors refused to do so as well. It was too dangerous, but everyone knew they were mostly the younger, fresh-faced punks who, after dodging the draft, became loyal associates of Tony Spinuzzi. New bold, brash boys proud to be Tony's Cronies. They used their connections to become essential persons, but most hadn't earned it.

Altered union personnel records showing phony ages and dates of employment – that was all the proof they needed to become essential persons overnight, to serve without honor and to be shielded from flying bullets and exploding artillery. In most of these ugly cases, the local draft board accepted the doctored documents as fact, never questioning, never challenging. Special rules for special people. Carlo was sickened by the stench around him, but he kept quiet.

In contrast to the around-the-clock production schedule at the steel mill, there was one enterprise that seemed to be on hold, taking a break from the big-time action. It was Jimmy Clemente's business. Not his goat cheese business at his little stand out on Route 50 east and along the river, that business was doing fine. Jimmy had the best cheese in town and people lined up to buy it. It was Jimmy's other businesses that he had put into a temporary state of hibernation.

The town knew Jimmy was lying low. Things were too quiet in that dark corner to think otherwise. You just knew it. You could feel the calm and most people liked that feeling. But Carlo assumed that Jimmy and dozens of his gangster peers were becoming anxious and increasingly frustrated by all of this war business, because it was hurting their business. Carlo was certainly enjoying the calm that came without the criminals constantly in their midst. He kept an eye on the situation from his position on the outside, and he had a few friends, one in particular, on the inside, who kept him informed just in case anything changed.

Carlo was careful to never mention the names of those who spoke freely with him about the thugs because some were still involved, a few at their own choosing, and others who weren't given a choice. Carlo was one of the very few lucky ones who had gotten out, extracted from the Mafia mire only with the help of a trusted friend. Most of those who had once been Carlo's lowlife goomba buddies would never be so lucky.

There were probably patriotic reasons that ran parallel with practical reasons for Black Jim and the rest of La Costa Nostra to hibernate during the war years. Carlo didn't know which reason outweighed the other. But he did know that the mob's mantra for all of its members during the war was patriotism. But their definition of patriotism was not like that of the rest of America. Lucky Luciano and his counterparts, all the way down through the ranks of Black Jim's mobsters, were, for the most part, staunchly pro-war and pro-American, even though most saw fit not to enlist, a good number of them paying big sums to avoid service and even the draft, opting to buy their way into the corps of corrupt essential persons. Still, they were one hundred and ten percent behind American troops fighting on all fronts, and they prayed on bended knee before the altar of the martyred Christ for quick victories in the Pacific and in Europe.

Yes, a fast ending to the war was foremost in the minds of the Mafia. Gangsters desperately needed the four million or so in uniform to come home as soon as possible to resume their proper places as the targeted recipients of the numerous goods and services the Mafia had to offer. They were waiting for the troops with open arms. During the war, it became impossible for the mob to earn the profits it was used to with so few patrons for their hookers, their extortionists, their numbers rackets, and their hijackers, or from the emerging drug trafficking that was taking hold in most of America's major cities even before Pearl Harbor. The Mafia couldn't possibly be as profitable as it needed to be without homeward bound GIs.

Through his trusted sources, Carlo paid close attention to what was underway in the underworld. It was clear that Lucky and the boys had put the traditional criminal activities on hold and had ordered Black Jim and his counterparts to temporarily turn their attention to other endeavors, less lucrative as they may be. Julia Gail's father had given Carlo the best of the insider's view of what was going on in the underworld, even though he was technically an outsider. Thomas had earned his way out, and that was rarer than a bad piece of cheese from Jimmy's stand. He would never say how or where he got his information, but it always seemed to prove out in the long run. One of Thomas' hard and fast predictions was that the U.S. government itself was being taken to the cleaners by the Mafia as it concentrated on building a corrupt corporate infrastructure that would be the future linchpin to a greatly expanded empire when the war ended.

"And a brilliant corporate strategy it is," Thomas would say during his conversations with Carlo when they were safely tucked away in the basement of his Bessemer bungalow, with Julia Gail upstairs, wanting desperately to be included in the conversation.

"Why won't you let me hear what you're telling Carlo?" Julia Gail asked once. "It isn't right. It isn't fair. What in the hell are you two talking about?"

"Don't you use that language around me," her father had scolded upon hearing his daughter's uncharacteristic remark. "What I share with Carlo is my business. I am doing it to help him and you; to protect both of you, but you cannot, you must not know what I say."

"I don't understand father," she would plead. "Please help me understand."

But Thomas 1 would simply look down on her upturned face. "I'm sorry, my dear, you must trust my judgment and not question what I do."

When they were alone again, Carlo asked, "Taken to the cleaners, how?" Julia Gail was upstairs, still fuming but no longer questioning.

Thomas told Carlo about how the massive amount of war material being shipped to all parts of the globe was ripe for the Mafia-infested longshoremen to skim just a little here and a little there to keep the warm hearths of the bosses' Long Island palaces burning brightly. And there was little to stop them from sending a few inflated billings or phony invoices to unsuspecting and overworked government procurement and payment offices.

"Just a few hundred million here and there; that really doesn't matter when tens of billions are being spent,"

Thomas said, shaking his head. "No, they're just earning their rightful share, rebuilding their criminal network for when the war ends and they can get back to the real business at hand. It doesn't hurt anyone all that much. They deserve it," his voice dripped with sarcasm as Carlo sat and listened, fascinated by the Mafia's remarkable business tactics.

Another new and very profitable scheme, Thomas went on, was the black market in cigarettes. Billions of cigarettes were being shipped from the tobacco companies to the troops overseas. Well-placed suppliers, or "brokers," would buy the smokes direct from the companies and sell them at another price to the military, a price five times what it should be.

"Our hoods, who just yesterday were mowing each other down in the streets of Brooklyn over a block of territory for their hookers to work in, are now sophisticated middle men merchants fleecing their own government while we're at war, and turning a few Army supply sergeants near the front lines into crooks just as rotten as they are," was Thomas' way of describing it.

Carlo's sessions with Thomas would go on for hours at a time. At one point Thomas moved an old couch and chair to the basement with a coffee table, lamp and smoking stands where he and Carlo could relax, smoke, and Thomas could teach. He told Carlo that it was important that he become equipped with as many facts about the people and circumstances around him as possible. It was Thomas's way of warning him, but also, Carlo had decided, of ridding himself of some of his own guilt. If he could convince just one person, with Carlo maybe being the most important one because of his relationship with Julia Gail, that mob life was putrid to the core, evil in every respect, then perhaps he could edge toward making amends.

Was Thomas looking for redemption, or was he sharing experiences and bragging about how much he knew? Carlo chose the former. Thomas was like his brother in that respect. He needed to shed his past, an unbearable part of his life growing like an incurable disease, just like me, he needed a way to sweep away some of his experiences in the war. Were Thomas's dreams as bad as mine, the nightmares as haunting? Carlo wondered. So Thomas's lectures, although enthralling to Carlo at first, became like a painful purging of his father-in-law's soul. Carlo grew weary as Thomas began repeating himself, almost as if he needed to double-check on his cleansing.

Of course, there were new and exciting bits woven throughout Thomas' tales. One of Carlo's favorites was finding out that while the Mafia was conducting a carefully crafted scheme to fleece the government during the war effort, as only crooks like them could, there was a problem in the front office. The Boss of Bosses, Mr. Luciano was in jail. No bail. Indicted on numerous counts, and word was leaking out despite the best efforts of the Feds and the thugs alike to keep the high-profile case under wraps. It was a trumped-up charge, Lucky had alleged, but he was going nowhere fast and needed a way out. Not out of the rackets, but out of the country.

Lucky had been heading for his fall after the then Manhattan district attorney and future presidential candidate Thomas E. Dewey garnered an indictment on extortion and prostitution charges and was shooting for a conviction and sentence of thirty to fifty years. Lucky's predicament became well known across America not long after Thomas told Carlo about it. The Dewey-Luciano fight appeared in all the newspapers, capturing headlines for days. But Carlo's father-in-law knew more than any newspaper reporter, by far.

Thomas explained that La Cosa Nostra was especially anxious for the quick liberation of Italy and Sicily, and every gangster celebrated in unabashed jubilance when the Allied troop carriers lined up in the Mediterranean to deposit their rampaging soldiers along the shores of their former homelands. Lucky's clever spies had made him well-aware that their wise guy recruiting grounds had been greatly depleted, and the fear was that the crop of new Mafia recruits would take too many years to harvest if the war lasted too long and resulted in too many casualties.

"Lucky had more than his own skin to worry about at the time," Thomas explained.

History records but historians debate whether Luciano and his spies had much of an effect on the highly successful invasion of Italy and Sicily by the Allies. But Thomas gave the Boss due credit for contributing to the Allies' victory in that part of the world. Lucky, over the strong objections of Mr. Dewey but with the support of more than a few high-ranking generals in the War Department, found his ticket to freedom, and cashed it in quickly. His spies came through for him and swiftly sent their information across the Atlantic, somehow reaching inside his jail cell. It was a clandestine covert chain of intelligence, in Thomas' view, that became the envy of the American and British spooks that couldn't come close to duplicating the accuracy of what Lucky was learning and shelling out.

Lucky cut the deal of the century with the insight, debatable as it was, that he had gained. Thomas maintained in the end that Lucky and his lawyers got Dewey to drop the charges in exchange for using his Mafia connections in Italy and Sicily to perfect an incredibly sophisticated spy network that provided highly sought-after information to the invading American forces. Needless to say, Dewey was not pleased when his prize catch and his future ticket to the

Republican nomination and the White House was deported to Rome after its liberation in exchange for numerous tips on Nazi troop movements and deployments as they prepared to defend against the marauding American and British troops. To this day, few like to admit that the invading forces planned and executed counter movements from the information provided by Lucky's loyal foreign associates, Thomas said, but he was a believer. He suspected champagne corks popped particularly often and most loudly in Mafia dens on the day Mussolini and his mistress were stripped naked and hung in the Roman square for all to see and jeer.

With Thomas's help, Carlo continued to follow Lucky as best anyone could even while the Boss was in exile. Even though overt Mafia activity waned during the war years in our town as it did across the world, the bosses, lying low and lurking in the shadows, were just waiting for VE day and the defeat of the Japanese. Victory couldn't come soon enough for anyone.

So despite a steel mill churning out millions of tons of essential wartime products, Pueblo was a fairly quiet place while Carlo's brother was gone. There were a few murders, although not one, as anyone could tell, mob-related, but a few just the same – from a domestic quarrel or two old drunks in a fight. Carlo watched the people of his town go about their daily lives with their heads lifted high saluting Old Glory, their eyes focused and their hands clasped tightly on the machinery, making steel as fast as they could.

Following the example of their superiors, even Tony's crowd was docile. They left Carlo alone, for one thing. And he left them alone. He remained cautious and by design encountered no out-of-the-shadows surprise attacks. He figured, actually hoped and prayed, revenge for his "disloyalty" had already been extracted. He hoped for now his debts had been paid.

While he kept one eye out for Tony and his bunch, Carlo went about his job with a renewed sense of commitment and dedication, telling himself he had made the right decision, and his good work would lift the nagging guilt that constantly crept into his thoughts, especially after reading one of his brother's letters. He continued to rise through the union-controlled hierarchy and with overtime, he was bringing home close to one hundred and fifty dollars a month. He and Julia Gail were living well. Julie was a healthy little girl and her new baby sister, Rose, was robust, too. Julia Gail's second delivery came easier than the first, so they were planning for their third child. Life was good. Life was peaceful, at least at home. But heartache came swiftly and unexpectedly.

Julia Gail's mother died from pneumonia a year after the war began. She had caught a bad cold, and a week later her infected lungs filled and her breath and life were gone. After the funeral, during the solemn visitation at her parents' home, Carlo helped his wife exorcise her grief, and watched and worried when her father didn't move from his living room chair for the longest time. Thomas sat there for hours after the service with his eyes closed, speaking to no one, until he waved for Carlo to come to him.

"God is punishing me for what I did. She didn't have to die. You must prepare Julia Gail for my death. It will come soon," he whispered, and then he closed his eyes again, ignoring all of the dozens of mourners passing by.

Carlo did not relay his father in law's message to his wife, but in the weeks to follow, he spent long hours with him gathering greater insight into the mob and helping him organize his personal affairs.

Among other things, this process involved accumulating, assembling and trying to make sense out of numerous scraps of paper found in Thomas' desk drawer with various numbers scribbled about on them. Carlo sat for hours attempting to decipher their meaning until he finally asked Thomas for help.

"Account numbers," was all the man would say.

"You mean bank accounts?" Carlo asked.

"Yes."

"Where are these banks?" Carlo prodded further.

"Can't remember," Thomas said, lifeless.

Weeks of letter writing and telephone calling to banks across the country finally produced results. The numbers turned out to be tied to actual long-dormant deposit accounts at banks in dozens of American cities.

"Have you been to all these places?" Carlo asked

"I guess so," Thomas answered.

"What were you doing there?" Silence. Omerta. Thomas would look away and cough. He had caught a cold he could not shake.

Carlo could not detect any particular pattern to his father-in-law's travels, and when he pressed him for details about those trips, he always would remain silence with a frown and a headshake no. Carlo strongly suspected how his father-in-law had earned the money, but after awhile, he never raised the subject again.

In all, Carlo received confirmation of accounts from banks in seventeen different cities. Over Thomas' signature he provided them with instructions to close the accounts and send cashier's checks to a single account at the First National Bank of Pueblo. The local account was set up in Julia Gail's name only. Carlo was unaware of the total amount on deposit until the Monday following her father's death. Pneumonia had struck him down as well, following his wife's death by a mere six months. When all the money was counted there was fifty four thousand two hundred and fifty three dollars and thirty-seven cents on deposit. A fortune by all estimates. The money began earning interest compounded at three percent.

Carlo told Julia Gail about the money on Tuesday, the day after he found out the total amount. He lied when he said it was from a paid-up life insurance policy he had discovered in the metal box on the top shelf of her parents' closet. He could never tell her the truth. Carlo's pledge of silence to her father would never be broken. Carlo, Julia Gail, Julie and baby Rose moved into her parents' house that next month when the lease was up on theirs. There was no mortgage to assume. Her father had paid it off before he died. It was one of the few houses in Bessemer now owned by a family, and not the new owners of the steel mill.

Carlo should have been a happy man; content with a beautiful wife who loved him without condition, two healthy, adorable, rambunctious children, and a home that he owned outright. Neither the bank nor the mill could get their hands on it. Plus his wife had a pile of money sitting in the bank. A twist of fate stemming from the simple infatuation with Thomas' daughter had led Carlo away from a disastrous path to a life of relative safety and security.

What more could he ask for? He was charmed. Yet Carlo had a demon circling overhead like a flock of hungry vultures. He could not shake his guilt. No matter how many production records his crew broke; no matter how many awards he received for outstanding supervisory performance on nearly every mill line, it was never enough for him. It gave him little satisfaction.

He should be over there, fighting along side his brother. No excuses. He told himself he was a coward. He could never forgive himself, or forget. My letters to him made it worse. He kept them anyway. Not once, but four times, he walked into the Army recruiter's office in the old Post Office Building to wait his turn. Yet every time he turned and walked out as the recruiter called out his name as next in line.

Chapter 33
Snipers Falling From Trees

I wrote the next letter to Carlo during our down time in England just before the 101st flew into Holland. My division's second airborne D-Day came on September 17, 1944. I wrote the night before we once again lifted into the sky toward an unknown fate.

16 September, 1944

Dear Carlo,

> *It's nighttime here, and tonight, like the last two nights, it's been hard to sleep, so I thought it might be good to write to you again. Twice now they've alerted us and we've had to move out quickly to what they call the airdromes, a fancy word for the C-47 transport planes, and both times they've sent us back to barracks with stand down orders. It gets on your nerves when that happens. The adrenalin starts, and then you have to calm yourself down again.*
> *Those of us still left kind of know what to expect. The new guys, replacing the ones who didn't make it, don't know, so it's like when mother used to tell us only about the happy times of her days in Sicily with father, we don't tell*

the new guys too much of what to expect. The new guys aren't stupid. They know it's going to be hard, but they have no idea how hard it will be. Our job is to pump them up and get them excited, but we don't want to tell them too much about the fighting. Mostly we talk about the pretty girls in the liberated towns (like it's nothing to get them liberated), and how they kiss and hug us while we're passing through.

Rumor around here tonight is we are going to fly again tomorrow. We're not sure where we're going, but the officers keep telling us that our next mission may not be in France. The word we get is our guys are still kicking butt over there and the Germans are on the run into Belgium and Holland. Remember, we're the guys that like to hit them by surprise, behind their lines, and attack them from the rear, right up their asses, as the saying goes around here. So with our guys moving real fast and the Germans on the run, it's hard to find the right place for us to land and run up their asses. I expect that not knowing where we're going won't last long. They will put us in there real soon, I bet. Maybe tomorrow, who knows?

I have other stories to tell you from when we were in France, before they shipped us back to England, but they're not that important to me now. It's funny, even though it's been only a few days since we were there, in the fight, a lot of what happened is mixed together now in my mind. The dreams are mixed up too. I dream about being home. I dream about Mrs. Montlero, and then all of a sudden I'm dreaming about the German in the foxhole, or before we got to Carentan and the German sniper in the tree.

Maybe I didn't tell you that one after all. Well, it's short. We're along this causeway before we get to the swamp, and one of our guys who's two in front of me takes one right through his helmet and drops. We all hit the ground and soon, another guy is hit in the back, and then another is hit in the head, through his helmet. We know the Krauts have these high-powered sniper rifles that can hit you from maybe 500 yards away, and if the shooter is good, he can put the bullet anywhere he wants in a guy's body. Another one is hit, but this time our platoon sergeant, Bristol's his name, yells that he sees where the Kraut is, in a tree, a good 325, maybe 350, yards away. He's got him spotted with binoculars.

So a few of the guys who have taken good cover start shooting at him, but their range is bad and they keep missing. Meantime, the Kraut is still hitting our guys. Two more. This is getting real bad. I'm able to get into a ditch and behind cover, but all I have is the machine gun, so I'm no good. Then this guy shows up beside me, with what looks like a 30.06 with a scope on it. I ask him where he got it and he said he took it off a Kraut at St.-Come-du-Mont. I said, well shoot that bastard. So he tries and misses him by a mile. So I take the rifle, and you know I've got pretty good eyesight, so I've got the guy in my sights and I get him, right through the throat. I was aiming for his head because I could see he didn't have a helmet on but, you know, bullets fall a little over some distance and, knowing that, I suppose I should have aimed a little higher. Anyway, he falls out of the tree and it's over.

Meanwhile, though, he's taken out 12 of our guys, either killed them or wounded them pretty bad, but you know, that Kraut didn't move from his spot in the tree. I know he didn't, even after our guys were shooting at him and missing. He just stayed there. Maybe he didn't think we had a rifle with that distance, didn't think we might have a rifle like his, and a guy with pretty good eyesight. Or he didn't care. He just wanted to kill as many of us as *he could before we got him. I don't know. For some reason my dream about the sniper is a happy one. I'm not sweating when I wake up after a dream about the sniper.*

I don't want you to worry. When I get home, if I get home, I'm not going to try to see Mrs. Montlero at all. I'm going to try to find a girl my own age, who's not married. I'd like to find a virgin, and maybe I can, since there are not as many guys still in town now that the war is on. If I get back in time, maybe I can find one who's not been touched. That would be nice. Although I'm sure Mrs. Montlero had some experience, and that was good, if you know what I mean. She taught me some things that made her and me feel real good, and maybe I can try those things with the girl I find when I get home, if I get home. Maybe you can keep an eye out for a girl like that for me, but don't tell her about my experience, let her find out for herself. But don't get me wrong; I'm not just looking for a girl for the sex. I want one that likes it but that's only part of a good relationship. Right, big brother? Like you have with Julia Gail. I want one like her.

You know, I'm tired now, maybe I can sleep. Please give my love to mother and the sisters and your babies. And I guess, the brothers-in-law. Man, I forgot their names again.

Your brother,
Johnny

PS: I almost forgot, I got promoted to corporal and may end up a squad leader. Squad leaders always take the point.

Chapter 34
A Handsome Man, Indeed

Silvio

Silvio Bustamonte knew he was indeed a handsome man. Angelina sure thought he was. His thick, wavy, shiny black hair, steel grey eyes, his fine physique, the way he carried himself to Mass each Sunday in his cream-colored suits with his plastered-on smile, that sly squint in one eye and that curled up lip made him a schoolgirl's dream. He had the attitude, and he had the demeanor, but below the shallow surface it was all an act. His pick-up lines were redundant, even he knew that, and when they worked, he quickly became condescending when he passed from one easy feminine target to the next. Outwardly, he was a sincere and fanciful dandy. Underneath, he had a hard edge.

Nicole hadn't chased after him and that's what made her desirable. At first, she hadn't cared for him. She actually ignored him. I have to admit she was the most beautiful of my five sisters, perhaps the most beautiful girl in town, and Silvio saw her as the grand prize. Silvio came calling for six months before Nicole accepted his invitation for a first date. Long before her acceptance he had routinely appeared at her door with flowers, candy and a certain irresistible charm. It didn't take long for Silvio to conclude that he had become a favorite of my mother's. Angelina became partial to him because, as he knew from stilted conversations with Nicole, he reminded her of Nick, in physical appearance and because of his baritone singsong delivery of a superb alternating mix of Sicilian and Italian dialects.

Silvio suspected that my brother was leery of him from the start, and that Carlo had told Nicole of this distrust. Sometime after the wedding, to Silvio's disappointment, Carlo had discovered that Silvio was one of those whose counterfeit employment records at the mill documented a work history of fourteen faithful years of service. Silvio didn't realize when he purchased the false records that if they had been true, he would have been six years old when he first manned the mill furnace. Child labor laws were fairly lax at that time, but not that lenient. But no matter. Because of the doctored records and other connections, Silvio was never subjected to a draft board hearing.

Silvio wasn't sure about Nicole's youngest brother's opinion of him either, and frankly he could care less. He had spent very little time with him during his courtship of Nicole, and now that I was in Europe I presented one less problem for him to deal with. Once his formal courtship had begun with Nicole, it blossomed quickly, running headlong into marriage, which came within the year. Silvio had his prize.

There was always tension between Carlo and Silvio, and the animosity was apparent each time they were thrown together at family gatherings. Yet Silvio wasn't worried about Carlo, because he knew that on the subject of Nicole's and his other sisters' love lives, their brother had no real status, nor could he influence their decisions. Carlo's presence at their wedding and the before and after festivities was welcomed by his fiancée for sure, but in Nicole's eyes, despite her brother's sincere efforts, Silvio knew she thought her brother remained a poor stand-in for her father.

So Silvio plowed ahead, becoming a crafty, manipulative family insider plying his craft at every opportunity. He would boast to his father, his reliable benefactor and the one who had shelled out the cash for the phony pilfered personnel records, that he had cracked open the shell around Carlo's family, and that he was "sucking the sweet juices right out of them." His father was proud. Just the way they planned it.

Silvio had actually been employed at the mill, but just long enough for the outcome of the war to tilt toward an Allied victory and begin its grinding, merciful descent into history. He waited until the draft board filled its quotas, and just at the right time, quit the mill and set out to open a restaurant and tavern. From conversations around Angelina's dinner table, he knew that it was just about the same time I was engaged in my first battle in Holland.

Poor sucker, Silvio likely mused to himself. *We need stiffs like him over there. He's there; I'm here, can't get any better than that. I'll bet he's as dumb as his brother.*

Silvio's idea of presenting an upscale restaurant and tavern to the bustling steel mill town had real merit. He was smart enough to perceive there was demand for a quality establishment in a proper downtown location. To attract plenty of customers, the restaurant had to be far enough away from the mill, yet convenient to the neighborhoods and government employment centers. He saw a need for good Italian food to appeal to that huge segment of the growing population. He had the right idea. He just had to make it work. He went to his father with a convincing argument and quickly gained his endorsement. After that, money for his venture became no object.

Silvio's family had had a tragic string of mysterious fires that had destroyed a family clothing store; later, a family drug store, and still later, the garage in the back of the family's home that housed a hardly-used 1939 Cadillac four-door. The car was a total loss. Three different insurance companies paid off systematically, all three times, no questions asked, because all of the premiums had been paid up just in time. The insurance adjusters were pleased to settle the claims, but even happier with the two one-hundred-dollar bills each received in a sealed envelope in exchange for full payment of the inflated amounts. They couldn't write the checks fast enough. Right on the spot. No further questions.

So Silvio's Bar and Grill, offering the finest Italian cuisine, swung open its doors with fanfare and more glitter and gilt than Pueblo had ever seen before. Gaudy, blue-velvet-cushioned chairs surrounded tables covered with starched Egyptian cotton cloths. Fine china. Crystal chandeliers lighting the main dining room. Waiters in tuxedos, and a scantily clad hat check girl. A bar was stocked with a wide assortment of liquors ranging from a special label **Four Roses** to ports and brandies imported from the homeland. The wine cellar boasted sixty-two different labels, but none from California; all were French and Italian origin.

Admittedly, the food, however, didn't come close to the ambiance, or the booze. Standard fare was meatballs, pasta, with either a bland, watery red marinara or white sauce, often too thick and gummy, almost like paste. The bread was plastered with way too much garlic butter. Lasagna noodles stuck to the roof of your mouth. Silvio fired two chefs in the first two weeks after opening. Nonetheless, the grand opening of SB&G, as it became known, was a smashing success. Every table turned three times during the first evening. A small combo played Glenn Miller classics from an elevated stage in the corner of the dining room. The bar grossed more than five hundred dollars on the inaugural night alone.

Within two weeks the place was nearly empty. All of the mill line supervisors and administrative managers who could afford the food and booze had been there once or twice, but failed to return a third time. Silvio suspected they were waiting for a special event to celebrate, or, more likely, for another chef to arrive. He knew the novelty was quickly wearing off of SB&G, and for the first time in his life, Silvio couldn't contrive a solution. His father told him one Saturday night while they sat together at a table in the back watching the idle waiters smoke their fifth cigarettes of the evening that his son owed him forty thousand dollars for "this rat trap dive" of his.

"You have six months to pay up," his father warned.

Silvio was his father's only son and he had always been an easy mark for Silvio since he was a child. His father had been strict and many a time his barber's razor strap raised welts on Silvio's blistered backside. Yet when the strap was hung back on its hook, his father would embrace him and soothe the sting with a fire-engine-red wagon and ice cream cones for a solid week.

Silvio thought he knew exactly how far he could push his father, and was shocked when he realized that this time, he had gone too far. He would have welcomed a beating in return for more cash, but when his father rose from the table and walked straight to the door without even the usual cold, distant farewell, Silvio was suddenly, for the first time in his life, alone. He felt abandoned, and looked for someone on which to vent his frustrations. The night of his father's demand for the cash was the first night Silvio struck Nicole. It wouldn't be the last. She was six months pregnant at the time. He embraced his wife after the beating and held her head in his lap and dabbed her split lip with a cotton ball. Like father, like son. The next day two dozen roses arrived by special courier along with a sweet hand-penned love poem. Silvio knew she would keep the abuse to herself.

And then a miracle, a savior, came knocking on Silvio's door. On another very slow Wednesday night at SB&G, the very lovely Lola, voracious eater and wife of Guiliano, arrived for dinner. Despite a succession of failed meals at Silvio's, Lola insisted upon returning to the place each Wednesday. Silvio greeted Lola and Guiliano himself. He had laid off the hostess. He was yet to fire the hatcheck girl because he still hoped a friendly encounter with her in the stock room might be in the offing.

"Good evening, Miss Lola and Guiliano, how lovely it is to see you. May I show you to your special table?" Silvio gushed.

Since the place was empty but for an assistant roller mill production manager, still in his business suit, sitting alone in the opposite corner wolfing down a bowl of fettuccini, Silvio had no problem finding the couple their quiet, dark romantic table opposite from the end of the bar.

Lola may have had a nip or two before making her appearance that evening because after only the first carafe of Chianti she began to cry. "OH, Guiliano, I am so sorry. I have deceived you all these years. I am unworthy of your love," she squealed.

As her shrieks echoed across the vacant expanse, Silvio immediately wondered how this two-hundred-seventy-five-pound specimen could possibly attract a love interest. Had she strayed and was now confessing a forbidden tryst?

Impossible, he thought. *I can't even stand looking at her.* Then she began howling even louder.

"It was Angelina. Angelina cooked those meals for you. Not me. She's the one. I paid her and I would bring them home from her kitchen just in time for your dinner. She is a wonderful cook. A master. The best. I am but a potato peeler by comparison!" At full speed now, Lola bellowed, "She cooks for many of her neighbor's husbands. Their wives buy from her. They pay her just like me to satisfy their men, to make them love them more. How can you forgive me?"

Silvio could not believe his ears. He was quite familiar with Angelina's truly miraculous meals, but now, as he listened closely, he conceived his potential salvation.

Guiliano comforted his nearly hysterical spouse through the rest of their tasteless meal, and they left more than a little embarrassed by the spectacle they had caused. Silvio now realized that Lola and Guiliano's persistent patronage was because Angelina must have been too busy to fill Lola's cooking pot with hot delicacies. Silvio hastily closed the place early that night and immediately went home. The hatcheck girl would have to wait. Silvio was especially kind and loving to Nicole when he arrived, as she was now in her third trimester. As they lay in bed, he told her he planned to visit Angelina the next day, reminding his wife that he had not seen her mother since Sunday, and wanted to make sure she was content. Nicole paid little attention as she rolled on her side and brought her knees up to seek greater comfort.

Silvio suspected that Angelina had money stashed away in many secret locations. Beside swelling bank accounts and numerous real estate holdings, Silvio envisioned dozens of coffee cans filled with cash buried in her backyard, and he often plotted schemes to relieve her of the burden of overseeing her fortune. Little time lapsed between his pointed questions to Nicole as to how and where her mother's wealth was walled away. At first, Nicole would gaze back at him, bewildered, but as the questioning persisted, he could tell her wariness of his gushing attention toward her mother was growing. Even though he knew his shallow, unending, yet lavish treatment of his mother-in-law had become more than an irritant to Nicole, he could not stop. He was definitely seeking more from Angelina than her motherly affection.

The next morning Silvio was at Angelina's door just in time for breakfast. In perfect Italian, he said, "*Mama, come e' delizioso il tuo sguardo questo mattino.* How lovely you look this morning." He hugged her tightly. "I told Nicole that I wanted to see you first thing today to start my day off just right. So she is still sleeping and I am here to be with you."

Angelina gushed in response. "Oh, Silvio, *achne tu illumini il mio giorno.* You brighten my day also. Please, sit, and I will fix for you the most wonderful frittata."

Dutifully, he sat and watched in silence as she delicately and with loving care scrambled eggs, ground and added sweet Italian sausage, chopped and added onions, green peppers and fresh basil. She stood for a moment to inspect the wonderful concoction as it sizzled in just the right touch of olive oil. The balanced aromas of sweet sausage against the tart of the sautéing onions, peppers and mushrooms overtook his nostrils. Silvio lost track of the true purpose of his presence and rested his head on the back of his chair; eyes closed to savor the delightful smells. They did not speak; rather Angelina sang as she worked. Silvio had not heard her sing before. He listened and was truly enchanted by the sounds and smells.

She placed the heaping mound of goodness in front of him and sat to watch him quickly devour it along with a cup of steaming black coffee. When his meal ended he addressed the subject that had been on his mind since Lola's revelation the night before.

"Mama, I need your help. You know your next grandchild is due next month and we are so happy. We promise you, Nicole and I will be the best parents and love our child with all our hearts. But, for us to care for our child as we should, Mama, I must ask you to cook for me, not here in your kitchen, but at my restaurant," he stated flatly. "My business will not survive without you."

Wiping her hands on her spotless apron she turned from her stove. She frowned, obviously bewildered by his proposal. Her forehead wrinkled, and her jaw set tight, yet her voice remained calm. "I do not understand, my boy. You ask me to cook in your restaurant? I do not cook for no one other than for my family. It is my gift to you. I not share that gift with anyone."

"Mama, forgive me, but I know you cook for your neighbors. I know you have done this for a long time, and it is a secret, but people are now talking. Your beautiful secret is out. Everyone knows that you make your heavenly dishes for the ladies in the neighborhood, and they take them home and tell their husbands they have cooked it all, just for them," he said, comforting, soothing and complimenting her with every word.
She was shocked.

"No, no, Silvio, *il mio lavoro e'il mio segreto*. My work is my secret," her voice, no longer calm, was cracking with emotion. "*Io non tradiro' i miei amcii.* I will not betray my friends."

"Mama, it is okay. You have not betrayed anyone. Your friends are already telling their husbands. *Tutti sanno.* Everybody knows. And they all agree that if you come cook for me, it will make them even happier. They can come to my restaurant, as often as they want, and there will be no more hiding," he reasoned with her. "You can help more neighbors and more of your friends. They will come in great numbers to enjoy your cooking and Nicole and I will save our restaurant."

Angelina fell silent. The dismay had not left her face. Silvio chimed in again to interrupt her thoughts. "Mama, I also know your friends pay you for your work. I will pay you for cooking for me. I will pay you more because you will bring happiness to the many people who will come to my restaurant. Together, we will make money. Plus, Mama, you need to leave your house sometimes. You need to go places other than just to Mass. You are young. You are beautiful. You will make new friends and have fun," he pressed, gaining momentum with every word.

"*Tu mi paghi?* You pay me?" she asked, her expression now changing from one of consternation to curiosity. She removed her apron, hung it in its rightful place and sat down, face-to-face with her son-in-law.

"*Naturalmente.* Of course," he answered, taken aback somewhat by her direct quizzical stare, but managing still an ear-to-ear grin of reassurance.

Exactly two weeks after their breakfast table discussion, and following rather intense negotiations that Silvio neither wanted nor ever expected, Angelina walked out of her house at precisely nine o'clock on a Monday morning to an awaiting Silvio sitting patiently in her front driveway in his 1940 Ford two-door.

It was the first time she had left her house that early since Nick's death. She always attended eleven o'clock Mass, so there was no need for her to leave before ten. She still wore only black, but a key part of her negotiations with Silvio, other than her compensation, was the full-length white aprons she would don the moment she entered the restaurant. Silvio insisted and she had agreed to cloak herself this way until her work was done each evening.

Once she had consented to Silvio's proposal, and the wearing of aprons, next had come the amount of her pay. He first offered her ten dollars a week. She laughed out loud. Her neighbors were paying her ten dollars a dish now, she told him, and if it were really an emergency, such as an unexpected guest joining her customer that evening, the price went up to twelve dollars.

Ever polite, she responded with, "*Mio caro, tu devi quindi trovare un altro cuoco.* My dear, you then must find another cook."

In the end, they settled for an amazing fifty dollars a week, and Silvio had to get permission from his father for the hire. He also had to borrow another two thousand dollars from him to restock the pantry, meat locker and produce shelves to meet my mother's demands. Plus it took him a week to find the special seasonings she needed.

Thankfully, Silvio's father forked over the extra money after devouring and drooling uncontrollably over one of Angelina's luscious linguini and clam sauce dishes at a private chef's table gathering on a late Sunday night. With a little money left over, Silvio took out full-page ads in the morning and afternoon editions of the *Chieftain Journal* newspaper and printed new daily menus that he proudly displayed in the front windows. He hired two Mexican sisters from Arizona who were new to town and had aspired to clerk jobs at the mill before he lured them to Angelina's kitchen as her assistants. The women communicated fairly well even with the language barrier. A basic understanding of the age-old romance languages bridged the gap just enough for Angelina to prod the sisters along to her speed and to conform to her style. Silvio noticed with satisfaction that the sisters learned quickly under Angelina's demanding guidance.

The second grand opening of SB&G occurred on a Saturday night, just like the first, and again, the wait for a table ran over an hour. The new menu was sent from heaven, or at least, inspired there by Angelina. It was printed in larger, classic Roman script, both in English and Italian, and placed in prominence by the front door on a music stand. It was entitled, *"Stanotte Delizie paradisiache da Angelina.* Tonight's Heavenly Delights from Angelina."

Among many other superb fares, the menu featured:

Insalata di Pepperoni e Capperi, and
Sformatini di Gunghi,
Minestra o Passato di Zucca alla Mantovana,
for appetizers;
Pomodori al Riso Verde
Polenta con Mascarpone e Tartufi
Triglie al Cartoccio
Involtini di Pesce Spada
Carpaccio (a meal in itself)
Luccio alla Mantovana
Piccioni Ripieni in Umido
Galantian di Anitra, for main courses, and
Schiacciata con Uva
Crostatine di Frutta Fresca, for dessert

The *Chieftain Journal*, which didn't have a culinary critic or anyone on the editorial staff even close to a designated writer of cultural affairs or entertainment, assigned Ruby Mizzaro, the Bridal Page editor, to cover the big event. Silvio dominated the interview with Ruby and was proudly taking all the credit for the successful debut of the restaurant, when the reporter interrupted him in mid-sentence and asked to speak to Angelina.

"Oh, she's too busy. She's in the kitchen. Too shy to talk with reporters. I can answer for her," Silvio tried to duck the request.

"But she's the grand dame of the chefs as I understand it," retorted Ruby. "She's the one who created this wonderful cuisine. Without her, no one would be here tonight. Right, Mr. Bustamonte?"

"Wouldn't you like to see our wine list? More than sixty labels. All French and Italian," Silvio ducked again.

He made certain that Ruby never got her interview with Angelina that night, but was shocked when he saw the newspaper the next morning. Apparently, Ruby's photographer had waited for the head chef to leave from the back door after the third seating. Angelina was photographed smiling at the cameraman and blowing him a kiss. Silvio noticed with irritation that Ruby had neglected to print even a single quote from the restaurant's owner. Even so, Silvio could not contain his excitement as his fine stock of booze and wine and a few bottles of exquisite port and brandy were whisked off the shelves on the nights that followed Angelina's glorious debut.

On the next Sunday night, Silvio, stuttering and stammering and shaking like a leaf, personally seated the cheese man, Mr. Clemente, at the best table in the house. La Cosa Nostra's finest was accompanied by three other gentlemen, all nearly twice his size. Silvio thought they would enjoy the table farthest in the back. They tipped the waiter twenty dollars and tipped their hats to Silvio on their way out. They further depleted Silvio's liquor supply, finishing off his best port while sucking on after-dinner Cuban cigars. That was the first and last time Silvio ever saw Black Jim. But he was thrilled just the same.

Chapter 35
Eagles Make Lousy Pets

I'm glad I didn't know anything about my new brother-in-law at that time. If I had, I might have gone AWOL and jumped a troop carrier going home to show up one day and wring the bastard's neck.

No, Silvio and I hadn't met yet, but we would about a year later and it wouldn't be pleasant. Meanwhile, I had other things to worry about – like staying alive. None of us had all the facts about how the second invasion of Europe unfolded, and at the time it was impossible to keep track of the sequence of battles and the towns, roads, rivers, bridges and all manner of territory captured, held, abandoned, recaptured, lost and retaken during this frenzied war-driven period.

The news got back to us in dribs and drabs from officers and enlisted alike, but the best place for us to go for the accurate summaries was still the *Stars and Stripes*. Those guys helped us all fill in the blanks. The skies over the English Channel were once again filled with Skytrains and gliders in the early morning hours of September 17, 1944. The aircraft were on their way to deposit a pretty good bunch of skillfully fierce fighters belonging to the 101st. Again German flak met our huge air armada, and often found its mark, downing many of our planes both before and after they unloaded their gutsy cargos. But this time, the seasoned pilots and navigators spotted the drop zones much easier, so the drops were more accurate, allowing our troops to assemble quicker and in greater numbers. Again we took the Krauts by surprise.

The names of the towns I jotted down in my notebook were different from those in France, but just as difficult to spell, so I still had to concentrate on getting them right. The ones that stood out were Eindhoven, Vechel, Wilhelmina, and St. Odenrode. And there were many rivers and canals whose signs were either gone, their names impossible to read, or I didn't have the time to stop and write them down.

Our liberating forces were charged with seizing and holding a twenty-five-mile stretch of highway from Vechel to Eindhoven. It was mighty difficult going, especially when the Germans realized our presence and counterattacked on all fronts. But in less than a day's fighting, St. Odenrode was the first to fall to the Screaming Eagles. The next objective was the town of Best. Capturing this, our second key city, took three days and cost hundreds of lives. When it was over the 101st t, supported by British armor, destroyed fifteen of the German's massive 88s artillery, captured one thousand and fifty six German soldiers and left three hundred dead on the battlefield.

My 506th Regiment marched toward the town of Zon, next on the list and an even bigger challenge to seize. Just as our assembled Allied column approached the town, the Germans dynamited the bridge over the Wilhelmina Canal and charged straight into our fortifications. A massive firefight ensued, but we Eagles held our ground and beat back the enemy. With the bridge gone, a few volunteers from one of the flanking platoons swam the canal under heavy fire and established a beachhead of sorts on the opposite side. That maneuver, and other flanking movements, served to seal off the area and its Nazi occupants. The Germans fell to the Eagles but our victory was short-lived. A seesaw battle began with attack and counterattack along the road to Eindhoven that would last for five horrendous days until our GIs, again supported by British artillery, established perimeters along the road and made it safe for travel for the Allied armor and supply convoys on their way through.

The next day the 101st was moved to an area that quickly became known as the Island, a strip of land located between the Nederijn and Waal Rivers with Arnhem to the north and Nijmegen to the south. I had the toughest time with these names. I never did spell the Waal River correctly, forgetting the second "a," but I did have some brief down time to record all of the local landmarks before the Germans attacked in force. Within twenty-four hours, the seasoned elite German 957th Regiment plunged headlong into the defensive position of the Eagles. We were encamped on the Island, and we threw back extraordinary resistance.

The German troops were initially decimated, but were soon reinforced and reorganized to strike again. This time we were forced to withdraw to the town of Opheusden and were engaged in another vicious firefight that lasted three days. When I got there, I had no idea I was in Opheusden, and when I left, I had no idea where I'd been. There was no sign anywhere identifying the place. The town was nearly reduced to rubble during the battle. It wasn't a place I like to talk about.

From that point on, fighting in Holland was mainly confined to patrol skirmishes and probes across the Rhine. The major German defenses were riddled and retreated across the great river to prepare for what history later recorded as Hitler's last great counteroffensive. Hundreds of Germans surrendered to the 101st and readily provided valuable information on their troop movements, tactics and strategies. Traitors to their demented leader, yes, but to their country? I don't think so. There was no intelligence, however, on the sick, maniacal machinations swirling around in Hitler's twisted mind, nor his plans for his final, fatal thrust to unattainable victory.

My Eagles and I returned to base camp in November, but this time, we went to France. Again exhausted, and in need of licking and patching our wounds, we were no less spirited from victory after victory.

I wrote to Carlo the third night after we settled in outside the liberated City of Lights.

7 November, 1944

Dear Carlo,

You won't believe this but your little brother is going to Paris tonight.

There I go again, only thinking about myself and not asking about mother and our sisters. I finally got your last two letters after I got back from Holland. We didn't fly home this time. We came back across France by truck to the rest camp here, but I doubt we'll be staying long.

I'm real glad that everyone is okay, and the babies keep coming. But what is this about Nicole and this guy Silvio? I don't like how you describe him and that restaurant of his. When I get back, we will have to take him out behind his joint and teach him a lesson.

It's cold here. Winter set in without the cool days of fall, especially in Holland. Remember when we'd go to the mountains in September and see the trees change their colors? I miss that stuff. It was pretty.

There's not much to see around here that's pretty, but they say Paris is. They also say the Krauts stole everything in sight from the French but they didn't destroy the old buildings, which is nice; that's if the Krauts ever did anything nice.

Other than all the dead bodies and blown-up towns we saw coming across France after Holland, the other un-pretty thing we saw was how the French were treating each other after we kicked out the Nazis. We'd go through these towns and the people would be out, waving American flags and such, but they'd always have some poor woman up on a stand that looked like it was built for a hangman, and just as we would drive by, they would strip her down and shave her head. They were pretty women too, before they shaved their heads. They tell us they are doing this because the woman screwed a Nazi or something. So, they were punishing them, marking them for life.

It's funny, but I wonder if they deserve it. I don't think these women fell in love with those Nazi bastards. They were destroying their country. How could you love someone for that? I think all they were trying to do, well some of them may have thought they loved some Kraut, I guess, but most of them were just trying to survive. To me, over here, you do just about anything you have to do to survive, and since these women, or at least most of them, couldn't shoot a gun to defend themselves, they spread their legs instead. Is that wrong? I don't know.

But you know a few of our guys, even while we were in transport from Holland, were able to sneak off the trucks when we would stop for awhile in these French towns, and they would get with the French woman. And these guys would later talk about how the French women would say they hated the French men and would beg to come back with us to America. I didn't find one of these women in those towns, but believe me, I'm going to look for one tonight. Not that I want to bring one back with me, don't get me wrong.

They've just told us we're relieved and the trucks are waiting for us to take us into the city. I will write again before they ship us out. I need to tell you about some things that happened in Holland, but I don't want to do that now. I want to go have some fun and not think about the stuff I need to tell you.

Your fun loving brother,
Johnny, Corporal, 101st Airborne

14 November, 1944

Dear Carlo

I thought I'd be able to write again sooner than this, but this is the first time I've been back to base. They gave us a whole week's leave, which nobody ever expected. I was in Paris the whole time and I was lucky to get back to base when I did. If it hadn't been for two MPs who spotted me and this guy from Bozeman, Montana, coming out of our favorite house in Paris, I would be in real trouble. There's much about this past week that I don't remember, but I do remember finding Chloe at this sidewalk café the second day we were there. Paris is as beautiful as they say it is. All of the buildings, the streets, the neighborhoods are just like you see in the travel books. I even went to Notre Dame, the cathedral on the Seine River that runs through town. I didn't go to Mass there, but I looked inside and walked around. You could fit our cathedral in the middle of the first floor of Notre Dame and have plenty of room left over.

Anyway, as I've told you before, I am a gentleman, so my time with Chloe will be private, but it was a good time, and I can dream about the good things and remember them, and sometimes they crowd out the bad things in the dreams. I will tell you Chloe was very pretty, just like Paris. She couldn't speak much English other than to say, "Good soldier, good American, I be good to you." But that didn't matter much. Soon we were able to kind of know what the other one was saying even though we couldn't understand the words. We spent six nights and days together and I spent all of my money, every dime. They had given us back pay and some other money for combat duty, I guess, so I went to town with over 200 bucks in my pocket. Now I have nothing, not even enough to get into a crap game. But it was worth it. Chloe showed me everything, and we didn't just stay in bed all day. Keep that to yourself.

The only trouble we had was when I would have one of my dreams and wake her up at night. She had this little apartment, so that's where we stayed. There was a whole bunch of other GIs doing the same thing as me with other French women. The French men sometimes got really pissed off and there were a few fights in the bars, but they pretty much left us alone with their women. I expect they will get most of them back when we leave. Anyway, I would have these dreams and they would wake Chloe up and she would have to shake me to stop me from yelling, because I would actually wake up yelling sometimes.

I will tell you about one experience that keeps coming back to haunt me. You might know from the newspapers that we landed behind the German lines in Holland and our mission was to capture and clear this long road between these two towns so our heavy equipment and supplies could get through. This piece of road was as long as the road between our town and Walsenburg, and it's

324

hard to think of the fact that we needed to control every inch of that long road when there were like 30,000 German troops trying to keep control of it themselves. But we did.

It took us almost two weeks, but there's not a German within 10 miles of that road now, and I'll bet there's a traffic jam of our trucks and tanks and stuff on that road as thick as the traffic in Paris is sometimes.

I told you they promoted me to corporal and corporals walk point on patrol. Maybe I told you that, I don't know. Anyway, they do, so I had to walk point every time we went on patrol, which was every day we were there because we were advancing so fast the main body of our regiment had to know what was ahead of them, and so it was the job of my platoon to find out. We thought at first this was going to be a piece of cake with little resistance, until the Germans decided they wanted to try and take back this little piece of ground we were defending as part of keeping the road open on the way to this town called Arnhem.

It got real nasty when the Krauts came at us, and like it always seems to be, we didn't have any artillery support or heavy weapons to help us fight them back. Just machine guns like mine and a few mortars. And one of them damn mortars, the Germans', not ours, got too close to me once. I had set up this parameter position and was firing that damn thing as fast as I could when it hit close by. When I got blown off my feet in France that time, I didn't feel any pain, because I wasn't really hurt, but this time it hurt like hell. Immediately. The shrapnel caught me in the back and neck all at the same time. I rolled over in the dirt and saw the blood. My jacket was ripped like someone had taken scissors to it; neat, straight lines from the collar to my butt. The guy next to me was dead, I could tell. When I turned him over his guts were hanging out through his shirt and his eyes had already rolled back in his head.

I yelled for the medic and by then the mortar fire was coming in real heavy so it took the medic a little while to get there. But he did finally and by then I felt real sleepy. I must have passed out because the next thing I knew I was in the field hospital in the rear. They stitched me up, gave me some blood and morphine, and here I am. It still hurts like hell, but it's healing up good. The doctor said the shrapnel missed my spinal cord by a half-inch and said I shouldn't go to Paris, but I did anyway, and I'm glad I did even though it hurt sometimes, especially when I was with Chloe. She was careful when she woke me up at night as to not touch the bandages along my back. The bandages are supposed to come off next week, the doctor says, and he'll take out the stitches.

We don't know what our next mission will be, and because we're here in France now, I shouldn't tell you even if I knew. It's really cold and if we go back to the fight I expect it will be even colder. Like I said, winter comes early here, no fall. Not very pretty.

Your brother, still alive and still a little sore,
Corporal Johnny

PS: The other reason I'm broke is I gave Chloe my last 50 bucks. When I did that, do you think I made her a prostitute?

Chapter 36
You're Too Late, General Patton

While some of us on leave in Paris were trying to grab reservations for the best tables in the best joints in the city, Adolf Hitler was making his reservations for the best table in hell. But before he got there he would put me and the 101st through an inferno of agony. Hitler didn't survive, but the 101st and I did.

In a desperate last-ditch move to reverse the German army's relentless retreat, Panzer divisions broke through Allied lines, and on December 17, 1944, rolled westward across Luxembourg and into Belgium. They overran numerous American units, and others were staggering from the surprise blow of a still powerful *Wahrmacht*. When word came of the German *blitzkrieg*, all units, including my Screaming Eagles, were called back to the front. There was no time or opportunity to organize an airborne counterattack, so our parachute forces were loaded into trucks for ground transport back to the fighting.

This didn't make the Eagles, our commanders, or me very happy. We were supposed to fly to our missions. We were airborne commando fighters, specialists at our craft, but now we were stumbling onto troop trucks to be hauled like cattle to some unknown pasture to shore up a crumbling line instead of stampeding behind the lines in a rear-end assault. Less than forty-eight hours after Hitler screamed out his order to charge, over loud protests and thousands of cuss words, we crammed into those trucks and headed west out of Paris for the front. It didn't take long for us to accept the assignment; concluding we would just as soon jam it down the German's throats instead of up their asses.

Hitler's objective was immense, ambitious, and daring. His main target, we were told, was the capture of Liege, Namur and ultimately the recapture of Antwerp. Word was leaking out even then to our intelligence officers that the Fuehrer's generals, almost to the last, objected to the strategy, but he overruled them and threatened them with death if he heard further dissent. To make his victorious vision possible, according to one of the captains briefing us during a welcomed piss break alongside the road, the Panzers had to take and hold Bastogne, a vital geographic and manmade commercial hub that brought together the spokes of seven highways and three railroad lines.

As we sped back across France and into Belgium, piled "assholes to elbows," there was no time to stop to connect with the French ladies. The 101st got to Bastogne first, well before the enemy, to lay in for the impending assault. And I was right when I told Carlo it would be cold. It was damn cold. It was December and it started snowing almost the moment we jumped from the back of those trucks. Man that was different then coming from the sky.

Here came the snow and here came the Krauts. A lovely combination. The first contact with the German front came just a day later when an organized resistance force of Eagles beat them up pretty badly in a skirmish on the outskirts of town. However during the fight, the Germans captured the Eagles' entire Medical Company and attached surgical teams, rendering our main force without supplies or medical personnel for the upcoming siege. Just thirty-six hours after the alert went out, the Eagles had established headquarters in Bastogne, and units were set up in circular defense positions ringing the town. I was positioned with one of those units at an outer ring. Machine gunners usually were put in places like that. Just like corporals are put on point during patrols.

The attacks by the Panzers came from the east of town and they were steady with bombardment after artillery bombardment in advance of frontal ground assaults with tanks and determined troops. Yet the Eagles held and repulsed the assaults time and again. The German commanders got the message, and over the next few days, shifted their tactics to come at us from the north and south. With the Panzers attacking from those directions, supported by reinforcements and their own parachute divisions, Bastogne and the 101st were soon surrounded. The Krauts now held the roads leading into and out of town. There was no escape, no retreat; no means of rescue. Okay, now what? The Germans clearly had the upper hand. They had the manpower, elements of seven divisions, the supplies and a deadly war machine coming down our throats and up our asses, this time. Plus the weather was cooperating for the Germans with thick fog banks protecting their front and flanks as they advanced, mercilessly probing the Eagles' defense.

We knew the German's time was short. If they didn't take the town soon Hitler's master plan would fail. With not a minute to spare, and feeling quite confident, I think, the Germans, under white flag, gave their surrender ultimatum. And as the world quickly learned, the order to give up or be annihilated was followed by General Anthony McAuliffe's famous reply of "Nuts." The *Stars and Stripes* later told us that that the *dumbkauf* Kraut general Heinrich Freihrr von Luttwitz and his aides took two hours to figure out that

McAuliffe was fundamentally and without proper protocol between commanding officers telling those Nazi bastards to go straight to hell.

No way would the Eagles ever surrender. So the siege continued and intense warfare gave way to desperate thrusts by the faltering elite Nazis corps. The Germans threw everything they had at the 101st; armor, infantry, parachutists, *Luftwaffe*, night after night, day after day. Christmas approached, the snows came, and the cold got colder. Frostbite was as worrisome as the next *Luftwaffe* dive-bomber coming in low.

Despite no place to hide, no place to take the wounded, and with supplies running low and the rationing of shells and ammunition, the Eagles held on and fought back and prayed. A few miniature Christmas trees and menorah candles were lit in the midst of the carnage. Reports came in that General George Patton, silver six shooters and all, was on his way with the Fourth Infantry Division. Then on December 23, the weather finally swung in favor of the good guys, and supplies and fresh equipment drifted down from the skies. As each German tank and infantry force ventured out into no man's land, they were struck from above by American fighter aces and driven back or crushed. The Eagles had a front row seat and we cheered with delight. The German offensive was broken. Hitler's grand scheme had fizzled. His suicide was weeks away. General Patton would finally arrive on December 26 and immediately claim credit for the rescue.

I never really liked Patton for a variety of reasons, but probably foremost was his unfounded boast that he saved our butts at Bastogne. Never happened. What really kept us going until the end was General McAuliffe's message to his weary men sent on Christmas Eve? That was our inspiration. Patton could have stayed home.

I read it by flashlight inside my outer perimeter machine gun bunker. I think a Jewish kid from Boston was beside me as my bullet belt feeder. He had just wished me Merry Christmas when a runner dropped the envelope in our lap. I didn't know what to wish him, my feeder that is. I didn't know anything about Hanukah. He said it didn't matter. Anyway, the letter read:

> *"What's merry about this? We're fighting. It's cold. We aren't home. All true, but what has the proud Eagle Division accomplished with its worthy comrades of the 10th Armored Division, the 705th Tank Destroyer Battalion and all the rest? Just this: We have stopped cold everything that has been thrown at us from the north, east, southwest. We have identifications of four German Panzer Divisions, two German Infantry Divisions and one German Parachute Division. These units, spearheading the last desperate German lunge, were headed straight west for key points when the Eagle Division was hurriedly ordered to stem the advance. How effectively this was done will be written in history; not alone in our division's glorious history, but in world history. The Germans actually did surround us, their radios blared our doom. Their Commander demanded our surrender.*
>
> *We are giving our country and our loved ones at home a worthy Christmas present, and being privileged to take part in this gallant feat of arms are truly making for ourselves a Merry Christmas."*

The final and almost kamikaze-like assault came early on Christmas Day, but that too we drove back, and the 101st and its support divisions began to take German prisoners. The Nazi offensive turned once again into defensive maneuvering, but the fight kept on until January 9. On

January 19, 1945, the town square of Bastogne was filled with weary but celebrating GIs with their commanders handing out a whole bunch of medals for valor.

A sign on a bullet riddled wall near the town square put it best:

This is Bastogne,
Bastion of the Battered Bastards
Of the 101st Airborne Division

But still, it wasn't like the music magically stopped and we all got up to go home from the party. Skirmishes continued with our guys probing defense perimeters as the Germans continued their massive retreat. For nearly a month, GIs were still dying and hearts were being broken at home, but the bloodiest part was over giving way to a feeling of relief, coupled with warm toes and fingers around the cook stoves in the rear base tents. We were bone-tired to the point where any victory celebration was cancelled for lack of sheer energy.

The Eagles were withdrawn from our post some weeks later, but we continued to see limited action, much devastation, and, worst of all, we would bear witness to the height of inhumanity. The only easy part ahead for us was the taking and occupation of Hitler's remote retreat in Austria, ironically called the Eagle's Nest, which occurred with much fanfare that spring and into the summer of 1945. The hard part was seeing the destruction of nearly the whole of Europe. The fighting that lay ahead for the troops didn't remotely compare to what we had endured. And endure we did, to come away victorious.

In August 1945, my division left Germany a final time for Auxerre, France, to begin training for the invasion of Japan. Japan surrendered two weeks later, rendering the operation unnecessary, and on November 30, the 101st was deactivated and I was close to going home.

During the fighting, I received a few more shrapnel wounds, two moderately serious bullet wounds, plus more bumps and bruises than I could count. My feet and hands had been severely frostbitten during Bastogne, and from that point on, even at the height of summer, or while sitting before my fireplace at home in the winter, my feet and hands would always feel cold. My shrapnel and bullet wounds would heal with little long-term effect on my strength and agility. All in all, I was grateful. All my digits and a good deal of my sanity were still intact.

While on leave, much of my remaining time in France was spent with Chloe, and she joined the legions of those who begged to accompany the GIs home to gobble down a piece of the American pie. Leaving her behind was a hard decision for me.

My dreams continued while Chloe was by my side, and they were worse when she was gone. My letters to Carlo grew more infrequent as the time for my departure for America grew near. I didn't think there was a need to put all the stories down on paper. I could tell Carlo about the dreams in person now, if I chose to remember. But when a particularly bad dream came, I still felt the need to write my brother to get it out.

Chapter 37
Medals Don't Mean Much
When the Graves are Full

16 May, 1945

Dear Carlo,

I really don't remember the last time I wrote to you. The other day one of the GIs in the mess hall said it had already been a year since we flew across the channel and started the fight. I have to tell you it seems like 10 years. I'm a sergeant now. I lead a platoon when we go into the field, which I hope we don't have to do any more. I'm sick of it. But I think they are talking about sending us to Austria. It's pretty much a cleanup operation now. There are still plenty of what they call pockets of resistance, but most of the commanders around here are saying it's only a matter of time before the Nazis surrender. Some guys even think Hitler's dead. If not, I would like to be the one who puts a bullet in his brain. But most people think he won't be captured. He'll take the easy way out.

Okay, there I go again, not asking about you and the family. I want to hear more about Nicole's husband, this Silvio guy. In your letter about him (and by the way, I think I've only received three or maybe four since I've been gone, but that's okay, probably some were lost since I've been moving around so much), you didn't seem too impressed with him. For some reason he bothers me and I haven't even met him. I did get one of your other letters after we were relieved from Bastogne, but I lost it. I'm sorry, but that was a pretty rough time and a whole bunch of us lost things coming back here to France. I don't think I was thinking too straight for a while. I was jumpy all the time. You know, nervous. Even though I was bone-tired, I couldn't sleep because I would wake up thinking I heard shelling again. You know, they shelled us all the time, day and night. They didn't stop until I think they ran out of shells. And I wake up cold even though I wrap myself in blankets, and you know what's really funny, the other night I woke up on the floor of the barracks. I don't think I fell out of bed. I think I may have been thinking I was sleeping on the frozen ground again, and the soft bed was wrong for me. Boy that is strange, I'll tell you.

The one thing that isn't a problem is eating. We eat all the time and the food is good, especially when we are on leave in Paris. But still, nothing is as good as mother's cooking. And what is this about mother cooking in Nicole's husband's restaurant? Try to get another letter off to me if you can. Who knows how long I'll be here this time and maybe it has a chance of finding me, so write and tell me everything you can. Anyway, I am getting to know the city, that's Paris, pretty well. When I am with Chloe, she takes me to some interesting places. I like the museums and some of the artwork. I want to buy a nice painting and bring it home, but that probably won't be possible. Anyway, I am feeling a little better, but I still don't want to go to Austria if I don't have to.

The other day, they showed us a newsreel in the mess hall during breakfast about the 101st and our defense *of Bastogne. They said we were the hole in the donut or something like that, since we were surrounded most of time but the Krauts couldn't get through us to take the roads and rail yards. This newsreel had us all smiling and waving and happy. Yeah, we were happy to get out of there and we were proud of what we did and no one else did what we did either, let me tell you. The newsreel said General Patton and the Fourth Army came to our rescue. That's pure bullshit. We had them beat before they got to us. Don't let anyone tell you different.*

I'll tell you one story that happened while we were there. When I got back to France, they gave me a Bronze Star for this. I really don't know why. And I really don't know what it all means because I don't think I did anything any of the other guys wouldn't have done, but somebody thought it was special, I guess.

Anyway, like I said, every goddamn night and most of the day, they would shell us. At night, especially when it was foggy out, the Nazi patrols would advance to our perimeter. I was out on the outer defense ring because of having the machine gun and all, so one night, and most of them were the same, but this one night, there's about 20 of us in pretty close ranks, some in foxholes, others, like me, in our nests, just waiting for the bastards.

Through the fog, I see what looks like the whole goddamn German army coming at us. I open up and all the rest of the guys do the same, but they keep coming. I've got pretty good eyesight so I can see where they are, but I'll be damned if my gun doesn't jam. Up until then, the fire we had been laying down stopped the Krauts for a minute, but they soon figured out why I wasn't firing, so they started at us again. There was really no choice, and since I'm a sergeant now, I tell my guys to hit the road. I'm screaming at them to move back while I'm trying to get the gun un-

336

jammed. None of them will move, but the fire my guys are putting down isn't enough. I have to get the gun to work or we're all dead. So, I tell them it's an order to move back — and I can give orders now, because I'm a sergeant -, and the guys have to obey, so they finally move back. I am there by myself now, and Carlo, I knew then, or at least I thought for sure, my time had come. There were too many to them coming at me and they knew where I was or at least it seemed that way because they were heading right at me through the fog. And the last thing I'm gonna do is surrender.

Finally with my teeth, because my hands were too cold, I got a shell to come loose and was able to reload. By then the first group of 10 or 15 Krauts were maybe 10 yards away. I just let them have it. They were almost on top of me, so I couldn't miss. I just kept firing until I was out of bullets and the gun went silent. Then I just laid there waiting for them to shoot, but no one shot. I was alone. So I just lay there. I had wool gloves on my hands with the fingers cut out and my hands were so cold I wrapped them around the barrel of the gun and the gloves burned off in about a second and I burned my hands, but at least they got warm for a minute or two. I just lay there, but nobody came. I must have fallen asleep because the next thing I knew, it was morning and I woke up to see this GI staring down at me with this shit-eating grin on his face. They took me back to the rear on a stretcher because I couldn't walk. My legs and feet wouldn't move. When I got there and took off my boots, my toes were grey, almost black. They let me sleep all day and my feet and hands got warm. Two days later I was back out on the outer perimeter, but this time with two other machine gunners kind of in a pyramid shape to try to prevent leaving one guy out there alone if a big swarm of the bastards came at us again.

337

Even though I sleep with two pairs of socks on and when I'm not with Chloe, and with gloves on, my hands and feet are still cold. Damnedest thing. Maybe when I get home I won't have to do that anymore, or maybe it's warmer in Austria, although I don't want to go there. I put the medal away so I won't lose it, like I did your letter. Sorry about that. Write me again. Maybe I'll get it before we ship out. I wanted to tell you about what they call the concentration camps, but I'm too tired right now and my hand just got cold again and I can't write too well with gloves on.

Your sergeant,
Johnny – three stripes and all

PS: I chipped my front tooth getting that bullet out so I look like some bojon hack we used to beat on the snooker table. Maybe I can find a dentist to fix i, when I get back, if I get back.

2 August, 1945

Dear Carlo,

In this letter I'm only going to talk only about one thing. They are shipping us out to Austria in a day or two and I really don't want to think about that. I really don't want to think about what I'm going to tell you in this letter either, but I need to anyway, since there's some really good stuff to remember and some really bad stuff to forget.

If I go to hell when I die, which now is a real possibility, I plan to tell Saint Peter when he kicks me out that I've already been in hell so I don't give a shit anymore. Plus I've already met the Devil and he doesn't scare me.

338

For some time there have been rumors that the Nazis had rounded up as many Jews, and some Catholics and some Gypsies, as they could to force them into labor camps to keep their Army and Navy going, since all the men had been put into service, the old men and the young ones. A German surrendered to us at Bastogne who said he was 70 years old, and he looked it. Also there were kids, maybe 12 or 13 years old, who we'd find dead in the field after a night following one of their charges at our outer perimeter.

Anyway, our officers said that we might stumble onto one of those camps so we should be prepared to fight off the guards as best we could and then try to help the people inside with supplies and such. Well, we did come across one of these places, but it was no labor camp, if that's what they called it. It was like I said, hell. The worse kind of hell the Devil could have created. We had a couple of patrols out, maybe a mile out from where our main body was, and when they came back to tell us what they'd found there were two or three pretty tough guys who couldn't even talk; one was actually bawling like a baby. And as we stood there listening to these guys, the wind must have shifted and you could smell it. We were a mile away. And as we got closer the smell got worse. It was like being in the middle of the stockyards at Lamar and someone throwing a bucket of shit in your face. You couldn't help but get sick to your stomach. Plus there was this other smell, like when some of the guys we shot snooker with at Joe's would have us over to pick up their extra deer meat after they'd butchered one, or maybe an elk. Remember, they would burn the carcasses, hair and hide? That's what it smelled like, when they were burning the leftovers.

Anyway, the rumors are true, but there wasn't one person, if that's what they still were when we found them, who could work. There were piles and piles of dead bodies all over the place. They were rotting out in the open. Hundreds of them, maybe thousands, I don't know. Piles of what were men, women and children, and piles of shoes, piles of clothes, piles of shit, all in piles. We just stood there and looked. They were all naked. Soon some of us realized that some of the piles were moving. There were some people still alive. I found one man, and picked him out of the pile. He had no hair, and I'll bet he weighed only 75 pounds. He looked up at me and tried to say something but I couldn't understand him. I gave him some water. I carried him over to the temporary hospital that had been set up and handed him to a doctor. But the doctor looked at him and said he was already dead. So I took him to the big grave that had been dug and put him in. We had to spread lime over the bodies to keep the disease from spreading, and our medics made us burn all of our uniforms after we were done to make sure we didn't spread disease as well.

The few people we found alive and who I think survived were stacked in these buildings lying on these cots. There might've been five or six people on one cot. Usually those on top of the pile on the cots were dead. And those on the bottom were still alive. I don't know why those on the bottom made it. I guess they were kept warmer by those on top. There wasn't any food anywhere, or water other than piss water, and I saw one woman trying to drink that out of a bucket before we stopped her. And then we found these big rooms, and one guy said these places were where they gassed the people. Can you think about that for a minute? They would herd these people into these big rooms, all airtight with no windows, and turn on the gas and everyone inside would try to get out but would die from the gas, like if you put your mouth around an exhaust pipe and sucked in the fumes.

340

In one room at one end toward the door, you could tell the people had tried to get out. But they were all piled up by the door, dead, still trying to get out. And you could still smell the gas. It made you choke. The guards told them they were going in there to take showers, to get clean for a change.

We spent the whole day there. Hauling bodies to the graves. Giving food and water to those people still alive, and executing the Nazi guards. I didn't do it, but I heard our guys took 50 of those dirty bastards out into the woods, beyond the fence and shot every one of them dead. We were so mad and so sick at what we saw and what they had done to these people... I would have liked to have killed a few myself, but I missed it. For some reason, I found the man I had carried from the pile and put some clothes on his body and carried him to a special place and just sat there with him for a while. God, how I wish we could have got to him sooner.

And you know I wonder, what if the Germans had spent their time trying to figure out how to kill us instead of killing those people? I'll bet we would have had a much harder time winning this war like we are. And if they had fed them enough so they could have worked in a real labor camp, the war also would have been harder for us to win. Instead they did this. How could you hate someone so much to do that? It's one thing to kill a soldier in battle, for a good cause, but it's another thing to just slaughter people for no good reason, just because you think they're different. I'll never understand that for the rest of my life.

Anyway, we're going to Austria. They tell us it won't be too tough. Just mop up, they say. I hope so.

All of us try not to think about being the last one to die, but you know I'd rather die fighting these bastards than die like the man I carried from the pile. He didn't have a chance.

Your brother,
Johnny, wishing he was home

PS: I said in the beginning of this letter there was good stuff to tell you, but I can't remember any right now.

PSS: Most of the dead people in the camps were Jews. You know we were taught that Jews were different. They were odd or strange and they weren't as good as us because they didn't believe in Christ. You remember Father Bernard? He hated Jews, it seemed. Anyway, no matter what these people did or who they were or what they believed, nobody deserved this. All the more reason to put a bullet in Hitler's head.

Chapter 38
Bullets Resting Nicely in the Brain

Like some in my unit had predicted, Hitler took the easy way out with a bullet he lodged in his own brain. Despite the war winding its way into history, the 101st was still being called upon for the most dangerous and difficult missions. Before the surrender, the division would ride into Bavaria in search of what turned out to be a phantom force of Nazi die-hards trying to organize a resistance force, and finally into Austria to capture Hitler's famous Obersalzberg complex. Or more accurately, the Eagles flew there to roost in the Eagle's nest. We were camped out in Hitler's luxurious lair when VE Day came. I joined in the celebration, and the next day, our fighting forces became occupation forces. We immediately complained about everything including not liking Hitler's supply of German wines. The French vintages were much better.

As our bodies, minds and souls rejoiced in survival and think about a life to follow, word came that training would begin in a month for the invasion of Japan. As we did at Normandy, the Screaming Eagles would take the fight to the Japanese mainland in what was forecast to be carnage beyond anyone's imagination. Word was leaking out to our division and others still in Europe that the brass was predicting at least one million American lives would be lost in the invasion force and five million Japanese would die before the end would finally come. They left us hanging for a few awful weeks until news that the Enola Gay had flown and the big bombs had obliterated those cities. So, the end came just days before the 101st was to report to the transport areas for our return to France and commencement of training for the invasion.

I wrote one last letter to Carlo before I left the places I had grown to love and grown to hate. Austria, Bavaria, France, Germany, Holland, Belgium, England and places in between. I would never return again despite pleas from my son in later years when reunion invitations would flood my mailbox. The snot-nosed teenager from Colorado who had seen the world in all its glory and all its gore had no desire to retrace his footsteps to the places where so much misery had been endured.

I did visit New York on my way home. By then, my home with the 101st was never more. The division was deactivated after VJ Day and merged into the 82nd Airborne. The Screaming Eagles didn't participate in the victory march down Fifth Avenue. I watched the festivities from the sidewalk while still in uniform, the Bronze Star in my pocket, but my Purple Hearts pinned to my chest. After the parade I walked past the bright, gleaming Plaza Hotel and into the renowned Central Park, and I laughed to myself how my own Central Park didn't quite compare. At the time I would have given up the three thousand dollars in my pocket to be home instead of being where I was.

3 September, 1945

Dear Carlo,

I'm here in France again. Today we had a jump, and it was just for fun, but they paid us anyway. They pay us a little extra when we jump, calling it "hazardous duty pay," but some of us joke about how much they really owe us for all the days over the past four-and-a-half years that were really hazardous. Jumpin' out of an airplane is nothin'. Anyway, we've been here for about a month, I think, and up until just a few days ago, nobody was having much fun. After we left Austria and all the wine Hitler left behind for us to drink, they told us we had to get prepared for an even a bigger fight in Japan. God that was a bad day. I got so drunk on some vodka we had swapped with the Russians for some Kraut wine that I was sick that whole next day, and laid in the back of the transport truck all the way back through the Alps.

None of us could imagine having to take the fight over there. We had made it through this past year or so here, and to ship out halfway around the world to fight the Japs on their own home territory was something none of us could even think about. You talk about bitching and moaning and cussing and all that.

Anyway, from what we hear, we dropped these huge bombs on two of their cities, and the Japs gave up, so now we don't have to go. You probably know more about it than I do, with it being such big news around the world. Boy, am I happy. We all got drunk again, but this time not on vodka. I don't think I will ever be able to drink vodka again.

None of us know when our orders will come through to disembark, as they say. Mine could come any day, and I will go to some port and board the ship for home.

345

You know, it's funny, but I will miss the guys around me, and I will miss some of the things we did. I think I've become more of a man, and I think from what you've told me about our father, he would have liked what I've done. I hope our mother likes what I've done, even though I won't ever tell her about everything. Maybe just a few of the good things. She doesn't need to know the rest. Most of the stuff in my letters to you is private, between you and me, and I expect you've thrown them all away by now, which is good. No one needs to see them.

Last night I told Chloe that I was leaving soon, and she wouldn't be coming with me. She cried and threw a lamp at me, just missing my head. She yelled and yelled, mostly in French, so I don't know all the names she called me. Anyway, I did understand from her yelling that she wanted me to leave her apartment, so I went to the door. Then she was begging me to come back, to take her to America, but I just left, not saying anymore. I don't think I will ever see her again, but I will always remember her. She's one of the good things to remember. Other good things are the guys I served with and my talk with General Eisenhower. I'll remember those things, forever. I'll tell you about Ike, and I'll even tell mother that story too.

I'm going to try to go through New York City on my way home. I want to go there to see all I can see, including the museums like they have in Paris, like the ones Chloe showed me. That will be another good thing to remember. You never know, I just might show up some day soon and surprise you and mother and our sisters and, I guess, all the babies you've had. I would like to be a father, like you, that is if I can find someone to have babies with. I'm going to try.

Your brother,
soon to be ex-GI, Johnny

Chapter 39
Yale Isn't For Me

My discharge papers finally arrived on February 15, 1946. I already had my duffel bag packed when a young, fresh-out-of-West-Point lieutenant stood at the foot of my barrack's cot and issued me my last order.

"Rise and come to attention," the lieutenant shouted.

It took me a few minutes to respond. That made the lieutenant furious, until he saw the Screaming Eagle patch on my Army-issue jacket hanging in the locker beside my cot.

The sandy-haired, freckle-faced twenty-one-year-old from Des Moines stopped yelling and quietly said, "It's okay, sergeant, sleep a while longer if you like, sir, you deserve it." He turned and walked away.

I had given some thought to re-enlisting. There was bonus pay for such a decision, and some cushy jobs were available to veterans of my defunct division. They told me I could have been an administrative staff sergeant, or a warrant officer, or a drill instructor, even a paratrooper trainer. One re-up recruiter said I could go to Officer's Candidate School. He said my eyesight was so good I should apply for flight school in the soon-to-be revamped Army Air Corp being morphed into the U.S. Air Force. And soon, they explained, the GI Bill would become law, enticing those who desired the pursuit of a free college education to stay in the Army until it was time to go to college. I might have even enrolled at Yale. Who knows?

No, I decided, I wanted to go home. I'd had enough. I'd paid my dues. I had a pocket full of medals to prove it, and a lifetime of experiences, most of which I was struggling to obliterate from my mind. Back to a simpler life, that was my goal. Maybe I would go to college, maybe not, but I wasn't staying in the Army any longer while making up my mind. So with a hundred and forty five dollars in my pocket, I boarded the Queen Mary at harbor in Portsmouth, England, and headed west. Like going across the first time, I joined the enlisted NCOs who occupied the lower decks while the returning officers took the staterooms above deck. And like going across the first time, I occupied much of my time being seasick and gambling.

The first two nights at sea, I slept. From then on, I played cards around the clock until we reached New York. It came down to the last card in a five-card stud poker game with everyone but an Ensign from Connecticut dropping out of the hand. There were three thousand dollars in the pot. I drew a straight to the nine. I had the hand with the first five cards. It was amazing. I don't think I remember ever drawing a straight on the first five cards.

Naturally, I didn't take a draw card. I think the Ensign thought I was bluffing. He had two pair, aces and queens. He thought he had me for sure on the first four cards with those high pairs, but he missed the full house. We shook hands when it was over. I cashed out after that hand, having the strongest feeling that I should quit right then. The Ensign was a good guy. Most guys would have started a fuss over me quitting a winner without giving him a chance to win his money back, but it was four or five o'clock in the morning and I guess we were all pretty tired. Anyway, the game broke up after that hand. I never saw the Ensign or any of those guys again. I stuffed the money in a sock and put it in the bottom of my duffel bag.

We docked in New York harbor to cheering crowds and a blizzard of confetti. The sights and sounds were big and blasted into my head, and I can't say it wasn't exciting while it lasted. All the dancing in the streets, pretty babes, and free booze just for the asking. I hooked up with some sailors from one of the destroyers docked at the harbor for a couple of nights and "painted the town," as they say. But that got pretty old, pretty quick, so I found my way by myself into Little Italy where I paid a number of visits to many of the finer restaurants featuring the food I loved the best and missed the most. I practiced my Italian ordering from one great menu after another.

Often, I wouldn't be charged for my meals once the restaurant owner recognized the Eagle patch on my shoulder and heard a "grazie" instead of a "thank you" for the Chianti. I wasn't there to eat for free, so I often objected to the owner pushing the food and wine at me, but it was almost like I would have offended them if I had paid. Anyway, I would always leave a good-sized tip wherever I went.

I visited the museums and marveled at the art, thinking often of Chloe and what would have been if I had bowed to her wishes. I had wanted to return home alone, and while sitting in one of those quaint eateries on a lazy Sunday afternoon, I decided I wanted to be in the restaurant business. I would ask Carlo to be my partner.

The three grand at the bottom of my duffel bag, which was sitting safely in a footlocker at Grand Central Station, would be enough to get us started. Before I left the dancing in the streets of a still rejoicing, post-war city, I wrote to Carlo one last time, but this time it only took a postcard to record my message.

12 March, 1946

Dear Carlo,

> *On my way home. I want to make you an offer. I want you to be my partner. I want to start a restaurant. Not like Silvio's. American food. We'll make the best cheeseburgers in town. Maybe even turn it into a nightclub.*

> *See you soon,*
> *Johnny, the civilian*

Chapter 40
Sleep No More My Antagonist

Carlo

Carlo admitted he couldn't wait for my return, but he was agonizing over what awaited his little brother at home. It was Silvio and Silvio's head chef that were causing Carlo so much anguish. Not to mention their hometown, which was already changing even though the war had not been over for three months.

Silvio's Bar & Grill had been renamed after the debut of its new chef. "Angelina's" became the new name, and all of the town, including many of Black Jim's associates, paid their respects and turned over a good portion of their legitimate and illegitimate paychecks each week when the new menu was published.

Silvio and his restaurant dominated Carlo's family's life. Katrina and Sophia worked as hostesses, and occasionally, on busy nights, they substituted for the tuxedo-attired waiters. Even Julia Gail had casually mentioned to Carlo her desire to volunteer on extra busy nights, but Carlo squelched that idea immediately. Not his wife. Never.

At first, Angelina would not allow her name to be unscripted in neon above the doorway to the restaurant, but, in so many other instances, her resistance to Silvio's persistence quickly subsided. Soon the renaming ceremony was held, as the sign was unveiled before an approving crowd awaiting the Saturday night eight o'clock seating.

At Silvio's insistence, Carlo could never pay for a meal during the rare occasions he dined there. He would watch his brother-in-law glad-handing those in the familiar pinstriped suits as they disappeared into to the proprietor's back room office.

He is such a suck up to those guys, Carlo told me he thought. *Just like I'd been, once upon a time.* Carlo knew they were setting a trap for another unsuspecting sap.

Carlo abhorred the thought that his brother would be returning home to witness the re-emergence of a once-hibernating mob. More than most, Carlo could sense the hungry animal crawling from its cave after nearly five years of self-imposed slumber. Already there was a noticeable pick-up in activity around Black Jim's goat cheese stand. There were more hookers on the street corners to entertain the returning GIs. And the whole town knew about the shakedown that had occurred one recent afternoon at Mr. Loretto's hardware store when poor Mr. Loretto failed to make his first protection payment on time. Then there was the rumor about a shipment of tax-stamped Canadian Club whiskey hijacked south of Denver.

With all of this going on, Carlo had grown wary and spent many nights at Joe's playing pool and quietly sharing his concern with the trusted owner. Along with these hushed conversations, Carlo and Joe were also planning a special gathering for my return and first ceremonial snooker challenge.

One morning, Carlo had rushed to our mother's and found the last letter from his little brother lying in the mailbox. He always checked the mailbox each day to make sure Angelina did not get to it first and stumble onto one of my letters from overseas that might contain something she shouldn't be reading. That day, Carlo was especially glad he had gone searching since this particular letter, actually only a postcard, contained my plans for the future. Plans that should not be revealed to anyone else.

His brother was on his way home. Carlo wanted my homecoming to be extra special, not tainted by internal family squabbling, especially involving Silvio, or marred by a mob killing at the corner of Fifth and Main. The former he could prevent, the latter, no one could.

~

I arrived on April 3. I didn't call anyone in advance or tell them when the two o'clock from St. Louis would pull in. I had seen so many of those station platform ceremonies along the way from New York with all the hooping and hollering, bands playing, flags waving, and tears flowing, I wanted my homecoming to be different. I wanted it quiet when I got there. I wanted to ease into being home.

I struggled to contain my emotions and was glad that no one was there to greet me except the smiling station manager, Mr. Valdez, who told me he had made it his business to be the first to shake hands with each returning GI as they disembarked. After Mr. Valdez paid his respects, I collected my duffel and took a seat on the bench outside the depot.

I needed a few extra minutes to collect my thoughts. In city after city along the route of my rail journey across the country, I had collected the local newspapers and read the stories of the parades and the parties and the town square speeches honoring homecoming war heroes. And with each story in each town, I grew more anxious. I didn't want to be the center of attention. I didn't consider myself a hero. Those left on the battlefield were the heroes. I was just a lucky stiff. Sure, I had had a few scares that wouldn't fade any time soon, but the deadly bullets and shrapnel had simply gotten someone else less lucky than me. They were the ones who made the sacrifice that really mattered.

The fact that the 101st Airborne Division had already become a household name only added to the glamour and excitement generated by the homecomings across America. The stories of our successes on the battlefield and our many colorful commanders had caught the attention of the press, which almost immediately began to blow the Eagle's exploits out of proportion. And with each story came those Eagles who liked to bask in the limelight and fuel the journalistic flames to make their own contributions to Hitler's defeat exceed reality. I could not play that role. I was, in fact, disgusted by it. We had a job to do. We did it well. Those who came home like me should be thankful, and we should honor those who didn't make it back. That's all anyone should be talking about.

I had to put the war behind me as quickly as possible, but I didn't want to offend those I loved, so I decided I would go along with their party plans and smile and say thank you each time I was slapped on the back or kissed on the cheek. I guessed it was okay to be this way, and I guessed I could take it for a while as long as I could finally tell everyone exactly how I felt. Eventually, sooner than later, I hoped, the celebrations would be over and life would go on.

~

Carlo

Carlo told me he sat in his car watching his brother perched all alone on the train depot bench. He said my head was down, my hands clasped together and elbows on my knees. I didn't realize any of this at the time. I probably looked like a hobo. Since the postcard had arrived the day before, Carlo had driven by the depot eight times to check the arrivals and view each disembarking passenger from each idling train. He had been there late last night and early this morning as the trains had rolled into town. On his ninth drive-by, he spotted his brother.

Carlo admitted he wiped a few tears from his eyes as he waited and watched from across the train station parking lot. He patiently but anxiously observed his favorite soldier. His brother remained frozen in that posture for the longest time.

He looks good in that uniform. Are those four stripes on his sleeve? There's three on the bottom and one on the top. Does that mean he got out as a master sergeant? Where are the medals? They're not pinned to his chest. He looks tired. He's lost weight. He looks older, but probably not wiser.

Finally, I apparently stretched my back and turned my neck side to side. I looked up and was looking around.

It still wasn't time to go to him, Carlo decided. But he was back, thank God. Finally, I rose to collect my belongings. Carlo swung the car around and drove up to his brother from behind, rolling down his window.

"Need a lift?"

Part III

Chapter 41
Don't Make Excuses For Me

The days that followed were a whirlwind of activity I had never expected. My town waited for about a hundred of its soldier citizens to return before organizing a series of celebratory events. Most of the events were sponsored by the USO whose volunteers had fanned out across the country to make sure not one homebound soldier would feel slighted. I had no choice but to participate in the festivities. My family insisted that I take my place as honoree at each of my town's special occasions.

I wasn't happy about all the attention. In fact, I was embarrassed by the way I was being treated, like some kind of dumbass king, with people I'd never met calling me their hero or their savior. All of this business of glorifying people for simply doing their jobs was ridiculous in my opinion. One kid even asked for my autograph. He didn't know who the hell I was, but I gave it to him anyway. He was happy. I felt like an idiot.

I guarantee you one thing, the Bronze Star stayed in its velvet-lined box in my duffel bag, safely stowed away in my mother's attic. I did decide, however, to wear the Purple

Heart and the Meritorious Service medals on my tunic to each of the events around town.

The first night I played snooker at Joe's, I stripped down to my shirtsleeves to give me a little extra free arm movement, but that didn't help much. I lost in a three-hour match to a thousand points to this seventeen-year-old kid named Timmy Marconi. The score was four hundred and fifty five to five hundred and fifty five. After he cleaned my clock, the boys all told me it was still a close match for a guy who hadn't had a cue in his hand for nearly five years. Still, I was pissed off losing to a kid. I made too many dumb mistakes and let him run two tables after missing three easy bank shots on high number balls.

"No excuses," I said to Joe and Carlo later. "Don't you dare make excuses for me," I said.

One thing was bothering me that I didn't tell anybody about for the longest time. Now, I'm not trying to make excuses, but I had this nagging little handicap that I got saddled with on that frigid day after Christmas at Bastogne. And it wasn't my cold feet and hands. Truth is, the doctors told me they couldn't remove three randomly scattered scraps of shrapnel from a well-placed Nazi mortar shell that had ripped into my neck and lodged between the third cervical vertebra and the fourth and fifth lumbar vertebra. Lovely little mementoes to carry around for the rest of my life. I didn't even mention them to Carlo.

One tiny, stinking nickel-sized shard of metal was too damn close to my spinal cord, the doctors said. They called it "precariously close." The surgeon had decided to leave it there or risk paralyzing me for life. It had tumbled its way in so tightly within the bone structure that it now hurt like hell to pivot my neck. Even the slightest rotation sent a shooting hot-iron pain down my neck into my right arm. The other two were snuggled up next to the bone so they could rub and scratch away the surface. So each time I bent over the snooker table to take a shot I could feel the spots where those damn things were grinding into the bone and tickling the nerves.

Like I said, I missed a number of shots I normally would have made. It was difficult to concentrate under those circumstances, but that was still no excuse blowing my first homecoming match. From then on when I played snooker I tried real hard to whip my opponents quickly. Three-hour matches were much too painful. But the pain in my neck and back seemed to melt away each time I hit the dance floor at the USO parties. I must say they were fun. The women were abundant, the music loud, and the booze plentiful. And all for free.

The last USO-sponsored dance was held at the Minnequa Club, a big public meeting hall on the south side of town on the banks of Minnequa Lake, the only natural lake around town. The lake was still fairly pretty despite years of neglect and tons of nocturnal trash dumping. You couldn't fish on it, or water ski; only swim in it if you dared, and only if the water was clear that day. Anyway, that night, I got reacquainted with Maggie Danna.

This may sound like bragging, but I had grown accustomed to spending most of these long evenings on the dance floor jitterbugging with one local dame after another. They weren't actually standing in line to dance with me, but when the great old music of Glenn Miller, Spike Jones, and Tommy and Harry Dorsey blared from the bandstand, they weren't exactly bashful in grabbing my hand and occasionally pinching my butt. I can't remember having to ask any of the ladies to dance. Except for Maggie Danna.

It was funny. Before the festivities around town began, Julia Gail and Sophia had teamed up to teach me the latest steps, but much to their surprise I had snatched each one of them and, in turn, showed them a few steps right out of the Arthur Murray textbook. My moves had been choreographed over many late nights at the Paris dance halls under Chloe's very patient, expert instruction. I missed her some, especially on the dance floor, and I must say, in the bedroom. It had been a long time and I was getting real tempted to latch on to one of the local babes who sure appeared willing.

When Maggie Danna walked into the Minnequa Club that night I was real happy, but somehow I felt intimidated having her around. I don't know why. Maybe I was bashful or something. The other dames didn't make me feel unsure of myself but she sure did. Maggie had a strange effect on me. And it really kind of pissed me off. I was out there to handle the broads, not let them handle me. Maggie's blonde, curly hair, her sweet smile and her voluptuous figure made her a very popular dance partner. So that night, I mustered up my courage, and for the last dance on the last night of USO-sponsored events, I took her hand before anyone else could.

She accepted, and the enchanting sound of Frank Sinatra and Ella Fitzgerald's "Blue Moon" reverberated around us. I have to admit, I was enthralled. Her smell, her skin, her breath on my neck, the wisp of her hair across my chin when I pulled back to look into her eyes – man, all of that was hard to handle. I didn't want the song to end, and when it did, I stammered and stuttered like a schoolboy to get the words out.

"Can I see you home? You do remember me?"

"Yes, I remember you, and no, my cousin is here and he has a car," Maggie retorted. "But you can come by my house tomorrow if you like," she threw her nose in the air and strutted off.

Bitch, I thought, but that opinion soon melted away as I eyed her graceful, spike-heeled stride through the exit and into the darkness. Great legs. Great ass. And bad attitude. Just what I was looking for. Not like the wallflower she was in high school; that's for sure. I would definitely stop by her house tomorrow. Wait a minute. Stop by her house? I'd heard she still lived at her family's farmhouse east of town, and it would take me forty-five minutes to drive way out there; that is, if Carlo would let me use his car.

Later that night I went to my brother's house, a little wobbly and a little lonesome. I woke him up. He quietly let me in, guarding against waking Julia Gail and the babies. Hot coffee on the stove and a little brotherly love were what I needed. I asked him about Maggie Danna. He said she worked at the Army depot, and that she was some of kind of math and chemistry whiz.

As far as her childhood, I knew some about the murders, but Carlo knew more. What he knew of Maggie's story was a real shock, and by the time Carlo was finished, my coffee was cold, my head hurt and my heart had dropped to my stomach.

I decided if I had one ounce of strength left in me in the morning (and that might be tough to muster with what I knew would be a rip-roaring hangover), I vowed to drive that twenty-two miles east of town just to see her again. Carlo said he would let me use his car if I put gas in it.

~

Maggie

I came to learn dear Maggie was tough to pry things loose from. Particularly her private thoughts. I took me years to get this out of her. As she drove home with her cousin

Louie that night, Maggie admitted she regretted her offer to the stout, shy, silly little Sicilian boy whom she once liked in high school, but soon promptly forgot about after graduation. Not very flattering, I would say.

She said was trying to remember what she had liked about him. Maybe it was his reserve and his reticence, even though she knew by his reputation that he was a rough and tumble sort who, despite his size, could handle his own in the frequent backyard brawls between the wops and bojons. And that night, despite her professed anger for extending the invitation on a whim, she found his bashful beam and his timid, ill-at-ease approach rather cute and somewhat alluring. Now that's better.

Maybe what little affection she had for the pipsqueak was returning. *My God, no!* She had to dismiss her feelings as childhood infatuation. No other way to handle it, she thought.

Plus in her high heels, which she immediately kicked off the second she closed the car door because her feet hurt like hell, she was at least two inches taller than him. But, boy, could he dance, and that last dance was the best of the night, perhaps the best ever.

Wait a minute. What are you thinking you stupid woman? Yet he moved in such a sensuous way. Maybe she underestimated him.

Maggie had had plenty of offers from plenty of men of every size, shape, age, rich and poor and of just about every national origin. She became very skillful with her consistent rejections, mostly remaining polite but direct in repulsing their solicitations. There had been no lovers in her life so far, just a few dates and a little front seat petting, with each episode turning out unworthy of follow-up and her squelching the notion with little hesitation.

But why this little guy? Why was he different? Why had she offered the invitation? She didn't do that kind of thing. Men came to her. She never invited them, and she couldn't understand why she had done so this time, especially when she knew her family would be gone that next afternoon and she would be alone with him. She would make sure she cut things short, real short, she decided. What she needed to be doing was composing her response to the job offers she'd received so far and make up her mind about which company to join. She was not about to waste her time with some horny little ex-GI who acted like the schoolboy.

But he was so cute, and God, could he dance, she thought. *God could he dance.*

~

Believe it or not Maggie and I spent quite a bit of time together during the weeks that followed that last USO dance. But it darn near ended before it got started that very next day. I drove out to her place on what started out as a glorious Saturday afternoon, and yes, I was nursing that hangover and, yes, I was hoping for the best with her. Anyway, I will get to that later. What's important is, as we got to know each other, I began to understand how this woman was shaped. Not her hourglass figure; that in itself is beyond comparison, but rather what molded her, distilled her and polished her into the person she is. Gore and grit were the two words that came to mind at a first blush description of Maggie Danna's ascension through her life so far.

I also soon discovered that with Maggie, you never got it all from her in one chunk. She would slowly peel back layer after layer of the shell in which she had encased herself for her own protection. Maggie told me that when she had returned to her family's farm from the orphanage (now this was before high school, one layer at a time, you see), her Uncle Vincennes and his family had embraced her and each worked in their own special way to help her forget her past and concentrate on her future.

She thought she responded well. Night after night, she said, she fought the demons that haunted her dreams. Sure sounded familiar to me. Meeting the Devil and all. Every day, she panicked if she found herself enclosed in a room with no visible sunlight or means of immediate exit. She hated basements. She wouldn't go into elevators, although there weren't many in Pueblo that she had to worry about.

It quickly became apparent that Maggie's strong will, her grit, was clearly an outgrowth of her early childhood trauma; the gore was the burdens of growing to adolescence in the orphanage. You either went insane from those demons or you cast them off and built up your resistance, as Maggie had, to become extremely independent, self-disciplined and in absolute control of your emotions at all times. She would never let herself become vulnerable again. Boy, I found that out the hard way.

She made it clear that she loved her adoptive family, but she knew she had to make it on her own. There was no doubt when I'd sit and listen to her gradually ease out of her shell that she relied on her wit and brains first, and her charm and her beauty later, if those secondary attributes ever became necessary.

Julia Gail also helped fill in some of the blanks about Maggie. Julia Gail had worked part-time during the war at the munitions manufacturing and storage facility that the Army was building on the main rail line south and east of town. It was the same facility at which Maggie was also eventually employed. Julia Gail didn't know Maggie very well at first, she said, but the girl's image and reputation at the plant grew as the months went by. According to Julia Gail, as soon as the war broke out, Maggie was one of the first women to volunteer as a technician at the plant. Most women at that time went to work as clerks, typists or accountants. But not Maggie. She used her skills to work her way up through specialized channels. The Army recognized, and soon the key people at the plant realized, that because of the flat, open terrain in that part of the state, the facility could become an excellent location to test the rapidly expanding arsenal of conventional American weapons. Maggie had been one of the first to come to that conclusion, and wasn't about to miss out on being a part of making that a reality for the war effort.

The mission at the plant and the job of every employee was to find ways to kill more of our country's enemies and destroy more of their real estate with better and more efficient lethal detonations. Maggie was one of the few women, Julia Gail said, to quickly advance on the assembly line which, at the peak of production, turned out ten thousand rounds of one hundred five-millimeter artillery shells a day. Maggie had particularly liked the intricacies of assembling the triggering mechanisms, and soon became a chief quality control inspector. That position led to a role supporting the assembled staff of engineers and scientists on the testing range.

Maggie had stellar mathematical skills that brought her into the inner circle of the calibration and trajectory teams, and she became a key member of a select group that worked day and night to perfect a shell that was at least as potent as the German's fabled '88 artillery round. She admitted to me once rather sheepishly that what gave her the most pleasure from her job was observing the test firings and visualizing the destruction that her bombs were making on Hitler's and Tojo's military apparatus.

Maggie eventually became one of only three women on the design and test firing teams, and at twenty-one years of age, she became somewhat of a celebrity at the facility, more with the men than with most of the women, however. She certainly would have photographed well for one of the famous Rosie the Riveter posters, but Julia Gail described her as better suited as a surrogate model for a Betty Gable pin-up. Her beauty was striking, and as she realized this more and more, she purposefully dressed down in work shirts and baggy pants to hide her shapely curves. Makeup remained at home on her vanity, an imperative lesson Julia Gail also learned and used to avoid the catcalls and smirks.

Maggie told me that shortly after the war ended she had gotten two offers, one from Lockheed Aircraft and the other from Raytheon Corporation. Both offers included advanced training and free college tuition if she wished to attend. Maggie was giving both offers serious thought the night she wandered back into my life, only to promptly step out of it once again.

Chapter 42
Hangovers and Mobsters Can Last for Days

On that bright clear Saturday afternoon while my headache and I were on our way to visit Maggie for the first of many lively, gut-wrenching discussions, I drove Carlo's old Buick right past Jimmy Clemente's cheese stand. I didn't realize it was about halfway between the outskirts of town and Maggie's farm. I noticed that behind and slightly to the side of the cheese stand stood a lovely two-story brick and dark-wood-sided Tudor-style house. I slowed down to take in the beauty of the place with its dark shutters, wrap-around porch and slate roof. Three gables across the front accented the lines of the house, but the dirt yard in front adorned by an old dusty brown Chevrolet, possibly a '37 or '38, detracted from the scene.

I didn't remember the house being there when I would occasionally accompany Carlo to Jimmy's to retrieve Angelina's weekly order of goat, cheddar, Romano and mozzarella. Jimmy must have built it since I'd been gone. Whatever the case, I hadn't given much thought to the scum who had severely strangled my town for so many years, and it was strange since I'd gotten back that Carlo and I hadn't had one conversation about Jimmy, the mob, or any of that stuff that had at one time dominated so much of our lives. I wondered as I sped past that little big man's establishment when my town's menace would rear his pointy, ugly little head once again with a new, reinvigorated sense of purpose.

That day, Jimmy's great cheese emporium looked as if it were closed. I glanced in my rearview mirror past the empty parking lot to the decrepit old storefront shack that served as Jimmy's place of business, wondering what truly went on behind those cracked, whitewashed walls and under that leaky roof. I wondered if Jimmy worked on Saturday. Just then the car behind me turned into the dusty lot, and I caught a glimpse of a tiny fellow step out the rickety front door of the house to presumably greet his customer, or maybe shoo them away.

Five days a week must be a work heavy load for the old man, I thought. I knew he didn't work on Sunday. That was the Lord's Day. What I didn't know was that Jimmy was actually working overtime – not making cheese, but making horrible mischief once again. It would take nearly thirty years for Pueblo, my family especially, to fully appreciate the breadth of his evil and to understand who the little Mafia ringleader really was.

Jimmy's true identity became known to my town and the rest of the country thanks to a grizzled, pot-bellied cigar-chomping veteran newspaper reporter by the name of William J. "Wild Bill" Gagnon. I got to know Wild Bill around 1962 or '63 shortly after he came to town. He didn't gallop in on a white stallion with his guns blazing, like most of Colorado's wild Bills, but instead drove into town in a rather ancient '54 Ford wood-paneled station wagon filled with his clothes, his old yellow newspapers and not much more.

I served him a bowl of spaghetti and a Coke his first night here. He didn't drink anything but Coke, but he drank it by the gallon. Bill told me he'd arrived from San Diego to work for the *Chieftain Journal*. By then, he'd been in the newspaper business for fifteen years, working mostly in the West. Up until then I didn't like newspaper reporters much, mostly because they never seemed to get the facts straight, always slanting the stories one way or the other to suit their own opinions. But Bill was different. This old codger played it straight down the line, every time, right from the start.

I fed Bill a lot over the years and read everything he wrote with the best by far being his unauthorized biographical series on Pueblo's most famous crook. Come to find out that Bill had been chasing Jimmy Clemente for years and exposing the little cheese man had become an obsession for him. That's why he took the job at the *Chieftain Journal*. But it was after Jimmy left us for good that Wild Bill got the story of a lifetime.

~

Wild Bill

William J. Gagnon, with a two-day growth of salt and pepper beard, reeking of cigar smoke and aimlessly wiping a stain from his ever-present red, white and blue striped tie, was slumped over his gun-metal grey metal desk one afternoon studying a beautiful red leather-bound book. Wild Bill seldom smiled unless he had some public official whom he'd caught with his hand scooping cash from the city coffers sitting uncomfortably in his office stammering to answer his razor-sharp questions. But today Wild Bill was grinning from ear-to-ear. He couldn't believe what he was reading. His spit-soaked stogie hung from the corner of his mouth, the flame long extinguished. His reading glasses, streaked with grime, were pushed up to the crown of his hairless head. He leaned back in his swivel chair, taking a breather. He started to chuckle, which because it was such a rarity to hear Bill laugh, startled city editor George Lowry, who sat ten feet away reading wire copy off the Associated Press ticker.

Bill was old school. He was a man who took his profession of journalism as seriously as he took his Catholicism. He was a crusader. He fought evil and corruption with a poison pen as potent as the bite of an angry rattler. And now, in Bill's hands, was a gift from the god of scoops, delivered that morning wrapped in brown paper with a white string in a neatly tied bow. No return address, just the familiar seal of the Federal Bureau of Investigation stamped in the top left hand corner. Bill knew who had gone to the trouble of wrapping and sending the greatest gift of his career, but he would never tell. Bill would go to his grave protecting a source. The year was 1971. Bill would be seventy next month.

Lying opened before him Bill had the five-hundred-page personal, intimate diary of Black Jim "Jimmy" Clemente. Written by hand in simple bold print with a blue fountain pen, Jimmy had told it all, pulling no punches and keeping no secrets. Most of Jimmy's contemporaries were either dead or had long ago disappeared, but if they had been alive when the FBI found this diary among the Mafia don's personal effects, the federal prisons would have had a surge in population. It took Bill only a few days to verify the authenticity of the journal and Jimmy's telling descriptions of the main events. Bill's stories began two weeks later with a front-page banner headline. It took a dozen articles to tell it all.

This is the way Bill told it, bringing to life in stark, vivid prose the many facets of the mysterious little man and his sinister accomplishments. Black Jim Clemente attended Mass each Sunday at Saint Teresa Parish Church on Lake Avenue. Jimmy was a creature of habit. He liked things orderly. No loose ends. His wife and lifelong love, Lizzy, sat with him in the second row pew. They had no children. It was just the two of them.

For twenty years, until he bought a new one for a special trip back east, Jimmy drove to church each Sunday in a seldom-washed brown 1937 Chevrolet, parking always in the same space. No one else ever parked in Jimmy's space. Jimmy liked brown cars. They blended in well with the dusty, windswept town in which he lived and over which he presided. He also liked Chevrolets. They also blended in. In fact, Jimmy himself blended in. He was the typical height and weight of his Sicilian brotherhood, and at about age twenty-five, began to lose his curly black hair. His creeping baldness bothered him a great deal, he told his diary, so what was left he combed over from side to side in a futile attempt to conceal the shiny dome.

His closest friends, and he had few, called him Mr. Clemente. His employees called him Boss. He always wore brown work pants and a white shirt, except to Mass, where he wore his brown suit, white shirt and brown tie. Not a pinstripe anywhere on him. He blended in so well, sometimes Jimmy liked the idea that people thought his car was driving itself. Then he would straighten up in his driver's seat to reveal his stern, dark-skinned face topped by his ever-present brown Fedora peering over the steering wheel, both hands clasped tightly to each side. He always drove the speed limit.

Jimmy was a lonely man, Bill told his readers. Men at the top usually were. Those were Jimmy's words. He worked very hard, and he kept to himself. He was polite, yet tight-lipped with his customers. He didn't tolerate idle chitchat. Without daring small talk, his customers entered his cheese stand and quickly exited, taking home their weekly supplies. Lizzy manned the hand-cranked cash register. Jimmy knew the aroma from the stand would strike his customer's nostrils from thirty yards up the road. He was proud of that, reveled in it, in fact. He devoted two whole pages in his diary to the various odors permeating from his place.

Those who visited Jimmy, those other than his cheese customers, never entered his stand through the front door. He made sure of that. They always entered from a door to the side and they always entered at night. They always parked their cars under a big, sweeping weeping willow, which rooted about fifty yards from the side entrance of the cheese stand. The tree obstructed the view of the cars from the road.

Jimmy always conducted his second, more important business at night. His nighttime visitors also were polite, uttering scarce words to him. During the war, he had the carpenter's union build Lizzy's dream house right next to the cheese stand. Although it was right next door, none of his customers ever got near the place. Neither did any of his associates, those nighttime visitors who entered through the side door.

The after-hours business was housed and conducted in a deep underground man-made cavern twenty feet beneath the floor of the cheese stand. Inside the huge dugout that penetrated the side of a sloping ravine was an enormous forty- by fifty-foot luxuriously appointed room. The front of Jimmy's cheese stand sat far back off the side of the well-traveled Colorado Highway 50 heading east. Jimmy took great pains in describing the engineering and architectural design of his sanctuary in his diary, and Bill spent one entire piece for the *Journal* on the subject.

Construction of Jimmy's hideaway was made fairly easy through the side of a natural dried up creek bed that dropped off a good distance behind the cheese emporium.

His elaborate headquarters was safely nestled beneath the earth's surface, secure from unwanted intrusion and hidden by the natural slope of the creek-carved ravine.

Even though Jimmy's bunker was sufficient distance below grade, the smells from the cheeses nestled in their display cases could not be ignored by those visiting Jimmy at his lair late at night. They were intoxicating, and Jimmy loved to describe their effect on his men long after he closed up shop for the day. Jimmy no longer noticed the aromas. He had grown use to them. Each one of his nighttime visitors had important things to hear from him as well. And important things to do for him when given the word.

Jimmy's underground refuge was well equipped with every modern-day feature. Since it was underground, there were no windows, and the door looked like any other cellar door, or Dorothy door. Dorothy doors were common around town, but not ones protecting underground multi-million-dollar, multi-faceted, multi-state business enterprises in rooms furnished with the finest Italian antiques, paintings and statuary money could buy. Jimmy's bunker and the businesses it shrouded were protected not only by a locked Dorothy door, but also by an elaborate, state-of-the-art security system. Trip wires surrounded all approaches to his property, encircling the perimeter and guarding the single, outside entrance. Jimmy was always concerned about the Feds discovering his hideaway and launching an invasion force to capture the king and his pawns. But the king was never captured because the cops never came. Once in a while a lone fox or coyote would wander by and trip one of the wires. With the sound of the alarm Jimmy's visitors would leap from their seats, and one among them would be assigned to investigate by scurrying through the twenty five-yard escape tunnel that ran at a steep angle out of the room and down the north side of the ravine. One could tell from which direction the un-welcomed guest was approaching by the location of the alarm that had gone off.

In one passage, Jimmy wrote vividly about a particular disturbance that prompted his uncontrollable anger. Rocco Vencenso was the unlucky one that night chosen to find the cause of the alarm. Rocco was too big to scurry off; rather he lumbered through the tunnel and for a long time, Jimmy watched his associates squirm in their seats while the racket of the alarm echoed off the walls. When it came the gunshot sounded like a cannon going off. Finally, Rocco came back with his prize trophy. Dangling by its tail in Rocco's bear-sized paw was a three-foot long silver fox that had tangled up in the trip wire. He had blasted the animal with a .357 magnum revolver drawn from his shoulder holster.

When the poor bastard returned with the dead fox in his hand, Jimmy beat Rocco about the head and shoulders with his blackjack so badly that he nearly died of a skull fracture. No one was ever allowed to fire a gun in or around Jimmy's compound. Those were the rules, and Jimmy's rules were never broken. Rocco's friends were not allowed to take him to the hospital until after the meeting ended and Jimmy had dismissed them for the night.

For these meetings Jimmy always sat behind his desk. His desk was an exact replica of the desk behind which his mentor, friend, and staunch supporter Lucky Luciano sat to conduct his business from his East Harlem headquarters. At the time of this diary entry, Lucky was five or so years in exile after cutting his wartime spying tit-for-tat deal with the United States government. Jimmy missed Lucky, he wrote, but he got along well with Lucky's handpicked successor to lead the Genovese family, Vito Genovese. Lucky had to leave his desk behind when he was deported home to Sicily. Vito had the Boss of Bosses' mahogany monstrosity put in storage. A fourteen-foot-long, hand-carved black walnut conference table with comfortable seating for six on each side ran perpendicular to Jimmy's see-your-face-in-the-shiny-surface-top desk. There were never more than twelve men attending Jimmy's meetings. They always arrived in no more than three cars, and they always parked under the giant willow tree, out of sight of passing vehicles or nosey pedestrians.

The meetings always began at eleven p.m. and ended at three o'clock the next morning. A late dinner of spaghetti and meatballs with plenty of grated goat cheese sprinkled on top was served at midnight. There was a kitchen in an anteroom off to the side of the main meeting room, and Jimmy made sure one among the invitees knew how to cook.

The designated cook would miss the first hour of the meeting preparing the meal for thirteen. Jimmy told his diary that he wasn't superstitious like so many of his fellow dons, so thirteen at his table didn't bother him. Lizzy could have cooked the dinner, but she was never invited to the meetings. No one attending Jimmy's meetings ever met her. Jimmy's guests never attended Mass with him, so they never saw Lizzy there, and Lizzy knew none of Jimmy's business associates. They didn't know what she looked like, or even if she really existed at all, and Jimmy liked it that way.

The meetings were held once a month. The agendas were prepared the week before and assembled by Jimmy alone. Some of the topics were issues on his mind; others were important matters to one or more of his invitees, or they were subjects important to New York and Mr. Genovese. No one was allowed to attend more than two meetings a year. It was against the rules for anyone to know more, or even nearly as much, as Jimmy did.

Jimmy wrote long passages about his meetings and the topics they covered. He waxed and waned philosophically about his moods, the tactics he implored and his leadership skills. He relished his power and wrote with huge self-aggrandizement. The meeting agendas were packed, especially after the war ended and restrictions on imports and exports were lifted. Jimmy wrote with glee that rationing was over. Once again, goods and services began to flow freely. Millions of Americans were coming home, getting married, starting the baby boom, and were looking for fun, excitement, and entertainment. The war was won. Life should be enjoyed. Returning veterans needed plenty of cheap booze. They needed to gamble. Their new businesses needed protection. They needed new fresh, young hookers to satisfy their carnal needs, and there was growing demand for help for the thousands who couldn't cope with the traumas of war. The white opium extract easily eased the pain, and the supply was plentiful. Good times were ahead, and in Jimmy's part of the country, the mob was on its comeback trail. He was ecstatic. Jimmy wrote rather eloquently and with precision-accuracy that he knew these demands would only multiply as the population around them exploded. So, as Jimmy kept saying, urging himself as he wrote, it was time to get busy.

"Our sleep is over," Jimmy would remind his audience when he gaveled his meetings to order. In his book his meeting-opening salvo was written in inch-high block letters and underlined thirteen times.

It was necessary for his new businesses to operate like his old businesses, but even better. For ultimate success they needed legitimate fronts, like his cheese business, through which daytime activities could protect one's nighttime ventures. However, the new businesses must be more sophisticated than Jimmy's cheese business, Jimmy preached. They needed white-collar businesses, not just bars or restaurants or food stands, from which to operate and from which to shroud their criminal enterprises.

Jimmy told his men and later wrote, quoting himself, that, "we need to buy car dealerships. We need to own insurance companies, gas stations, hardware stores, building supply outlets. We even need a few good lawyers in well-placed law firms. And we need contractors who can build for us and let the unions control the workers on the job sites. We need financial experts and accountants who can keep the money circulating through the right places and through the hands of the right people. Good accountants to help us avoid paying taxes. We need friendly bankers. Loan sharking isn't profitable enough, plus it get messy at times."

Jimmy speculated that these types of businesses would help him become more respectable and help influence the politicians who provide the ultimate protection. Jimmy was a self-taught student of economics and business management. He had only been through the fifth grade. He was embarrassed about that, and never disclosed it publicly, only to his diary. But he didn't let that hold him back. He started with the principles of Adam Smith and moved through those early texts to appreciate the later works of John Kenneth Galbraith and John Maynard Keynes. He loved the so-called robber barons, particularly stories about railroaders Jay Gould and Commodore Vanderbilt. Of course, books about the life and times of Mr. Rockefeller also were on his reading list. Jimmy was particularly fond of and fascinated by the story of fellow kinsmen Amadeo P. Giannini, the founder of Bank of America. Jimmy fantasized that someday he would shed his cloak of secrecy and move his prized desk into the executive suite on the top floor of one of those new skyscrapers now dotting America's cityscapes.

Jimmy's absolute sway over his territory and his people came through his contorted brilliance coupled with uncanny business acumen. That's what made him very effective and very dangerous, Bill concluded in installment six. Jimmy's orders were precise, and he expected results.

The money was flowing in at an accelerated pace and proper investment of those abundant funds spelled a prosperous future. By instinct Jimmy knew his country's appetite for the old days and old ways of corruption would subside sooner or later. The old ways of doing business must be abandoned for new ways, because the new ways would shield the operations of the old ways. Owning and controlling legitimate businesses was the only alternative. Plus he had his eye on new opportunities. His territory included the great but barren state of Nevada, the least populated state of them all.

By the end of the 1940s, as Jimmy was just hitting his stride, he revealed to his diary that discussions already were underway about the creation of another gambling Mecca out West, one not vulnerable to foreign influence, particularly from the crazy, untrustworthy Cubans. To carry out this assignment, Jimmy needed plenty of money, plenty of power, and all the right people. Jimmy eventually got his money and lined up his support for early control of Las Vegas. Even Bill was shocked as he read this entry. Nobody had a clue that Jimmy's tentacles had reached that far.

Bill emphasized in installment eight that Pueblo couldn't have known these details about Jimmy Clemente, the little cheese man on Highway 50, especially in those early days. Yet its citizens had always been leery, wary and cautious when the Boss' name was even uttered in their midst, always in hushed voices. After the war people soon realized the Mafia was back on the rise, but few knew of the power Jimmy wielded from his shielded fortress until Bill received his gift from the FBI so many years later.

So Wild Bill told it all, all that he could tell from that red leather bound journal. His pursuit of Black Jim had finally come to an end. He told the stories in great, fascinating depth, right through installment twelve which spanned the forties, fifties and most of the sixties. Right up to when Jimmy checked out for good.

Even though Bill knew more than anyone else by far, and even though Bill and I became trusted friends, there would have been a few more installments to Bill's sensational series if he had learned the truth about my involvement with Black Jim, and how the little cheese man almost took my family down. But Bill never knew that part of the story.

Chapter 43
A Wet Sloppy Kiss and a Friendly Collie

When I think back on that bright, beautiful Saturday afternoon and my first time alone with Maggie Danna, I remember joking to myself as I pulled into her driveway that I was more nervous then when I faced down that Nazi platoon. She seemed like an incredible specimen of self-confidence and downright brilliance, and I have to admit, I was a little intimidated.

I wondered if there was a vulnerable side to her. I wondered if she had a soft spot, and if I could find it. Carlo said from what he knew she was double tough. He called her a real ball buster, but I've always liked a challenge, finding an opponent's weakness, like in a snooker match. It was the best analogy I could come up with. Once you've discovered the weakness, you had the advantage. If this woman gave me a chance, I sensed she would present the equivalent of the snooker match of the century, and the stakes would not be a penny a point.

The place was quiet and seemed deserted when I pulled to a stop to the side of the sweeping front porch of the house. It was very similar to Jimmy Clemente's front porch accenting the lovely farmhouse architecture. A lazy old Collie snoozing in the shade of an enormous maple tree stirred awake and made a half-hearted attempt at a bark, then wagged its tail and seemed to smile as I approached him to pat his head.

I called out, but there was no answer. The heavy wooden front door was open so I rattled the screen door with a loud knock. No answer. I went around to the side, toward the barn, and called out again. Still no answer. I stepped off the porch and strolled across the side lawn to the barn, opened the double doors and went inside. It was cleaner than some living rooms I'd been in. A third call, and still no response. When I turned to exit, there she was in the doorway of the barn, straddling a bicycle, staring at me, not saying a word.

"Hello soldier," she finally said. "I was just out for a ride. I saw you pull into the driveway, but wanted to finish my ride first."

The sun was to her back, its rays bouncing off the chrome fender of her bike, and the flash blinded me temporarily. I shielded my eyes and started toward her. I could tell she was smiling but it was a smile that somehow lacked sincerity. She was dressed in a red and black checked flannel shirt and baggy overall work pants held up by shoulder straps secured tight by brass buttons. A red bandanna tied back her hair, which was clumped, and hanging from her crown in several blonde, skinny ropes soaked from the sweat that sparkled from her forehead. She looked a mess and I could tell she gave a damn less. It was quite plain she hadn't bothered in the least to gussy up for my visit. In fact, she was making the opposite point, no doubt. She looked exactly like she'd just finished the overnight shift at the steel mill.

"I'm a civilian now," I reminded her. "I wasn't sure anyone was home, so I was about to leave."

"Why didn't you think anyone was home, when the front door was open?" her voice held more than a hint of sarcasm. I wasn't a fool. I didn't need to be slapped in the face to find the facts – I knew my instincts were right. It was going to be a real test dealing with her.

"I don't know. I was hoping you weren't being careless, although I haven't heard of any crimes in this neighborhood for some time," I blurted out as I approached her. The second the words were out of my mouth, I wished I could choke them back. By then she was already pedaling away.

God, what an asshole, I thought to myself. How could I even mention something like that? Maggie peered back over her shoulder at me with a harsh look.

"No there hasn't been a crime here for some time," she called out, a tiny trail of dust drifting above her bike's back tire. "Well since you're here, I made some iced tea before I went for my ride. Why don't you take a seat on the porch and I will bring it out?"

I hated iced tea. Why did all the desirable women in my life want to serve me iced tea? Thank God Chloe hadn't liked tea either. Mostly all we drank were espresso and wine while we were together.

Maggie parked her bicycle along the side of the house and strolled rather nonchalantly to the rear kitchen door. She was in no hurry to fetch my tea, I could tell. And I was in no hurry to have it. I stood in the driveway and watched her intently. She swayed as she walked, the baggy pants trying hard to conceal what I imagined to be the fine flesh beneath.

I did as I was told, stepped up onto the porch and took a seat in the white wicker rocker next to the coffee table and front porch swing. The Collie joined me. She was gone a long time. Time passed slowly. This was getting ridiculous. I must have sat there waiting for her for twenty minutes. I tried to rationalize the wait thinking she was cleaning up and changing clothes. Time slowly marched on.

I was about to leave when she emerged, still in her bike riding best, carrying a tray with two glasses filled with dark brown liquid that looked more like burnt coffee than tea. I didn't see any ice floating at the surface. She had topped off the gourmet serving with a plate of what looked like little dark brown bricks. I guessed they might have once been offered as chocolate brownies. At least the colors of the food and drink were coordinated, I thought.

"Sorry, no ice. And I baked these about a week ago so they may be a little hard," she proclaimed, bending to scratch the Collie's head and turning her back to me to look out across the yard. I could have sworn I heard her snicker.

Boy, this will be interesting, I thought to myself, and despite my recent shameful remark, I couldn't help but go on the offense.

"Look Maggie. I think that's your name. I appreciate the lovely snacks you prepared. You shouldn't have gone to so much trouble. You know, you really didn't have to invite me all the way out here last night. Nobody twisted your arm, so I can leave right now. It was nice meeting your dog," I declared and rose from my hard, uncomfortable seat to walk past her and down the steps.

Out of the corner of my eye, I caught a mischievous grin crossing Maggie's lips as she turned to place the tray on the table. "Johnny, see, I remember your name, please sit down. It's such a common name. How could I forget?"

I just kept walking, then turned for one last look. I noticed her smile had faded. She continued, "I won't blame you if you leave. I'm sort of sorry, I think, and I know I am acting like a bitch by the way. Look, I'm not sure why I invited you at all, but I did, so let's spend a few minutes together pretending to get to know each other again, and then you can leave, and then we'll both be happy."

I wasn't too far off the steps, so I stopped. Acting on nothing more than pure, unconscious impulse, I turned back, climbed up to her, grabbed her by the waist, pulled her to me and kissed her full on the mouth. A big, sloppy, wet one. Don't ask me why. At that moment I couldn't stand her and I should have kept walking, but I kissed her anyway, crazy as it was. But before I let her loose, I sensed her stiff resistance had slackened.

I took my seat without another word. She did the same. A few tense, silent moments passed. Neither of us even looked at the other. And then as she swung on the porch swing and sipped her warm, nasty, stank dark tea, she declared, "I should call the sheriff and have you arrested for assault."

I ignored her. I had already watered the bushes with my full glass of the nauseating liquid, and I just sat in the rocker, looking out across the lawn and taking my turn to scratch the Collie's head.

"What's the dog's name, by the way," I asked.

"His name is Killer," she responded, expertly keeping a straight face. I couldn't help but smile at that one.

"Nice doggy," I cooed to Killer as he looked up at me with droopy, sleepy eyes.

Other than that the conversation hadn't progressed much since our spontaneous encounter, and I was pondering whether she was serious about the assault charges and if I should actually leave this time before the sheriff came.

"But I won't," she suddenly proclaimed. "Have you thrown in jail, that is, unless you try that again."

"What? Scratch Killer's head?" I joked.

She ignored my rather ingenious stab at humor. "My aunt and uncle will be home soon and if you get to meet them, they will think you are just like all the rest of the GIs who invite themselves out here only to be made fools of before I send them on their way."

Casting my unblemished arrest record to the wind I turned to her. "What are you anyway? Some kind of freak? In France they called them lesbians, girl queers who used to perform for us in the strip joints. They seemed to like each other better than the men. You hate men, or only yourself?"

"Wow!" Maggie exclaimed. "You really saw two women perform on stage and make love to each other? That would have been very exciting. No, even though it's none of your business, I'm not a man hater, and no I don't like women in that sense. However, I have many other things on my mind these days other than hooking up with some horny GI, screwing him and getting pregnant to help re-populate America."

"Whoever said I wanted to hook up with you in the first place and what's this about screwing? I should have you arrested for soliciting. I think they call it prostitution," I came back.

"You're insufferable," she huffed.

"Look Maggie, I came out here today in what was one time a sincere attempt to get to know you better. I've heard a lot about you since I've been back and I remember how you openly flirted with me in high school so I was curious, that's all. I heard you were some hotshot at the Army depot. You like to make bombs, artillery shells, grenades and the like. That's pretty interesting work for a woman and all. I'll bet you impressed a lot of people," I said with a sincere tone of interest, hoping my questions would bring something meaningful to the conversation. But even my bold act of sincerity didn't seem to work.

"I never flirted with you. Ever! And what do you mean, for a woman and all?" she spat angrily. "I worked my butt off out there. I learned everything I could, and I took risks to get ahead. I stayed late and I put up with all the bullshit from the supervisors and assembly line workers, especially the women, who were jealous of me. They were the ones who thought I got ahead by working on my back."

She stopped, only to catch her breath. "Now I have a chance to leave this hellhole and go to work with a big company. Not because I am a woman, but because I know damn well what I'm doing." Her fist was clinched and her arm slashed through the air as she made that last declaration. It seemed if she'd said it many times before for the benefit of people around her, at least those interested in more than her good looks. For the others who cared only for her boobs and not her brains, it was easy to tell they were instantly cast aside.

How could I make her put me in the category of brains over boobs? My next attempt was feeble. "There aren't any companies around here that do that kind of work; at least that I know of," I offered, trying not to sound too stupid. After I said it, I really felt like an idiot.

She sighed. "No there aren't any companies like that here. The most we have here are fireworks stands on the Fourth of July. The companies I'm talking about are back East with big government contracts to maintain our munitions stockpiles so we're not caught with our pants down again, or should I say, with our guns unloaded, if, for instance, the Russians decide to get ornery," she explained.

Christ, I'd never heard a woman talk that way before. She's unbelievable, I thought. I'll bet she did hold her own with those snotty bitches at the plant and the men who thought she was a pushover. I tensed, fully expecting another ambush from her, and hoping I could react this time with an ounce of intelligence.

"My mind is really out there, trying to figure out what to do, so I'm sorry if I offended you or made you feel unwelcome. I have a lot to think about," she said. I was beginning to get the feeling she was about to come around when I blew it again.

"So, if you take a job, would you go back East?" Fucking idiot.

"That's what I said, the companies and the jobs are back East, in New Jersey mainly," she responded all-too-politely.

"Oh," was all I could muster. "That's nice."

With that last remark, it was like I had dropped my guard and some burly staff sergeant in basic training was about to right cross me into an unexpected nap. And I was right.

"Nice? Is that all you have to say?" she shot at me. "What about the technical process. How they're made. You know, the bombs. Aren't you curious? Are you curious about anything?" she swung with another verbal punch that landed right where she aimed. I saw it coming but couldn't duck.

"Look, little Miss Maggie, to tell you the truth I could care less how you make those goddamn things," I struck back. "I've had them drop around me, twenty at a time. Breaking my eardrums and killing everyone in sight. I've seen them destroy a hospital full of wounded American GIs and sick babies. I've seen them take the head off one of my buddies standing right beside me, and I have a few of pieces of them stuck in my back and neck. So, lady, I can tell you that learning about making them from you doesn't interest me. I wish we had no use for them, and there wasn't a job for you to go to in New Jersey or wherever the hell you think you're going. But I know there's a reason for you doing what you do, and it's probably a good reason, for our country and all. So, go do it. Good luck."

"Okay, okay, I got it. Don't be so sensitive," she replied.

We continued to go at each other, back and forth, bantering; berating, riling, and recoiling for the rest of the afternoon. It was dusk by the time both of us seemed to grow weary of the verbal rugby match, and as I rose to leave, I extended my hand to for a manly shake. I didn't expect more and was unsure if I wanted more. She stood from her porch swing and extended her hand. It was warm to the touch. It was the hand that held the glass filled with awful tea. She had held it grasped in a tight clench during our entire debate.

She came close and her eyes narrowed as if burrowing into my brain, looking for something, anything to attach to. She looked away at the sound of an approaching car, breaking the all-too-brief moment. I held my gaze until her eyes returned, but by then the link was broken. But I had felt it. It had been there for an instant. She pumped my hand like that recruiter welcoming me to the Army, and I turned and walked down the steps.

I saw what appeared to be a new Buick park beside Carlo's car in the driveway. I walked over as the car doors swung open and made a point to greet each one to emerge warmly. I hadn't met anyone in her family before, so it took a few minutes for the polite but awkward pleasantries. It was strange, but almost immediately I felt a connection to her Aunt Carmella and Uncle Vincennes. They had kind eyes. Their children, Tanya and Terrance, were detained by their parents long enough to shake hands with me with a straight look in my eye before being dismissed to romp in the yard with Killer who had suddenly perked up at the sound of the children's shrieks.

As I was ready to leave, Carmella grabbed me by the shoulders and leaned in to whisper in my ear, "be patient with her; she's worth it." I nodded and turned back to the porch to see if Maggie was still there. She wasn't. I got in and drove off toward town.

Neither one of us had asked to see the other again. I didn't want to make the first move, and I was sure she wouldn't either. So we left our next meeting, if one were to occur at all, up in the air. Even though I was exhausted from the head-butting match, I wanted to turn the car around and go back for more. But I didn't. I knew we were probably at a stalemate. Stubborn, yes. Stupid, likely. Who knew what was next? I sure didn't. I thought both of us were snookered, unable to shoot at a money ball. In fact, both of us were left without a shot at all. The score was tied with very few points to the advantage of either.

Chapter 44
A Good Head Taller Than Me

Although the marathon deliberations with Maggie that afternoon had left me ready for either a long nap or two shots of pure scotch, I couldn't head home just then. I had agreed to have dinner at the restaurant with my mother, Nicole and Silvio that evening at seven o'clock.

I had eaten Angelina's a few times since I'd been back and concluded that even though my mother's cooking was still spectacular, it had lost something in that setting. When Angelina cooked for my brother and sisters and me at home it was different. When she made the sauces for the pasta or she baked the eggplant in her special seasoning and spices, her love flowed through her spatula. Here at the restaurant the ingredients may have been the same but she something was missing. Maybe the love. It didn't taste the same somehow. Or maybe I was jealous that others were sharing in my mother's delights.

Anyway as I drove along, passing Jimmy's cheese stand again, I was tired and cranky and wanted a bath, and wished I hadn't tossed that glass of Maggie's terrible tea into the bushes. I detested iced tea, like I said, and hers was the worst I'd ever tasted, but at that moment I was so thirsty I would've drunk that stuff if I'd had some. The last thing I needed right then was a night of more mental jousting, so the thought of putting up with Silvio for the next three hours was not the least bit appealing.

My first meeting with Silvio had been awkward to say the least. Both Nicole and my mother had begged me to be nice and cordial, so I did my best to tolerate the little squirt (I call him that, even though he's a good head taller than me). It was easy to see that Silvio was the master of false sincerity. He was transparent as a clear glass window. Right off, he embraced and kissed me on both cheeks as a phony expression of his affection. When men do that, it had better be for real. His effort landed flat and I think even Angelina realized the gesture was half-assed. Yet she told me later how much she "so loved having all three of her boys together as a family." When she said that, I nearly lost my lunch. But I had to give the guy a chance. At the very least, I gave him credit for bringing my mother out of her hardened, self-imposed shell after all those years mourning my father. Even though all of us, with the exception of Angelina, suspected his reasons for giving her something other than her house and church day in and day out were purely selfish (Carlo said she was the only thing between him and bankruptcy and his father's boot up his ass), it was a good thing, so what could I do but give him a pass for now?

On the other hand, Carlo wasn't quite sure about the pass. He couldn't stand to be around the guy and he kept telling me that I'd soon find out that he was everything he had warned me about, and more. Carlo said the business appeared to be making loads of money, and he attributed that solely to my mother's cooking, but he was convinced that most of that dough was only lining Silvio's pockets.

As I drove, I tried to push Miss Maggie out of my weary brain. I told myself I would go into this next meeting with Silvio with an open mind. I would try to put aside my brother-in-law's brand of superficial crap and instead concentrate on his good points, if he had any. One of the many good things the Army taught me was to size up a man on his actions, not his loud mouth. There were many times when at first a GI would come off as the biggest pain in the ass you could imagine, but when it counted, like in a firefight, he would come through, like save your goddamn life or something. All that stuff about not judging a book by its cover, I found to be good advice.

Carlo had made up his mind about Silvio. For me, the next card hadn't been dealt. Dinner was waiting and so was a good, stiff drink. That was worth looking forward to. I also knew tonight there would be a new menu at Angelina's Fine Italian Restaurant. Every week my mother changed her menu, which assured that the restaurant would be full for next six nights running. Angelina insisted any establishment with her name on it be closed on Sunday, so they had to make their profit from twelve, six-night seatings, two servings each night. Occasionally they squeezed in a third seating if food supplies were still sufficient to avoid sacrificing quality.

My mother cooked only one full meal each week and never repeated the same dishes twice. Her command and control of the kitchen was much like a military operation. She required that her subordinate chefs only observe her initial preparation and presentation of each new appetizer, entrée and dessert, and for the next five nights, they were responsible as best they could to reproduce each of her perfected delicacies, but in quantities sufficient to meet the two or three-seating demand. If any of her chefs failed her nightly inspections and tastings, they were given only one more chance to improve to her standards or be fired.

As I pulled up to the restaurant, my stomach growled as I spied the menu. Tonight, I would be enjoying:

The appetizer: *Crema di fagioli;*
The first entrée: *Risotto con aragosta e gamberi;*
The second entrée: *quaglie con uva;*
The vegetable: *Melanzane al forno;*
The dessert: *Crostatine di frutta fresca*

I decided when I arrived at the table I would concentrate on the food and try my best to ignore the impending conversation. As I walked into the restaurant my mind wandered back to Maggie. How was she spending her evening? I suspected she was composing her letters of response to the corporate job offers. Then she might be fielding questions from her family about her afternoon guest. I was willing to bet that she was trying like hell not to think about me, this wonderful guy who had become such an intriguing, obstinate, yet alluring household guest. As my ego really caught hold I speculated that I would be the topic of the evening. But then I reasoned, as my ego deflated, she would probably dismiss most of their questions with monosyllable responses. Yet maybe, just maybe, she found me the least bit interesting, even if she wouldn't admit it.

Before I got too close to the table I diverted my path to the bar to grab a fortifying cocktail. A double scotch it was. I hung at the bar and took in the aromas from the kitchen, trying to concentrate on the forthcoming meal and not the forthcoming forum. They were in between seatings so the place was only about half-full. I could tell activity in the kitchen was at a frenzied pace in preparation for the eight o'clock seating.

They were all there at the table waiting for me. I moved toward them, sipping my scotch, feeling the flames lick my throat and the warmth hit my stomach. Big, genuine smiles, except for Silvio's, greeted me when I arrived. Even though I'd seen my mother and sister two days before, I could not hold back my affection for them, and the gratefulness I felt at seeing them again. Our hugs and kisses were abundant. I shook hands with my brother-in-law and avoided the pecks on the cheek.

Immediately, the volume at the table rose as the conversation, mostly dominated by Silvio, intensified. I drained my scotch. When the first course arrived, I tried to follow my own advice and concentrate on the food instead of the nonstop chatter, all in Italian, going on around me. The topic, as it was most often these days, was the restaurant. Silvio was going on about personnel, supplies, future menus and possibly purchasing new bar stools, when the discussion suddenly turned to me.

I stopped with the fork halfway to my mouth when Silvio said to me, "*E madre terzo tu affar venire in affair con mio eessere mio socio.* And Momma thinks you should come into the business with me and be my partner." Ignoring my gaping reaction, he continued in English, "We would make excellent partners. I suspect you have a flair for managing supplies, the food purchases, the personnel, and even the accounting, while I am only good at greeting people and making them feel comfortable, like they are at home. This is a family business. We need you."

Angelina said nothing; rather watched my face for a reaction. Nicole, as always, was quiet, but her eyes revealed an expression of concern. I slowly put down my fork, wiped my chin and took a sip of Chianti before responding.

"Silvio, I appreciate the offer, but I am not interested. I don't know if anyone told you this, but I hope to convince Carlo to go into business with me. We are thinking about opening a restaurant ourselves," I said as calmly as I could.

Silvio's reaction came swiftly and, typically I imagined, was displayed without much thought behind it. He slammed his fist to the table, rattling the china and spilling Nicole's wine on the white linen table covering. "What are you talking about? How could you do this? You and Carlo, in business against me! Against me and your own mother! I thought you were a stupid bastard all along, but I didn't know you were that stupid," he ranted. I saw then how he could switch from calm sweet Silvio to abusive prick at the flip of a switch.

By then the other patrons were watching the exchange at our table, Nicole grimacing and wiping up the spilled red Chianti, the house special that evening. Angelina was stunned, I could tell. She started to speak. I held up my hand in a gentle but direct way for her to remain quiet. I did my best to stay calm. I stared into my brother-in-law's face and waited for his tirade to subside. I spoke very quietly and in English, hoping my mother might have lost her ability to translate my remarks after years of being out of practice.

"The first thing, dear brother-in-law, if you ever use that kind of language again around my mother and my sister I will rip your tongue out. And second, I wouldn't be in business with you if you were the last man alive. I can't tell you how much I hate the thought of my mother and my sisters working here for you. How you scam them out of good wages and probably even their tips. My mother is the only reason anyone comes to this dive of yours, and the minute she stopped cooking for you, you'd go broke again."

My voice was nearly a whisper so he had to lean close to hear me spit out the words. "And for your information, if Carlo and I do this, we plan to find a place across town from here, to avoid competing for your neighborhood crowd. And we're not planning on serving Italian food, only American, and maybe Mexican. So why don't you calm down, apologize to everyone here and let me finish my dinner," I strongly advised.

"Hey, man, I was only kidding. I didn't mean anything by it. I knew you wouldn't do anything to hurt you mother or me. Let's just forget it," he sheepishly responded.

"Good idea," I said, without looking up from my food, which now was getting cold.

Silvio took my advice and remained quiet through the remainder of the meal. Angelina and Nicole took up a conversation about the new priest at Saint Teresa's, Father Danilo. He had apparently just finished a year's training at the Vatican and was thought to be in line, if he met the expectations of the Cardinal in Denver, to become bishop, but that might be many years off.

When the meal ended, I tried to excuse myself, begging off on the short glass of Amaretto, but before I could escape, Silvio asked me to join him at the bar. He said he had something important to say. So we excused ourselves. I left my mother and sister at the table and followed him to the bar. An Amaretto was waiting for me. I drank it down in one gulp, which is not the way you should drink that good stuff. Too sweet.

He spoke, now with a hint of a slur after finishing off a bottle of the house special by himself. "I know some guys who can help you get started in business. Real good guys. They can make things happen for you and make sure things go well, particularly with your liquor supply, vending machines and other things that you'll need. I can make the introductions. You'll thank me."

"No thanks," I said, trying extra hard not to lay him out. I tried to keep my distance by adding, "Listen to me, if we do this, Carlo and I will take care of those details. We won't need anybody looking out for us."

"You'll be sorry if you don't make the contact," Silvio warned.

"Is that a threat?" I asked. "Or are you just giving me some more good advice?"

"Oh, no, dear brother-in-law, I wouldn't do that. You're so damn smart. You and your fucking brother. You know it all. Go ahead, open your own place. I'll run you into the ground. I've got the connections. I know how this town operates, and who pulls the strings. You are either on my side or you're nowhere, out in the cold, sinking in the shit." He was slurring even more. His eyes were now a little glassy.

I couldn't hit him. It would have been too easy to put him in a heap. What good would that have done? So, I just reached out and snatched a good grip on his cheek.

"Good night you little scum. I will be watching you real close. Thanks for the dinner, and here's my warning to you. If I find that you ever lay a hand on my sister, or if you don't pay my mother on time and in the amount you agreed, I will fry your balls in that imported olive oil you have and feed them to you in nice, bite sized pieces."

All the while I kept a good grip on his cheek and a menacing smile on my face. I finally let him loose and returned to our table to retrieve Angelina. A drunk Silvio was her ride home, and I wasn't having any part of that.

I heard Silvio angrily call out to Nicole, "Get your coat; let's get out of here."

My mother and I sat in silence as I drove through the night. I was furious – everything Carlo had warned me about Silvio and more had just been proven true. No doubt in my mind now that inside Silvio's book cover were pages filled with conceit and selfish contempt, with more than a little larceny running through his veins. I turned to my mother beside me. She was staring straight ahead into the darkness.

"*Mio non comprenda?* I don't understand?" she finally said. "Why do you not like that boy? He is a good businessman. He is trying to help you, if you want to be businessman too. He is a big mouth sometimes, and he should not swear, especially at you, but he is nervous around you. I like cooking for his business. They call me head chef. I run a good kitchen. Make good food for the customers. Why you not like to work with me? You a big man around town. He just has the restaurant. He takes care of Nicole. He just wants you to like him," she continued, all in English. I guess she hadn't lost her ability to translate after all.

Her words were filled with anguish. It brought back the memory of her, Carlo and me in her kitchen the night I told her I was volunteering for the Army. That night the fear was apparent in her voice, and it had been there again just now. Was she fearful of what I would do, or what Carlo might do? Or was her fear for her daughter? Was she finally beginning to see through Silvio's vanishing veil? Was she trying to convince me of his goodness, or was she trying to convince herself?

Finally, gently and soothing, but direct as I could, I said, "Mama, please, I would like to work with you. You are the best chef west of St. Louis, and he knows it. Everybody knows it. But I can't work with him. I don't trust him. I don't like the people he associates with. Carlo won't work with him either. The people around him are not good people. If they don't control him now, they soon will. It scares me to have you work there, but I know you love to do your cooking, to make your masterpieces, so it's okay for now, but you have to promise me that you will watch him real close," I pleaded.

"*Tu pensi la Costa Nostra?* You think La Cosa Nostra? Lo so. I know. *Forse non e cosi' cattivo*. Maybe it not so bad," she corrected herself.

"*Si mamma cio' e' cattivo, veramenta cattivo*. Yes Mama it's bad, real bad," I responded as I pulled into her driveway. I escorted her to the door, and kissed her on the cheek goodnight.

I drove around town for a while after leaving Angelina. Suddenly I wasn't tired. My mind raced. I pulled to the side of the road and stopped to sit and ponder. My instincts foretold of big problems ahead, maybe even battles to be fought. I wasn't up to another battle, let alone another war. I knew this wouldn't be easy. Could this guy already be connected? Was he capable of delivering on his threat? Should I heed his warning? He was a punk, a no-good. I should have broken his jaw.

I pulled myself together. Now I had to convince my mother and Nicole. We could control him. Carlo and I would work on him together; bring him around; maybe even help him once in awhile. Good thing to do for Nicole and Angelina. I was a little drunk, I guess, because the next thing I knew it was three o'clock in the morning and I had a flashlight shining in my eyes and a cop staring at me through the driver's side window.

"You're the paratrooper. I saw you at the USO dance. I'm corporal Stafford. Proud to make your acquaintance. Why don't you start your car and I will follow you home, just to make sure you get there in one piece."

"Sure, officer," I said with no resistance.

Chapter 45
Untangling the Parachute Strings

I loved a lot of things. I loved the blue sky. I hated it when the sky was clouded with dust. I loved the mountains to the West with their snow-capped peaks. I loved pink and white peonies. I loved playing snooker. I loved to dance. I loved beautiful, strong-willed women and I loved pistachios. I eat them all the time. I always had a bag of the tan-colored shelled nuts in my pocket, on the car seat next to me, or on my bedside stand. I missed having pistachios while in the Army, and when I returned home, the first thing I did after disembarking from The Queen Mary was buy a bag from a street-corner vendor near the peer. I ate them like candy, not only were they delicious, they served to help curb my smoking habit. Like most of the GIs I took up smoking cigarettes while in boot camp and continued puffing long after the war.

Cigarettes were supplied free to fighting soldiers, so there were vast quantities of *Lucky Strikes* and *Camels* which made it very easy to get hooked. I once knew a supply sergeant who somehow maneuvered his way in to become the sole source of cigarettes to several Army divisions. This made him very popular, and rumor had it, very rich, as the war progressed, by creating his very own black market.

When I got home I had more than a little time on my hands, so I spent many long hours at the library. I wanted to research the tasty little nuts – I was curious about them. I don't know why, other than I get that way sometimes when my mind isn't otherwise completely occupied.

In the library I read everything I could get my hands on about pistachios. To me, they were fascinating. I discovered the pistachio tree was native to western Asia and Asia Minor, and today is found in regions stretching from Syria to Afghanistan. There is archaeological evidence in Turkey indicating that the nuts were a food source as early as seven thousand B.C. The pistachio was introduced to Italy from Syria in the first century A.D. Since that time, the nut has been a staple snack in the Sicilian and Italian diet. Maybe the craving for them is in our genes.

In 1954, the pistachio was introduced in the United States by one Charles Manson, a famed horticulturist (not the famed maniacal murderer). Mr. Manson planted pistachio tree seeds for experimental purposes in California, Texas and in other southern states where the trees would thrive in cool winters and hot, long summers. I knew pistachios were also found in France because once, while on a date with Chloe, I spotted a small bag in a Paris candy store. I paid twice the going rate, but didn't care. It was the only bag left in the store, maybe in all of Paris. I savored every bite, and offered only a few to Chloe.

The nuts were very popular in my town, and you could find bowls filled with them on the bars in just about every tavern. They were always free when you were drinking, but I always wondered if people would pay for them, and thought maybe they could be sold through vending machines, like cigarettes and hard candy and music from juke boxes.

After I had read up on the subject I began to wonder if the trees could be grown in my part of the country. On my second day at the library, I happened to read an article about the emerging pistachio market in California. The article said the nuts were drought-resistant and very tolerant to high summer temperatures, but could not withstand excessive dampness and high humidity. The pistachio tree has about the same cold resistance as almonds and olives but flowers later in spring than almonds. I knew you couldn't grow either almonds or olives in Southern Colorado, but I wasn't sure about pistachios. I decided right the to find out.

I figured the climate conditions around my town fit the basic needs of the pistachio tree somewhat well, except that the winters here can be much colder than those in some parts of northern California. I wondered if a tree could be made adaptable to the slightly harsher climate, or if the climate could be altered to adapt to the growth and reproductive needs of the tree.

Exploring the possibility of growing my favorite snack became a priority of mine, but in the meantime, I needed to talk with Carlo about my restaurant plan; the money I had to invest and the proposition I wanted to present. I needed to concentrate on making things happen soon. Pistachios would have to wait. I needed to put my money to work and begin to make a living.

The thing was; I was getting bored. I wanted to find my own place to live. I had taken my old bedroom in my mother's house temporarily, and before I knew it, it had been six months of sneaking home late at night for fear of waking her. I felt like a teenager again and that was intolerable.

It wasn't practical to think about women with all this planning to do, but my brain wasn't cooperating much since thoughts about Maggie kept creeping into my head. Plus I was having a harder time resisting the street corner temptations that seemed to become more numerous and more inviting by the minute, especially after midnight every time I drove past the corner of Main and Fifth Street.

I had asked to visit with Carlo and Julia Gail on the next Sunday afternoon, after they got home from Mass, and I intended to sit down with them and get right to the point about the restaurant idea and our future. On the Sunday morning of my scheduled meeting it became very clear that I had to move out of my mother's house much sooner than later. I woke that morning to Angelina knocking loudly on my bedroom door announcing rather harshly that it was time to get up, or we would be late for Mass. When I ignored her demands, I heard her leave the house in a huff. Mass began at eleven and it was ten minutes to eleven when I looked over at the alarm clock on my old bedside stand.

I could tell Angelina was becoming very unhappy with her son. I cautiously peeked out the bedroom window and saw her crossing herself, probably asking God to forgive me, as she stalked down the walkway toward Silvio sitting in his idling car in our front driveway. Silvio never missed Mass.

Such a good boy, I thought with disdain.

Soon thereafter I was dreaming of falling toward earth with a tangled, unopened parachute and just as I was careening toward my certain death, my fall was suddenly slowed, and I began gliding down like a delicate peony petal into the arms of an awaiting German soldier. But before I could get to the outstretched reach of the Panzer corporal who looked strikingly similar to the one I met in the foxhole, an incessant buzzing jolted me out of my half-asleep daze. The piercing sound wouldn't stop. The German soldier was gone. My mind finally clicked in to realize that it was the telephone ringing in Angelina's kitchen. I climbed out of bed and ambled off to answer it.

"I knew you were there. I knew you would ignore your mother's fervent wish for you to attend Mass with her. You are an ungrateful, disrespectful little snipe. Your mother should never cook for you again. She should throw you out of her house!" she hissed into the telephone.

"Who is this?" I growled into the receiver, knowing immediately the answer to my question.

"You know damn well who this is, so don't try to get smug with me," Maggie shot back.

"What do you want?" I asked, coming at her a little softer while I unsuccessfully tried to hold back a smile.

"I thought it would be nice for you to take me on a road trip up to Colorado Springs. Perhaps for a late lunch date at The Broadmoor Hotel," she said, now with a distinct and – dare I say – friendly lightheartedness. "What do you think of that idea?" she asked after a slight hesitation.

I paused for some time, more for effect than in not knowing the answer.

"Hello, are you still there?" Her voice rose with a hint of concern.

"First of all, I don't have a car. I borrowed my brother's car to drive all the way out to your farm the other day only to be treated like a naughty schoolboy by an old hag of a schoolteacher. Second, I am not going to spend my money buying you or anyone else an expensive lunch at that place. And third, I have better things to do than spending the afternoon with you, like playing on the railroad tracks next to the mill," I finished, proud of myself for such a fine spontaneous rhetorical performance.

"I will pick you up in a half-hour. If you haven't bathed, please do so," she ordered, and hung up.

I was standing by the front door, bathed, with my hair slicked back and a splash of cologne on for good measure when she swung her blue 1946 Oldsmobile convertible into the driveway and blasted the horn. She was right on time. One half-hour to the minute. I had purposefully avoided wearing my only solid blue suit – the one I'd purchased in New York – opting for slacks and an open collar shirt, not wanting her to think I was going to too much trouble and thinking that a suit might be too formal for a Sunday afternoon drive. She had changed out of the baggy pants and flannel shirt and was wearing a yellow sundress with a neckline just low enough to expose the top of her amazing cleavage.

"I didn't have anyone else to call. I wanted to celebrate with someone. I got a job offer this morning from a company in New Jersey and I didn't even have to send in my application." The words came tumbling out of her mouth as I slid in the front passenger seat beside her.

"Well, hello to you," I said, pretending to disregard her announcement and the rudeness attached to it.

As she backed out of the driveway and ground the Olds into first gear, she went on, without looking at me and still ignoring my greeting. "Didn't you hear me? I'm taking a job at a factory in New Jersey. Probably going to leave in about a month. Isn't that exciting?"

"Yes, I heard you. Congratulations. Now, why are you telling me all this? Why not one of those mangy GIs, as you call them, who supposedly line up to come knocking on your door? Why didn't you call one of them? I assumed when we didn't even talk about seeing each other again, that was just as good as formally calling this whole thing off. It seemed a good idea at the time that at least we would avoid making each other miserable, or beating each other up, or sending one or the other of us to jail." It was my second great speech of the day.

This time she didn't answer right away. The giddy, schoolgirl smirk had left her face and she just drove on in silence, eyes straight ahead on the road.

Finally she spoke, and for the first time I saw a slightly different side to her. I actually could detect vulnerability bubbling toward the surface. "I don't know what to do," she began," and I don't know why I'm even here with you and about to ask you this question, but I have this job offer. Its in New Jersey, and it's for a large company that will continue to supply the military with munitions, even now, after the war has ended. They heard about my work, my background and interest in math and science, and I suppose since I am a woman and somewhat unique in my field, I guess for a variety of reasons, they came after me to work for them. I hate to say this, but I'm scared." I knew she had more to say, so I remained quiet.

"I've lived here all my life. I suppose you know some things about my childhood, or at least you seemed to know when you made that awful comment about crime on the farm. So, yes, I had a tough childhood growing up in the orphanage, but I was lucky to have my uncle and his family come after me when they did. They gave me everything. They treated me like I was one of their own children, so I think I had the best possible teenage years any one could hope for. I was allowed, even encouraged, to go in any direction I wanted. Now, I have this big chance to be a big shot woman with this big company, but I can't decide what to do." Her voice tapered off at the end to a volume I could barely hear.

Now it was as if she was talking more to herself than to me, but I didn't mind. I found this earnest, open side of her much more appealing than her put-on toxic side, and I wanted her to continue her self-examination. That way I could try to understand her even better. But then she stopped and the harshness leapt back in.

"You haven't said a word. Are you a mute? Or are you just stupid and can't come up with an original thought?" she sneered.

"Okay, just relax," I said, trying my best to gloss over the outburst. "You were doing pretty good there for a minute, and I think you said some things that you really felt, so why don't you take a deep breath and try to go back to where you were, and stop trying to be such a hard ass. You're not very good at it. Your play-acting really stinks." I was trying to turn her inward for more revelations. It didn't work. She just glared at me and didn't respond.

By now we had driven north far enough up Highway 85 and were approaching the turnoff to the wide, tree-lined Lake Avenue, which leads back West, toward the opulent Broadmoor Hotel. As we crested a slight incline heading up the avenue, the building seemed to rise up out of the ground to greet us with its grandeur. The afternoon sun was setting behind the mountain and its spires of orange illuminated the facade and surrounding grounds to capture the breath of even a jaded, hardened character like me.

Sure I had heard about the fabled hotel, but I had never seen it before. One thing I did know was it was very expensive to stay there, and you'd better be prepared to shell out big bucks just for drinks and dinner. I also remembered from one of my history classes that the hotel was originally built by Philadelphia railroad baron, land speculator and gambler Spencer Penrose in 1891. It sits at the base of the majestic Cheyenne Mountain, in the shadow of Pikes Peak. It had fallen into some state of disrepair during the war, and I could tell repairs were still underway by the scaffolding off to the right. Nonetheless, the Grand Old Dame of the West, as it was called, still held its allure. The light pink stucco structure with its center tower and expansive wings was renowned by its international clientele. I certainly wouldn't fit into that crowd even if I had worn my blue suit. The joint reminded me of the Plaza or the St. Regis in New York City.

"Isn't that lovely?" Maggie declared excitedly as she slowed the Olds to make the turn into the circular drive in front of the main entrance to the hotel. "I will never get used to seeing this building grace this end of the avenue. It is truly magnificent," she gushed. "But I suppose you've grown used to it by now, right?"

There she goes again, I thought. She knows damn well I've probably never been here. She just can't resist taking her pot shots. One minute I'm enchanted by her and the next I could bop her with a pool cue.

"Oh, thank you," Maggie chirped like a songbird as the uniformed door man with his top hat and red-tailed coat clasped her hand to help her from the car. "Please park it for us. We don't know how long it will be. We may be back in just a few minutes, or this may take hours," she told the valet as she slipped him a dollar, showed him a slight wiggle, sounded a slight giggle and made her way to the entrance to the main lobby. I gave a shrug to the valet who smiled, winked in return, and instantaneously shifted his gaze back to her swaying behind. I followed her quickly, thinking I might get lost if I didn't keep up.

We ordered drinks and watched the sun set behind the mountains in the terrace lounge on the second floor of the main hotel foyer. Long pauses interspersed our conversation, but when we did speak we were cordial and our brief exchanges were void, this time, of the typical banter that had characterized our prior heated conversations. It was as if we might be getting comfortable in each other's presence and I began to wonder if the silence might help bring us closer, or at least keep us from fighting. Either situation would be all right with me.

I finally broke the stillness with the question that had been on the tip of my tongue since she announced her looming departure. "So, the job offer would take you back East but you're scared to leave. What are you scared of? Besides your family here, what's holding you back? You seem like the kind of person who has to be independent to be happy. It seems to me the last thing you want is to be dependent on someone for your future."

Maggie stared at me with an impassionate look. "I don't want to talk about it now. What I want is for you to tell me about your experiences while in the Army, the war, how you survived and came home with your sanity. That is, I'm assuming you are sane. I understand you saw a lot of combat. Did you kill anybody?" she asked, turning the tables back on me completely.

Somehow I knew as soon as she shifted the subject and began asking about me, that questions about the war and killing would be inevitable. Those questions always seemed to come up in almost all conversations, so it was no surprise that it would eventually be on Maggie's mind as well. I was not offended by her natural inquisitiveness, nor was I especially reluctant to answer. And in this case, I knew dodging the answer at that moment might be unavoidable, but I tried anyway.

"Just like you before, I'd rather not talk about it, if you don't mind. Why don't we just enjoy not talking to each other for a little while longer? I'm sorry I brought up the subject of your job and you moving away," I said, rather pathetically attempting to deflect her line of questioning. But I did add, "The only thing I will say right now is, yeah, I think I am quite sane, considering."

"Are you sorry I'm moving away, or are you sorry you brought up the whole subject?" she asked, which probably meant she couldn't resist the temptation of exploring my deeper feelings.

"Both," I proclaimed.

"Both what?" she continued to probe.

"Both nothing. I don't want to talk about my experiences and you don't want to talk about your future, so let's drop both subjects," I demanded. "Now look, I'm getting hungry and I don't mind telling you that I would rather not foot a big bill here for dinner. This is a beautiful place, and by the way, for your information, it is the first time I've ever been here, but don't be so high and mighty with being so familiar with the upper crust. Is there another place we can go for dinner that won't set me back enough to equal a month's Army pay?"

"I'm buying, so, yes, we are staying here for dinner. We have reservations in the main dining room. Ten minutes to spare," she said. "Please excuse me. I need to powder my nose."

This woman doesn't miss a beat, I thought, enjoying my turn to watch her wiggle her way across the lobby lounge. I guess I would have to reschedule my meeting with Carlo and Julia Gail for another time.

Chapter 46
Kilos and Fresh Tomatoes

Silvio

Silvio liked his restaurant business. He liked the attention and the admiration and respect owning the fine establishment brought him. Having to share the limelight with his mother-in-law was another matter, and the fact that he employed other family members who also sucked away his notoriety as owner made him angry and frustrated. The only reason he had made the offer to me was he thought it would give him opportunity to spend full time "out-front" meeting and greeting his patrons and making connections instead of worrying about Angelina's supply of fresh tomatoes.

Through it all and at whatever cost he wanted to keep his personal affairs to himself. And that was hard. There were people, family members in particular, around him all the time. It was no one's business what he did, or who he did it with, not even his wife's. He had to protect his privacy no matter what.

What Silvio did like was how his restaurant helped him make new friends. His new friends knew how to live. They knew how to make money, big money, not the nickels and dimes from selling a few plates of spaghetti and a few bottles of cheap wine to mill workers. No, his new friends were wired in, and they were going to take him along for the ride. Silvio was headed straight to the top. But before Silvio could assume a permanent, respectable, position with his new friends, he had to prove his loyalty. This meant making sure when his new friends needed a meeting place, they would have it, no questions asked. And when certain valuable commodities had to be moved from one spot to another, his storage rooms would provide a convenient and safe way station. And when one among Silvio's new friends showed any sign of disloyalty, disobedience or disrespect, Silvio's backroom became the late-night location for re-training sessions taught by those who appeared to Silvio to be the leaders.

Once he heard the word "capo" used in reference to one of those leaders. And another time he heard the name Clemente uttered by one of the capos. Silvio hadn't connected all the dots yet as to who was who and who answered to whom, but he soon learned that some guys gave orders and others took them. And apparently the guy in charge was Mr. Clemente. After a while Silvio was told that Mr. Clemente liked his restaurant and thought it would be a good place to conduct business. Silvio was flattered. He couldn't be more pleased and thankful that they chose him, so when Silvio's job was to mop up the blood after those re-training sessions and before Angelina and her chefs arrived to prepare the menu for the next day, he didn't mind at all. He was paying his dues. Earning their respect. All he had to do was obey.

The magic white powder, or in its raw cut form, the Mexican brown cake, was one of those highly sought-after commodities that needed a safe place for storage until it could be cut and moved to market, and diluted a hundred times to its miniature dime-sized packets. Demand for narcotics was growing and the prices were rising, so trafficking was expanding exponentially. The mob had always had its toehold in drug trafficking, but after the war, the toehold became a stranglehold and the sky became the limit. And Pueblo, under the tutelage of Mr. Clemente, was becoming a major collection and distribution center for an elaborate drug trade network serving a dozen-state region or more.

So, when one of Mr. Clemente's representatives asked Silvio to store a few small packets for "just for a day or two" he was more than happy to accommodate him, especially if Mr. Clemente really was the one doing the asking. A few small packets soon became several large packets and the volume went up from there. At its peak a hundred kilos of pure heroin were stored, cut and packaged each week at Angelina's Fine Italian Restaurant. None of us knew any of this at the time, but it eventually all came out.

Silvio got the job of seeing that each kilo of the stuff was safely stored in secret compartments built in the basement behind the canned goods shelves, produce bins and meat lockers. Steadily activity increased and Silvio found himself working eighteen hours a day trying to keep up with two thriving businesses. It wasn't easy carrying such a burden, trying to keep his after-hours bosses happy while making sure Angelina and all the rest of his employees didn't suspect a thing. But he was good at that. Sly and shrewd. He had them all fooled and the money rolled in.

With Silvio's help Mexican heroin boomed onto the marketplace, and the gangsters in his midst were exploiting the drug cravings in their territory with an unparalleled distribution system geared to meet the exploding demand. Heroin was cheap and it was strong and it was plentiful. The coveted product was flowing freely by the gallons into the veins of the weak, the thrill seekers, and the hard-core addicts from Missoula to Malibu; from Seattle to San Diego.

Black Jim was known to say: "It's a hell of a lot easier to hide and move around than a barrel of scotch whiskey."

Silvio met Black Jim only once, when he dined that one night with his men at Angelina's but the don's influence could be felt as each kilo was packaged and shipped unknowingly from the basement distribution center.

Silvio loved the action, and for his cooperation, he was quickly pocketing an extra two thousand a month on the side. As volume increased, it became three thousand a month. No questions asked.

Naturally Nicole never saw any of this money. Silvio still constantly griped to anyone who would listen over how much he was paying out to his relatives and employees. The cost of food and booze and all the cheap bastards who passed through the doors to buy only one round of drinks instead of three really got him.

His point man was a fellow by the name of Julio "Strawberry" Torino. Strawberry quickly became Silvio's pay-off link, chief mentor, was his source of inspiration. Strawberry was a bona fide capo, Silvio was sure of that. Silvio was told by the others to call him Strawberry after Mr. Clemente had named him that because his fat cheeks were always red and sprinkled with scar pits from persistent childhood acne.

Silvio liked the fact that Strawberry was the epitome of a mob enforcer. He looked and acted the part, and without reluctance or remorse, he would complete the Boss' orders and enforce whatever decisions Mr. Clemente made. Strawberry carried his three-hundred-and-fifty-pound frame with nimbleness, a light step and the quick hands of a junior welterweight. Every Tuesday, Thursday and Saturday he ate two orders from Angelina's single item menu and drank a bottle of Chianti at each setting. He never paid. He answered only to the cheese man and his business was dope, the more the better. If anyone got in his way of increasing production and distribution, they were targets for quick elimination.

At first, Silvio only knew that Strawberry was there to guide him, to solidify and expand the network, and each month, hand over the crisp new bills that went directly to his private account at the First National Bank of Rocky Ford. But Silvio had ambition too. He wanted to go places, to get out this rat hole of a town and move on to places where he could truly make a name for himself. Maybe Los Angeles or at least San Francisco. He liked California, although he'd never been there; he'd only read about those places in travel books. As his ambition got the best of him, Silvio began to pressure Strawberry, and in the beginning, Strawberry was patient and understanding.

"I want to be more useful Mr. Torino," Silvio announced late one night, while Strawberry was resizing and repackaging the latest shipment for transport that next night to Albuquerque. It was four in the morning. They were toasting an unusually large five-hundred-kilo shipment from Angelina's basement with a bottle of Dom Perignon straight from the top shelf of Silvio's wine cellar.

"What do you mean, little man? You already are useful. Hey, we couldn't do this job without you." Strawberry said, playfully jabbing him in the ribs.

That was one thing that Silvio hated about his new friends. They all called him "little man," after Strawberry had come up with the name late one night while delivering a loving squeeze to Silvio's neck and a ruffle to his carefully coiffed black hair.

"No, Mr. Torino, I want to be in the middle of the action, in on the distribution. I want a city to run. People to

415

work under me street selling, where I'm in control, where the big money is made. I'm good at it. I know how to manage people. I'm loyal. I can do it. I need to get out of here. I can turn the restaurant over to one of my brothers-in-law. In fact those pricks want to start a restaurant themselves. They want to be my competition. Can you imagine that? Those pricks. I should stick an ice pick in their eyes," Silvio ranted.

Strawberry just grinned at him until he was finished. "Silvio, you're a good boy. You *are* loyal. You've proven yourself to me and to the Boss, and I will talk to him to make sure he understands your plan. I'll see what I can do. Don't you worry little man."

Strawberry seemed to be thinking about something. "You think your brothers-in-law would take over the place. That so?" he asked.

"Yep, Johnny and Carlo, those pricks. They'd do it. All I need to do is give them the word. They'd be here tomorrow, if I'd let them," Silvio boasted.

"I got it. You may be right. We'll work on it," Strawberry assured him.

Silvio knew Strawberry would take care of him. So as Silvio's vision of his future grew disproportionately to reality, so did his personal intake of the magic powder. Skimming the product was a death sentence, but Silvio had convinced himself that he could disguise his thievery as well as his burgeoning habit. Besides, he deserved some relief, some happiness. He was carrying immense responsibilities. He could handle the dope just like he was handling all of those around him, including Strawberry. No problem.

Chapter 47
Bombs, Bombs Go Away

"So, you really like this woman. Is that right?" asked Julia Gail as she stood at the sink rinsing dishes. I was sitting with my brother at the kitchen table, relaxing after devouring a breakfast of scrambled eggs and sweet Polish kielbasa. It was the Sunday following my trip to the Broadmoor and my growing infatuation with the lovely Miss Danna.

All of us had skipped Mass, me for the second time this month, and all of us were destined for eternal damnation in the eyes of our dear Angelina. I was enjoying my second cup of coffee and preferred not to answer questions about the gracious when-fangs-not-bearing Miss Danna, but I needed to be polite to my favorite of all relatives; I loved Julia Gail as much as my own sisters.

"Yes, I like her. Actually I like her a lot, but she's moving away. She tells me she's taking a job with a big, fancy company in New Jersey. She's going to make ammunition, maybe even bombs for the military. This company has a big contract with the Army and as you know she was mighty successful at her old job at the depot, so they offered her a job with this big company. Pretty important stuff," I explained as dispassionately as possible.

"Is she going to make bombs like the ones they dropped on Japan?" Julia Gail was quick to ask.

The atomic bombs were still big on everyone's minds since they had obliterated two cities and left all of us with either a great sense of security or outright terror that someone else could get their hands on one to return the favor. But the fact that their ungodly destruction had kept me and the 101st out of Japan still made me thankful for their creation.

"Gosh, I never thought of that. Maybe she will," I pondered. "As you know Jules, they didn't make the atomic bombs here at the depot. They made them down in New Mexico; at least that's what I read anyway, but maybe they'll start making them in New Jersey and Maggie will be a part of that. Point is she's moving away. I think next week in fact. She told me the last time I saw her that she's leaving next Saturday." I thought of Maggie actually turning into a full-time mad scientist bomber.

"You going to see her off?" Now it was Carlo's turn, his head buried in the morning edition.

"Damn, you two are full of questions today. Can't a man enjoy his breakfast in peace?" I asked, scrambling to latch on to the sports section of the *Sunday Journal* lying under Carlo's out-stretched palm. "I'm sure glad the bojons make that kielbasa we just had. Sometimes I like it better than the sweet sausage from Stefano's," I continued, trying to change the subject.

"No, you're not gettin' away with that. As long as you're at my table, eatin' my food and drinkin' my coffee, you'll answer my wife's questions," Carlo replied, folding his section of the paper and snatching the sports section back from me.

Actually, that was your question, you nosey bastard, I thought. But I didn't say anything except, "No, I'm not plannin' on seeing her off," I flailed at the section of newspaper I wanted. "Look, I think we had a pretty good time, the couple of times we were together. After the trip to Colorado Springs, we had coffee at Karen's restaurant day before yesterday. Some good conversation, some not so good. You never know how it's gonna go with her. One minute she's gentle as a kitten, and the next she'll scratch your eyes out. She's damn pretty, and she's damn smart. Next to you, Julia Gail, she's the smartest woman I know. She has a quick tongue, and she's quick to flap it at you if she thinks she can make you squirm. She likes to keep you on your toes. I suspect she scares off many guys 'cause of her ways, but to me, she's just another challenge, you know, like climbin' a hill or catchin' a big brown trout out of the Arkansas," I said, trying to convince them that, despite her strengths, I still had the upper hand. I'm not sure how convincing I was.

"Or like fightin' the Nazis," Carlo smiled.

"Not quite that bad." I said solemnly.

"Why don't you follow her? Go to New Jersey to be with her, because I know you well enough that's what you're thinking," Julia Gail said as she sat down between me and my brother and placed her hand over mine and her husband's.

"Come on. I don't want her that bad. To move to New Jersey? I just got home. I'm not interested in chasing some woman all over the countryside. There are plenty of women right here in town. She's just passin' through as it is; I mean passin' through my life. Besides, I didn't come here to talk about women, I came here to talk business," I tried again to veer the conversation away from Maggie.

"What do you know about runnin' a restaurant other than you've watched mother cook and you've cleaned the dishes a few times," Carlo asked, increasingly patronizing with each word.

"Look, I know that," I began, "but you and I would make good partners." I fought back a bubbling anger as I was reminded of our days as children and Carlo's way of putting me down when I would challenge him with something that made him uneasy. "We could buy a building, gut it out ourselves and set it up. There's already too many Italian and bojon restaurants in town as it is. And there's that new Mexican joint. What's it called, Garcia's or something like that? But, there's not a good American food place where you can get a good hamburger, steak, mashed potatoes. You know some good old fashioned American food. Fried chicken. Right?" I pleaded my case.

"You know where you ought to be workin'. Where the money's good, where there's a pension and there's not gonna be a bunch of punk wop gangsters tryin' to get in your pocket for protection from burnin' it down." My brother added insult to injury.

"We've been over this before. It started with you ten years ago, so let's get off me goin' to work at the mill. It won't happen, so please, let's talk about somethin' else." I congratulated myself for keeping my temper.

"Okay, Carlo," Julia Gail injected, squeezing both of our hands and raising them off the table like a referee declaring a draw after a hard-fought boxing match. "Let's think seriously about what Johnny's saying. He might have a good plan, and he's right that you two, if you can bury these old stupid complaints about each other, would make good business partners, in the restaurant business or just about anything the two of you decide."

"See, why don't you listen to your wife?" I asked, pleased to at least have some support. I raised my sister-in-law's hand in symbolic victory.

But Carlo extracted his hand from Julia Gail's and took on the air of seasoned brigade commander addressing his troops. "Let me tell you something. Right now we don't want any part of the restaurant business. Certain things are about to happen that could make the restaurant business one of the last you want to be in. You've been gone a while, and things have changed around here since the war ended. You have to understand that the goombas are back, bigger than ever." He had turned stern. Like the President's annual State of the Union Address Carlo went on to describe the current state of the Mafia in town.

For an hour he told about Black Jim's rise to power; how he now controlled operations throughout the West and how the mob's emphasis had changed from booze to dope while at the same time their lifeblood enterprises of prostitution, extortion, protection, gambling and bootlegging liquor absent tax stamps had re-emerged with a vengeance.

"And restaurants are the natural spot for them to spread their venom," Carlo explained. "That's where people gather. That's where people interact with others, sometime daily. That's where their guards are down, where service is provided, where a little dope, or a little sex, or a little gambling are easily provided on top of a good hamburger. My brother, it's been that way for a long time and it's gonna get worse, believe me," he was almost pleading with me now.

"Jimmy Clemente doesn't look the part and he keeps it well hidden, but he's meaner and smarter than Charlie Blanco, the Smaldonis, the Carlinos or all of the rest of them put together. That's why he's runnin' the show in our town and everything else between here and Los Angeles," he continued. "Our town is like an experimental laboratory for them. Kind of like a test market, or in your former job, a front line patrol scouting for the main troops," Carlo seemed

421

like a tactical officer, explaining the terrain his troops were about to cross.

"What the hell does that mean?" I nearly shouted out of frustration.

"I thought you were smarter than that. Don't you get it?" Carlo was beyond patronizing, but he was beginning to make sense.

"They use our town to test their operations; their procedures. How to take over a new business, let's say. When a new business comes to town, for instance a lumberyard, they experiment with ways to get to the owner, convince him to pay up for protection, in a gentle way at first. They are slow and patient in the beginning, but the pressure gets greater if he resists. Then things begin to happen. Like a burglary, stolen tools. Then they vandalize the place a little; then there's a small fire, then they burn his car, or scare the hell out of his kids while walking to school, or some big bastard knocks on his door while he's at work and makes advances at his wife. It's the experiment. The test. How fast do they turn up the heat, and what works best to bring the guy in line? If he continues to resist, there's usually a big fire or someone close to him gets hurt bad; maybe not his wife and kids, but his brother or his sister has a bad accident. They usually don't kill the target unless he's already one of them and he gets out of line. They just scare the hell out of him until he comes around, or he moves out of town," Carlo paused for a moment. "Remember, Tiny's place. The auto repair shop?" he asked.

"Yeah, what happened to him?" Now the pieces were falling together.

"Long gone. After his brother got hit by the truck up on Sunset Drive and died the next day," Carlo said, his eyes drilling into my head for emphasis. "These guys can't afford to play too much out in the open anymore. They have to stay underground, just enough, to keep the Feds or the state cops off their backs. They don't care about the local cops; most of them are on the take as it is. They've become a lot more sophisticated, like extorting money out of the insurance companies; like faking someone's death, or collecting for arson if one of theirs owns the business outright."

He didn't stop there, although I wish he would have. "Meanwhile they've become the best dope peddlers around. They deal with the Mexicans and they have their sources mainly in Mexico. In our town, they have experimented with how to set up their labs for cutting and mixing, and how to operate their distribution networks. We're talking about pure heroin. The cops, even the Feds, haven't figured it out yet, or they just don't care about some dope fiend droppin' dead in the back alley. Just yet, that is. The Mafia knows that dope is gonna be bigger than bootleggin' ever was, and just like booze, they want to make it available to the junkie in the back alley as well as some executive in his glass office skyscraper. There're plenty of new customers now, those back from the war, to satisfy them, and the Mexicans are growin' the stuff by the acre and hauling it in by the truckloads. There are even bigger supplies coming in from South America. So how do they make all of this happen?

"Same as it goes for everything else, but they pretty much know how to run gambling and prostitution. But that last one is interesting. Since they now have the heroin, they give it to the whores. It makes them a lot easier to organize and control. Just keep them on the stuff, and they can do pretty much what they want with them; that is, until they die and they have to get rid of the bodies." Finally, he was running out of steam. But he had definitely caught my attention.

"So that's how it is. I know what I'm talkin' about here, 'cause I've lived with it, closer than you think. Julia

Gail knows enough, just so she's careful with what she says about what went on in the past. We are out of it now, and we don't ever want to go back. Ever. It's like a disease. Understand?"

I was not as naïve as he thought, with all the research I'd done in the past, but I hadn't realized how much influence these guys had assumed. I was amazed at how much Carlo knew. If I didn't know better, I might have thought he was wearing his old pinstriped suit again.

"Carlo, you think I'm a moron?" I couldn't resist. "Remember, I saw you burn your clothes that night, out in the backyard. Yeah, I was a kid, but I knew you weren't dressin' up on a Saturday night to go to Mass. But then you stopped, and something had to have happened for you to be able to get out, but whatever it was, you were one of those guys who wouldn't put up with them. Well, I'm the same. I don't want any part of them either. We're Sicilians. They expect us to join up, especially now, since bein' in the war, or stayin' at home with an important job, makes us special. Like top recruits, or something. I don't know as much as you do about how they operate these days, but I do know they can't have everything they want. Somebody can tell them no. Somebody can have a business here without workin' for them, and it may as well be us," I finished with a bang.

All three of us just sat there at the table for a while without speaking. My coffee was cold and black as a hallow cave and was just as uninviting. I stared into the cup. Julia Gail finally got up to clear the dishes.

"Shall I get you another cup of coffee?" she asked.

"No thanks," I said, the acid in my stomach churning. I turned to my brother. "We're not gonna break their backs ourselves. The Mafia will go on, probably forever, but I'm not gonna' run off to New Jersey hopin' to convince Maggie Danna to marry me. To me, that's like runnin' away from a fight with the Krauts. I never did, and I never would. I knew I couldn't beat the whole goddamn German Army by myself, and I know I can't beat these goddamn wop gangsters by myself, either, but I knew then, in the Army, I had a job to do, and if I did it well enough I'd have a better chance of surviving and everything would turn out all right. Back here, I also think I have a job to do, and I need to survive, but more than that, I need to prosper. I don't know how I'm going to do that yet; maybe it isn't the restaurant business, but whatever job I do, I'm gonna do it right, and if I have to fight those bastards to make my way here, I'll do it. Let's figure out how we can do it together, and do it," There was a force and conviction to my voice he damn well had to appreciate.

Carlo got up from the table to help Julia Gail finish the dishes and I got up to leave. But before I did, I asked, "From how you're describin' things around here, with the dope experiments and all, do you think Silvio's place, or maybe Silvio himself, might have been taken in by them? Seems like a guy like him might be attracted to that type of life," I speculated.

Carlo, standing next to the kitchen sink drying the glasses, did not turn around. "I told you earlier things were about to change. Just remember that," he said, slipping back into his Big Brother Professor role.

"Oh, that's real helpful," I said. "You're just full of bullshit advice today. Sorry, Julia Gail."

He turned toward me, leaned against the counter and said a soft even tone, "Little brother, I don't know if or when those sons-of-bitches out there will come at us, maybe ruin our lives, but we're Sicilians; we're like those trout in the reservoir. We have two choices in the matter. Either we take that juicy worm on the hook and let them reel us in, gut us, filet us and have us for dinner, or we swim right past the

425

worm and feed on the fresh moss at the bottom of the lake. You can bet, though, they'll keep throwin' out the bait. The worm will be bigger and fatter with each cast. They want us real bad, I think. You're right. They had me once and I got away. I spit out the hook. I'm not goin' back, ever. But now they want you, too. War hero and all. Good for their image. Good for their cover. The mill gives me my cover for now, and if I leave, to ever so slightly step back into their world, that hook might just catch my tail. Maybe Silvio has taken the bait already. I don't know, but if he has, we'll find out sooner than later. For now, just let it go. Relax. Go play for a while. Do something completely out of the ordinary. Let's let some time go by. Say, six months. We'll talk about this again. Please."

His words struck true and quickly sunk in deep. His expression reinforced his message, a sense of concern, but not fear. He was right. And I was right. We had some time. I knew it then, but I paused for a moment, dropping his gaze to stare at my shoes.

"Okay, I hear you. Tabled for six months," I conceded. "I promise. I'm goin' over to Joe's to play some snooker. Want to come?" I asked.

"No," my brother replied. "I'm stayin' here this afternoon. I have too much to do and quite a bit to think about."

Chapter 48
So, You Think You're So Damn Smart

A week later, I stood on the Union Station train depot platform facing Maggie who was wailing away at me, arms flailing and tears streaming down her cheeks.

"Goddamn you, why don't you tell me not to go?" she cried loud enough for the dozen or so who also were waiting for the noon train North to Denver to hear. "You shit, you won't say anything. I invited you here to see me off and you just stand there like a tree stump." She had muffled her tone, but it was still quite shrill.

"Maggie, sure, I don't want you to go. I like fightin' with you all the time. Gives me real pleasure. If I told you not to go, and somehow or someway you decided not to, you'd blame me forever. You need to go. See for yourself what's best for you. If you don't like it back there, then come back, but don't do it for me. Do it for yourself, and don't ever tell me it was my fault or my idea," I reassured her as gently as possible.

"Well, aren't you the smart one," she scoffed. "You have all the answers when you finally open your trap. Okay, big boy, I'm going, and I won't come back no matter how hard you might try to convince me. I'll go there and make a whole lot of money; move on to New York and marry some millionaire with a penthouse overlooking Central Park."

"I saw Central Park once. I was pretty impressed, but I don't need to see it again," I retorted. "I like the one here better."

"Oh, there you go again, trying to make me smaller than you, Mr. World Traveler. Well I'm telling you I won't have any regrets leaving you here to scrape by, trying to make a living, trying to run a restaurant, or grow pistachio trees in a cold climate like some idiot, or whatever harebrained scheme you might have up your threadbare sleeve. By the way, my uncle says you can only have a half-acre on the farm to play with your tree branches, but if they grow, he wants a percentage." She folded her arms across her chest.

"You didn't tell me that. Why didn't you tell me? That's great! I'm going to make them grow. You'll see!" I exclaimed, accidentally loud enough for everyone on the platform to hear.

"You're so foolish. Like a little boy," she continued her lashing. "Mr. World Traveler, and now your a scientist, and you think you are going to make a new tree grow where none has before. Mr. Optimist to boot."

The train arrived and she broke down again. I pulled her to me and kissed the tears away. I cupped her face in my hands and kissed her mouth, tasting a hint of salty snot from her nose, but not minding at all. We released each other and I took her hand to help her up the portable metal stairs to the passenger car. I watched for her to find her seat and she peered at me through the window. I smiled and waved and walked away.

I will miss her, I said to myself. *God, I hope she comes back, but on her own terms, not mine.* The train pulled away and she was gone. I went to Joe's to shoot snooker and tried to think about pistachio trees instead of the taste of her tears.

~

A month later, I was back at the train depot to retrieve two long wooden boxes from the baggage department. In them were two matching infant pistachio trees whose roots were carefully wrapped in burlap. The pencil-thin braches snuggled close to the trunk, tied with twine. They had been shipped from a farm outside Fresno after I had called the farmer and negotiated a price of fifty dollars each including the sapling graphs. The article I read in the library said the farmer's trees were the highest producers in the San Joaquin Valley.

I loaded them in the green 1940 Ford pick-up truck I'd brought for three hundred and fifty dollars from Ralph Luby's used car and truck lot and pulled away from the loading dock, heading for the Danna farm. I also loaded some tools in the truck; two-by-fours for framing and a clear canvass tarp bought from Pueblo Tent and Awning. I was building a temporary greenhouse.

For the first time since my return home, I had a plan, a project, a real purpose, something tangible to latch on to. It was probably a stupid plan, an unachievable dream, but why not? I had nothing to lose in trying my hand at being a nut farmer. People were doing nuttier things. Ha! I was almost relieved that Maggie was gone, and a good part of the month had passed before I asked myself why I felt that way. Time with her drove home the point that I was literally drifting from one day to the next. Maggie had her sights set high and straight. But what was I doing? Where was I going?

That relief was mixed with uneasiness, because being with Maggie was never dull, and with her gone part of me feared that dullness would return. I was used to action, actually thrived on it, and now, if life became dull, I feared I'd look for action in the wrong places before I found my path.

I was taking Carlo's advice. Relaxing as best I could, thinking about things out of the ordinary, things far removed from the routine, if there was such a thing. Like trying against all odds to grow pistachio trees, which were about as foreign to me as an opera or ballet. Chloe took me to a ballet in Paris one night. We left after the first act. It was completely out of my league. I was bored stiff. She was pissed off at me for a week.

I exited the parking lot of the depot and steered east with mixed emotions, feeling more content than anything. The plan with Carlo was on hold. We would give it six months. I still had about two thousand dollars in the bank. Much of that wasn't going anywhere soon. I would be conservative with my cash, for now, so I could afford "playing scientist," as Maggie had put it, and being optimistic. I wanted more than anything to grow these trees, and even though my chances were pretty slim, by God, I was going to put my heart and soul into it.

I knew my timing was right to start my experiments. The weather was becoming warmer by the day. The soil at the Danna farm was black and hearty. The rains had been generous, and my head was filled with information from three books from the library on hybrid trees and grafting techniques, with four more on order. I was optimistic, even with the odds against me. I had nothing to lose, and I had six months to play scientist, or – more precisely – horticulturist. I loved pistachios, and I had plenty of time.

I was waiting for the traffic light to change to green at the intersection of Ninth Street and Highway 50, thinking about my trees, when I looked up and saw her stepping into the crosswalk. The lovely Mrs. Montlero. At first I didn't recognize her, but as she passed in front of my truck and glanced at me through the windshield, our eyes caught and both of us connected immediately. She looked spectacular. I gobbled her up with my eyes. Her bright pink dress clung tightly to her luscious frame and the wind whipped at its hem to reveal the lace bottom of her white slip. As she strutted gracefully before me on her matching pink high heels, all the delightful memories swept back in an instant.

I rolled down my driver's side window and greeted her politely. "Hi, how are you?"

She opened her mouth as if to respond, but paused and didn't say a word. She just shook her head no and stepped up her pace to the other side of the street. She stopped then and stood there with her back to me. Hesitating, thinking, remembering; I was sure.

Even though there was plenty of traffic this time of day as people arrived to pick up passengers and cargo at the depot, I ignored the commotion around me and sat there through two more changes of the traffic light, waiting, hoping for her to turn around. Car horns blared behind me. A driver shouted, "Move it, you bastard!" Cars and trucks sped by, blasts deafening.

I recalled the strange description of her actions in one of the few letters I received from Carlo while in the Army, and his account of Mr. Montlero's angry admonishment. Maybe she told her husband about her overly friendly fix-it man, or – more accurately –boy. Or maybe she had rejected her husband after I left her bed. I didn't know, and I really didn't care all that much, but I began to feel hurt by her refusal even to acknowledge me.

Finally she pivoted and looked back. Tears glistened on her cheeks. She smiled, but then again shook her head no, ever so slowly. I smiled back at her and we both knew it was never to be again. She continued on her way, out of my life for good.

No, turn around again! It's not over! I shouted inside my head.

Having completely lost my sense of where I was or what I was doing, I popped the clutch on the old Ford and killed the engine. Another horn shook me back to reality. The light was green. I re-started the engine and turned the corner onto the highway. As I drove to the farm, I thought mischievously that I might telephone her, or even drop by her house knowing her husband would not be home. That would be a terrible thing to do, I thought, but it had been a long time. Chloe had been my last. No, I had to accept the silent agreement we had just reached. If she had wanted me I would have known, but she had decided against it, for whatever reason. I had to respect that, but still I toyed with trying to change her mind. Was it my head or other parts of my anatomy doing the thinking?

Instead I tried to focus instead on finding and mating compatible trees. That was really sick. I had been strict in my order to the Fresno farmer. I must have a male and a female pistachio tree. Pistachios are dioecious, with male and female flowers on separate trees. Both trees must be present for fruit to set, I had learned, and if I were to create a heartier tree to withstand a harsher climate, I needed male and female trees planted closely together for pollination and grafting. The male tree goes by the name of Peters; the female tree is a Kerman. Funny names for males and females, I thought. Well, maybe not for males when you really think about it.

Anyway, why not call them by regular names, like Johnny and Maggie? I decided to call my first pair Johnny and Maggie to see if they became compatible and maybe even copulate. I wondered how difficult it would be to make them do both. Perhaps my ambitions were impossible.

The pistachio is a broad, bushy tree, which grows slowly to a height and spread of twenty five to thirty feet with one or several trunks. The trees are inclined to spread and droop, and when they are young they need to be staked for support until the root system takes hold. A blooming pistachio produces a small brownish green flower that is not very pretty. The flower doesn't have petals, and it should appear in early summer, so I had time to get my mates in the ground and nurse them along through the spring before they were expected to copulate, like compatible trees and people should, you know, get to know each other.

By the time I swung into the driveway at the farm, my head was clear and my loins relaxed. Unconsciously, I looked for Maggie on the front porch sitting in her swing. Empty. Deserted. I've got to get these women off my mind, I thought. Not forever, that's for sure. But I had other things to worry about.

Within a week, working every day, I had fashioned a ten-by-fifteen-foot rectangular greenhouse that now covered Johnny and Maggie, both of which had been planted with great care in the middle of my tiny plot of mother earth. I had staked both samplings while they adapted to their new environment and welcomed the nurturing I intended to provide. Every day, I greeted Mrs. Danna and drove to my half-acre on the southwest quadrant of the property. I brought along a desk and chair for my long days of reading, waiting and caring for my precious couple. All of the books I ordered from the library had arrived and I was slowly absorbing each one.

Since the pistachio produces such a highly sought-after, tasty nut, they are called cultivars, and because they have been cultivated for thousands of years, a great many varieties have been created. The different species had names too, like Irbrahmim, Owhadi, Safeed, Shasti and Wahedi. There were also the Bronte, Buenzle, the Sfax and the Trabonella. I soon realized I needed more samples with which to experiment so I placed four more orders with the farmer in California and soon had eight more males and females in the ground; a colony of ten all together. I expanded my oversized makeshift greenhouse tent to twenty feet by thirty feet with a second supply of lumber and another sheath of canvass. I became a regular customer at Pueblo Tent and Awning.

By summer, as the temperature at mid-day rose to nearly a hundred degrees, and during the nights it rarely dropped below eighty, my saplings began to flourish. Four pairs did anyway, six pairs died. Maggie and Johnny made it through the season, producing the ugly flowers and defying the odds. I ordered more samples to replace the ones that hadn't made it, and I made sure I mixed them up this time with Irbrahmin matching with Safeed, and Buenzle and Trabonella, seeking a more perfect union.

The hot days continued through September and into October as fall was delayed, replaced by, on most days, warm, wet afternoons. The dusty wind still blew through on its normal path, but my small plot of beloved ground was partially shielded from the gusts because it sloped into an ancient creek bed below the surface of the planted fields. Also the Dannas' brilliant crops of corn, soybeans, alfalfa and hay helped block the relentless blowing and swirling of the wind. The welcomed rain seemed to keep the humidity higher than normal, allowing my first growing season for my tiny grove of infant trees to be abnormally extended. Only two trees died toward the end of October, so I entered the critical colder months preparing for my trees' survival with some advantage.

I would have to wait for my first experimental grafts until next spring. Most of my books described grafting as a delicate art. I was good at planting, but wasn't so sure about my grafting skills. First you have to recognize which branches, or branch stubs should be cut and removed from one small tree and grafted to, or attached and secured, to another. That was an acquired skill. So I read more on how to spot the good grafting branches and reject the others. And then I practiced the various cutting and re-attaching techniques on the dead trees for the time when this part of the process would be best applied. A good horticulturist wouldn't think of grafting in the summer or fall even with a real greenhouse controlling the environment. Grafting happened only in the spring.

Meanwhile, on the Danna farm, the long growing season had resulted in two plantings and two harvests of the main money crops – alfalfa and wheat. I had the privilege of helping with the harvesting of both. At least half of my days were spent on the tractors and combines, or with the hay balers. I liked the work. My skin turned a dark chestnut brown and my muscles hardened once again to their Army basic training peak. I was in tip-top shape by the end of harvest. I kept to the routine, taking my main noontime meal with the family nearly every day, and hearing Mrs. Danna read the letters she received each week from Maggie. I suspected my hostess was omitting some parts of the letters since it appeared that the sentiments Maggie put to paper often lacked continuity. Occasionally, Maggie's aunt would read where Maggie would mention my name in her correspondence, but only in passing when she asked about my plantings or if I was earning my way as a hired hand.

The farm crews working the harvest for the Dannas' labored hard each day until dark, and after a light supper, I would usually retire, exhausted like them, to my greenhouse

435

for further reading. Often I slept in the bed of my truck or on a cot beneath the white canvass. Vincennes allowed me to string wire from the main house and barn to my greenhouse providing a power source for ample lighting. I preferred sleeping out there rather than returning to Angelina's house even though both my cot and the bed of my truck were hard and uncomfortable. I liked my bed at home but I didn't like all the questions from my mother and sisters about my plans for the future, nor did I like waking them up with my screams in the darkness. Out in the field, all I awoke were the rabbits and coyotes.

Six months went by in a flash. I was surprised when the time came, I wasn't ready to go back and re-start the conversation with my brother. Right now, I *was* content and maybe even happy. I needed more time and told Carlo as much. He agreed. Take more time if you need it, he said. He wasn't going anywhere.

I didn't go near Mrs. Monterlo that summer or fall or winter, or ever again for that matter. I admit I tried to telephone her once, but hung up after the first ring, thinking better of it at the time, but later wishing I'd had the guts. I drove by her house a couple of times. Again, it wasn't my head driving the car, or my actions. Control and discipline, like the Army taught me. How could I forget? Still I yearned, and there were a few times that I traveled to town for the sights, sounds and pleasure one could enjoy while visiting the clubs and backrooms featuring the girls from Trinidad.

The first snowfall didn't occur until late December in that first Year of the Pistachios, as I like to call it. And when the cold finally came, the greenhouse gave the trees cover and kept them warm. When the sun went down and the temperature dropped into the thirties, my nights were spent stoking fires at each end of my big tent and coaxing smoke to rise through the holes in the provisional roof. I didn't have time to think about much else.

Luckily each day that first year the air temperature climbed back into the forties during the daylight and most often the snow was gone in a day or two. By spring of 1947, six pairs of trees, each about ten feet high and about eight inches around, had survived and were budding their ugly flowers, ready to mate and put forth their bounty. I ordered ten additional pairs from Fresno.

I was down to five hundred and thirty five dollars in my bank account, but my head was full of confidence and more theories about my miniature forest than I could count. Time to start grafting. Formal experimentation would begin in late March, or so I thought. But life unexpectedly had other plans for me.

Chapter 49
Sweet Choirboy

Strawberry

Julio "Strawberry" Torino became what he was through a circuitous, calamitous route. Unlike many of Julio's compatriots, from childhood on he was destined for great things. Odds were back then that Julio Torino would become the first male in generations on either side of his family to become a priest.

Julio knew he was a special child. He was an only child, adored by his mother, ignored by his father. By his nature he was quiet and reserved, introverted and studious. He learned to read at age three. The books of Solomon in the Bible and Alice in Wonderland were among his favorites. Even as a child, he shunned the outdoors, despising the slightest speck of dirt on his short pants, knee socks, shirt and tie. He preferred poetry to baseball or bicycle racing. Self-taught, he loved the pipe organ, and at age twelve he was the youngest in the whole of the Diocese ever to play for an evening Mass. And he did so without missing a note. He sang in the men's choir at age thirteen and never missed a practice. He was a model student, even mastering advanced Latin by the ninth grade. His mother was convinced that an early, glorious ordination awaited him. His only flaw in an otherwise perfect, reverent psyche was his gluttony. He ate often and in great quantities. It gave him wild satisfaction.

At age twelve, he weighed one hundred and seventy pounds. The other kids ridiculed him relentlessly, mercilessly, casting him out. He became self-absorbed and increasingly reclusive. His mother didn't care. She fed him and kept him close. When his father was away, which was often, she would bring Julio to her bed. He rejoiced in her warmth. Her love gave him comfort well into his teenage years. They memorized Bible verses together and he prepared for seminary. He ate. She encouraged. He grew into manhood, confused and frustrated. Despite the haunting demons, meeting the Devil often, he was on the sacred path to a life in Christ.

On a rainy night while walking home from choir practice, Julio took a shortcut through the alley between Main and Spruce, just a block from Father Mario's rectory. He heard the grunting and muffled panting before he saw the shadowy figures of Timmy Costello taking Teresa Florentino from behind. Timmy was standing on an apple crate, enveloping Teresa. She was bent over, willing, skirt over her head, hands bracing her thrusting body against the building wall. Standing close by, waiting his turn, was Paulie Pagnatto. All three turned at the noise of Julio's heavy steps. They stopped and stared.

"Hey, Fat Boy, want some?" Paulie called. "But you have to wait your turn. I'm next." Julio didn't move. He watched with gaping mouth and wide eyes until Timmy finished. Teresa pulled down her skirt. Timmy stepped down from the crate.

Finally, Julio spoke. "You're hurting her. Leave her alone," he said timidly.

To his amazement, Teresa laughed loudly, shrilly. "Fat Boy, you wouldn't know what to do with it if I put it in your face!" Timmy and Paulie cackled hysterically.

"Come on Fat Boy, try it. You'll like it. Teresa will let you," Timmy urged.

"Wait a minute, I'm next," Paulie reminded his friend.

"No, I want the Fat Boy next," Teresa interjected.

Timmy walked up to Julio and took him by the arm. "Come on, what's your name? Julio? Come on; you can do it. You'll like it. Feels good," Timmy cooed.

Julio allowed himself to be guided toward the apple crate and Teresa. Before he knew it, his pants were around his ankles. Teresa's bare rump was before him. His response came quickly. He began. And continued, and continued.

After a time, impatience grew and tempers flared. "Hey, Fat Boy, that's enough," yelled Paulie. "My turn!"

"Yeah, get your fat ass down," Timmy demanded.

Julio ignored them. Teresa's panting became anguished. "Stop," she cried. "Stop, you're hurting me."

Julio kept going, heaving even louder, thrusting even stronger. Timmy and Paulie rushed forward and grasped at his thick flailing arms from opposite sides. Julio swung one of his massive limbs and then the other, catching both of his antagonists square in their Adam's apples, knocking them aside. They staggered back, choking uproariously. Julio interrupted his motion to look their way and thought for a moment how effortless his blows had been. It was the same sense of amazement he had when he broke that little grey kitty's neck the other day, swatting it so gently just one time beside the head. When he started again Teresa was crying in pain. Timmy and Paulie came at him again. Finally Julio stopped. He withdrew. Teresa slumped down the brick wall into a fetal position on the ground.

Julio met his enemies as they cautiously approached. His pants still around his ankles, Julio head-locked both Timmy and Paulie with ease. His strength was overpowering. They couldn't escape; their arms thrashed harmlessly in the air. When Julio brought their heads together in front of his protruding belly, the cracking sound of skull meeting skull was none he'd ever heard. But it felt good, so he did it again, and again, and again until Timmy and Paulie were as lifeless as sandbags in his grip. He carefully laid them on the asphalt.

He hiked up his pants, and then turned his attention to Teresa. He helped her to her feet. She was weeping uncontrollably. He brushed back her matted, sweat-soaked hair with his catcher's-mitt-sized hands and ever so gently placed each on either side of her head. Her eyes were wide with terror. He began to delicately twist; her chin moving to the right, too far; her neck muscles straining. He went farther and farther. Her muscles tightened, resisted even more, and then all she could do was gasp. He continued the movement until he heard the snap, like the breaking of a tree branch. Her struggle stopped and she slumped in his arms. He placed her back on the ground near the boys, pulling down her skirt to cover the exposed flesh. He adjusted his clothing, surveyed the scene without emotion and calmly walked from the alley to continue his stroll home to the arms of his waiting mother.

According to the newspaper, while out for a morning saunter with his pet Irish setter, Alfonso, Father Mario stumbled upon the bodies around five the next morning. Blame was placed on unknown random killers most likely passing through town. In Father Mario's sermon that Sunday he mourned the fallen victims of a crime too horrific to have ever been committed by anyone from their town. It must have been a maniac, a stranger no one knew, Father

Mario told the congregation. The police said robbery was the motive. Despite all the evidence to the contrary a sex crime was never mentioned, even in the official reports. Those things never happened in Pueblo, people said. Mob killings, yes; sex crimes, never.

Julio entered seminary after graduating from high school with honors. He studied only two semesters before leaving. He didn't tell his mother why or where he was going. Julio disappeared for five long years. He came home only after his mother's death, and on the direct orders of the bosses in New York. Julio had achieved the highest recognition for his skills. He was meticulous at his craft.

Black Jim welcomed Julio back to Pueblo with a private celebration in his underground hideaway. There were eleven other guests, so with the Boss and Julio, the correct number of thirteen was in attendance. That was the night Jimmy gave Julio his nickname. All applauded Jimmy's selection. They always did. No one ever disagreed with the Boss. Julio wasn't so sure he liked his nickname and didn't quite know why it was Jimmy's choice. Julio thought it might have been Jimmy's way of showing some sort of affection toward him. "Sweet as a strawberry;" yeah, that must be it, Julio concluded.

Jimmy had been happy that night. He needed muscle and he demanded loyalty. He was getting both from Strawberry Torino, and Strawberry was more than happy to supply it. Nearly seven years to the day after Strawberry got his nickname, he tapped on the rear entrance door of the restaurant bearing Angelina's name.

Silvio told us how it all went down. Strawberry had arrived precisely at the appointed time. It was two o'clock in the morning. The street was dark and the alley pitch black except for a lone dim bulb suspended by a wire above the doorway. The door opened a crack, stretching the heavy chain securing the interior to the maximum possible extent. Strawberry eyed Silvio peeking through from the other side of the door and heard him slide the chain from its place to allow the door to swing open. Before the unsuspecting Silvio could speak or even extend his hand, Strawberry hit him with the full force of his three-hundred-fifty-pound bulk. The blow, square to Silvio's nose, flung him off his feet and into wooden pallets of lettuce stacked three high. Blood spewed and splattered across the crisp green leaves and the heads of produce scattered across the floor around where Silvio lay. Blood stained Silvio's heavily starched pink dress shirt. He was dazed, bewildered, and most assuredly terrified. Silvio tried to speak, but instead sent blood dribbling down his chin.

Strawberry stood over him with his hands on his hips. To either side of the big man stood two of his accomplices. One had closed and locked the door, this time using the inside deadbolt. No one spoke as Silvio struggled to regain his senses. But before he could he slumped back to the floor, his eyes rolling back in his head. Strawberry had seen that look before, not necessarily from people he was assaulting at the time, rather from the heroin-induced stupor his regular junky customers took on after a heavy prick from the needle.

Lucky for Silvio, Strawberry thought, *his pain is dulled somewhat from the high he is on. Strawberry noticed the fresh needle mark in the vein in Silvio's neck. My God, the punk is farther along than I'd thought.*

Strawberry stooped down, popped the cufflinks off Silvio's French-cuffed shirt and pushed up the pink sleeves to expose numerous injection points where his veins at the bends of both elbows, just below the biceps, had received the venom many times over. Strawberry could tell from seeing far too many injections that Silvio's veins had long ago collapsed; used up, no good to him any longer. The vein in his neck was a convenient alternative. Ample blood flowed through that source.

Strawberry was patient. He had all night. Silvio could take his time recovering. Strawberry would wait in silence for the crumpled, rumpled slug in the blood-spattered pink shirt to come to so they could talk before he beat him some more. Still trying to speak, but hindered by gaping holes in his upper and lower jaw from three missing teeth, Silvio got to his feet, holding on to the shelves of canned goods behind him for balance. Strawberry took him by the arm and steadied him as they walked together into Silvio's office. Strawberry's goons followed closely behind. Strawberry sat Silvio in the visitor's chair while he took the proprietor's chair behind the desk, telling his accomplices to stand at each side of the chair supporting the needle-pricked arms of the battered boy before him.

Finally Strawberry spoke. "Little man. We have a serious problem. I think you already know what it is, so we can make this conversation real short. I am going to have my friends here break both of your legs in a few minutes with a baseball bat. Then we will take you to the hospital. I assume you would prefer to go to St. Mary's. Correct? I thought so. You will stay in the hospital as long as necessary to heal up and think things over. When you get out of the hospital you will disappear. You will probably need to have someone help you do that since you will be in a wheelchair, so it won't be easy for you to, let's say, run away and blend into the crowd. However, figuring out how to disappear is your problem, and you need to do it the minute you're released from the hospital.

"You will not come back here to the restaurant. You will not come back to town. You will not tell anyone where you're going, with the exception of, I suppose, the person who will be wheeling you around in your chair. They will probably need to know. Maybe you'll bring that person along. I don't know and I don't care. I also don't care how you get the money to disappear, but I suspect you have some stashed away somewhere. You didn't buy that many pink shirts with the money I gave you or you stole from us.

"I like you, little man. But I told you when we first started; there would be trouble if even an ounce of our product ever turned up missing. I thought you understood that. But you've probably shot an ounce a day up your arm for who knows how long. So, I think you would agree some of our goods are missing. That's why there's trouble here tonight.

"I don't care how bad you're hooked on the stuff, but I do know junkies are careless. They are stupid and they make mistakes. They're loyal to no one other than the needle." Strawberry paused. He stared at his bruised and bloody victim. "You are there, little man, you are there. You're a full-blown junkie, a waste, a disgrace, so now you have to go. You make this real difficult for me because now I have to find another place to operate from, and find someone to replace you. I like this place. It makes things easy for me. Your mother-in-law is the best cook around, and I'm real angry that you've made things hard for me. And when things are hard for me I make them hard for people who've made them hard for me."

Strawberry paused again as his associates brought Silvio upright in his chair. He had slumped forward, and from experience, Strawberry knew he was struggling not to faint. Undaunted, Strawberry continued. "Now, this might hurt a little."

Strawberry swung around in Silvio's swivel desk chair so he no longer faced the tear-and-blood-streaked face of the pathetic figure in front of him. He waited as one of his companions took a forty-two ounce Louisville Slugger, engraved with the forged signature of Joe DiMaggio on the fat end, and swung it across Silvio's outstretched right femur. The snap of the bone was as sharp as an exploding firecracker. Strawberry jumped in his chair at the sound. Silvio screamed and then went silent. Strawberry didn't flinch with the second crack. Then he turned around. He stared at the pieces of shattered bone that protruded through the purple welts, which immediately rose from the point of impact on both of Silvio's quivering legs.

He turned to his comrades. "Find us a nice bottle of California burgundy to share gentlemen. This will be a long night."

~

Nicole

Nicole told me later that she hadn't bothered checking on her husband that night or even early that next morning, since she had grown accustomed to his long absences. Often, especially recently, he would be gone for two or three days at a time without word or explanation, and long ago she had stopped her frantic pacing through their house, waiting and worrying.

Around ten that morning, the day shift nurse at St. Mary's called to summon her to the hospital, but Nicole took her time getting there, since, again, she had grown accustomed to Silvio's binges, two of which in the past six months had required overnight hospitalization for observation.

When Nicole arrived two hours later and saw a gathering of nurses and doctors standing outside her husband's room, she felt uneasy for the first time. She entered the room and caught a glimpse of the two bloodied, bandaged stumps lying atop the bed sheets, and wept for him the first time in a long time. Her emotions ran to extremes, from grief to anger, from remorse to revenge. As she stood in silence, her eyes fixed on her husband's pathetic form. She hated in one breath and grieved in the next. She thought of her children, her two daughters, who barely knew their father, but in his presence were enchanted like so many others who encountered him. She thought of herself, a selfish thought, how he had deprived her of hope, denied her a future, lied and cheated, deceived and deprived. Then she wept again, loathing herself for lack of sympathy. Where was the outpouring of her heart for his man, her husband?

She must be depraved herself, but her self-inflicted wounding soon left to be replaced only by numbness.

At about that time a surgeon entered the recovery room to give Nicole his report. His arm around her shoulder, he whispered gently to her how hard he had tried to repair the damage and save her husband from a crippled life.

"Was it an accident? Did he wreck his car?" she asked, now having gained her composure.

"We don't think so. We found him next to the emergency room, on a gurney, like someone had carefully placed him there. But he was unattended. Alone, and in great pain. Someone brought him to the hospital and left him, it seems. The police found his car at the restaurant. It was not damaged." the surgeon replied. "His wounds were horrific, inflicted by someone or something with great strength. His bones were shattered in so many pieces. So many I could not repair. I so wish I could have done more," he sighed.

"Oh God, it's awful, so awful," Nicole wept again as she gazed past the stumps to the ashen face of her husband.

"Mrs. Bustamonte, may I ask you? Is your husband diabetic?" the surgeon inquired.

"No, well not that I know of," she replied. "Why do you ask?"

"Please, look here," the doctor instructed, leading her over to the bed and pulling away the sheets to reveal the undersides of Silvio's arms. The pinpricked marks and the bruising surrounding them were striking in contrast to the stark white sheets.

Nicole gasped; then took a deep breath to regain her self-control. It was if she was staring down at the arms of a total stranger, someone foreign, an alien to her. Where did these come from? She turned away from the sight.

"Doctor, I've never noticed these. Silvio and I haven't seen much of each other for some time. When he comes home, if he comes home, it's late at night and I'm asleep. He then sleeps late in the morning and is dressed when he comes to eat, so I haven't noticed, but there were no signs of him taking insulin if that's what you mean," she calmly explained.

"That's what we thought, Mrs. Bustamonte. We tested him for diabetes. It came up negative. Those aren't needle marks from a diabetic injecting daily insulin, but we wanted to check with you to make sure. We believe, Mrs. Bustamonte, that your husband is injecting narcotics, probably heroin, and in great quantities," he said, attempting to move her away from the bedside.

But Nicole would not budge. She turned back, grasped Silvio's hand and stretched his arm straight out. "So this is why you abandoned us?" her voice raspy with anger. "This is why you stole from us; to feed your habit. Why? You had everything. People loved you. I loved you. You have children. You threw it all away. To get high! You're weak; you're a weak man, and when you hit me when things didn't go your way you were even weaker. Now look at you. Somebody hurt you to get back at you for something you did. I can't help you now. I cannot grieve for you," Nicole broke down again and collapsed in the chair by his bedside.

The surgeon, consoling, said, "We will take care of him the best we can."

"Good, because I won't. I won't any longer," Nicole responded defiantly.

Angelina, Carlo and I arrived a short time later. Angelina was inconsolable, but by then, Nicole's grief had subsided, perhaps indefinitely. She led her mother out of the room leaving her brothers behind for their bedside vigil to begin. She knew how they felt about Silvio, but we did it for

449

her and our mother, demonstrating a family bond, fragile and contrived as it was.

When Silvio awoke three days later, Nicole was in the room. She had reluctantly yielded to her mother's demand that she attend to her husband in his hours of great anguish. Both of her brothers were there, too; Nicole didn't know what she would have done if they wouldn't have been. Over the days, Carlo and I had endured alternating twelve-hour shifts to support her while she spent her days and nights curled up in a chair on the opposite side of the room, as far away from her husband as possible. Her daughters were in the care of our sisters, having been told their father was again away on a business trip and not expected back for some time. Her children also had grown accustomed to his long absences, so to them, at their pre-school ages, not having him close made little difference. She would worry about what to tell them later.

She was asleep when I had arrived to relieve my brother and was startled awake as Silvio bellowed out a wailing, nightmarish sob. Carlo and I waited at the foot of his bed unwilling to go to his aid, calling for the nurses instead. Nicole sat still in her chair in the corner of the room. She knew he couldn't see her, and prayed the nurses would come quickly. They did, two of them, rushing past the men at the foot of his bed, probably wondering why they stood by without a sound or motion. The nurses calmed him, re-dressed his wounds and cleaned the bedpan of his waste.

Groggy and disoriented at first, Silvio finally regained his senses and spoke haltingly after the nurses left the room.

"Hey, you guys, what are you doing here?" Silvio slurred. "Where's Nicole? Well, no matter. She's such a pain in the ass. Man that was a hell of a night. Really laid one on. You should come with me some time. I could show you both where the action is. We could tear up the town, you know. Plenty of strange pussy out there."

He plopped his head back on the pillow, and moaned, "Man, I don't feel so good. I must be gettin' old; feelin' a badass hangover coming on, you know, but I got to pee, man."

Silvio propped himself up off the pillow and attempted to position his body to step out of bed. But then he stopped and looked down. He howled for twenty minutes before another dose of morphine from an accommodating day-shift nurse calmed him and took him back to his tortured dreams.

Many times in those nightmares he shouted, "It was Strawberry…..It was Strawberry!"

That evening, the family gathered around Angelina's dining room table. Carlo, at the opposite end from his mother, at my right hand. Our sisters, as always, down either side descending by age from their mother. Nicole was seated in her usual spot to the left of her mother, in the third seat down. Our sisters' husbands sat behind them. Julia Gail placed behind Carlo. Our ritual continued no matter the occasion.

Carlo spoke first. Our mother was weeping quietly into her lace kerchief. Nicole was stoic, unemotional, rigid, waiting for her chance to tell us all, to seek our help.

"It will be up to Nicole and mother whether we keep the place or sell it. They have to decide. Silvio, once he dries out, if he dries out, will probably go to a handicap home where they'll teach him to ride around in a wheelchair all day, but he won't ever be able to work again, or really make any decisions."

He turned to Nicole. "I will have Mr. Parlipiano, a lawyer friend of mine, look at the papers to see if you have control of the place as his wife. I suspect you do, and I suspect you should have the law on your side whatever you and Mama decide to do," he paused and then continued. "I understand it's a good business, but I don't think any of us know where all the money goes. He's not been paying any of you workin' there all that much, including Mama, but he always seems to have new clothes and lots of money to throw around on himself."

"He's taken all the money, Carlo," Nicole interjected. "He gave me just enough to get by on, to pay the household bills and all, and he kept most everything from the restaurant for himself, to buy his drugs," she spat.

"Drugs, what do you mean drugs?" Angelina demanded. "That boy drank a little. That's all. Don't you accuse him of that."

Nicole didn't answer. After all those trips to the hospital she wondered how much Silvio had paid the doctors to tell her he was there drunk and sleeping it off. Silvio must have been released each time before withdrawal symptoms set in.

Nicole eyed her brother intently. He took solace in his presence. Without official designation, but certainly by silent acclamation, Carlo was chairing the family meeting and leading the discussion. He demonstrated a calming, soothing, yet forceful leadership recognizing that quick, decisive action must be taken to protect Nicole's interests and wrest control of the business from her husband. Nicole felt cold inside. She had tried desperately through the preceding days to collect, restore or resurrect some inkling of sympathy for her husband, lying there, not too far away, in his agony. But she could not. She had no feelings for him other than disgust. He had betrayed her. He had stolen her love; abused and discarded it.

In one brief moment of lucidity Silvio gave me the horrific details of his beating and mutilation. As if he were telling it about someone else, his graphic description was torturous even to hear. In turn I summarized his ordeal for her so in the clearest sense she knew by forsaking him it would be his final blow. It didn't matter. She rejected his pleas for help, for compassion, even for recognition. He was a monster. She existed only then to protect her children and her self interests.

She watched Carlo; considered him differently than before. He had wisdom and poise. How she wished she had listened to him before; those many times he offered his gentle advice, but she was headstrong then, she knew her way and he was not her father so he didn't matter then. Her thoughts were interrupted as she looked away from Carlo to her mother. She could tell that Angelina wanted no part of what Nicole was saying. By the look in her mother's eyes, Nicole could tell she was denying all she was hearing, still refusing to accept what her darling Silvio had become.

"Mama," Carlo said gently, "Silvio is not a drunk. He drank a little just to cover it up. Silvio's a heroin addict, a junkie, he's been heavy into the dope for a long time. I'm sorry, but it's a fact. He probably would have been better off if those guys would have killed him."

Angelina's fist came down hard on the table. "*Che cosa fare tu meschino Silvio e' junkie.* What do you mean, Silvio, is a junkie. What is a junkie, *e' spazzatura?* He drinks a little wine. That's all. He is still a good boy. He loves his wife and children. He had an accident; that's all. We must help him now. He will not go to a home. *Egli volonta vivo qui se egli guerra.* He will live here if he wants," Angelina sternly proclaimed.

"Mama. Please understand," Nicole said, surprisingly in a very calm, deliberate manner. "I don't want him here, with me or the children any longer. I don't love my husband any more. I haven't loved him for some time. He hurt me.

453

He hit me when he was drunk, or whatever he was, when he would come home. You never saw that about him. I have a duty to take care of him now, but he has to live somewhere else, not with you or with me. We have to decide where to put him. We have to decide about the restaurant. Do you still want to make the food, and do we as a family want to run it? I love you Mama, all of us do,

but *Silvio e' cattivo*. Mama, Silvio is bad.

He always will be bad, and now that he's crippled I know that he will be worse. Please believe me."

Angelina lifted her hand to shake her finger and scold her daughter for speaking that way, but Sophia gently took her hand and coaxed it back to rest on the table.

"We won't decide tonight. Let's all sleep on it. We'll come back together after Mass on Sunday and decide then," Carlo instructed.

Chapter 50
Keep Out of Utah and White Powder Residue

Strawberry received a last minute "invitation" to Jimmy's monthly meeting the afternoon after the *Chieftain Journal* published a short article about Silvio's hospitalization in the section next to the obituaries. No details were given about his injuries in the one-paragraph story, but word was on the street about their severity and mysterious cause.

Strawberry had been to the meeting the month before, but Jimmy's call to attend again so soon was not unexpected, even though it broke the Boss' pattern of staggering attendance among his capos. Strawberry had expected the call from Jimmy, and knew he'd better be prepared to answer serious questions about the junkie in the hospital with no legs.

Jimmy waited late into the meeting to address Silvio. "So, tell me why you decided it was right to hurt that boy the way you did," he asked while the spaghetti was being served.

"Boss, I had no choice. That punk is a junkie," Strawberry responded defiantly. "He was hittin' the supply once a day and trying to cover it up with powered sugar. He is so stupid. He thought I'd never catch him. Plus he was bombed out all the time. I couldn't trust him to keep his mouth shut. I was afraid he'd break if the Feds or the state ever got wind of the operation. I had no choice Boss. He had to go. I didn't think they'd have to cut them off, but he deserved it."

"You're so smart," Jimmy growled. "You think you're smart to take these matters in your own hands? Is that right? You think you're smarter than me? Did it ever cross your mind that now we must find a new place to cut and distribute, or someone else in that family to recruit so we don't have to move? That easier than just roughin' him up a little as a warning? What do you think? You're so smart!" Jimmy was in a rage.

"No Boss. I have it figured out," Strawberry, having now lost his defiance, tried his best to cajole his don. "We can keep the place. The boy's brothers will take it over to run it, and everything will be okay. As before. You'll see. No problem. Just as before."

That seemed to calm Jimmy slightly. The aroma of the heaping plate of pasta, marinara and sweet sausage which had just been placed before him probably helped, too.

Thank my precious Lord, Strawberry thought.

"Yeah, we'll see," Jimmy tucked his napkin into his collar. "You'd better be right. I trust you. I respect you. You must respect me. I put you in charge to make that business run well. It is a good business, maybe our best business right now, and it can get better, as long as there is no problem running it smoothly. I don't want problems. Don't make me any problems," he warned. "Next time you want to teach somebody a lesson, check with me first. Understand? No more problems." Jimmy picked up his fork and began to eat heartily.

"Don't worry, Boss. Everything is taken care of," Strawberry offered assertively, hoping desperately that was the end of it for now. Much to his relief, Jimmy moved on to the next item on that night's agenda, which Strawberry thought he understood was a new numbers game being introduced in Salt Lake City, but he wasn't sure. He was still too nervous to concentrate.

One of Jimmy's new young recruits, attending his first meeting after having spent six months in Utah scouring the market for opportunities, spoke up. "Boss, them Mormons are tough customers. They don't give a shit about how we operate the numbers as long as they can play equal to everybody else. They want their cut, maybe five percent higher than we're used to, but they can guarantee returns like I never seen. They seem to have no vices with their religion and all, so gamblin' just about makes up for all the things they're missin'."

Almost immediately Strawberry forgot about the confrontation with Jimmy as he listened to the young thug sitting at the other end of the table speak, occasionally, nonchalantly between sentences, stuffing his mouth with a meatball and a twirl of spaghetti from his fork.

Strawberry watched Jimmy nod as the little shit spoke, furiously jealous of the time and attention Jimmy was giving to the sassy, arrogant punk, even though just five minutes ago he had been thrilled when the subject shifted from severed legs to the untouched territory of Salt Lake and its strange inhabitants.

"A damn hooker would be broke there in two days," the boyish, less-than-bashful, pint-sized hood continued. "Bootleggin's no good neither. They got the craziest damn liquor laws in that state I ever seen. You can't get a drink from a bar over the counter, and there ain't no liquor stores anywhere. So these people ain't got nothin' to do 'cept gamble a little and go home and fuck their wives and have more kids. Damnest thing," he said, trying desperately to stifle a grin. "We'll make good money goin' in there, but it won't be like nowhere else. We sure can't strong-arm anybody, 'cause if we do, we won't make it outta there alive. They'll get us 'fore we reach the border, for sure. Vigilantes, damn sure. Them people stick together. Protect each other. They will let us in, if we want, but I'll bet we give up control in five, maybe ten years after they figure it out and boot us right out. One thing though, they got the prettiest goddamn women I ever seen in my life. Pure as snow, most of 'em, all blonde and virgin and the like. Goddamn strange place to be, Boss. Let me tell you," he concluded.

Strawberry watched with disdain as Jimmy and the rest of his associates punctuated the slimy little scum's monologue about Utah and its people with chuckles. Strawberry sulked in his seat and steamed with envy. When the laughter finally died down, Jimmy led a serious discussion through the majority of the evening's remaining hours debating the hot topic of the Mormons and the Mafia. In the end Jimmy tabled the discussion pending more research. Like all good businessmen, Strawberry knew Jimmy was weighing the investment capital needed to penetrate the market – a commitment of staffing and equipment – and a timeline for the first signs of a return on that investment. Before the matter was officially pushed aside, Jimmy espoused, as he often did, on his overriding philosophy. He said he was reluctant to set up shop in that mysterious part of the country with only one marketable product.

"You need many products, not just numbers and gambling, but the usual array," he preached. "Offer many products and services; whores, loan sharking, protection, dope. This broadens our profit potential, and reduces our risk. Otherwise, we sink before we swim."

Before Jimmy dismissed the gathering in the early morning hours, he brought the discussion back to the narcotics trade in general. Strawberry tensed, he knew what was coming – the question of continuing operations through Angelina's Fine Italian Restaurant.

"Strawberry, you really think that junkie's relatives, you say his brothers, would step in? Just like that? Take things over as if nothing happened? What makes you think so?" Jimmy probed.

Strawberry took a deep breath. "That's right Boss. I have them by the balls. I think they were prayin' for their brother-in-law to fall so they could take over 'cause of all the money that was slippin' through their fingers and landin' in the punk's pocket instead of theirs," Strawberry tried to sound reassuring.

"Well, I hope you're right. I hear the older brother works at the mill, pretty high up too, and the other's some kind of war hero. They're Sicilian, and that makes them good, but they might need a little persuasion to bring them in line; you know, to give up other things to come over. Especially the ex-soldier; he might still have an honest, patriotic streak in him. The other one; working at the mill; he might be more willing to leave that shithole for good. Might be real easy for him. In fact, wasn't there something about him awhile back, before my time? I remember something," Jimmy stoked his chin, thinking. "There was a young punk killed some years back; in Blanco's days, and a kid who was recruited at the mill saw it all. Then the kid wanted out, a real chicken shit, I remember. We let him off the hook when one of our top boys called in a chit. I think this is the same little wop bastard. This time you get him to come to his senses. But like I said, I want no more trouble there. Any more trouble will bring attention to the joint and to us, and it's your job to keep things quiet; make things run smoothly. *Capice?*" Jimmy warned.

"Don't worry Boss; I got lots of ways to go at this one. You'll see. Don't think no muscle will be needed, but if it is, it'll be real quiet; they'll go down easy," Strawberry promised.

"Better go down easy," Jimmy said before he brought the meeting to a close.

~

The following Sunday afternoon after Mass my family gathered back in Angelina's to take our designated places around her table. Neither Carlo nor I had gone to Mass. We had met early that morning at the closed-up restaurant to inspect the premises and rummage through Silvio's office for evidence of a bookkeeping record, inventory, or anything we could read to try to understand how the place was being run.

Not long into the investigation, we realized it would be very hard for us to gain any insight about anything that had gone on there before. It appeared all of the business transactions had been paid in cash. There was no general ledger or schedule of accounts to provide any guidance whatsoever.

"It's all in that slimy bastard's head," I said as I leafed through a stack of papers I found in Silvio's desk drawer. "Question is, where's all the money he skimmed?"

"It's stashed some place, and unless he gets his wits about him, we might never know," Carlo responded from the other side of the room, where he was sorting through hundreds of documents, most without relevance.

"This must be where they smashed his legs," he said as he stooped to rub his fingers over the expensive oriental carpet that accented the room's interior. "There're two stains on either side of the chair here. Looks like somebody tried to scrub them out with lye soap. See, the fibers of the carpet are dried and hard."

"What are you, some kind of a detective? Who cares, we know they whacked him good with somethin' real sturdy. Doctor said the bones were broken in a million pieces, like breakin' a china cup on the floor." My frustration was growing and I had very little patience or sympathy.

We then decided to tour the underground storage room and the two large, walk-in refrigerators stocked with perishables and meat. We headed to the basement. As we descended the stairs the temperature must have dropped by twenty degrees. It was cool and dark, but not dank or musty. The smell of sweet freshly cut basil, hanging and drying from a line stretched across one section of the room, was pungent in the air. Carlo switched on the lights as we reached the bottom stair and our eyes canvassed the large expanse.

I inched my way through the crowded but neatly kept rows of produce, vegetables and hard cheeses toward the refrigerated meat lockers. My mother demanded top quality ingredients in her cooking, so the canned goods that lined the shelves were mostly foreign brands. No telling where Silvio got them, but one thing he did right was to meet Angelina's strict standards for the best money could buy.

"I guess Mama must have told him what to order and the quantities she needed, and it looks like he did a pretty good job keepin' her supplied," I said. "I'll give him that much credit."

"Yeah, but what was kept behind these shelves here?" Carlo wondered aloud, pulling one wooden plank away from the wall. A drawer sprung out of nowhere. Both of us moved in closer to inspect.

"Well I'll be damned," Carlo muttered as we peered behind the shelf. There was a whole wall hidden back there, maybe twenty by thirty feet, with at least a dozen, floor to ceiling drawers running the length.

We could see how ingenious the design of the hidden compartments was. Some damn good carpenter had built a mechanism that when the exposed shelf containing the food was lifted slightly and moved towards you, a drawer literally popped out of the wall. Unless you knew how to work it, no one would ever know. Carlo had been lucky to accidentally shift the shelf in just the right direction to spring the spring. Heaped inside the drawer that had popped out of the wall was a mound of dusty white power.

"Damn, that's remarkable," I said. "Looks like our brother-in-law was hidin' more than his money, the rotten little prick. What do you suppose that chalky stuff is there?" I asked Carlo as I rubbed my finger through the thin layer of dust and collected a bit on the tip.

"What do you think that is little brother?" Carlo asked sarcastically.

"No! You really think so?" I felt like an idiot.

"Now, why do you think Silvio nearly got killed? Why would somebody go to so much trouble to build these shelves here and keep them hidden so well? Not much doubt about it in my mind. Hidin' a lot dope for them I would guess," Carlo concluded.

"Looks like there's storage here for enough dope to supply this part of the country for months. And I suspect he was skimmin' some of it for his own use. You don't do that kind of thing with the boys in town and live very long. Can't understand why they just didn't kill him. He probably deserved it by their rules," he added, without a hint of regret. I tasted the powder residue on my finger. It was strikingly bitter, and I immediately went to a nearby sink to wash out my mouth before joining Carlo again.

"So now that he's out of the way, what do you think they'll do? Think they'll want to keep storing the stuff here?" I asked him, but thinking I probably already knew the answer.

"Sure, suspect so. Question is, how insistent will they be?" We both stood there in silence for a moment, lost in our own thoughts.

By noon we had covered nearly every square inch of the building, including the basement and the restaurant. In addition to the ones behind the shelves lining the basement, we discovered more hidden shelves behind the walls of the walk-in coolers, in storage areas and through a trap door under the canned goods shelves leading to an earthen sub-basement and a cache of fine French wines. Behind the rows and rows of wine bottle slots, all made of finely crafted red clay, were more shelves, floor to ceiling. All were empty but few still displayed the dusty remnants of the contraband they once concealed

In the wine cellar, I identified a few of the finer selections of wine from the Bordeaux region of the liberated French Republic. Geographically, the cache hailed from the farthest point to the south. I recognized several labels. The Nazis had stolen and shipped tens of thousands of bottles of the best harvests to Paris for their hoarded selfish pleasure. They hadn't had time to drink it all, however, having made a quick exit after the invasion, courtesy of the good ole USA.

I picked up a bottle of Chateau Lafite de Rothschild Pauillac, vintage 1932, a fine red, deep crimson in color, aged now twenty odd years. Superb with lamb or veal. Chloe had taught me well. For a moment, cradling the outstanding creation in my hands like a newborn baby, my thoughts returned to Paris, its lights, its allure, its charm, its tastes and its temptations. Chloe and our frequent toasts from bottles like this slammed into my consciousness. I was lost in the memories until Carlo snatched the bottle from my hands.

"Where'd you go little brother?" he smiled. "Taste some of that way back when?"

I snapped back to reality, longing to stay where I had been just a while longer and not be here in this moment uncovering a den of balled-up snakes. "Some pretty special customers, I think, would be askin' for this stuff," I said smartly as I pulled another dusty bottle from the rack. "Suspect you'd have to have good connections to get this here, especially without the tax stamps," I added, now reluctantly fully back in the present.

We took two bottles of the best of Silvio's cache with us before climbing out of the wine (and dope) cellar to make one final sweep of the basement and main floor of the building.

"I'll tell you something right now," Carlo announced after we had locked up and were climbing into his Buick for the drive to Angelina's. "If we decide to keep the place, we're gonna have to contend with the boys. I think this place is real important to them. This joint's not only their hangout, but I have a feeling it's a pretty important distribution point. Too much storage here for a small-time operation. I say we burn it down. If we don't, they'll surely come knockin'."

On one hand, Carlo's declaration about keeping Angelina's was music to my ears. On the other hand, his predictions were more than a little disturbing. I didn't respond. I decided to ignore what he said about burning the place down.

As we drove toward our childhood Bessemer bungalow, I said, "Why would we let those bastards drive us off? That is a hell of a business we got there. Yeah, we don't know if the Mafia makes up half of it or not, but we do know there's plenty of good people who go there as regular customers, and they pay good money for Mama's meals. Our sisters need the jobs, and this would give you and me the chance to be in business together. It's been nine months since we had our little talk. This could be our chance, maybe our best chance. We could do it. You and I could stand up to them. We could take over that place and run it legitimately," I boldly declared.

"How stupid are you, anyway?" Carlo didn't hesitate. "Did you forget what happened to your girlfriend's family? Huh? Seems to me they were splattered all over the inside of that farmhouse you go to every day just because the old man stood up to them, like you think you can do."

"She's not my girlfriend, and that was twenty some years ago. It's settled down now. They aren't as powerful as they once were. You and I could reason with them. Just tell them no, and make 'em understand Silvio was not like the rest of us," I said with conviction.

Carlo jerked the steering wheel hard to the right and brought the Buick to a screeching halt at the curb. He turned to face me. "Damn, you really are ignorant. Didn't the Army teach you anything? Jimmy Clementi might look like a kind, gentle old man, but he's the meanest son-of-a-bitch to walk this countryside, ever, and he don't take no for an answer. You ever seen that big, fat prick they call Strawberry? Huh? Yeah, the same one who busted his legs in half. I've seen him in there nearly every time Julia Gail and I've been there. All by himself, sittin' at a back table, eatin' like a pig. Silvio was all around him like a pesky fly, bringin' him pasta and wine by the wheel-barrel-full. He's who you would stand up to. Him, and probably four or five others just like him. Ready to do that little brother?" Carlo's question hung in the stale air of the Buick's front seat.

465

I rolled down the window, needing to breathe. I surprised myself though. I was calm. I was not offended. "Brother," I said. "Let's not get excited. We'll take it a day at a time. We don't have to hurry."

"You're so full of shit," he declared, and the Buick surged forward from the curb with a cramming of the gears and popping of the clutch.

We pulled into our mother's driveway at the same time Katrina and Sophia were arriving with their husbands. Carlo hesitated before opening the driver's side door and I sensed he was giving me a signal that he wanted to hear more from me on the subject.

"Look, big brother," I took a deep breath and began. "I did learn a few things in the Army, not the least of which was how to defend myself, confront the enemy, and fight for something I thought was right. You think for a minute those goombas scare me? You think for a minute I couldn't mop the floor with any one of those wop mother fuckers? When you and I fought back to back the last time in Joe's place, we got the shit beat out of us, yeah, but I've learned a few things since then. Carlo, I know how to fight and I can fight just as dirty as they can if I have to, and if I want to. But I fight smarter than those guys do. And that's what will make the difference. We have the advantage. Outnumbered, yes, but we can still beat them. You're the one who has to make up his mind. I already have, and you know our sisters have as well. Mama has too. You're the hold out here today, big brother. You know I'm always there watchin' your back, now I'm askin' you to watch mine," I finished, opening the passenger side door and stepping out.

But before I went inside, I leaned back in through the open window. "I'll do this by myself if I have to. You can go back to that nice, cushy job at the mill, all safe and sound like a baby in a warm blanket. Be my guest."

I walked towards the front door before Carlo could respond. I must admit my knees were shaking just a little. Okay, I thought to myself, you've laid it out there. Now you must follow through. He may not be with you. And you may have to go it alone. Are you ready? I really didn't know. Hell, I'd probably just jumped into another foxhole.

Chapter 51
Try the Calves' Feet

Louie Parlipiano, esquire, sat shuffling through a stack of papers, his reading glasses to the tip of his nose, his moustache twitching, his fine French-cuffed shirt starched to the maximum. He had been at his immediate task for some time. Carlo, Nicole and I waited patiently, seated in his three office guest chairs across from his wide, brightly polished mahogany desk. Heavy deep-purple velvet curtains hung at the windows and a symphony played softly in the background on the *Motorola*, placed prominently in the corner of the spacious room.

Finally, when it seemed his glasses would slip from his sweat-beaded nose, he removed the frames, raised his massive baldhead, and spoke. "In our state, the spouse can petition the court to declare his or her counter party incapacitated, by mental or physical impairment, thus exercising their rights to gain possession of subject real and/or personal property including all assets related thereto," the esteemed barrister of the Pueblo District Court declared.

"In that event, unfettered possession can occur without probate or other legal proceedings, once a court of jurisdiction declares said petitioner's petition valid. Of course, competent legal counsel must be present at all times to initiate the petition and marshal it through the complex court system to properly and expeditiously secure a favorable outcome. It would be my pleasure to assist you and your family in undertaking this serious matter, and I assure you my actions will be effective and discreet, protecting the interests of each of you, and of course, your beloved husband, my dear," he looked at Nicole. "We all pray for his speedy recovery, but realize only God and the Blessed Virgin have authority over the outcome of that situation."

Despite the seriousness of our circumstances, I couldn't help but chuckle at the demonstration before us. None of us had had much experience with members of the bar, but I had seen the lawyer, his equally large wife, and, at last count, seven children, march proudly into St. Teresa's for Sunday Mass many times. They always made a grand entrance, with Louie leading the pack and his lady and children in single file close behind. He was one of the few members of the congregation who finagled a special greeting from Father Constanza each time he held out his right hand, pinky ring and all, for the priest to grasp. More than once I could have sworn the priest stooped to kiss it like he would the Pope's ring but caught himself just in time to raise back and instead give it a shake.

By all counts Louie was probably the biggest, most consistent contributors to the offering plate each week, which I suppose, warranted the attention he always received. Our goal in meeting that morning was to carefully weigh the advice he was giving and firmly keep our hands tight around our wallets.

"Plus, I might add," Louie continued. "On a personal note, I and many of my friends and colleagues would be greatly distressed if your establishment were to close. There is no finer eatery for a hundred miles around. My fee is twenty five dollars an hour, with a fifty-dollar retainer," he inserted as an oh-by-the-way.

The three of us sitting across from the barrister quietly took in his commentary; then looked at each other. Simultaneously, Carlo and I shrugged. Nicole sat quietly, intently, and quickly riveted her attention back on Louie.

I spoke first. "I guess that means we have a case. That is, you believe Silvio doesn't have to die for us to take over the restaurant. We can gain possession, as you say, or at least I think that's what you said, by going to the court and having him kind of pushed aside, like he doesn't exist anymore. Is that right?"

"Well sir, I am not suggesting he be pushed aside. It is up to you how you address his future physical and mental rehabilitation and the court will act upon the evidence we produce testifying to the extent of his current incapacitation. You must bear in mind that if, by the grace of God, he does recover his faculties, the court could reverse its decision, and he could regain control of the physical property and monetary assets, but he would have to disprove his current condition and convince the court, beyond a reasonable doubt, that he had fully recovered. That would be quite problematic for him, however. It is a rarity that someone, shall we say, so far gone, ever convinces a court they have returned, shall we say, to one hundred percent," he explained.

I found this part of his speech quite useful and I think all of us realized what he meant with the fancy words. "And I might add," he went on, "that once you have garnered power of attorney and right of receivership with respect to his assets, you also gain quite broad decision-making powers over his future medical and psychiatric care. To a very large extent he will be relying quite heavily on you to determine the speed and the, shall we say, scope, of his recovery."

That last part was even clearer to me. I looked over at Carlo and he back at me with growing appreciation for what Louie was telling us. But Carlo and I didn't have a chance to relish the lawyer's observations very long before Nicole spoke up.

"I got it. We are in agreement, then. Draw up the papers," Nicole ordered. "The sooner, the better."

Carlo and I sat back in our chairs a little stunned as we watched our sister take charge. There was little hint of emotion in her voice. Rather, a stern, forceful direction.

In days preceding our meeting, Nicole went about her business stoically and with purpose. She had been at the restaurant every day, scouring records and assembling what she believed was essential information for her case against her husband. She also was determined to have Angelina's re-open with a fanfare a week from today, and had assumed all along that Louie would confirm her conviction that she stood on firm ground. She had no legal training. What she had was instinct and her gut was telling her she had been wronged for way too long. It was time to make things right. Carlo and I had been skeptical but she told us repeatedly before the meeting not to worry.

I glanced over at her and she turned to me and winked.

"Very well then. My retainer agreement is before you. Please execute it, and I will accept a check," the attorney instructed.

It was over before we knew it, and only Carlo momentarily hesitated before rising to leave. We each signed the agreement and Nicole dug the fifty from her purse to hand over to our new legal counsel.

"I found this money in the bottom of his sock drawer," she said. "He must have forgotten it there. If he hadn't, it surely wouldn't have made its way into my purse. Please make this happen quickly, Mr. Parlipiano."

"I shall do my best." The lawyer wiped away a sweat bead ready to drip onto the freshly signed paper.

As we drove home, Nicole said with clear vengeance in her voice, "I'm going to take real pleasure in making sure that bastard never recovers."

A week from that day, we met Nicole's goal of reopening the restaurant by completing a proper inventory, purchasing new supplies in strict adherence to Angelina's culinary lists, creating a legitimate bookkeeping system and establishing new work schedules for the dining room, bar and kitchen employees.

Silvio remained in the hospital under heavy sedation and was transferred to the psychiatric ward, which was isolated behind locked doors from the main facility on the ninth floor. He was placed on twenty-four-hour suicide watch after the nurses discovered that he had hoarded his pain pills and one night took twenty. We were told that his efforts only resulted in a thirty-six-hour non-stop slumber. When he woke, they said, the stream of obscenities spewing from his mouth was even more intense than usual.

The next time we gathered at Angelina's house to decide the fate of the restaurant, we voted to move on and not look back. There was only one who abstained. Carlo was still undecided. If he quit the steel mill he would sacrifice at least half of the fairly decent pension benefits that he had accumulated after nearly twenty years on the job. Quitting now only made him eligible for about fifty percent of his weekly pay. A new union contract provided partial benefits for employees with less than a full thirty years with the company. His shop steward was president of the steelworker's local 27, and loved the restaurant and promised Carlo his support if he left. Still, big brother could not decide. Julia Gail was all for it, and his sisters were all applying pressure. Angelina was praying. There was no question where I stood.

We re-opened on a Saturday night to a packed house and turned the tables three times before eleven. Angelina's menu for the evening was nothing short of divine. She began the meal serving *Purea di Fave con Cicoria*, made extra sensual with her favorite fava bean, topped with dandelion greens. The *salada* that evening was untraditional and spectacular. She chose *Carciofi Ripieni*, small stuffed artichokes for this course. Then came an unbelievable plate of *Carpaccio* presented with lemons, champignon mushrooms, thin slices of *scaglie*, topped with paper thin slices of raw beef, and of course, only the leaves of the sprigs of Italian parsley. The main course took the diner's breaths away – *Galantina di anitra*. With it Angelina introduced *Risotto con Fiori di Zucca*. That year, the yellow zucchini blossoms were particularly vibrant. She chose aspic over the piquant for her poaching sauce, preferring its clearer reduction. She wanted the food just perfect for the restaurant's rebirth.

Angelina's helpers, frantic in their attempts to present the dish exactly as instructed, stepped to the line and performed to her expectations. She made it clear that there must be a delicate balance between the duck meat, pancetta, and chicken breast.

At Angelina's side that night watching every move her grandmother made, was Julie, the youngest of Carlo's three children. She was a beautiful child, striking in appearance with blazing blonde hair, almost platinum in color, when it shimmered in the sunlight; unusual for parents with hair as black as night. I knew my mother loved that Julie would jump at any chance to hover nearby as she mixed, blended, sprinkled, tasted, tested, poured, sliced, diced and dispensed her amazing concoctions. Although Julie was a sweet, kindhearted kid full of charm and inquisitiveness, she could be mischievous, and would hide behind her grandmother's apron for protection from her mother's occasional angry reproach.

I stood in the corner of the kitchen that night and watched the master at work. She said none of the meats must dominate the other, specifically the *prosciutto*, since it has a tendency to do so if not to the precise proportion. I watched the team add cloves of garlic to accentuate the spicing, and then whole black peppercorns, onions, cloves and celery to contribute to the multitude of flavors. They prepared servings of twelve.

Sparking further wild discussion was the offering of a small calf's foot with the meat dishes. It is a whimsical delicacy presented in various parts of Italy, and on this special occasion, Angelina insisted they be included. Kind of an Italian alternative to pig's feet, I would say. I had to make a special trip to the slaughterhouse out near Lamar to bring the baby bovine hooves to her when the local butcher failed to fill the order. All he had that day, he said with a chuckle, was cow brains, not feet.

My mother decided to cap her menu that night with peppermint Spumoni ice cream and dark chocolate bars. However, there were more refusals for dessert than takers since everyone had eaten like kings, and I'm sure few had room in their satisfied bellies.

Carlo watched the proceedings from the sidelines. He nursed one too many glasses of a less-expensive Pinot Grigio during the evening, and after Julia Gail seated the last of the diners around ten-thirty, she had to drive him home. That next morning, despite a crashing hangover, I'm sure, he drove back to the restaurant to see me. I had spent the night on the couch in Silvio's old office.

I woke with a start as my brother came through the door, announcing, "Okay, I realized last night you sure as hell can't run this place without me. You'd be broke in a month. All the employees would quit. Mother would be embarrassed as her hero son failed at his first and only business venture. Our sisters would be out of work. I can't let that happen."

I rubbed my eyes and yawned. "You're right. I can't run the place without you. Let's see. We only made seven hundred dollars last night; that's after paying the help. The food and wine and liquor probably cost us three hundred, so that's a four-hundred-dollar profit. I figured that out about two hours ago before I got this great night's sleep. Now, if I have to pay you, that reduces my profit by, say, fifty dollars, so I'll have to see if you're worth it. Why don't you leave your application there on my desk and I'll let you know if I can use you."

Carlo grinned. "Smart ass; let's get to work."

Chapter 52
I'll Pass on the Cognac, Thanks

Six months passed before late one Friday night, Julia Gail escorted Strawberry to the table he had requested at the rear of the dining room.

It had been an excellent span of time since the re-opening. Our routine had been perfected with Carlo and me alternating shifts of four days on and three days off and each covering every other weekend of the month. This allowed me to spend precious time at the farm with my trees and nuts, and Carlo to spend time with his family. Profits from the restaurant remained strong; traffic was steady and patronage loyal. In fact, just the day before, we had totaled our profit over the past half-dozen months and the families had each taken twenty five hundred dollars in extra cash, and Angelina and I had both pocketed a cool one thousand. With that and the stash buried in a Folgers's coffee can in her backyard, she brought a brand-new shiny 1950 Chrysler Imperial four-door for three thousand and fifty five dollars, and demanded that one of her sons teach her to drive. As with the restaurant, we also rotated shifts with this challenging task.

The rookie driving episodes that followed were terrifying, especially for her teachers. At the end of her training and a short trial period (which involved repeatedly circling the parking lot of Central High School until her instructors were dizzy), she declared herself ready for the road. The first night she drove to work alone, following receipt of her first-ever driver's license, she took up two, possibly three parking spaces in front of the restaurant. We had watched her park, a very unsettling experience. No longer was she dependent on anyone. A career woman. Head chef. True independence.

"*Io no avere unbisogno per tu a strada me. Io sapere fare esso me stesso.* I no need for you to drive me. I can do it myself," she declared as she proudly entered the restaurant through the front door, not the rear door to the kitchen, as she had always done before. From that point on she always came through the front door to survey her domain before taking charge in her kitchen.

The first time she came through the front entrance Carlo and I stood at the bar in shock as she walked up to us and placed her order. In English, she declared, "A shot, please, Johnny Walker Black." I couldn't speak. Dumbfounded, I turned to the bar shelf behind me and grabbed the most expensive bottle we had, placing in on the bar with a shot glass in front of my mother.

"Please pour," she requested politely, keeping her eyes on the empty glass. I did as told. She gulped it down with one swoop to her lips and placed the glass back on the bar. She reached and kissed me on the cheek and turned to her other son to do the same before walking back to her kitchen. Angelina was a free woman and remained a bad driver.

That Friday night, I saw the big fat bastard come in. I thought I knew who he was, and Carlo verified it. We both tried to ignore him, but when Strawberry finished his meal and asked for the check, he also requested that Carlo and I join him at his table.

"Gentlemen," said Strawberry as both of us were seated. "Will you please join me in a glass of cognac? You have the finest selection. I am particularly fond of the Elysee 1934." He lifted his glass to the dim light and twirled its contents to substantiate the color and texture.

"We're ready to close and still have a lot of work to do so we'll pass on the drink, thank you," Carlo responded coolly. "What can we do for you?"

"Gentlemen, I come as a friend. I come representing other businessmen in our community who wish to establish a friendship and a long lasting business relationship with you," Strawberry proclaimed in a manner that reminded me of lawyer Louie. "We believe we have a lot in common, and only wish to share in one or a number of endeavors that can prove to be very lucrative for you."

"Again, we don't have much time here. We have to close. What sort of business proposition do you and your friends have in mind?" I asked.

"There are many opportunities that present themselves for gentlemen such as yourselves," Strawberry declared as he swirled his cognac and took a delicate sip. "As you may have come to realize, for some time, prior to his unfortunate accident, my associates and I had a close relationship with your brother-in-law. We wish him a full and speedy recovery. In his absence, we would like to re-establish that relationship with the two of you. I don't need to remind you that keeping it in the family is always the best way to go," Strawberry winked and smiled, his fat chins quivering.

Carlo was losing his patience. "Let's get to the point. What do you want?"

"Alright," the fat man said with a slightly harsher tone. "I am in a generous mood tonight having thoroughly enjoyed your excellent food and superb hospitality. I am prepared to offer this. In exchange for the normal ten percent of your gross receipts for our uninterrupted insurance protection, we would be granted full access to your basement storage facility, to which, by the way, we have made quite costly renovations to accommodate the storage and modifications of our products. One or both of you would assist me and my colleagues in securing the products and the shipments, in and out, as the demand for those products increases as we believe they will. Like I said, in that event, with your assistance, we would waive the monthly payment for the insurance."

Now it was my turn. "We have a very simple response to your very attractive proposition," I said in a mocking and sarcastic tone. "Get the fuck out of here. Don't ever come back and we're warning you and your associates to keep your filthy hands off our place, leave our family alone, and go find another place to run your dope business. You aren't our friend, and never will be." "And, just to show you that we are also in a generous mood tonight, your dinner's on us."

Carlo added for good measure. "Now it's time for you to leave. It was very nice meeting you, and please tell your esteemed colleagues they are not welcome here either."

We waited. Strawberry sat silently, still twirling his nearly empty glass of cognac. Still smiling, but in more a menacing way, he finally spoke.

"I am very sorry you feel that way. I will relay your sentiments to my associates. I'm sure you will be hearing from us in the near future. By the way, since you insist, I accept your offer of a free meal, but you must understand your decision tonight will cost you the price of my meal many, many times over before we are through." He took a final sip to empty his glass, wiped his chin, and folded his napkin. He rose to his feet and walked away.

"Good night, gentlemen," we heard him say as he crossed the dining room floor.

When our final guest of the evening was out the door, Carlo turned to me. "Well, now you've done it. No turnin' back now."

"Seems you were takin' a big part in that little conversation we just had, big brother," I responded.

"Yeah, I guess so. I don't know what got into me," Carlo admitted. "Let's close up this joint. I'm tired. This might be the last good night's sleep we have in a long time."

The next week, since I had been spending most nights on the couch in Silvio's old office, Carlo and I worked to move furniture around, allowing room for a cot, armoire and nightstand to make my accommodations a little more comfortable. From now on I would sleep there permanently. To adjust to our new situation, we purchased two 20-gauge Winchesters. One was placed in the armoire, next to my cot, and the other under the bar at Carlo's easy reach. Just in case.

Apparently, Julia Gail had watched the proceedings with Strawberry that night from the open door to the kitchen and later demanded that Carlo tell her what was going on. He did, holding nothing back. Our dilemma was how to inform the other members of our family. Same way, we decided, hold nothing back.

At the end of our next gathering around Angelina's table, at the insistence of each of their husbands, all of our sisters quit their jobs at the restaurant. Their lives and the safety of their families could not be threatened or compromised. No one blamed them for their decision. The meeting was not confrontational, but rather sad, knowing that such power and intimidation could force a family to separate from the one thing that had bound us together. Angelina, however, would remain at her post. She would cook and run her kitchen. They would not drive her away, she insisted.

"I die first!" she shouted that night, not at her family but at the world outside. She told us she hoped she would live long enough to spit in Silvio's eye for putting her family at risk. Our mother had remained loyal to our broken brother-in-law until Nicole told her all there was to tell. She too held nothing back. All the beatings, all the insults and all the deceit came out as she sobbed on Angelina's shoulder.

On top of that, Nicole told me that one day when they visited Silvio together, he denied everything and pleaded for forgiveness. When she rejected him, he let out a lashing tirade of hatred for us all, including Angelina, the one he despised most for the credit she received for making his restaurant what it was.

Angelina was adamant that until her dying day, she would keep up the fight against the evil that her son-in-law had brought upon us. Our father would have wanted it that way; she made that clear. She would not disappoint him, and said he was standing right behind us for the decision we made. But she wished we had someone else to help, that we didn't have to fight alone. She was angry at that, above all.

"*Perche' erano sinistro nudo in facciata di far pagare toro?* Why are we left naked in front of the charging bull?" She could not accept the fact that there was no one to turn to. The cops wouldn't help. Other families were surely either already compromised or soon would be, either by intimidation or direct payoff. My mother was right. We faced a charging bull, horns sharp and not even a matador's cape to distract him. Yet we were defiant, most of all her.

"I will run them over in my car," she said.

We had to laugh at that one. That night, it broke the gloom, relieved the anxiety for just a moment. In fact, we howled until we ached.

Chapter 53
Pursuit of the Perfect Pistachio

A very uneasy calm settled over Angelina's Fine Italian Restaurant. The dinner crowds remained heavy and the money rolled in. There was no sign of Strawberry or the easily spotted hoods that often accompanied him around town. Time passed, and Carlo and I almost wished something would happen so we would know what we were up against.

For me, it was like waiting for the next Nazi charge across the winter landscape at Bastogne. Show yourselves, I silently pleaded. Reveal who you are. Come out of the shadows. Let's fight fairly. The waiting was making us crazy.

We changed our routines. None of us ever took the same route home at night. Sometimes Carlo and Julia Gail stayed at the restaurant with me, their children at Sophia's or Helena's. Other times, the children stayed with us at the restaurant. That was a thrill for them. They had their own secret places for hide-and-seek and they usually got to stay up late. When she insisted on it, Angelina drove home alone, but I usually took her instead, despite her willful objections. Sometimes she would stay at one of our sisters' houses. We couldn't change our hours of operation at the restaurant; that would've hurt business, and let our adversaries win. All of the kids in the family were closely watched. They were driven to and from school and never allowed to play outside alone.

But Carlo and I both knew our enemies, too, would change their routines. We didn't know how or when they would strike, only that they would. It was impossible to guard everyone and everything completely. We found ourselves living on a cliff's edge, peering over. We shared precious moments of joy and laughter, but were always mindful of what lurked outside, unseen, unknown.

Our shield was our grit, and a stubborn resistance. Our trust was kept among ourselves. Acquaintances were many. Trusted friends were few. We longed to break out, to return to a life before, but we believed in the righteousness of our choice, and with that knowledge we stiffened, grew stronger and more resourceful. The money was plentiful, but it lay there, accumulating, waiting, and even begging extravagance. Yet our self-imposed discipline held. We resisted the temptation. Our growing prosperity must remain hidden. To reveal it would spell greater danger. The more they saw, the sooner they would strike. But were we clever? Shrewd like them? They could see the crowds at the restaurant, night after night, spending freely. Our hoarding, our self-denial, may have bought time, but also might only have served to bring on a larger force, and a more determined foe.

We witnessed the dawn of the 1950s. And more of Truman. Korea, more war; although he said it was only a police action. He lied, and I couldn't understand; it was war just the same and he knew it. The whole country knew it. But I didn't much care. Self-absorbed, yes. I was detached, balancing high above the world, preparing for my own war.

My only escape from the spinning cycle of fear was my pursuit of the perfect pistachio. It captured every moment of my spare time. The trees in their neat, straight rows were my sanctuary, and I anxiously awaited the leave they granted me. I traveled to the farm every chance I could. My only companion was the Remington 12-gauge, always by my side.

My second and third growing seasons were marked with two rounds of early spring successes followed by late season kills from early, inconsiderate winters. Nevertheless, I managed to save about seven of every ten new plantings, and my three-year-old trees produced their first edible crop. My favorite pair had sprouted earliest and laid dormant the latest. Johnny and Maggie grew to the biggest of them all. The nuts produced by my tiny grove were different than the typical California kind, a little dryer and slightly bitter. I had to work on sweetening them up, but that would come after I figured out how to keep more of my precious trees alive.

I was pleased with my success so far. I continued to experiment with different techniques of grafting using the whip graft mostly on the young saplings and the cleft graft for top-working to encourage the trifle trees to expand at the top and spread their branches to eventually droop, heavily laden with their production. I was amazed as I watched my fledgling friends perform as the books described they would once my planting and grafting procedures were somewhat perfected. The cleft graft was particularly good for the more mature top branches. I worked with a mixture of road tar and rubber budding strips for the grafting. The tar worked well in preventing wood tissues from drying out while shielding the exposed area from the colder air. Because of the more frequent and sudden drops in temperature to which my town was prone, I soon discovered the inefficiency of my canvass-covered greenhouse. I was forced to tie the shoots growing out of my grafts with twine to support the braces. I tested the modified cleft graft and the side graft repeatedly, finding they were adaptable to certain trees depending on their individual growth patterns.

It was long and tedious work but it kept my mind off the day-to-day grind at the restaurant and the constant, nagging fear of retaliation. I also was growing weary of my confinement to the basement office/bedroom, hoping soon to begin creating a home of my own, with or without a mate to share it with. At the end of my third growing season, I paid Vincennes two hundred and fifty dollars for the right to construct a permanent glass-roofed and sided greenhouse on the half-acre plot, and set out to finish it by November.

To celebrate my first cash crop, I bought an old lever-action glass-encased gumball machine and filled it with two pounds of still slightly bitter nuts, which mostly came from the generous branches of Johnny and Maggie. To add a little curious color to the presentation I dipped the cache in red food coloring before filling the ancient cast iron disperser to the brim. I lovingly placed my treasure at the end of the restaurant's bar. I set the slots to charge a nickel a handful.

The machine ran out of produce after a week of steady sales, and I packaged the five one-dollar rolls of nickels collected from it and put them in the cash register. At that point I was only two thousand six hundred and fifteen dollars in the hole. Not bad for three years' work. The only complaints from my nut-filled-bellied-patrons were their crimson palms and fingertips, but they liked the color just the same. There was no taste to my food coloring, just the red smears to lick from fingers and hands. Red-shelled pistachios would become my trademark.

The tedium and tension of our lives continued, lapsing only in fleeting fragments of time with the occasional conscious discard of caution when we ventured out to tempt them with our public presence.

But then, when least expected, the first sign of trouble. Just a taste, but a bitter one. The winter after my red-dyed nut's debut, Julia Gail was driving a new route home. There was a light snow falling, and Carlo had remained at the restaurant. Following close behind her with was a dark sedan with its bright lights glaring. At the stop sign on Eighth and Spruce, she felt a slight touch to her rear bumper. Not thinking, she got out to check for damage. The sedan backed up and slowly steered around her, barely missing the spot where she was standing. An arm came out the passenger side window and waved to her with a middle finger as the sedan crept passed. She told Carlo. He told us, and we went on alert.

All of us feared there would be more. But nothing came, for months – 1951 then 1952. Ike's election, a landslide. Finally Eisenhower, I rejoiced. How I longed, once again, to hear him speak his encouraging words as he did on Britain's airfield tarmac. I needed to hear him now, to inspire me. To tell me the coming fight was justified, that it was right, and honorable. But he wasn't there to lead me, not this time. There was a truce for our troops between the Koreas at the thirty-eighth parallel. Good for them. Good for America.

But a truce in my town? A truce for us? Impossible to believe. And then, more than a year later, another encounter; this time more serious. We may have grown complacent. Sophia's two daughters, Jennie and Joyce, were walking to school just two blocks from home; walking alone. School began at eight-fifteen. It was a lovely spring day; peonies blooming, birds chirping – Sophia forgot. Or she thought, just this once, no harm. She was tired. She needed her coffee that morning.

A woman stopped her babies on the sidewalk, commenting on their pretty dresses. Taking them by the hands, she walked them to a nearby drugstore with a soda fountain and bought them milkshakes. They were late for school. The principal called Sophia to check on their whereabouts. She drove through the streets in a panic. We all joined her, frantic, petrified, blaming ourselves. We suspected the worse. Complacency is deadly in this game. But at three o'clock sharp, Jennie and Joyce were let out of a strange car in front of their school just in time for dismissal. The principal called Sophia again. They are safe, he told her.

"Mommy, she was such a nice lady," Jennie told her mother. "We had milkshakes, cookies, sodas, ice cream and candy all day. We drove out to the reservoir and had a picnic; then she took us back to school. It was a fun day; sure better than going to school. Can we see her again, Mommy? Why are you crying?"

"Who is she, Mommy? Why are you crying?" asked Joyce.

Police conducted a half-hearted manhunt for the kidnapper. No one matching the description was found. Months passed again. This time we remained diligent, cautious, and protective. Everyone vowed not to slip up again. Life as we knew it returned to normal – the normal we had grown used to, anyway. Shotguns were kept within easy reach. There were erratic schedules, little venturing out. We remained sheltered, hunkered down. Eyes always searching, ears always listening, keeping watch. It got tedious, sometimes depressing. It was often lonely, especially for me with no one to keep me warm at night. The girls from Trinidad were off limits.

Our task was to prop each other up; to find pleasure in the little things, like a birthday or a christening, or a good bottle of wine. We got by. We embraced each other and believed in ourselves. And then Maggie came back into my life.

I was tending bar on a rather slow Wednesday night when she walked through the door. I was only halfway listening to one of Carlo's old co-workers who had become a regular begin his latest joke about the farmer and the skunk. Gus drank way more than he should have, and was known for his string of off-color humor. The more gin he consumed the raunchier he became. The skunk was doing something inside the farmer's overalls when I saw her reflection in the mirror behind the bar.

Maggie took a stool seat at my counter. My heart thumped in my chest. I took a moment and a deep breath in a failed attempt to snatch back my composure. Disguising my elation pretty well, I thought, I turned to face her. I stuck out my hand. She took it and pulled me across the bar to kiss me on the cheek.

"Hello, Mr. Optimist. I see you got your wish, but I hear it didn't happen exactly as you planned," she said, catching me off guard as she had so many times before, leaving me bewildered, immediately wondering what the hell she was talking about. And in the very next instant, I heard, "I will have a Vodka Collins, if you please.

"It would be my pleasure," I declared, now beaming like a baby with a new orange sucker.

I mixed and poured three more for Maggie before the night ended. She ate handfuls of my pistachios, and her words began to slur. We had time for conversation since few were seated for my service, but our exchanges were sparse, trite and never got beyond the pleasantries expected between new acquaintances. Right before closing, her cousin Louie came to take her home. I closed the place; lonely again, knowing my bed would be cold.

Chapter 54
A Festering Sore

Jimmy

"Boss, why can't we hit them?" Strawberry demanded after the others had left. "They disrespected you." He and Jimmy were meeting privately following the regular monthly gathering. It had been six months since Strawberry had last been invited to attend, and since his last plea to Jimmy to allow him to permanently settle the score with Angelina's wop family.

Jimmy hadn't wanted Strawberry around. He didn't want to hear him whining about how he was treated that night nearly three years before when Carlo and I politely asked him to leave Angelina's after impolitely rejecting his request to become fellow criminals.

"Those little scum; I could crush them like bugs!" Strawberry nearly screamed.

Wild Bill's expose taken from Jimmy's diary mentioned a local family that became a "thorn in his side" as he described it. Our names were not revealed; rather Jimmy wrote how his will was tested by this family but in the end he prevailed, as always, in reeling in dissident factions. I'm telling this part as I think it probably happened in his twisted mind.

"Don't ever raise your voice with me," Jimmy shot back. "I will decide when we make trouble for them and how. Not you. This is the last I hear about it from you. Understand?" he warned, poking his finger into the big man's chest. Strawberry pulled away and fell silent.

Prior to their bickering over the brothers, Jimmy let Strawberry brief the others that night on a favorite topic – dope, pure elicit narcotics. Strawberry reported, as expected, narcotics trafficking in the U.S. had literally quadrupled in volume since the end of the war.

"Our businesses," he lectured as if he were before a classroom of graduate students, "are measuring this advancement in the hundreds of thousands of kilos of heroin, opium and cocaine – the new wonder drug – and we are earning massive profits. We've got more fucking money than we can spend," he bellowed, momentarily losing his professorial demeanor to return to the crassness that normally dominated his soul. But he caught himself, straightened his tie, and went on. "The importation, cutting and distribution networks for narcotics are well-established now, and our Boss' position in the West," Strawberry boasted, "provides a vital link to major consumption points all the way to the coast, particularly California."

"The temporary loss of Angelina's restaurant to our highly sophisticated system was a blow, a setback." Jimmy could see Strawberry was about to lose it again, as his voice rose and his face reddened. "But adjustments have been made. Other loyal supporters have been recruited to fill the void, and new safe centers for storage and processing have been found. But let it be said, no one ever fucks us over and gets away with it. Never! Not those little pricks. Nobody. Never. Let that be a lesson to you," he nearly shouted.

Jimmy then decided it was time to take over. He raised his arm to quiet the murmur passing through the attendees. "Okay, we've heard enough," he commanded.

Jimmy moved on to other topics, but despite his objections to Strawberry, the wop brother's situation was a festering sore and he was not one to forget or to forgive. Jimmy's credo always was that disrespect, left unchecked, could grow like a radical tumor. It could spread, could eat away at a healthy, vibrant business. The brothers must be taught a vital lesson so that their rebellion, their insubordination, did not tempt others to copy their actions. That was an unacceptable risk. He must set an example. His authority could not be threatened with dissenting disease.

Jimmy's problem was the allocation of time to address the issue, and he was not about to leave Strawberry on his own to carry out his vengeance, unsupervised, and without very specific instructions. Jimmy well remembered the backlash from the Danna killings and how Lucky never hesitated to remove the perpetrator, even from within his own ranks. The murders had been unworthy and created unnecessary upheaval. Killing those on the outside was still considered unseemly; frowned upon. And under Vito Genovese's command that edict remained clear.

Besides, things were going too well to bring those boys down now. He needed to remind us that we had violated the unwritten code, whether we knew it or not, but he suspected we did. They were smart boys. They should expect something coming their way. Their only question was what and when. And his only question was how severe.

Meanwhile, Jimmy had other, more important things on his mind. Priorities, like that spot in the desert someone had named Las Vegas and the big meeting coming up back east. Jimmy was in a never-ending scrap to maintain control over how things were being done there in the desert. His long-time rivals Benjamin "Bugsy" Siegel and the other Jew Boy, Meyer Lansky, had been causing him trouble for a long time. It was good that Bugsy was long gone now, failing to survive the multitude of .45 slugs to his face inflicted while he was reading the newspaper in the front living room of his mistress' house in Beverly Hills. Now it was Lansky who was giving Jimmy heartburn. Vito had not ordered his hit, however, so Jimmy had to deal with Lansky's erratic behavior.

Jimmy had approved and helped raise the money to build the Flamingo Hotel and Casino in Vegas way back in 1946, and he remained frustrated over the ongoing maintenance problems of the sprawling pleasure palace and the lingering disputes over the splits of proceeds. Plus, now that the place was finally making money, other projects were being planned, like the one being called the Desert Inn, and another, the Riviera; yet five million was a big number to sink into the sand and pay back on time. Jimmy also had his reputation on the line to make Bugsy's successors toe the mark.

He had Joseph "Joe Bananas" Bonnano to worry about from his outpost in Phoenix. Joe was determined to run the narcotics trade from his town, and Jimmy was equally determined to maintain control from his perch. These were burning issues that had to be resolved, face-to-face, in the presence of Vito and the others who could arbitrate the outcome, if necessary. Vito had been trying to organize the meeting for months, but scheduling conflicts, the choice of location, time of year, and a host of other problems always seemed to get in the way. So, severely punishing the two young pricks for being obstinate several years past was down the priority list just now.

But Jimmy still had to act, to throw Strawberry a bone. If he waited much longer it could be seen by the others as a sign of weakness. Strawberry had an enormous mouth and he had to shut him up.

Finally, placing his hand on Strawberry's broad shoulder, Jimmy said, "Okay, let them know we're still around, but don't hurt anybody and don't mess with that restaurant. If you torch that place, I'll personally cut your throat. Leave it alone; it's too popular around here. People would hunt us down, and the cops would be forced to turn up the heat. Just be smart. Don't cause me any problems."

"Right Boss, no problems," Strawberry shook his head. "They'll know we been there, but no one will get hurt, just yet," the fat man promised like the good solider he was.

Chapter 55
Scorched Earth and Stairways to Heaven

Three nights after Maggie returned to town, I finally heard from her again. I finished closing the restaurant and had retired to my basement boarding house when the telephone rang. It startled me. No one ever called this late. The instant I picked up the receiver a chill scampered up my spine. At first, I could hardly recognize her voice. She was gasping between sobs.

"What is it? What is it, Maggie? What's wrong?" I begged with an urgency I couldn't control.

"Oh, God, Johnny. I'm so sorry. Your place is burning. The greenhouse. I can see it from the upstairs window. My uncle is out there trying to put it out, but I don't think he can. You need to come. I'm so sorry," Maggie wept. Without responding, I hung up the phone. I knew exactly what had happened.

By the time I got to the farm, my sanctuary was a charred heap of rubble. Maggie took my hand as we slowly encircled the blackened remains of my silly dreams. Yes, my time with my trees had probably been childish pursuit, yet losing them – seeing my trees injured and likely dying – brought on real grief, not like a child's death, but like the unexpected flight from earth of a dear friend. Like the few I lost in the war. Something like that. I could have, should have, saved them, protected them better, guarded them so they could've thrived. I hurt inside and feeling helpless made it worse.

Maggie and I kicked the chunks of charcoal in our path and didn't speak for the longest time. The embers had cooled by the time we returned to the farmhouse. It was nearly dawn. We were too tired and it was still too dark to inspect the trees. Had any survived the torching? We would have to wait to know. I held her hand tightly and brought her away from my despair, before it turned to rage. I knew it would. Anger, then rage, then revenge. But that was for another time. It would come later.

The remainder of the night and into the early sunlight found us together on the front porch, both swaying on the swing, the site of our first date. But this time we talked, and cried just a little. Having her there consoled me, and brought me peace. There was none of the verbal jousting that had marked our earlier times together. Maybe we were over that, or maybe it was just that night.

I wanted to rebuild the greenhouse. When Vincennes stepped onto the porch with fresh-brewed coffee and words of encouragement, he could see no reason why not Maggie agreed. We would rebuild together. She said she was staying for a while. She had left her job in New Jersey. She made all the bombs she could. She had not made the atomic ones they were testing in the South Pacific, now that the Soviets had theirs. If she had wanted to she could have gone out there to the South Pacific, on to the Bikini Atoll or to the Marshall Islands where routine mushroom clouds were evidence that another sliver of land had been obliterated. She could have made the triggering devices for the big bombs, but thought better of it. She got homesick, she said. She said she was embarrassed to admit it. I scolded her for that. She said she was missing something, but didn't know what. She was not satisfied, even though her position and all the responsibilities that came with it piled tremendous recognition upon her. Vice President of Technical Services and Director of the Department of Special Component Devices was her title. No man ever held that post before. Her opportunities were limitless. She didn't know why, but all of this became unimportant to her. Perhaps, she speculated, she sought a simpler life, a less complicated life, and a life more rewarding.

Often she crossed the East River to see Central Park, experience Broadway, the Metropolitan Museum; had even stayed at the Plaza and the Waldorf, several times in fact, both on business and on two occasions with lovers, both of whom fell short of her expectations. Her candor was surprising yet I sensed it was cleansing for her. She was quick to say neither of them remained important to her or stayed in her life beyond the one-night-stands. She admitted that perhaps things would not be simpler here, either. There were different complexities and different challenges. She didn't know. She said she needed advice from someone who was relevant to her. She said I was relevant. To her. She didn't know why.

Relevant. I wasn't sure what that meant, but despite the fire, that night might have been the best night of my life, and somehow I knew when I went to check for signs of life among the trees there would be at least two which had escaped the destruction around them.

When morning dawned, after Maggie's uncle's coffee had refortified us somewhat and the sun gave us a rich, red glow, she and I walked to the scorched site that had once nourished my thriving, now pathetic pistachios. We discovered that a few of the trees had survived, but most hadn't. Johnny appeared to be dead, his bark blistered, his limbs limp. But Maggie, standing near, was alive; green and glorious at her trunk near the soil, and only slightly injured.

I wondered how the flames licked their wrath upon him, and she, only a few feet away, escaped with only a scalding. Around them, wilted leaves and blackened branches were everywhere. I pointed out to Maggie my favorites of them all, and revealed to her my names for them. She cried again. She said Johnny would come back. Don't give up on him, she advised. He was strong. He had work yet to do. We would give him a chance. Others would be removed, their remains buried to replenish the ground, but Johnny would stand as long as he could. Maybe there was life in him under the surface.

We spent the rest of that next day cleaning up the site, and made love for the first time that night in her bed in her upstairs bedroom, from where she saw the fire blazing the night before. It was glorious being with her, having her beneath me and then looking down at my face. We were at ease, comfortable, uninhibited. Our passion was strong. It came easy, genuine, unreserved. It was relevant. Is that what we were? Relevant? Maybe that's all it took, maybe that's all that mattered during those first few moments we were intertwined. Being relevant was a beginning.

Later, lying quietly in each other's arms, we whispered to each other about things that mattered. Did her bombs matter? Once, they did, but no longer, she said. Did her career matter? Yes, but she wanted more. She could find a new career. Did my trees matter? Yes, I would try again. Together we would protect them this time. Did the restaurant matter? Yes. My family's life was wrapped up in it. We would fight to keep it, to protect it. Would we give in? No. Never. We would fight.

Now, I thought, I had a lot more behind me than ten police departments and the entire FBI. I had her, I hoped. I asked her if I did. She said, yes. That was better. I could win with her.

I called Carlo the next morning and told him I needed a couple of days off. Living in the basement of the joint never really gave me a full day away even though Carlo and I were alternating shifts. Point is I'd worked damn hard for the past three years with few days off so he couldn't say no. Carlo said he had ordered five Navy surplus fire extinguishers like the ones used on the battleships from a surplus supply outlet in California. They would be delivered in about a week, he said, and would be placed around the restaurant and in the basement. He and Julia Gail would spend the nights at the restaurant until I returned.

"Take your time, little brother," Carlo said.

Maggie and I drove south to Santa Fe, taking the route through the mountains and down through Taos. It took us two leisurely days to get there. We visited several of the lovely, idyllic Spanish missions that dotted the route, and bought two spectacular Navajo blankets from a ninety-year-old roadside vendor. We stayed at the Inn at Loretto and marveled at the winding staircase to nowhere constructed near the altar in the sanctuary of the church next door. The nuns told us that it was built with heavy wooden planks without nails or fastening pegs, shaped in a configuration that remains baffling to even the most esteemed architect. The nuns solemnly claim that the carpenter who built it for the good sisters a century-and-a-half ago just appeared at their doorstep one day. He was a mysterious man, warm, kind and gentle. He was a godly figure, the nuns say, who came, stayed a short while, and left them blessed with much more than a stairway suspended only by air. Some say it is a stairway to heaven. The nuns sure think so and when you gaze upon it, it's hard to disagree.

While standing under those marvelous, mysterious winding wooden steps, I asked Maggie to marry me. The words came out of me in a voice too loud for the sanctum we were in. The sound seemed to reverberate off the soft, cream-colored walls and rattle the stained glass windows. Maggie appeared stunned by my question, and didn't respond. I looked to the side to scan the pews opposite the altar. A lovely, angelic, milk-skinned lady with her habit-capped head bowed in reverence to her Lord stopped her prayer, her eyes rising to search for the source of the noisy interruption. I mouthed a silent, "I'm sorry," but all she did was smile broadly and raise her hand to bless us with a sign of the cross. She re-bowed her head and returned to her rituals.

Maggie watched the nun shed her grace on us, and then turned to me to whisper, "yes."

Later that night over a dinner of the finest green chili pork enchiladas I ever devoured, I told her I couldn't promise the life she had lived for the past three years, but she said it didn't matter. She had come home to me and had prayed every night that I had waited. We were tempted to marry the next day right there at the altar, near the stairway, but she wanted her uncle to escort her down the aisle and I wanted my mother to wear a new dress that was not black. And maybe her red scarf, too. There was an apartment above the corner grocery store, across the street from the restaurant, which I thought we could rent until things were sorted out. That was fine with Maggie for now, but she soon wanted a home of her own. For too long she had lived in someone else's house.

We drove home a different way to see another part of New Mexico. There were no winding mountain roads and mini white temples to Christ. All we found was red dirt and asphalt. We regretted the alternate route, immediately missing our missions and the serenity they shed.

Our wedding, six weeks later, was attended by nearly four hundred people. The cathedral was packed, with standing room. Maggie wanted me to wear my Army dress uniform, but I declined. We had a brief argument over that, but I won out. That was my past, I insisted, just like her past. Time to move on. I did wear my Purple Heart though, pinned to the pocket of my rented, somewhat ill fitting black tuxedo jacket. My Army dress was placed back in the closet, although I did try it on before I put it away and was dismayed that it had shrunk, especially around my belly.

My mother wore a pale yellow silk dress and the red scarf over her head. She was gorgeous, and sat alone in the front row pew as she always had at each of her children's weddings. I almost fainted when I saw my bride. Carlo steadied me with a firm grasp at my elbow.

After my priest-instructed vows, I asked Maggie to remember the good times, forget the bad times, and look with me to the future. She nodded as tears rolled down her cheeks. As my wife and I walked arm in arm down the aisle to the applause of our guests, I saw him standing on the steps just outside of the cathedral's front entrance. He tipped his hat and strolled on down the street. As she watched him amble away, Maggie asked me who the
fat man was in his fancy pinstriped suit.

"He sure seemed to know you," she observed.

"Nobody," I replied. "Never seen him before. Must've gone to the wrong church."

Chapter 56
Careful Where You Step

The same day of Maggie's and my wedding, my very good friend Sergeant Victor Bravo also was celebrating; not his marriage (at least not on that day), but his ninth year on the Pueblo police force, and the fact that he had just received his gold detective's shield.

I've known Victor since high school. We played football together. In most cases the Sicilians didn't mix with the Mexicans, but Victor and I crossed that invisible ethnic barrier early on when two bojons jumped me in the shower after practice one day and he pulled both of them off after snapping one in the balls with a wet towel and the other with a thump to the back of the head. From then on I kept a close watch on his back and he does the same for me.

In those days in my town it was very hard for an American Mexican (to me Victor always was an American first and Mexican second) even to get on the police force, let alone move up the ranks, especially to detective. The Anglo cops, especially the bojon and Irish cops, dominated the top and middle echelon of the department. There were three Italian and two Sicilian cops on the force, all of them patrolmen.

Sergeant Bravo was one of four Hispanic cops, and the only detective. The shift senior officers were all white. So were the top commanders. Chief of police was Thomas Kelly. His deputy chief was Paul O'Malley. They were Irish pals whose families had been friends in Boston. They grew up across the street from one another and were quite the celebrities around town; everyone knew their stories. They made sure of that by hounding the *Chieftain Journal* to do series after series of personality profiles on them. At eighteen years of age, Kelly and O'Malley came west together and were hired in Pueblo as rookie patrolmen. In tandem they moved up the ladder, especially during the war, since they remained at home as essential persons, generously granted that status by the friendly Irish-dominated draft board. That last part never hit the newspapers, or course, but it was well known how they both avoided the draft.

Rumor had it that Chief Kelly planned to retire in two years, and after that, Deputy Chief O'Malley was tabbed to take over. All O'Malley had to do was serve one year as chief and he would earn the same pension as his buddy Kelly. It was all planned out, and everyone on the force knew it. They also knew three years back our four-term mayor Michael O'Callaghan approved the deal in an executive session of the city council's law enforcement committee.

Bravo told me that the chief and his deputy were active in community causes beyond their duties as stewards of the law – each still attended Klan meetings held each month outside of Rocky Ford. Bravo speculated with caustic humor that between meetings, their sheets and hoods were probably stored neatly in cedar chests at the foot of their beds at home after their wives washed, starched and pressed them by hand. They weren't grand wizards, but their tenure allowed them to co-chair several subcommittees including the initiative to suppress voter registration of blacks and Hispanics during each election cycle.

And they remained part of a splinter group that still plotted the Klan's retaking of control of mob activities in the region, a position it once held before the Sicilians gained the upper hand some thirty years back. O'Malley and Kelly were comrades in arms in every sense including their hatred for all minorities, especially the rotten Sicilians who had dethroned the Klan as corruption kings. Despite their festering animosity, the chief and his deputy were not above extending their greedy hands for payoffs from those they despised. Each month, at a pick-up point at the rear of the Twin Peaks Bowling Alley, the two top cops gladly retrieved their two-hundred-dollar cash-filled envelopes, courtesy of the benevolent cheese man. The two were so brazen that they stood under the blazing light of a street lamp to make one of the drops, and Bravo had witnessed it through a pair of strong binoculars one night while standing on a rooftop ten blocks away.

It was hard to tell the crooks from the honest cops on the police force in my town. Staying an honest cop was probably about as hard for Sergeant Bravo as getting hired in the first place. But he was a damn good detective. No denying that. While still a patrolman, he became especially adept at inspecting crime scenes and collecting useful evidence. He was skillful at lifting fingerprints. He could measure blood spatter patterns, and tell you the angle of the bullet or the thrust of the knife. He could detect what kind of flammable liquid was used to torch a building, or a greenhouse, for that matter, using his wartime Navy training as an arms and munitions expert while serving in the South Pacific.

Sergeant Bravo was off duty the morning after the blaze at Maggie's uncle's farm, but had responded to my urgent request to inspect the site before the rain, wind and dust spoiled the evidence and washed it away for good.

503

After a twelve-hour shift and on little sleep, and before Maggie and I left on our trip south to Santa Fe, the detective had driven out to the farm on his own time, off the city's clock, out of courtesy to me and our longstanding friendship.

"Definitely, standard grade gasoline," Bravo told Maggie and me. "But it was lit by some sort of timer or remote switch, so the arsonist could get away easily before it went up. A professional job, no doubt."

Ever since I had known Victor, he always wanted to be a cop. He left the police department to join the Navy and served on the carrier Enterprise in the battle of Midway. He did not lose his rank or his seniority while he served for three years, so when he returned Chief Kelly, reluctantly, and over the protests of many of his Irish kinsmen, reinstated him with full privileges and benefits.

As we stood among the rubble, Maggie asked Bravo if she could see a twisted, blackened lump of metal that Bravo found among the debris, wrapped carefully in a handkerchief, and placed in his pocket. Bravo un-wrapped the tangled glob and handed it over to her. In spite of the fact that the lump was warped beyond recognition by anyone without special insight, that woman immediately identified it as a delayed action explosive timer.

"Yes, just as I thought," she declared. "These were the types of timers used for booby traps. They are pre-set to ignite when triggered from a remote location. The Germans and the Japanese had them but the Japs were the best at using them, and during the war, at the depot, we thought we needed some device of our own to counteract theirs. Never made many of them, however. It was not the technology that stopped us. We could've made them by the millions if we needed, and they would've been better than the Japs," she

504

shook her head. "But it was a political problem. Our guys were honorable warriors.

Our guys thought booby traps were for cowards, hidden away to kill the unsuspecting. The program never got off the ground. No telling how many of our soldiers were killed by these types of things. The 'cowering enemy,' we called them. But probably only a handful of Germans or Japanese were killed by them, and probably most of them died accidentally running into their own rigged-up buildings or wide spots in the jungle trails. Pretty damn sophisticated for a bunch of dumbass Mafia hoods, I'd say, and pretty damn effective here. I'll give them credit," she added.

"No real way to trace them, I suppose," Bravo said. "I could see if any of the devices have been reported missing, or if there have been any reports of break-ins out at the depot," he offered.

"Don't bother," Maggie advised. "My guess is any one of a number of those guys out there, if asked and properly rewarded, would walk off with a bushel basket full of these and hand them over for fifty cents apiece."

"No question, someone's got it in for you, old friend," Bravo looked at me. "I just wish I could help. Was this a warning? Is there something going on that I should know about? This wasn't vandalism, you know. Do you want to talk to me?" the sergeant asked, concerned.

"Look Victor, I appreciate you coming out here; giving us your time on your day off, but I can't get into it with you. Not just now. You've got to trust me on this. It's something we have to work out on our own. Involving you would just lead to more trouble. Besides, if you did get involved, you'd be on your own. If you looked around for help in your in the department, I'll bet the room would empty out in a flash," I predicted.

"Okay, you've made your point. I just want you to know that I'm here if you need me," Bravo relented. "Most of the time I work on my own as it is. I've established pretty solid contacts with both the state cops and the FBI. If I run onto something that might require reliable backup I go to them directly. If all of a sudden they show up on an anonymous tip demanding help from the chief and his deputy, then those two lowlife bastards have no choice. Last time it was that burglary ring you might have read about in the papers. There was some kind of a connection to one of the boys in blue in cahoots with the cheese man. The chief ordered me to watch the punks at the high schools, when all along I knew it was a much bigger, much more professional operation. He was steering me in the wrong direction deliberately, until the Feds showed up under the broad jurisdiction of investigating organized crime. You should have seen the look on Kelly's face. That can happen here, I mean, the Feds coming in and all, so just remember, if this thing gets out of hand," the detective instructed, "you must promise me you'll call."

"We promise," Maggie declared without hesitation. The sergeant collected the evidence back from her, rewrapped it safely in the handkerchief, and walked toward to his car, leaving us alone among the destruction.

We had decided to leave for New Mexico before Bravo paid his visit, so we didn't linger long after he drove off. As we watched him turn from the driveway onto the main road, Maggie pressed me to think another way.

"Why can't we talk to him now, Johnny? He's your friend. He could help us," she pleaded.

I shook my head. "You don't understand. These are not fights you fight out in the open, and the last thing we should do right now is run to the cops. The only reason we called him is that we can trust him. He'll keep this to himself. I don't know how this will turn out, but I promise you if Carlo and I can't handle it, I'll bring Victor in to help," I swore to her.

She put her arms around my neck. "I trust you, and also, understand you have me. I've been known to get pretty nasty when I have to. Your problems are now my problems. Remember that, and also remember that I have a score to settle with these bastards, too. I don't know if I ever told you how much I love fireworks, and not just on the Fourth of July," she grinned and pecked me on the lips. We turned, hand in hand, and headed back towards the farmhouse to continue packing the car.

It was at that very moment that I had decided to ask her to marry me, and I would do it on our trip to New Mexico. How could I resist a beautiful, bomb-crafting bombshell that loved fireworks and bad tea and told me she trusted me even though we are going up against a very big, ugly, monster with ten times, maybe ten thousand times, our resources and manpower? I guess she liked those odds.

On our way back from New Mexico, I told Maggie about the other incidents involving our family that preceded the fire, realizing as I spoke that each event had grown more cunning and sinister. Throughout our trip and the wedding that followed, the fire and those who caused it never left our minds for very long.

"They are driving the knife in a little deeper each time," Maggie had said as we crossed Raton Pass and re-entered Colorado on our way home.

"You have a pretty harsh way of putting it," I responded.

"No other way," she said. "This is a deadly game, Johnny. You know these goons play for keeps. Maybe it's time for a little of their own medicine." And just like that, she laid her head in my lap for a nap as we toured North toward home. I stroked her forehead as she snored softly, all the while trying to wrap my head around this amazing creature soon to be my wife. The thought made me smile.

After the wedding we rented the apartment above the grocery store for seventy-five dollars a month and settled into a day-to-day routine. Maggie alternated shifts as hostess at the restaurant with Julia Gail and spent long hours in the kitchen with Angelina, watching and listening to her new mother-in-law practice her craft. Maggie caught on quickly, and soon Angelina allowed her to supervise the apprentice chefs on the three days each week my mother rested at home. On our one-day off each week, which we scheduled together, we were at the farm, in the field, re-planting and re-building. We counted twenty-five trees in bloom that spring. Our crop would be small, but a harvest was in store nonetheless.

Maggie waited three months before telling me she was pregnant. She wanted to be sure, and she avoided the topic until the doctor confirmed her suspicions. Her news came a month shy of our first anniversary over a late night dinner at our favorite American food restaurant where we went for a change of pace from the pastas and meat sauces. With the juices of crispy golden-brown fried chicken dripping down my chin, I nearly choked and I nearly cried when she took my hand to pat her tummy in celebration. She started showing at month four. It was going to be a big baby, we both agreed.

The greenhouse we built was much larger than the last, actually gigantic in comparison. Upon completion in October, just in time for the change of season, it measured one hundred and twelve feet by eighty feet with a ceiling height at the peak of the roof of eighteen feet. We had much more room than needed for the number of tender samplings it sheltered at the time, yet we planned for a sizable expansion in the future. Plus we needed extra room to maneuver the young producers through the interior space of the shelter when they were ready for transplant to the field. Despite the minimal bounty that season, as more of a symbolic gesture than anything, I bought two more gumball machines and filled them with our first comeback crop from the field. Maggie the Tree contributed her share to the harvest by proudly displaying her drooping top branches. Even they were about half their normal production capacity. Johnny was dormant for that harvest, but we couldn't fault him. He wasn't dead though. He was still recovering and we celebrated in that. Eyeing green around his lower trunk and on the tips of a few branches gave us strong encouragement he would be back in full production by next year. He got a lot of our attention as we pumped gallons of special nutrients into the dirt around his base to feed his spreading root system.

"He's hearty," Maggie announced one day. "And he's fertile; we have evidence of that," she giggled, stroking her swollen belly.

I had enough nuts to refill my first machine at the restaurant, so I placed the second disperser at the grocery store across the street, and the third at the soda fountain in the drugstore on the next block over, where my nieces had spent a good part of a morning sipping milkshakes with the wretched, phantom bitch who had snatched them off the street many months before. When I went to deliver my machine, the drugstore owner, Stanislaus Polanski, asked about the woman kidnapper, identified by a few observant witnesses around my niece's school that day as a Rita Hayworth look-alike, with fiery-red hair, wearing a large hat with a plume feather jutting out the top. No one ever saw her again, or at least no one ever came forth to offer any information.

"I'd recognize her if I ever saw her again," Podlanski assured me.

"Sure as hell. Good lookin' wench, she was. Wish they would find her."

"Don't count on it. They stopped looking a long time ago," I responded gruffly.

It only took a week for all of my pistachio machines to empty, and Polanski told me his customers were already asking for more. They especially liked the red color, he added, assuring me that his patrons were convinced it added a tasty flavor found nowhere else. Food coloring had no taste, but I didn't tell him that. My secret recipe.

With this harvest, I noticed the nuts were less bitter, almost sweet, and when their shells cracked open, they presented themselves with a slightly deeper, richer brown color. I speculated that the ashes from the fire settling into the soil might have stimulated the growth of the trees during the summer and the slight change in taste of the nuts. I wasn't sure of this theory, nor was I sure if my further grafting experiments had done any good. I would keep trying.

When we were finished with the rebuilding, Maggie and I met with her family to give them a tour and a warning. Earlier that summer, Maggie took an afternoon off to visit with some of her old co-workers at the ordnance depot. She told me she had a wonderful day reminiscing and relaying stories of her experiences after the war in New Jersey. After her visit she walked out with five brand-new, still-in-the-box, but not yet armed, booby trap timers. She worked on them in her uncle's shop as Vincennes and I pounded framing nails and completed the sidewalls and glass-encased roof of the new greenhouse. She adapted the lethal devices in such a way to modify the impact, velocity and direction of an anticipated explosion. Our decision to arm the perimeter of the greenhouse came after an agonizing debate extending over several weeks. We were not killers, but we were not beyond retaliation. We had an absolute right, even an obligation, to protect our property, and it was time to send a signal back to Strawberry and his cohorts that we had entered the fight willingly. Just the fact that we were rebuilding was statement enough that we were not going away defeated. They had given us no indication whatsoever that they would hit our pistachio farm again, but the trees were easy targets and helpless victims. We would not be.

Maggie promised she would construct a device that would pack a punch but not a lethal blow. She knew what she was doing. We kept our plan to ourselves until she was finished. When she emerged from the workshop with the last little menacing clump of metal in her hand, we placed each in the ground in strategic locations around the foundation of the greenhouse, carefully burying them far enough away to avoid damage to the structure in case they were triggered, but close enough to inflict enough misery on any invading culprit for them to sorely wish they had stayed away. We showed Mr. and Mrs. Danna exactly where each explosive was placed, and how they were cleverly marked to hide their location from an unsuspecting intruder, yet be easily detected by all of us with forewarned knowledge.

Maggie explained how the triggers, set only at night, were fashioned to ignite the tiny explosive charges. Mini land mines, if you will. Her finished product also was crafted to protect animals native to the area from harm. It would take the thrust of a creature one-hundred-fifty-pounds or more to set them off, and there hadn't been a sighting of a bear around this area in a hundred years. No one that we knew of had ever seen mountain lions, either; those being the only two mammals large enough to plunge the ignition probe. Still there were risks, and we were

511

concerned. She was inventing technology as she worked, and I could tell her apprehension kept her determined to manufacture them to a set of high standards, meeting only a narrow parameter of specifications.

The Danna's were satisfied and in full support of our decision. They too rationalized Maggie's work, thinking they might also fall victim again to these scoundrels unless they sanctioned our stand. In the final analysis, Maggie convinced herself that she had restricted the strength of the charge to maim, not kill, however she could not be absolutely sure. That was good enough for me. Mr. and Mrs. Danna were frightened, as we all were, at the prospect of another incident at the farm, but understood what needed to be done. In addition to keeping their loved ones safe, they, too, harbored a long sought-after revenge.

There had been no sign of Strawberry since he stood at the steps of our church on our wedding day, but I felt him around me like a dog feels its fleas. In my gut I anticipated another attack soon. This was unlike anything I knew, unlike American soldiers fighting their enemy honorably. We were up against a shadowy foe that hid behind a cloak of respectability and snuck up on you in the darkness to strike without warning, never challenging face-to-face like brave opponents should. Even the Nazi's fought honorably most of the time. But these scum struck without cause, for petty, unwarranted offenses.

They always outnumbered you. It was like little boys who fought over toy trucks, and when one turned away, just for an instant, the other slammed him with a blindside punch, stole the truck and laughed at his victim for dropping his guard. And if the one who was struck, struck back, fair and square, the other brought in his friends for help. To even the score. Fair fights were never in the cards when it came to these people. There were no referees. Not once while placing the nasty little devices in the ground did we feel like cowards. Not once was our honor questioned. We were justified. We were not deterred, rather determined, and that was good.

Chapter 57
Don't Loosen that Tourniquet

That fall, two days before Thanksgiving, the early day shift orderly at the Colorado State Hospital for the Mentally Impaired found Silvio's body. Somehow, he managed to lift himself out of his wheelchair just high enough to get his neck through a noose he'd made from ripping the bed sheets in strips and tying them together in sufficient length to loop over the exposed water pipe bisecting the ceiling of his room. He'd been off suicide watch for more than a year, convincing the majority of his mind-probing counselors that he had adjusted well to being so seriously disabled.

After his death, Nicole was handed a dissenting diagnosis from one of Silvio's psychiatrists. This particular doctor was convinced that his patient had lived the past year with nothing more than his haunting apparitions. In fact, that shrink claimed his delusions were magnified by his unceasing dependency on heavy doses of morphine, which had become his substitute drug for heroin. He constantly professed unending pain, when, in reality, the shrink predicted, euphoric stupors were his only objective and the only way he could escape the reality of his predicament. He saw himself as a helpless cripple, a freak, and became a frenzied fanatic whose sole purpose in what remained of his hapless life was to exist in a fog of denial. We believed this shrink.

The frequency of Nicole's visits diminished over time, but this was of no consequence to Silvio. We knew the drugs had become his only means of mental support. One month before his death, Nicole stopped visiting him all together.

The funeral was held two days after his body was discovered. Only the immediate family attended. There was a graveside service but he was not given a gravesite in the family cemetery plot, which Angelina had purchased upon Nick's death for fifty dollars that came from the settlement claim from the steelworker's union life insurance policy. Nicole was unemotional through it all. She wore black as a symbol of her mourning, but she displayed none beyond that. Instead, she attended to her children who she made sure showed their respect for their father, and stood ready to comfort them.

For another one hundred dollars for his time, Louis Parlipiano accepted the death certificate and filed the necessary papers with the court to permanently eliminate Silvio's name or his relatives from any claims on the restaurant or other assets. Among Silvio's personal items Nicole found a "paid in full" promissory note to his father. Signed by both of them, it showed Silvio paid Mr. Bustamonte off within three months after my mother started cooking for him, so the old man couldn't take a greedy swipe at our property.

Parlipiano also formally launched a search among all banks, both in the state and in a wide circle beyond its borders, for accounts in Silvio's name. Within a week, he had notices of current balances at two banks in Rocky Ford, and one in Fort Garland, amounting to nearly fifty seven thousand dollars. We received another bill from him, this time for five hundred dollars, when he notified us of his discovery. We were happy to pay. That night, we closed the restaurant and celebrated until all the children fell asleep on the chairs in the main dining room.

Nicole left town shortly after the funeral. When she did, she was sporting a fat bank account, new clothes for her kids and a brand-new black and white 1955 Pontiac coupe. We protested loudly, but also recognized that she longed for a profound change in her life, to pick up the pieces and start fresh. She would head for San Diego where a close girlfriend from high school was living who had recently divorced and was raising a boy about the same age as Nicole's youngest daughter.

After only a month of searching, perhaps inspired by her experiences with the illustrious Mr. Parlipiano, my sister was hired as a legal assistant in a newly formed law firm in San Diego. She began dating a young lawyer fresh out of Stanford Law School soon thereafter. She would be fine. I had no doubt. Carlo and I bought out her interests in the restaurant, which we would pay in equal monthly installments over five years.

Life without Nicole was not the same, but her leaving seemed to grant us permission to close that chapter and start a new one, at least for the business and to some extent with our own lives. Maggie and I awaited the birth of our child while we braced ourselves for another assault. We never let down our guard, but we quickly fell into a pattern that restored some sense of order to our hectic pace. However that illusive calm was fleeting, shattered like broken glass when, one night, early that next spring, the telephone at the restaurant rang at about eleven o'clock.

The call was from Vincennes. I took it just before closing up on a rather busy Tuesday night. Maggie's uncle said it was an emergency and I needed to come quickly. I called Maggie, whom I knew was asleep lying on her side with a pillow between her legs, her only comfortable position with the baby inside her, as big as it was. I only called to tell her I was going out to the farm and not to worry about me coming home late. But before I could hang up, she commanded that I pick her up in no more than ten minutes. She would be dressed and ready. I gave up trying to talk her into staying in bed and put down the phone.

By the time we arrived, Vincennes had made the victim (I'm still not sure if that is the proper way to describe him) as comfortable as possible, laying him on the same workbench in the same shop where Maggie had plied her bomb-making skills. He was writhing in pure agony, his cries stifled by a handkerchief firmly stuffed between his teeth. Blood was pooling on the floor below the bench, steadily dripping from open wounds from both limbs on his left and right side. When I removed the blanket Vincennes had placed over him I saw that this boy's life had been irreparably altered in an instant. Yes, he was just a boy, I guessed maybe eighteen or nineteen years old. And yes, when I looked down at him, his eyes squinting tightly shut and tears leaking from their corners and streaming down his face, my gut wrenched and my hand shook as I placed it on his forehead.

Maggie stood away from the bench without speaking, her knuckles pressed tightly to her mouth. The boy's left foot and a part of his right hand were gone. Vincennes said he had looked for his mangled missing parts in a wide area around the site of the explosion. He hadn't been able find them in the dark. Apparently the angle of the small blast traveled from the ground left to right, ripping and tearing at the boy's body as it went. Vincennes had tied tourniquets at the wrist and lower leg. They were having some effect on slowing the blood loss, but in the quiet you could hear the drops splatter, enlarging the stains on the wooden planks beneath where he lay.

At the touch of my hand to his head he opened his eyes. A chill ran through him and he convulsed in a head to toe spasm. I removed the handkerchief from his mouth to try to aid his breathing. He convulsed again. His color was grey like the coat of a newborn coyote pup. Maggie stepped forward at the onset of the second seizure to offer comfort, and I leaned down in his face to speak. I didn't get the chance. He spit in my eye. Maggie stepped closer to the bench and clasped his damaged and permanently crippled right hand, sending a shriek echoing through the shop's rafters.

"You will live. We will see to it, but we need to know who sent you. Was it Mr. Clemente, or Mr. Torino? Which one is giving the orders?" Maggie demanded, her hand gripping the boy's forearm.

"Fuck you bitch," he spat.

I gently moved my wife back from the bench and leaned down upon the boy to whisper, "Okay, have it your way. I will loosen these tourniquets and use them to tie you down to this bench. In about an hour or so, maybe sooner, you will bleed to death. We will wait for that to happen, then clean up the mess and take your body out somewhere in the field and bury it. No one will ever find you. Maybe you won't be dead when we bury you after all. We're not doctors, you know, so it may be hard for us to tell if you've breathed your last breath when we put you in the cold hard ground," I continued dispassionately.

"Your other option is just to tell us whether it's Strawberry or Jimmy giving the orders. That's all we want to know, and then you'll live. We'll get you to a hospital. We'll tell them you've been in a car accident, and you'll live, without your foot, however, and with little use of your hand.

We're sorry about that. But you shouldn't have come here tonight to burn down our greenhouse again. You've done that once; it's not very creative on your part to do it again. We think all of this is because of Mr. Torino's obsession with us, and because he's not too creative. In fact he's rather stupid, don't you think?" My face was only an inch or two from the boy's grimacing profile.

After a few moments of quiet, with only the sound of the boy's labored breathing and the blood dripping into the crimson pools on the wooden floor, he finally spoke, now with a less menacing tone, perhaps because his strength was waning rapidly.

"Okay, you bastard," the boy gasped, gritting his teeth in misery. "It is Torino. He's the one who's after you. I never even met Mr. Clemente."

By sunrise, our victim was resting comfortably under heavy sedation in a small clinic just outside of Lamar, having been treated by a friendly family doctor who said he accepted the story of the car accident, but we knew he really hadn't. He worked until dawn cleaning and bandaging the wounds, and successfully reattached some of the blood vessels and main nerves to give the boy restrictive use of his mangled hand. The doctor had been with me in the 101st as a medic, and I saw him perform miracles on the battlefield. We called him "The Savior." He hated the name. He preferred the name "Mechanic" instead. Upon his discharge he went to the University of Colorado School of Medicine and completed his residency at Denver General Hospital trauma center. He was damn good at gunshot wounds and repairing the maimed.

Doc Mechanic told us later that when the kid regained consciousness he revealed he was only eighteen years, six months and seven days old on the night he lost his foot and fingers. He'd run away from his farm home in

Oklahoma and fell in with the wrong crowd, ending up as a new recruit in Strawberry's nest of petty thieves and strong-armed wise guys itching to prove themselves as big-time gangsters. He volunteered for arsonist duty that night, thinking such a bold gesture would draw attention to him from his warped superiors. From his bed in the clinic, he had the doctor contact his parents who drove the three hundred miles in one day to reach him and take him home.

Somehow the kid got attached to Doc Mechanic and they corresponded over the years. Doc speculated that maybe he was trying to redeem himself, to prove to the Doc, and maybe to us, that he was good for something, and would make something of himself in spite of his stupid early-life decisions. We never found out the kid's name. Doc held that from us. Doctor/patient confidentiality, he said. But Doc did tell us through his connections with disabled war veteran's organizations, he helped the kid get fitted with a crude but functional artificial foot and with physical therapy to aid him in regaining better use of his hand. Doc told us the kid returned with his parents to their Oklahoma farm where he remained after finishing high school. The kid learned to drive a tractor and run a combine with the best of them and won several Future Farmers of America awards for his driving and machinery operational skills.

We did what we had to do – but hearing about the boy's success sure made us feel a whole lot better. Two days after the incident, Maggie's water broke and she went into labor. On the way to the hospital, in between her contractions, we laughed out loud as we took turns imitating fat man Strawberry's reaction when he learned the greenhouse was still standing, had not been torched, in fact, was not even scorched, by his teenage emissary who had disappeared without a trace. Kind of sick humor on our part, I would say, but levity was good at that moment.

Scotty was born after a surprisingly easy first delivery for a woman of the size and with the narrow hips of his mother. He weighed six pounds and fourteen ounces, and I thought he looked like a dried-up prune until his normal color came to light, which didn't happen for several hours after he was born.

That night, I returned to the apartment to seek my first sleep in two nights, leaving Maggie and the baby to the care of St. Mary's nurses. Valarie, the head obstetrics nurse, was on duty by herself that night, but she seemed competent and confident, so I felt like my family was in safe hands. I could hardly keep my eyes open.

"Go home and rest," Maggie insisted, cradling our new baby suckling contently at her swollen breast.

~

Valarie

When my son entered this world Valarie had been sleeping with Strawberry Torino for more than a year. She was trying to raise two children on her own after her husband was killed at the fight to retake the Korean central highlands. She met Strawberry in the hospital – he had been sitting in the cafeteria for hours after his mother had breathed her last breath. She didn't think he had a chance to say goodbye. She approached him, and they started talking. Turns out they both had needs, and they worked out an arrangement.

After that, he visited her about once every other week and she explained to her children that the big man in her bed was their uncle and that Mommy let him sleep there while she slept on the couch. Each time Strawberry left her fifty dollars and two Tootsie Roll pops for the kids. The money helped pay for groceries and part of the rent. The candy made the children happy to see their "uncle" the next time he arrived. She would do anything to give her kids a little extra; and she was a little scared of saying "no" to that man.

Valarie was a good nurse. She loved it when she worked the maternity ward and nursery. It was her favorite duty station and she could usually handle the care of the babies in the nursery by herself. In fact, she was adamant about working that area alone most of the time. She considered many of the other nurses quite incompetent, and liked to spend time with the brand-new babies as their sole caregiver.

The day Scott "Scotty" Nicholas Gernasio was born, Strawberry was waiting for Valarie when she got off duty.

When she exited after an exhaustive eight-hour shift, she was surprised, and at the same time dismayed, to see him standing outside the rear employees' entrance to the hospital. She was apprehensive. She always was when he came around, but his appearance at the hospital heightened her anxiety. She hoped that he wasn't looking for sex. He couldn't be thinking about taking her in the back seat of his car; right there in the parking lot? God, she prayed that was not the case. Could he even fit in the back seat? He barely fit on top of her, sprawled across her double bed at home.

She was already feeling dirty when she cautiously walked up to him as he leaned against the front fender of his big blue Cadillac. When he wanted her, his habit was to smile with a smirk and curl his forefinger, beckoning her to her bed. This time, his expression was stern; no smirk, no obscene gesture, just a stoic straight face.

"Don't say anything, just listen. I'm gonna tell you what you are going to do." And that's how he greeted her.

The deal was one thousand dollars and a promise never to return to her bed again. All she had to do was go on break for a cup of coffee that next night precisely at midnight. When her shift began at eleven she would again insist on working the nursery alone. Her knees almost buckled as he growled his instructions.

"You'll do it, won't you my nasty, sexy little nurse," Strawberry coaxed in a syrupy bittersweet tone. "If you don't I will pay you a different kind of visit next time, without all the goodies I usually bring. And you won't be happy and satisfied when I leave," he warned, smirking, the veiled sweetness disappearing.

That next night Valarie stayed in the nurses' lounge for thirty minutes after her shift began, crying quietly and searching her soul. At eleven-fifty-nine she left her post in the nursery. Through the window of the break lounge,

Valarie watched a woman, dressed in nurse's garb, dash from the door leading to the rear loading dock area of the hospital. She cradled a blanket-wrapped bundle in her arms as she sprinted to a waiting car, one that Valarie knew was different than Strawberry's, even though she couldn't decipher the make or model, only that it was black as the night. She wept again as the car sped off with its tiny cargo. No one but her as witness and accomplice.

After awhile, she dried her eyes and stepped to the next room to inspect her locker. In it was a brown paper bag that hadn't been there before. In the bag were the bills, ten with Ben Franklin's mug stamped in the middle. Four months salary and no taxes. She took a deep breath and returned to her post. Thirty minutes later, she reported a missing child.

Chapter 58
Running Like Scared Rabbits

Jimmy

The night baby Scotty went missing, Black Jim and his lovely Lizzie were on their way to Buffalo, New York, for a long awaited vacation before continuing on to the site of the summit meeting. Jimmy had the perfect alibi for any criminal activity that might be laid at his doorstep while he was gone.

After months of planning, Vito Genovese called for the first of its kind national gathering of the leaders of America's organized crime families. Vito's meeting was critical for several reasons. His underbosses were impatient, frustrated, bickering, and backbiting as never before. Jimmy experienced this firsthand when he demanded resolution over territorial disputes, mainly in the West, involving Las Vegas, Phoenix, Los Angeles and points in between. Vito needed to settle these conflicts before open warfare broke out, so the meeting was finally called, and a date set for November 14, 1957.

Jimmy and Lizzy left Pueblo two weeks before the meeting to give themselves plenty of time to arrive in Buffalo and see the surrounding sites, including Niagara Falls. Breaking up their vacation time Jimmy would be forced leave Lizzie behind to head toward Binghamton and get down to business.

While in Buffalo Jimmy paid a friendly visit to his old pal Stefano Magaddino who ran operations in the city by the Falls. That convenient detail, coupled with the We turned the tables from being the stalkers to becoming the stalked. spurred Jimmy's idea to take the little vacation, just the two of them, before the meeting began. To support that notion, and promote a safe, comfortable trip, for the first time in his life Jimmy bought a brand-new car. It was a Chevrolet four-door sedan, two-tone salmon and grey in color with wide whitewall tires, a big V-8 engine, and automatic transmission. It was fancy, but not too fancy. It would not attract too much attention. He was a bit concerned about the color – he preferred brown – but he got over that after Lizzy said she loved the salmon tint. So they drove out of town and headed East in their Chevy, just like any other typical American couple on vacation. They heard Dinah Shore advise several times to "See the USA in Your Chevrolet" on the new-fangled push-button radio, and each time, they laughed and sang along.

Stefano Magaddino was the cousin of big-time hood Joe Bonanno who, until recently, was residing on the Upper East Side of Manhattan. They called him Joe Bananas, mainly because he acted that way sometimes. Joe was causing trouble for Jimmy and Jimmy needed Magaddino to convince Joe that his cousin was making a mistake by opposing him. Jimmy always made things right for Joe who at one time held a high post in the Genovese family syndicate. In fact, Jimmy made Joe very rich despite the fact that the hapless Bananas had just been exiled from New York to the Valley of the Sun for his wanton carelessness.

Joe was placed under Jimmy's thumb for safekeeping, and Jimmy generously made the rebellious, headstrong hood the don of Phoenix. Joe remained a flashy gangster who flaunted his power and his money; the exact opposite of Jimmy's style. Jimmy could overlook that pompousness, but he couldn't ignore that Joe's ambitions ran counter to his own. Jimmy didn't want to take the matter to Vito, because if Vito got involved, he'd have to rule for one or the other, meaning that someone would be on the losing end, and whoever that was – whether it be Jimmy or Joe – wouldn't go away quiet. Joewas a formidable opponent for Jimmy, clever and resourceful, plus he was younger which made his orneriness all the more irritating, if not precarious.

But Jimmy knew he had Vito's ear more often than Joe did, and he was confident that if it came down to it, the ruling would go in his favor, but he also knew that when Joe lost, his temper would get the best of him, and that could be a dangerous, explosive situation.

Jimmy and Lizzie arrived in Buffalo on November 7. For them it was a beautiful, pleasant drive across country and into upstate New York. An Indian summer had pushed fall back, and the unseasonable warmth made their journey through the splash of fall colors that much more enjoyable. Strawberry was the last thing on Jimmy's mind. In fact, he had no idea about any child kidnapping back home.

Jimmy and Lizzie spent several days at the Falls and Jimmy thought his meetings with Stefano had gone well for all he could tell, with Stefano pledging support despite Jimmy's request for an overt severance of bloodline loyalty. Joe Bananas, Stefano told Jimmy straight to his face, could not be trusted. Bananas, Stefano said, did not respect lines of authority. If his wings weren't clipped, he would hurt the organization. One had to think, plan and execute, especially in the narcotics business, and Joe Bananas just didn't have the brains for it, Stefano proclaimed.

Jimmy left the meeting feeling somewhat reassured, having applied the Mafia mantra of keeping your friends close but your enemies closer. Few in his business, perhaps none, knew better than Jimmy that one had no true friends. Blood relatives were those you tended to trust the most, and Jimmy was asking Stefano to break that code, a dangerous request, but one that had to be made.

Jimmy decided he had better follow up. After several telephone calls from a payphone midway between Buffalo and the motel where Lizzie awaited him, Jimmy knew of Stefano's deceit. Apparently, Stefano called Joe right after Jimmy left his office. Jimmy had been betrayed, and that only happened once. Vito would now be told of his problems with Joe, and things were likely to get ugly.

The meeting was scheduled to begin the next day, and Jimmy had to get an early start on the four-hour drive toward Binghamton. He and Lizzie had just enough time for a quick tour of the sites and a quiet dinner at the Niagara Falls Lodge before he set out for the rendezvous with his associates at six the next morning. Vito was right, Jimmy thought, as he drove south in his freshly washed and polished salmon sedan, things were bad among the Mafia troops even at the underboss level. All the more reason for this high browed get-together.

The meeting would be held at a large Pennsylvania bluestone house on an estate owned by Joseph Barbara, a prominent landowner and local businessman. The house sat on a fifty-seven-acre spread just outside Binghamton, near the Pennsylvania border in an area the locals called Apalachin. Because of its relative isolation and assurances from Barbara that there were "no cops for miles around," it was declared a safe and secure location. No one would bother the two dozen or so Mafia chieftains set to gather there, Barbara insisted. But he was wrong.

~

As later reported in many national publications, it turns out that young New York State Highway Trooper Edgar Croswell had been watching Barbara's estate for some weeks before the meeting. It all started after he'd pulled over a motorist heading onto the property for running a stop sign. The young hood driving the car presented the trooper a phony driver's license and registration. This was around the third week in October. Croswell got suspicious.

Later, after he had returned home, Jimmy, ashamed and highly disgusted, read those articles as they poured out of the national press. He couldn't believe how stupid Vito and the others had been to allow it to happen. He would shake his head in dismay as he read quotes in *Time* from the smart-ass Trooper Croswell, who said he smelled something fishy after his encounter with the punk driver, and asked himself why this guy would go to so much trouble unless he was up to no good and trying to hide something really important? So he started watching the place during his day shift.

Wild Bill's account gave a delightful chronicle of Jimmy's description of the events that followed. Jimmy threw the *Time* article into the fireplace.

Christ, Jimmy thought, *why didn't someone realize the place was being watched? And why didn't someone find this Croswell prick and pay him off to get him out of the way?* He picked up *Life* and according to that magazine, Croswell said he began noticing a steady string of cars with out-of-state license plates coming and going from the Barbara property as the date edged closer to the big event.

Croswell kept up his vigil until November 14, and by then, had noted two dozen or so cars with non-New York license plates hovering in the area. He was on duty early that morning when activity around Barbara's property really picked up. As more cars sped toward the estate, the young trooper had excitedly called for back up. The volume was too much for him to handle alone, and he was coming up with some rather startling names for the owners of vehicles he had previously traced and the new ones arriving on the scene.

As the hours of November 14 unfolded, Trooper Croswell and his partner witnessed a near traffic jam on the entrance road and into the driveway of Barbara's property. They called in for more reinforcements; there were just too many license plates to track all at once.

"You never planned on raiding the house!" Jimmy shouted into the empty room. "You were only taking down license numbers!"

Life went into the fire, but not before Jimmy read Croswell's account of one car that especially had caught his attention – a simple salmon and grey Chevy; new, but not fancy like the Cadillac's and Lincoln's that surrounded it. The Chevy was far away from home, Croswell said. He had never seen a Colorado license tag before, so he had taken down the number with growing curiosity.

Jimmy had to take a break from the damn magazines. He felt a little faint. It was rare for him to drink hard liquor, but that day before he snatched another magazine from the pile he picked up at the local news stand, he calmed his nerves with a two-finger shot–glass-full of The *Glenlivit* single malt, aged fifteen years. When he resumed his reading, the shot glass now empty, it was the same story, just a different publication. Croswell told *Colliers* that "just as more state police and local sheriff's officers arrived on the scene to begin their note taking, someone from the inside of

Barbara's stone estate yelled "Cops!" and all hell broke loose."

Jimmy distinctly remembered the chaos inside the house when the cursing and scrambling began. He sat dumbfounded, watching his band of fancily dressed sophisticates, each having been given by Barbara a white carnation for their silk suit lapels as a memento for the occasion, start tripping over each other, grabbing hats and coats, pushing and shoving, fighting for the exits. Jimmy remained seated, watching it all; stunned, bewildered, and totally pissed off.

Vito was screaming at everyone to stay cool, but his orders were ignored. Joe Bananas was sneaking off, squeezing through a side window, but getting stuck. Jimmy wished he had a gun. It would have been a good time to blow Bananas away, he thought. He could have blamed it on someone else, maybe even the cops. But Jimmy remained in his comfortable easy chair as his good fellows ran like scared rabbits through a lettuce patch. He remembered thinking at the time how childish they all became in an instant, transforming from pillars of strength, feared by most, into naughty schoolboys scattering about after shoplifting bubble gum from the corner grocer.

Croswell described Barbara's mansion as it looked from the outside. Out from every door and window in the place, he said, sprinted panicked weasels with Fedoras in hand wearing pinstriped suits and pointed-toed wingtip shoes. They came from every direction, some slipping and sliding into the mud. Croswell said his mouth literally dropped open in amazement. But he shut it quickly, and acted on instinct. With bullhorns blaring, he and his fellow officers ordered the fleeing felons to halt. They set up roadblocks around the perimeter of the estate, and moved in task force strength into the nearby woods to flush them out.

There, they rounded up even more of the hotfooting hoods. Strange thing, however, he said, these wise guys hadn't broken any laws.

"Yea," Jimmy blurted out from his living room. "You fucking idiots hadn't broken any laws! If you had stayed put, the cops would have gone away, empty handed. Now look what you've done!"

After nearly everyone had vacated Barbara's house, Jimmy lifted from his chair and calmly walked to the front door of the house, now in shambles. Gorgeous antique tables and chairs had been smashed to splinters. Vases and crystal bowls lay shattered on the floor. Sheared glass ground into the polished hardwood from the heels of the scampering suspects. Fine silk oriental rugs were soaked with spilled scotch, vodka and bourbon. Awaiting Jimmy at the front door was a deputy who couldn't have been older than twenty.

"And who are you?" the cop asked with a grin as wide as the brim of his cap.

After his interview with the juvenile trooper in Barbara's doorway, with Jimmy refusing to answer even if the sky was blue, fuming with anger, he drove the Chevy North from Binghamton to retrieve Lizzie. Their trip West was much less joyful than the trip east one week before. Jimmy couldn't believe his luck when his cursed Chevy broke down in Ohio and they were stuck in Columbus for two days awaiting a new generator and alternator.

Croswell admitted in the articles that he and the other cops could not charge their captives with anything. They had to let all of them go. Before they did, however, the cops got to meet the Mafia's elite, including Vito Genovese, Paul Castellano, Carlo Gambino, Joe Bananas, and to Jimmy's utter dismay and embarrassment, the owner of the little salmon and grey Colorado Chevy.

"It is not illegal in America for people to gather together," Croswell was quoted as saying, as if overnight he had become a legal scholar. "The Right to Assemble is in the Constitution, so all we could do with these guys was ask them a few questions before we let them get in their cars and drive away. We did search the house, and found nothing other than the place had been completely destroyed. It looked like a riot occurred, with everything in shambles, but Barbara said he had no intention of pressing charges against anyone for destruction of his personal property," Croswell added.

In all, authorities, by linking the license plates to names and names to faces, gathered information on fifty eight of the highest ranking members of La Cosa Nostra, all the while thinking these wise guys had been there for a friendly backyard barbeque.

The *Saturday Evening Post* declared that the innocent surveillance turned into the most important assault on organized crime in decades. Photographs of Barbara's home and surrounding land filled two pages of that edition along with a detailed account of events leading up to and after the ill-fated gathering. Page after page of glossy magazines, Jimmy read every word. The mug shots of prominent mob figures highlighted the stories, always alongside a smiling Croswell, who had inadvertently stumbled upon the sting of his life. The only aspect of this otherwise disastrous episode that gave Jimmy any sense of satisfaction was that Hoover didn't get the credit for the raid.

Follow up articles described how the notorious head of the FBI J. Edgar Hoover was even more pissed off about the bust than all of the rest of the mob bosses put together. The Director, as he liked to call himself, had missed the big one. Hoover's corps was no- where to be found when the boys ran for the woods with the local cops chasing them down. America's self-declared number one crime buster had been beaten out by one lowly cop and his buddies from surrounding small town departments who became the first to come anywhere near to trapping the illusive dapper dons.

It was no secret that Hoover vowed never to sleep until he single-handedly crushed all of his country's big-time crooks, and he could not stand the thought of seeing others take the credit. According to the papers, what finally dawned on Hoover and his G-men following the unintentional raid was that big-time crime in America was highly organized; functioning under a close-knit command and control system. It was not unlike the military, and Angela's kitchen, run by an officer corps, which basically issued orders to enlisted soldiers who carried them out on the front line of America's streets. Jimmy was sure that the true intricacy of the mob's internal structure had been a stunning revelation to Hoover, who probably thought they were nothing more than a loose collection of ornery Italian thugs. Territory was captured and controlled by violence under an elaborate code of checks and balances, and big money was made each day, in outrageous sums. That year so far Jimmy had pocketed nearly two hundred thousand dollars; paying taxes on twelve thousand from cheese stand profits. A mediocre year by all counts in Jimmy's mind.

After the raid Hoover immediately secured subpoenas from the highest of all authorities – the U.S. Congress. He hauled boss after boss before multiple panels on Capitol Hill, television cameras rolling and flashbulbs blinding each witness. In the end hundreds of hours of Congressional hearings followed the foolhardy Apalachin fiasco, and thousands of pages of reports on the crime syndicate were written attempting to describe the American Mafia and its intertwined network of cooperating crooks.

Jimmy's new *RCA Victor* black and white console television with its dual speakers and walnut cabinet blasted Hoover's crusade into his living room day after day until he threw an empty shot glass through its screen, causing a spark and a small fire he had to put out with the blanket that hung over his couch. After that, the hearings got redundant and awfully boring when all Jimmy heard from his comrades were unending pleadings of the Fifth Amendment to every question including if the sun had come up that day.

The silver lining was that Jimmy had dodged being hauled before Congress. By the time investigators worked their way West, after first snatching up the big fish Mafia witnesses on the East coast, the press and the public had grown weary of the daily hearings. Their attention was drawn to other headlines such as the Soviets and their crude satellite called "Sputnik" and how some commentators, columnists and Congressmen thought America would soon end from an outer space invasion courtesy of the Communist bloc.

The hearings were completed about two months after they began. Jimmy was never even subpoenaed, but was preparing for the worse with his version of the speech: "On advice of counsel I respectfully decline to answer your question, Congressman, on the grounds of protection against self-incrimination."

Jimmy quickly realized that he and the other bosses would have to go even deeper underground. Now he would never get his chance to settle with Bonanno, or Stefano, or to set the future course for Las Vegas. For the first time in his life he felt apprehension. Not fear, really, just an uneasy sense that his impenetrable shield had been pierced. He was frustrated in not knowing exactly what his next move should be. Did he take on Bonanno, or Stefano or both? Was there a power vacuum with Vito's mug shot plastered all over the newspapers? Would Vito be neutered, his balls in his hands?

All he knew is that his tactics had to change. He knew he would become more isolated than before. He had an island to defend on his own, and his supplies in manpower and money were likely to be reduced, if not cut off all together, by the pirates in patrol cars and plainclothes disrupting or capturing his lifelines.

Jimmy was good at fostering change, but he knew this would be the challenge of his life. He was exhausted, drained from the sensational scene unfolding around him, and wary of the fate that had befallen his brethren. Jimmy was older now and wondered if he had the stomach for it all, or the energy to fight for his turf within the organization while fending off the long arm of Hoover's reach that might eventually extend all the way to the front door of his cheese stand. He only hoped Pueblo was too far away from Washington for the FBI and those high and mighty Congressional snoops to think about. He didn't know how it would turn out. It was out of his control, and losing control could mean his downfall.

Sitting alone, deep underground at the head of his opulent conference room table, he glanced down at his hands holding a trinket; a cheap little painted metal figure of a gentleman in a tuxedo with a cane and a top hat. It was a very poor likeness of Charlie Chaplin. Lizzie bought it for him at a curio shop near the Falls. He liked the miniature metal man. He loved Charlie Chaplin. Lizzie knew that. Jimmy, just once in his life, had worn a tux and top hat when he accompanied Lucky Luciano to the Stork Club in New York shortly after it opened in 1929. He hated the outfit – way too fancy for him – but he loved the atmosphere that night; the glitz and glitter; the puffed-up power they all had. They couldn't be touched. Amazing how years later, one lonely, very lucky highway patrolmen came so close to bringing them all to their knees.

Jimmy sighed, rose from his seat, went into the kitchen and lit one of the burners on the big stove. He gently placed the tiny trinket in a soup pot and settled it on the high flame. Slowly, ever so slowly, Charlie Chaplin began to melt, his top hat going first, his cane next, forming the beginnings of a puddle at the bottom of the pot. It didn't take long for the heat to intensify and destroy the rest of Charlie as Jimmy watched. He became disfigured at first then unrecognizable altogether, leaving only a molten pool that stuck to the bottom. Jimmy threw the pot in the garbage.

Lizzie spent a hundred and twenty five dollars on trinkets at the Falls. Jimmy thought it was an outrageous amount. Charlie only cost her a dollar twenty-five.

Chapter 59
Blue Blankets in His Bassinet

I was waiting in the hallway outside the nurses'
lounge at St. Mary's Hospital where Bravo was conducting
his interviews with the nursing staff, doctors, administrators
and any other employee he could get his hands on who
could shed any light on Scotty's abduction. I had just left the
men's room after dousing my face with cold water in an
attempt to stun myself back to my senses. I stood there in a
fog, staring at my ragged face in the mirror, consumed by
the events, ripped open by emotions. One moment my
hatred shook me as adrenalin charged through my body
demanding deadly retaliation, and the next I was drained of
all strength, all will, limp as a rag. My eyes were red, and
they stung from the tears. My fury ebbed and flowed.

Julia Gail was with Maggie, trying to keep her calm.
Over her protests, Maggie finally succumbed to a potent
sedative. The doctors said she needed it to stem her rage,
fearing complications to her healing from childbirth only
hours before. Julia Gail said the drugs would help me, too,
but I refused to take anything, even though I was drawn to
the thought of a drug-induced escape.

Finally, Victor emerged through the doorway of the
lounge and beckoned me to walk with him down the
corridor. Valarie, the pediatric nurse with whom we had

entrusted the care of our child as Maggie rested the night before, had been the last to be interrogated.

Bravo told me he had listened intently as she described the moments before she went on coffee break and after she returned to find the baby missing. She was heartbroken, she said, and was blaming herself for being away from the nursery, even though the head nurse, Valarie's supervisor, told the detective earlier that it was common practice for duty nurses to step away from their posts for brief periods if none of their tiny patients needed intensive care.

Scotty was robust. He was thriving. There was no reason to be concerned. No one was criticizing Valarie for leaving for those precious few moments. There were no witnesses to the disappearance. At least no one willing to come forth. No one had seen anything. Bravo's investigation had already smashed into a brick wall.

As we walked, Victor told me something wasn't quite right with Valarie's description of events. Her responses to his questions, he said, seemed rehearsed. Fear was driving her, he suspected, not for my child, but more for herself. He couldn't quite put his finger on it, he said, but his experience in situations like this told him to probe deeper with her. He asked her to call him immediately if she remembered anything, and then he recommended she not blame herself for anything. He tried to coax the woman to crack her suspected code of silence, complimenting her as a good nurse who cares for her patients. Everyone knew that about her, he assured her. He was using his "good cop" methods as opposed to a frontal assault on her potential culpability in an attempt get her to break. So far it hadn't worked.

"I think she's lying, but I have no way of proving it now," Victor nearly whispered as we made our way to the cafeteria for a desperately needed cup of coffee. "Our only hope is for her conscience to get the best of her at some point. Kidnapping is a federal crime, Johnny, so I have a responsibility to call in the FBI," he added in the next breath.

"You and I both know who did this," I hissed. "Just let me go find the son-of-a-bitch and I'll get our baby back; that's after I rip his fat miserable guts out."

"I don't think there's any doubt you're right. But you can bet he's got a rock solid alibi. If I go for him, or if you go after him right now, there's a chance you'll never see your child again. Maybe he's doing this just to frighten you. I need to know the whole story here, if I'm to help. You've got to open up with me," Victor pleaded.

We had reached the cafeteria. I followed Victor to an isolated table and slumped down in a hard plastic chair. Again my fatigue, my overwhelming sense of defeat, overtook me. Victor went to fetch the coffee. I gathered myself together. I knew I couldn't hold the whole story back from him any longer.

When he returned, I finally laid it all out for my friend, from our original suspicions of Silvio's activities, to our discovery of the hidden drawers in the restaurant basement, ending with Strawberry's demand for our cooperation.

"You know the rest," I concluded, "The greenhouse fire, snatching Sophia's daughters, and then," I gestured helplessly, "this."

"Okay, we know Strawberry works for Clemente," Bravo asserted. "I don't suppose he takes a piss without Jimmy's permission, so we have to conclude that Black Jim either directed this himself or at least sanctioned it." When I offered no response, he continued.

"What I don't understand is why Clemente even cares. This is small time for him. He's got many bigger problems now. You'd think something like this would be the last thing he'd want to deal with. It's not like you're a rival Mafia don, or some federal judge harassing him. Besides, by now, they've probably set up five or six other distribution labs around here that make it much easier to move the product. I just don't get it," Victor shook his head. "Maybe it's as simple as revenge. You and Carlo humiliated Strawberry by throwing him out that night. So he sends his goons to scare Julia Gail, and then burns your greenhouse, and he doesn't stop with that; he goes after Sophia's kids now he's got your son," Victor said, trying to put the pieces together in his mind.

"I left out one part," I interrupted rather sheepishly, and told Victor about Maggie's handiwork and the maimed teenager.

"Jesus, Johnny, you people are something," Victor exclaimed, after I was finished. He stopped at that, withholding further condemnation but still refusing to condone our actions.

Victor and I sat in the cafeteria for hours it seemed, until I had to tell him to leave, to go home and get some rest. He refused at first, but I told him he'd have to sit there by himself because I was going back to be with Maggie. I watched him slowly amble through the door to the parking lot; his head down, looking dejected. He was a pro and he made his living solving puzzles. We had all the pieces to this puzzle, and over time, I knew he would fit them together. But our terror was that my baby boy could be dead before that happened.

Two of the longest days and nights of my life passed without a sign, a hint, a signal – anything. Maggie was too distraught to leave the hospital, so our anguished nights were spent laying together, holding each other on the narrow hospital bed. We were adrift, floating on a leaking raft in the middle of the sea. Lost, no compass to give us hope or direction; at the whim of furious forces out to tip us over into the depths.

In my fitful dreams, I returned to the war for the first time in many years, and as always, as I was fighting the Nazis once again. I was wounded, bleeding badly, always in pain and never confident I would survive. This time the German in the foxhole wrestled the machete from me and aimed for my belly before Maggie nudged me out of my hell.

Valarie returned to work the second night of our purgatory and looked in on us. She only offered more words of sorrow, prayers for my son's return, and hopes for Maggie's quick recovery. Were her comments and questions insincere? Was her kindness a cover, a contrived misdirection to throw us off her trail? I was no cop, but with Bravo's words hanging in the air from the night before, I could not hide my suspicion. She went on with her expressions of concern, too long in fact, and she was stunned when I told her to leave.

Later we were told by another duty nurse that she would be substituting for Valarie for the remainder of the shift. Valarie had gone home, she said, with the sudden occurrence of an intolerable migraine. We waited. No ransom demand. No telephone call. Nothing. Just a deafening silence. Maggie and I had run out of words for each other.

I knew Victor was working back-to-back eighteen-hour shifts, driving, searching in every imaginable location for signs of our son, and questioning everyone at those places for any information that might aid in his mad scramble for Scotty's rescue. Abiding to our agreement, he didn't call in the FBI. He was working the case alone. Also as part of that agreement, at Victor's insistence, I stayed off the streets. He was adamant that I remain by Maggie's side and not join the hunt. I knew my friend was right. If I had gotten my hands on any of those pukes even remotely associated with Strawberry or Clemente, it would have been carnage for sure. He also insisted that Carlo stay at home. Bravo reasoned with Carlo, making sure he got the message that a counter-strike would most certainly result in my son's life ending before it began. We both did as we were told. We didn't like it, but my friend was right.

Carlo, Julia Gail and Angelina visited us at the hospital at regular intervals, comforting as much as they could. Carlo and I avoided any discussion of retaliation, heeding Bravo's advice. Angelina surprised us with her strength, her quiet yet forceful reminders of God's compassion; His promised protection for those who trust in His will. It was hard to believe in anything good at that time, but it was harder to deny my mother's confidence that goodness would prevail.

At about four in the morning on the third day, when my dreams had become so haunting that they crowded out any hope of meaningful sleep, I slipped away from Maggie's side to take a stroll down the hallway. Just past the nursery, which I had passed by maybe a hundred times a day, always with a faint, mystical hope of Scotty's magical reappearance, I stopped and turned around. I backtracked to the big window where elated parents were allowed to peer through the glass at their wrinkled, pink creations. As I stood staring at the only infant in the room, sleeping soundly cocooned in her blanket, I heard a whimper through the open door. I stared harder at the pink-swaddled baby – she wasn't making a sound. It was my mind playing cruel tricks on me again. But there it was again; this time louder. I looked around, not daring to hope. Not a nurse in sight. Trying not to think, I followed the sound through the door of the nursery. Inside, it was dark and cool from a twirling fan overhead.

543

As I moved toward the sound, I slipped on something on the floor. It was wet, sticky. I caught my balance, grasping the corner of a crib close by. But that, too, felt wet. I brought my fingers to my face, using the dim light that now shone through from the cracked door. My hand was stained red. The smell made me nauseous. I repulsed, terrified at the sight of my blood-smeared hand. I instinctively groped for the source, searching frantically inside the crib I had touched. I felt a blanket, covering something small. I folded it back, and gasped as I stared at the pale face of an infant, not moving, not breathing; cold, flesh unreal. I lifted it from its bed, the light-colored blanket almost purple from the substance it had absorbed. My knees buckled. The blanket dropped away. I was left holding a doll, its lifeless glass eyes blinking open as if to greet me, acknowledging my presence. I almost let the artificial human plummet to the floor, but instead, I carefully placed the doll back in its bed, its mechanical eyes closing once again.

I stumbled away, catching the slightly opened door to edge it open further, allowing more light to enter. I found a chair to catch my weight and stop the room from spinning. Then I cried. Huge gulps of anguish erupted from me and I shook uncontrollably. Still no one came. Finally, I lifted my head and wiped my eyes, my sobs subsiding. Then I heard it again – the whimpering – this time unmistakable. I had forgotten the reason I entered the nursery in the first place. I jumped up and stepped toward the baby behind the glass – she was lying peacefully, fast asleep. I turned and splashed through the coagulating liquid on the floor. The light from the door faded as I made my way to the back of the room.

There, buried under blankets in a bassinet, I found my son. I heard myself whimper now much louder than he as I reached down for him frantically, unraveling him from the heavy cloth, like shedding him from the awful ordeal he had unknowingly endured. I held him high over my head; then brought him into the light. His body had no marks, and his infant mind would display no scars. I cradled him close for the short journey back to his mother. And then I noticed, pinned to one of the blue blankets that had swaddled baby Scotty, a note with crude, cutout letters. It read:

Next Time You Wop Bastard It Will Be Real

Chapter 60
Choose Your Foxholes Wisely

After two harsh winters, the first snowfall the year following my son's abduction didn't occur until early February. On Christmas day the temperature was in the high fifties. The exceptionally warm weather for such an extended period produced an outstanding growing season for my pistachio trees.

The prolonged warmth, coupled with intervals of days that brought cool rains, gave me plenty of time to test new grafting techniques and develop a means of warming the air with external, propane gas fired heaters encircling large areas of the field. I studied how the farmers in Florida were devising ways to protect their orange groves from unexpected frost, and from that research, I designed a network of strategically placed heaters along the pistachio planting rows. I now had two hundred and fifty trees rooted solidly in the ground, seventy-five of them in production stage. The greenhouse became a laboratory for my ongoing work to perfect a heartier tree and a sweeter nut. Each year, more of my hybrids were surviving and growing stronger, and each year, I was acquiring more land from Vincennes for my expanding groves.

During the latest of this unusually long growing season, I was afforded two harvests from the best producing trees, and I stocked my thirty or so pistachio machines four times each. With the profits I purchased ten more machines, which I filled and placed in new locations around town. By harvest time I had machines at spots stretching from downtown to the fringes of the East side.

When Maggie and I worked in the fields, we brought Scotty along. Even though he was a small child, we wanted him to experience the wonders of the soil, the expanse of the land, and the bounty of the trees. When he began to crawl, he usually did so through the rich, soft, almost-black earth. If given a choice, we would have lived on the farm permanently, but our restaurant responsibilities required us to live in close proximity to the business. We moved out of the second story apartment and into a small two-bedroom cottage in a neighborhood outside Bessemer called Rosemont. We bought the house under the new home purchase program for veterans, which was part of the GI Bill, and this made the payments more affordable.

To add to the challenges of running a business, it was apparent Angelina's Fine Italian Restaurant was crying out for expansion. Carlo and I needed a plan to accomplish that without the costs dipping too deeply into our profits. The immediate need was to enlarge the dining room and the bar, and to add space to the kitchen to accommodate larger and more frequent seatings. The single-item menu, encompassing the multitude of courses, was becoming unwieldy, as Angelina was constantly worrying about exhausting supplies of her selective ingredients. Even when stocks of the meats, vegetables, and other fine fixings were purposefully kept high, the volume of business often threatened a shortage as we strived to meet increasing demand.

This became all too apparent on an exceptionally busy Saturday night when we actually ran out of eggplant and veal for a succulent scaloppini dish that had become an overnight sensation. We had to turn away twenty people that night and they were as angry as we were about the lack of proper planning and preparation. In addition, our kitchen was just too small for the seven full-time apprentices and senior chefs under Angelina's supervision. They were getting in each other's way and the place was literally becoming chaotic at peak times.

Our mother needed more room, and a larger, calmer atmosphere in which to create her masterpieces. She was rapidly running out of patience and the endurance she needed to maintain the quality of her dishes. To lessen the stress until we could provide more space and better working conditions, we offered a two-item menu of an equal number of courses. This would not be easy if we were to maintain the high quality standards achieved when only a single menu item was featured. It was a major challenge for Angelina, but she prevailed.

For now, she coped with the size and capacity of the kitchen we had. We did make adjustments, however. We spaced out the seatings with the first starting as early as six in the evening and the last beginning at eight. That meant Angelina's workday began at three in the afternoon, but she was done and could go home by eight o'clock each evening. This was a much better schedule for her. Things were changing for my mother, an admission hard for me, Carlo or anyone close to her to make. Maggie was actually the first to point out Angelina's stepped down pace. We noticed a slightly slower, more deliberate motion of her hands as she worked and in her feet as she walked. Although still plenty vigorous, our mother was beginning to show and probably feel her age. She would turn fifty-nine this coming summer.

As we planned for the expansion, another idea popped up. In addition to the larger kitchen and dining area, we were also considering building a small, intimate nightclub, providing a dance floor and live entertainment. This was actually Carlo's idea, which was somewhat of a role reversal for us, since I was the one who usually advanced riskier initiatives. The concept was to create a first-class supper club and all-around entertainment center, attracting both families out on the town for the evening as well as couples, or even singles, looking for enjoyable adult diversions.

We rationalized that if we completed the expansion all at once, it would save money in construction and allow us to absorb the added costs more easily. On the other hand, the risks would be magnified, and I was the one, this time, who took the cautious stance. What caused the concern was the unrelenting threat from our tormentors. It had been more than two years since they had struck us. We had been left alone since my baby's kidnapping. No one from Black Jim's camp had come around to spread their terror. There had been no threats or incidents to prompt greater apprehension, although we always remained on high alert for signs of impending harm.

"Carlo, all of you," I began when we met to discuss the proposition, "This probably sounds crazy, but if we turn this place into a jewel, which I know we can and probably should do, it's like waving a red cape in front of an angry bull. If we flaunt our success, those bastards will flock around us like buzzards just circlin' up there, waitin' for the best time to swoop down and take their fill."

"Come on brother, now look who's actin' paranoid around here," Carlo mocked. "You accuse me of a rubber neck, always lookin' over my shoulder. Sure we have to be careful. Our erratic routines haven't changed, and probably never will, but it's been two years since they snatched Scotty and nothin's happened. Nothin' at all. Don't you think

Jimmy's made Strawberry move on to bigger and better things, bigger and more profitable victims?"

Then my wife joined in. "Johnny, I understand what you are saying, but you're the one who always preached about never letting those scum control our lives," Maggie gently scolded. "We can't just sit here, cramped in this building when our business screams for improvement and expansion. They took our son. They brought him back. They didn't hurt him but they could have. Sure it was a warning, but a warning for what? To cower in the corner? They win when we hunker down, trembling in our boots. But that's what I hear you saying. Am I right?"

"No, lay off, both of you," I demanded. "I'm just puttin' it out there, bringin' it out for all of you to think about."

"Well, stuff it back in your head," Carlo advised. "If you can't give me – all of us – one good reason not to go ahead, then it's time to end this meeting and get on with it."

Julia Gail spoke up. "Johnny, I can never get over the nagging feeling that they will hit us again when we least expect it," she said quietly. "And that's going to happen whether we stay small as we are or we shoot for the moon. We all know they never forget or forgive; they only lie in wait. So, yes, I think you're right. We will be inviting them to hurt us again, and yes, we are flaunting our success, but that's the risk we have to take."

I turned to Angelina. "Momma, what do you think?" She didn't hesitate.

"*Figli miei. Non potremo mai riposarci con la mano nera sulle nostre spalle. Sara'sempre li. Ma la loro maledizione diventa reale solo se scpiamo. Costruisci la mia cucina, la risposta di Angelina e dopo agguinse, e voglio ballare il mio primo ballo nella sala da ballo.* My children. We can never rest easy with the Black Hand on our shoulders. It will always be there. But their curse only becomes real if we run. Build my kitchen," she answered and then added in English, "and I want to dance the first dance in my ballroom."

"*Non ti stiamo costruendo una sals da ballo, mamma.* We're not building you a ballroom, Mama," Carlo said.

"*Per me sara'una grande sals da ballo, figlio.* To me son, it will be a grand ballroom," she replied.

I interjected. "Okay, but let's just spend a minute or two going over what we now know about our enemies."

"All right, go for it," Carlo allowed.

I had been thinking about the topic for some time so I was prepared to lay out the facts as we knew them. I presented a fairly concise summary. As far as we were concerned, Strawberry was nowhere to be found, but he remained a shadowy poison serpent.

I was repeating some facts my family already knew when I described how the mass of publicity surrounding Jimmy Clemente's attendance at the botched national mob conclave the press now called the "Apalachin Meeting" two years before had died down, but newspaper stories about him were still frequently planted, probably by the FBI. The stories contained allegations from anonymous sources of his numerous criminal activities.

There had been no arrests, nor were there even any announcements of formal investigations, yet the stories still painted a diabolical picture of Black Jim as a Mafia madman managing a vast empire of corruption and coercion. The press was keeping Black Jim in the spotlight and that seemed to be keeping his cohorts, including Strawberry, in check for the time being. Yet, I emphasized to my family, if we raised the profile of our establishment, no matter how much the Feds or anyone else ranted about them, it would likely mean that the mob would eventually come calling.

"You can bet," I asserted, "that they will first demand protection money, and then a piece of our profits and then, who knows; the sky's the limit." The more business investment one had, the more the mob wanted a slice of it. It had always been that way.

I looked at my mother thinking how far she had come, how strong she had been through all of this, yet she was growing weary. All of us could tell. Could we put her through another battle with the same kind who had tormented her in her youth, tried to steal her son, nearly ruined her daughter's life, and now threatened the livelihoods of her family? We had to take her into consideration. I was still not convinced, despite her outward strength.

I was reminded of my weeks clamoring for vengeance following my child's abduction. Sure, I was thankful for Scotty's safe return, but thankful to whom and for what? Yes, they could have killed him and gotten away with it and didn't, but was I to be grateful for that? No! God hadn't brought him back to the hospital, some lowlife motherfucker had, and I was out to find him and punish him. How could I not do that? I had argued with myself and those closest to me for action, for a counter-strike, a flanking move to catch the enemy off-guard, like we did a few times with the Germans, hitting them early in the morning while in the latrine.

For weeks I couldn't sleep as I planned and schemed and crafted an assault. I became obsessed. It was eating at my guts. But it had been Angelina who calmed me and soothed my nerves. In a few short sentences she helped me focus on what had to be done by telling me about our father and the plunge of his stiletto.

"Figlio mio, il tuo papa'ha odiato. Ha combattuto i demoni e li ha feriti. Ha avuto la sua vendetta per cio' che mi hanno fatto

ma cio' ha fatto lasciare la casa prima del dovuto. Tu anche puoi odiare. Ma sii paziente. Verra'il tuo tempo. Il diavlo sa che lo stai guardano. Il diavlo sa che tu non dimentichi. Gia' hai incontrato il diavlo. Tu gia'lo hai visto. Organizzati. Non reagire subito. Non far si che la tua famiglia se ne vada a causa delle tue azioni. Difendi la tua famiglia prima e poi colpisci. My son; your Papa hated. He fought the demons, and he hurt them bad. He got his revenge for what they did to me, but it made us leave our home sooner than we planned. You can hate too. But be patient. Your time will come. The Devil knows you won't forget. Plan well. Don't act too soon. Don't make your family leave by your actions. Protect your family first, and then strike," my mother had courageously advised.

I had listened in utter amazement. She spoke with such profound assurance. Guiding, not scolding. Coaching and instructing. She knew what I had to do, and all she was saying was wait until the time is right. Don't act prematurely, but act with devastating results. So we had waited. I fought the demons inside me and tried desperately to look with Carlo through a clear prism.

Now we were there once again − at a crossroads. Deciding a future course, but still haunted, still frustrated, still controlled, goddamn it, by an outside force. A force just as fearsome as before, even though the scourge had lain dormant at our feet long enough for its sting to subside.

Now, I looked once again to my mother for her wisdom. All she said this time was, "*Construsici la mia cucina e dammi un posto per ballare.* Build my kitchen and give me a place to dance."

Should we take the risk? Give up and stay small in our shell despite our success; hiding out, hoping they would go away? Would Strawberry kill the next time? He certainly could have killed my baby, and there would have been no proof of his involvement whatsoever. Even Sergeant Bravo's hands would have been tied. If we went ahead with the expansion, how could we protect the restaurant and our families from an inevitable assault? Wouldn't we have to pay for protection?

I think I knew what the verdict would be, even before we began our special family gathering that night. But I had to put my views – no, my fears – out there for all to see. We would go ahead. We would build my mother's kitchen and her ballroom. And, yes, it would be a grand ballroom. In the end we were not to be intimidated. We had no illusions that the Mafia would be muzzled much longer. Their problems with the law and the public's gnawing attention on them were only temporary setbacks prompted by a series of self-inflicted missteps and misfortune. That's all that was keeping them quiet, stalking instead of pouncing. The gangsters may have taken a shot to the chin, but like no other formidable opponent, they could counterpunch with the force of a sledgehammer.

It is the unknown and the risk that motivates people, I think. Not knowing, but anticipating how your lives can be made better by hard work, taking chances, planning and executing. But it also is the unknown risk that keeps people back, makes them reluctant to strive forward, allowing their dreams to fade. Those are the choices. We made our choice that night and we would not turn back. We broke up our family meeting with anticipation for the good things ahead of us, while fully realizing the likelihood of the bad times to come.

The next morning, I drove to the farm. Maggie stayed behind to tend to the baby. As I approached my grove, I remembered other choices I had made, meaningful ones, like refusing the steel mill, entering the Army; being a paratrooper; leaving Chloe behind; coming home instead of wandering off chasing Maggie back to New Jersey. And others not so important, like hanging on Mrs. Montlero when she answered in that voice that sent shockwaves through my loins. Spur of the moment choices, like picking out that one foxhole over dozens of others and finding myself in a battle for my life instead of securing a place to rest.

Had I – had we – chosen the wrong foxhole? I wondered. Would we awaken an angry enemy, and would my tortured dreams of the machete thrust into my gut become my fate – our fate? And would Maggie always be there to nudge me awake before the sharp tip of the big knife pierced my flesh? My brain was in overdrive.

When I got to the farm and roamed among my pistachio trees, I felt those concerns melt away, and I rejoiced in the choice we had made. The next Monday, Carlo and I made an appointment at the bank.

The bank officer at the Southeast Bank and Trust Company was none other than Herbert Prendergast. I watched him as he smiled and leaned back in his swivel desk chair, tucking his hands in his vest pockets and fingering a gold watch chain.

"This was my grandfather's," he said in a high-pitched squeal as irritating as a fingernail scraping across a chalkboard. "He was a conductor on the Union Pacific, originally based in Omaha. He'd come through Pueblo frequently on his runs to the West Coast and decided one day to move his family here. So I am a third generation resident. I suppose you could call me a native, by now. There aren't many true natives here in town, you know, except for the few Indians who still reside over on the West side. Some people think they're Apaches or Comanche. They could be wild, you know, if you believe the Western movies, but I wouldn't know since they never come in the bank. I guess they don't need money since they continue to live off the government."

Dumbfounded, Carlo and I sat there across from this scarecrow-looking guy with his ill-fitting vest, pointed head and sunken cheeks, patiently listening to him rattle on. We weren't sure if he'd ever shut up.

"I came to the bank ten years ago following two years at community college. I studied business administration. Never been late for work. Never. Thanks to his marvelous watch. My prized possession." There was a sigh of relief from both Carlo and me when he paused before asking, "Gentlemen, how can I help you? I sincerely appreciate the opportunity to serve you today. Now I see here from our records that the Bank recognizes both of you and your restaurant as loyal, long-term customers, and let me assure you, I will do everything I can, certainly within the confines of the authority I have here at the Bank, to present your loan proposal to our review committee in a most favorable light." Without taking a breath, Herbert went on. "However, as you know, your request for a fifteen-thousand-dollar loan for the expansion you have under consideration is a sizable one. It will require my utmost diligence in my review of your financial records and your projections for future income once the enlarged facility is up and running for my loan committee to favorably contemplate this request."

He paused again, but oh-so-briefly. "I take note here that, unfortunately, neither of you has measurable funds on deposit with us at this time. Is there any possibility that that situation might change?" he asked, keeping his head down, pretending to study the papers in front of him.

I, for one, was nearly been hypnotized by the bounce in Herbert's Adam's apple as he spoke. I hadn't heard a word he said in the last five minutes as a result of the anatomical spectacle before me. Thank God Carlo had been listening.

"Sir, I suppose if we had large deposits in the bank, we wouldn't be asking for a loan," Carlo said as calmly and politely as I knew he could.

"I see here that your wife has a large sum of money with us however. Is that your understanding?" Herbert continued without looking up or acknowledging what Carlo had said.

"Yes, sir, that is true. But that money is hers. It can't be used for this at all," Carlo patiently explained.

"But, is it not the case that you are married, and hence she shares in the responsibilities you are attempting to assume?" Herbert probed, still keeping his head down.

"You see here sir, I – we – need to do this on our own. The restaurant has been making money. Our records show it. We think we can make a lot more money if we can expand, and we think the Bank should understand that and believe in that as we do," Carlo pointed out, his voice beginning to quiver, which I knew meant his temper was beginning to flare.

"But her funds should be your funds," the banker retorted, this time raising his head, "and she should be willing to support this enterprise without hesitation. I don't understand," he added with just a hint of sarcasm.

I had enough. "Get it through your thick head, you fucker, you're not getting your grubby hands on his wife's money. If you don't want to make the loan, fine. Carlo, let's get out of here," I growled as I leaped from my chair.

"Now, now there's no reason to speak that way," the banker replied when the shock of my outburst finally wore off. "And even though I take strong offense at your remarks, please excuse me. I would like to speak with the senior loan officer."

"Man, what's got into you?" Carlo blurted out under his breath when rail-thin Herbert in his suit that clung to him like a wet sheet over a lamppost had walked off. But Carlo's question didn't hold much conviction. "I was just about ready to say the same thing," he admitted.

"I'm seasick watching his Adam's apple bounce up and down in his neck like it's going to fly out his mouth any second. He's so damn skinny; I could put my neck through his shirt collar along with his, and still have room. He struts like a red rooster with a cork up his butt," I whispered.

"Will you shut up?" Carlo giggled like a girl. "They're gonna throw us out of here, and we probably deserve it. But you're right. He is a little tough to look at and keep a straight face."

Two hours later the money from our loan was deposited into a new account in the name of the restaurant, to be used only for the expansion of the building, and some working capital. Both of our houses were pledged as collateral for the loan. Julia Gail's money remained in the bank, free and unencumbered.

Construction began two weeks later. In the early stages, we were able to keep the restaurant open since we were building the enlarged areas first. We planned to break through the outer walls of the existing building to attach the new wings. Carlo and I worked twelve-hour shifts alternating between the construction site and duties at the bar. Business dropped off slightly with the dawn-to-dusk hammering and sawing. That summer my pistachio harvest was a flop. I didn't have the time to tend to my groves and Maggie was in no condition to take on that task by herself. We were expecting again in October.

Every night when we walked off the construction job site or closed the restaurant, Carlo and I wondered and worried when they would strike again. Short of standing guard around the clock, there was no way to protect the exposed, vulnerable wood framing of the additions, nor could we shield the existing structure from any of the standard methods of destruction usually employed by our adversaries. More than once, each of us approached the other exploring, perhaps even suggesting, that we attempt to make peace with him. Not with Strawberry himself, but with the man at the top. But each time the topic came up we decided to hold tight.

Finally Maggie offered a solution.

Chapter 61
Don't Ever Refuse a Breath Mint

Sergeant Victor Bravo

Sergeant Victor Bravo ended his shift one Saturday morning around four a.m. He was more than exhausted. His workday had just passed thirteen hours. He rubbed the back of his neck and stretched his long legs, feeling the circulation return as he walked toward the side door of the police station after parking his unmarked cruiser in the adjacent fenced-in lot. When driving through he'd tipped his hat to the guard at the gate, who turned the other way, ignoring his friendly gesture. The rebuke didn't bother him. He'd grown accustomed to the snubs from his fellow officers.

He was dead tired of the night shift but took it during these summer months while construction was underway at Angelina's. He promised me while on his nocturnal tours around town he would drive by the restaurant several times in case there was any sign of trouble. But each night, as with this one, when he cruised by the site all was quiet. The whole town was quiet, in fact.

Uncanny this situation he thought as he opened his locker to retrieve his black metal lunch pail he forgot before hitting the road for the night. Actually, he remembered, he had forgotten to eat at all. His stomach was reminding him of his forgetfulness and he opened the lunchbox lid and began to hungrily chomp on the turkey sandwich his wife had made so many hours before. As he sat at the bench in front of his locker, his thoughts returned to the eerie quietness of his town.

It seemed much of the criminal world around him had fallen asleep in a swaying hammock under a crisp, clear sky. With the exception of a strange series of house burglaries, it was as if even the muggers, drunks, vandals and bunko artists were on sabbatical. He recalled the last case he wrote up was a week ago about a motorist driving off from the gas pump without paying. Later that same day, the guy returned to pay the station attendant. He apologized and no charges were filed. And yes, he did remember filing a report about a disgruntled neighbor allegedly poisoning the dog next door for killing two of his rabbits that had escaped from their pen after his son left the gate open.

Bravo thought the string of burglaries was interesting and worth studying some more to see if there were any patterns. He'd look at the files when he had some spare time, but meanwhile, his interest was focused on the mob. It seemed the real crooks remained underground. For the most part, the Mafia boys had been in their holes since the Apalachin meeting.

He finished his sandwich, left the locker room and headed for the parking lot for the short, ten-minute drive home. He longed for the luxury of cool sheets, soft pillow and the arms of his wife cradling him as drifted off to sleep. He couldn't wait to get there and he picked up his step, even though his legs stilled ached from driving most of the night. Bravo was a good enough cop to know that the tenuous peace with the Mafia wouldn't last long, and during this lull, he also knew there were no idle hands.

561

"Something is going on," he whispered to himself as he entered the driveway of his sleek but modest ranch-style home situated on the West side of town, just off Belmont Avenue. These guys do not go out of business. Ever. They simply change tactics. He tiptoed through his dark, quiet living room to check on his sleeping kids who both stirred in their beds when the hall light beam caught their upturned faces. The door creaked shut as he made his way down the hall to his room and his softly snoring wife.

Tomorrow he would try to figure out the new approach to organized crime. Tonight, what was left of it, he would rest.

~

Bravo remained a loner on the force, and he preferred it that way. He had a hard time fitting in with the other officers. He was not liked or appreciated by the top brass either. The new chief, Paul McCullough, had been handpicked by the old chief, Kelly and his deputy chief O'Malley, who also had since retired with a special pension slammed through the city council by an appreciative mayor. Bravo suspected McCullough likewise felt that Bravo had been jammed down McCullough's throat solely on the basis of his war record. The overwhelming numbers of Irish and bojon patrolmen were envious of Bravo's detective shield. His fellow Mexican cops, few in numbers, also were terribly jealous as well, wondering how the job. Everyone else just hated the fact that a Mexican had the job instead of one of them.

So he worked alone, and was very surprised at the beginning of a shift on a hot night in August a few weeks later when Sergeant Herman Borgstadt asked if he could ride along. Bravo was in his new unmarked 1959 Ford Fairlaine, inspecting the new multi-channel radio equipment squawking out position reports from other patrol cars when Borgstadt leaned in his driver-side window.

"I'd like to ride along. Any problem with that?" the intrusive cop asked. His breath made Bravo's eyes water. Bravo had known Borgstadt since the big German had joined the force some months before, and had immediately disliked him from the moment they met.

"No," Bravo replied. "Anything in particular you need to do?"

"Nope," Borgstadt answered. "Just thought it would be a good idea to get better acquainted."

Bravo looked across the asphalt. Several patrolmen standing by their cruisers waiting for their shifts to begin were watching the interaction between the two sergeants. Bravo could see the smirks on their faces. One tipped his hat to him as Borgstadt made his way around the front of Bravo's car toward the passenger's side. Bravo was calm but wary. He remembered all too clearly the conversation two weeks before with a trusted friend in the Internal Affairs Division of the Chicago Police Department. Bravo was uneasy about Borgsgtadt since their first meeting, and when Bravo walked around with a nagging feeling about someone or something, it became an itch he had to scratch.

After quietly leafing through Borgstadt's personnel file one afternoon before his shift began and finding records of his short stint on the force in Chicago, Bravo decided to call his buddy in the Windy City for a little background information. Bravo met his Chicago counterpart during a special forensic investigative seminar at the FBI Academy at Quantico, Virginia, two years before. The two had hit it off immediately, and Bravo knew he would get the truth from Detective Weinstein.

"Borgstadt? Oh yes. I thought I might be hearing from you. Ahh, my friend, do I have a story to tell you," Lieutenant Timothy Weinstein said when they had connected. "Where do I begin? Might as well get right to it. Borgstadt was a true honest-to-God Nazi. We started compiling a file on him when he first entered the country. The arrogant bastard never changed his name. It was easy to piece his history together from our sources in Europe and here in the U.S." At that point, Bravo thought he'd better sit down. He knew he was about to get more than he bargained for as soon as he had heard the word "Nazi."

Weinstein was a member of the American Committee for Holocaust Retribution and both of his grandparents, two of his aunts, his mother and two sisters all died at Auschwitz. Weinstein and his father were the only two who survived. The group's mission was to hunt down those criminals and make them pay for their war crimes.

"Borgstadt was actually a former full-fledged member of the National Socialist Party of the German Republic and had the credentials to prove it," Weinstein continued. " Thousands of German war prisoners brought to the United States during the war were able to immigrate legally if nothing in their backgrounds proved to be too sinister. As you know, many with questionable histories also slipped through the cracks and into the country, bamboozling immigration authorities, especially if they had a decent command of the English language.

"The sergeant was one of those who slithered in to the U.S. undetected. He had perfected his language skills interrogating American, British and Canadian POWs in camps located throughout the European theatre. I'm sure his command of the language and his interrogation techniques were excellent attributes when it came time for him to advance his national and personal causes. In 1934, as a young, idealistic anti-Semite, Borgstadt became an active member of Hitler's Youth Corps."

"You've got to be kidding!" Bravo exclaimed, as images of the goose-stepping troops on parade with their raised, swastika-encircled arms in salute passed through his brain.

"No, I'm not. Not for a minute," Weinstein's voice was solemn. "Borgstadt rose quickly through the Aryan elite to become a junior officer in the SS and eventually he advanced to officer corps status in the Gestapo, Hitler's acclaimed secret service. He was captured outside of the concentration camp at Dachau while fleeing from advancing American troops, including several companies from the 101st Airborne Division," Weinstein continued.

At that point Bravo wondered if I might have seen Borgstadt among the hordes of German prisoners taken by the Screaming Eagles during the final days of the war. But before his mind drifted too far, his friend's shocking story again riveted his attention.

"Before Borgstadt's capture by U.S. forces he managed to shed his jack boots and his black and silver uniform. You know the one – adorned with embossed lapel pins of skulls and crossbones. Rumor has it he stripped a dead Panzer private of his clothing and dressed quickly before waving a white flag at the American convoy passing close by in surrender."

It was a haunting description, and Bravo was stunned. "Absolutely amazing," he breathed.

"No, absolutely tragic someone didn't cut the bastard's throat," Weinstein corrected, and then hurried on again. "From pictures we've seen, back then, Borgstadt was a tall, blonde-haired specimen who looked the Aryan part so well he could have been a poster boy for Nazi Party Secretary Martin Bormann's propaganda machine. By the end of the war and his swearing in as a loyal American citizen, his hair had turned a silver grey. He made his way to Chicago to assimilate into a growing German population of immigrants.

"With fresh, new citizenship papers, Borgstadt joined the Chicago police department shortly after his arrival. His records show he was near the top of his class at the police academy, and in six short months, he was out on the streets busting heads in the big city. While here, he loved using his Billy club to prove his authoritative point of view to the chronic drunks, drug addicts, and even a few tipsy businessmen who'd lingered too long at the local pub after work on a Friday night. But his satisfying Windy City law enforcement career was abruptly ended when the overly zealous officer failed to recognize a prominent Chicago Alderman whom he had spotted staggering arm-in-arm with his mistress down the sidewalk near the Opera House on a Sunday morning at two a.m. Borgstadt handcuffed and hauled them down to the precinct house for booking then under the public drunkenness and lewd conduct ordinance.

"I am told the front of the mistress' dress was unbuttoned to her navel when Borgstadt approached the inebriated couple. The minute the desk sergeant saw them standing in separate holding cells, screaming obscenities at everyone around, he called the chief, who called the police commissioner, who called the mayor, and Borgstadt got a month's severance in his next pay envelope and a favorable recommendation to whom it may concern.

"The rest you know. Borgstadt was hired by the Pueblo Police Department five short days later after the personnel clerk in Chicago read his glowing Police Commissioner-dictated recommendation to the Pueblo Chief over the phone. Our guy was more than happy to pawn the scum off on your guy," Tim pointed out.

"Christ, Almighty," was all Bravo could say.

"Well, I wouldn't go that far," joked the lieutenant on the other end of the line. "The Jews hang together ever so tightly on this, as you know, and we have been given access to all the German military records, especially when there is a link to former Kraut soldiers who have immigrated to the U.S. either legally or illegally. Thing is, we can't pin anything on him directly. There doesn't appear to be any record of duty at one of the concentration camps, but we haven't given up yet," Weinstein explained.

When Bravo was sure his friend had finished, he said, "You've been a great help, Tim. I promise I will keep a close watch on this bastard, and let you know anything that might add to your case. You do the same. If you gather the evidence to deport him, or better yet, enough to throw his ass in jail, promise me you will let me arrest him for you."

"I will. So long my friend," Weinstein rang off.

Bravo replaced the receiver with a bad feeling in his gut.

Now, as the two officers eased out on to Main Street, Borgstadt struck up a conversation. "You know, Bravo," Borgstadt began. "We've been around each other for a couple of months now, but this is the first time we've had a chance to really get to know each other. I'm not happy about that, you know. I think you're a good cop, and you're real smart, but you know, you keep to yourself. You don't work with anybody and I don't think I've ever seen you having a drink at the Two & Nine with the boys after the shift. Is it that you don't like the rest of us? Or do you think, maybe, you're too good for us?" Borgstadt had an ominous tone to his voice, but Bravo kept his eyes on the road

"Look sergeant," Bravo chose his words carefully. "I don't know what you have on your mind ridin' with me tonight, but whatever it's worth to you; no, I don't think I'm too good for you or any of the other officers. I'm not big on the Two & Nine. I think their drinks are cheap and watered down. I just prefer to work alone, and after work I have family obligations that take me home."

"I hear you have a beautiful wife," Borgstadt said with a low, husky grumble. "Long brown hair. Those high cheekbones. She's got some hot Indian blood in her, mixed with the Mexican. That right? Maybe you're smart after all, goin' home all the time. With someone like that waitin' for me, I'd probably never leave the house," he chuckled.

Bravo resisted the temptation to smack him across the face. He ignored Borgstadt's sickening comments and changed the subject. "I need to drive over to the south side, near the community college. We had a report last night of a prowler, and this woman gave us a description similar to one we got of a man trying to break into a car in the parking lot near South High School. I want to go talk with the woman again," Bravo patiently and calmly explained.

"Sounds real exciting," Borgstadt said sarcastically as he leaned his head back on the car seat, brought his hat over his eyes and pretended to go to sleep.

When they arrived at the woman's house, Borgstadt stayed in the car while Bravo interviewed the prowler victim inside. When Bravo returned, he peeked through the window at what appeared to be a dozing Borgtsadt. He jerked open the passenger sidecar door.

"What the ...?" Borgstadt stuttered as he shook awake.

"Sorry Sergeant, didn't know you were sleeping," Bravo apologized with a suppressed chuckle. Bravo closed the passenger side door and moved around to the driver's side, ignoring Borgstadt's glare. He got in the car and eased out onto the road. There were a few minutes of strained silence.

"Now what, buddy? Got any more major crimes to solve?" Borgstadt finally asked with globs of sarcasm practically dripping from the corner of his mouth.

Bravo had just about enough. He pulled to the curb, the engine of the Ford still idling. Neither spoke. Bravo stared straight ahead; his hands tightly gripping the steering wheel. He was about to give this asshole a piece of his mind when, without warning, Borgstadt reached over from the passenger side and switched off the Ford's engine.

"Look here buddy boy," Borgstadt began. "You don't like me and I don't like you, but we need to have a nice, friendly conversation here. Some of us around the station think you've gotten a little too big for those skinny britches of yours. You're always sneakin' around, not talkin' with anybody; just pokin' your nose in places where it don't belong. Actin' like you're out lookin' for something that ain't there. Always actin' like a detective, even off duty. You're makin' people real nervous and you're playin' a dangerous game. What's on your mind, anyway? You got somethin' up your sleeve?" he prodded.

Ah, yes. Bravo thought. So this is the reason for your unwelcomed presence. For nearly a year, Bravo had been tracking a string of petty house and business burglaries around town. According to the log sheets kept on each case, investigating officers were spending an extraordinary amount of time at each crime location, much more time than necessary to gather information on what appeared to be short, inconsequential lists of missing merchandise. On two occasions, unknown to the officers assigned to the cases, Bravo contacted the victims to re-check their lists of stolen items against those attached to each police report. In both cases, the items didn't match the victim's lists of the most expensive items such as jewelry, antiques, cash, and in one instance, a missing red fox full-length winter coat. All of these items failed to appear on the official record. After he obtained complete lists from each of the victims, Bravo scoured the local pawnshops where he suspected the items might have been sold. No luck. Not one article had turned up in the hands of the town's pawnbrokers.

The only conclusion in Bravo's mind was that a fairly sophisticated fencing operation was underway, and it had become the victims' word against the cops, with the cops prevailing. If the cops were in on it by purloining the records, Bravo was fairly certain they were in much deeper than that by either protecting the burglars, or staging the burglaries themselves and then fencing the goods later. To pull all of this off, however, the cops needed help. They needed sophisticated, logistical support and an interstate transportation network to move goods out of state and into the hands of far-away dealers willing to pay big dollars for nearly untraceable merchandise. And who better to turn to for help than the local mob.

At this point, Bravo spun most of the strands of the crime web together, but he hadn't yet determined who was leading it from the inside. How far up the chain of command did it go? Now, as he stared, unblinking, into the steely blue eyes of the pale-faced, silver-haired German, he may have found one of the key players in the scheme.

Bravo also quickly realized that the antagonist in the front seat with him was on to his inside-the-department detective work. That meant he needed to change tactics, go deeper undercover while remaining in plain sight and keeping his attention riveted on the German cop with the wry smile and the horrible breath.

Bravo stuck out his hand for the car keys. But before handing them back, Borgstadt had a warning. "Whatever you're doin' Bravo, don't go too far. You have a beautiful wife and nice kids. Wouldn't want anything to happen to them. We're all here to protect and serve our community and ourselves. Remember that and you'll be fine. You forget, and well, it might get unpleasant."

Bravo held his temper, snatched the keys from Borgstadt's hand, started the car and reached in his shirt pocket to retrieve a breath mint.

"Here, take this. What's coming out of your mouth stinks like shit," Bravo spat.

Borgstadt's sneer was broken and his belly shook with laughter as he popped the breath mint in his mouth. As Bravo swung his new cruiser back on to Fourth Street he glanced over to Borgstadt who had already tilted back his head to rest on the seat.

"Look sergeant," Bravo said, "I have no idea what you're talking about, but be sure of one thing, if you or any of your rat fucking gumshoes ever come near my wife or my kids, I'll skin you alive with a dull knife. Inside this department, if I happen to smell something rotten, I'll go after it like a hungry jackal, and if your carcass is lying there, I'll pick it clean."

Borgstadt slowly raised his head and straightened his hat. His anger showed on his face, which took on a heightened reddish hue, but his voice was calm. "Now, now sergeant. Take it easy. Remember your blood pressure. You need to think about your health just now. For that wife of yours and those kids. What would they do without their daddy? All I said was I wanted to have a friendly conversation. I'm not lookin' for trouble. I want to be your friend, and so do a lot of the other fellows in the department. We just don't know what makes you tick, and we'd like to find out," Borgstadt said, pausing for effect before continuing.

"Like what are your hobbies, other than that beautiful wife of yours? You like good clothes, I can see that. You dress real well in plainclothes. You like good restaurants. I've seen you at Angelina's off and on. You're good buddies with the owner, or his brother, I hear, but that's still got to cost you a pretty penny to dine there as often as you do with your lovely wife. You like big fancy, fast cars? You need a bigger house for all those kids of yours? I'm just tryin' to get better acquainted. No harm in that. Is there?"

Bravo kept on driving, holding his tongue.

"Where do we go from here sergeant?" Borgstadt finally injected, breaking the silence, as once again, he leaned back in the seat and tipped his hat over his eyes.

Bravo sighed and shook his head. "That's up to you sergeant, strictly up to you. Have another breath mint."

Chapter 62
And the Band Plays On

The addition to the restaurant and the adjacent small dance club were finished in eight months and fifteen days, but construction costs came in over budget by seven thousand dollars. There were no fires, only minor vandalism at the construction sites that looked to be the cause of punk teenagers. We breathed a sigh of relief when the last nail was struck and the last brick laid and headed back to the bank.

We needed a supplemental loan, which we got, but we had to pay a higher interest rate, among other things, to get the extra money. Herbert Prendergast again asked for Julia Gail's money, but again, we refused, this time, more politely. Our banker appeared to be less interested in Julia Gail's nest egg, probably because of the higher interest rate they were charging, plus the fact we agreed to pledge ten percent of the net revenues from the restaurant for the first six months of full-scale operation. That extra hand in our pockets would last until the additional seven-thousand-dollar loan was paid off.

Our second grand opening (well I guess if you count the one Silvio had, it would be the third) was held on the weekend after the Fourth of July. Angelina loved her new kitchen with all the latest equipment and gadgets designed to ease her workload and further perfect her unmatched culinary skill. The rooms were divided and decorated differently. A more elegant interior, in classic Italian motif, dominated the dining room, while the supper club exhibited a New York style art deco décor. We hired eight more waiters and two additional bartenders since the supper club had a separate bar.

The dining room could now accommodate fifty guests at each seating. Two new menus were designed. One for guests just dining, usually at the early evening seating, and the other for guests out to enjoy dinner and dancing in the new club room, which could serve thirty and still have room for dancing to live music, provided by a well-screened musical group.

There were plenty of local groups from which to create a featured musical guest list. Competition came from numerous traveling bands passing through town. Maggie and Julia Gail formed a self-appointed two-member talent selection committee and received auditions each Wednesday afternoon. They had a grand time in the process and occasionally invited our sisters to comment on the candidate entertainers. Once in a while even Angelina would come by and listen. We paid the musical groups well, as high as two hundred dollars each night, but they were required to perform three sets and provide a full repertoire of music each Friday and Saturday evening. We debated the genre of music, and our wives and sisters all chimed in with their opinions. Maggie and Julia Gail prevailed, and the swing era sound won out.

Business boomed. At this rate, we could pay off the loan even with the higher interest rate within two years, we estimated, and the extra seven grand we borrowed would be retired in three short months. The one big issue Carlo and I had was we had to wear coats and ties while on duty, a "suggestion" from our wives to reflect the restaurant's new upper-scale image.

Our new establishment was introduced at just the right time to appeal to a more sophisticated and demanding middle and upper middle class population. Our customers crossed all ethnic lines, and they had more money to spend and more leisure time during which to spend it. Yes, Angelina's Fine Italian Restaurant was a hit. But with the good inevitably came the bad.

One Saturday night about six months after we re-opened, three uniformed patrol officers showed up at the height of the dinner hour, just as the band in the clubroom was striking up its first tune of the evening. When the cops hit the front door they announced with a bullhorn that their "friendly" visit was to check identifications of the patrons and inspect the booze on the shelves for proper tax stamps. Before they were done, the place nearly cleared out. No one wanted to continue their cavalier dancing and drinking under the watchful eyes of nasty looking cops clearly out to bust anyone for the slightest infraction.

I was on duty when the cops came in, and I called Carlo back to work to help me seek some explanation for what appeared to be nothing more than a good old-fashioned Prohibition-style raid.

"You're joint here is gettin' a bad reputation for servin' under-aged drinkers, and there's been some rumors out there that you might be slippin' in a few illegal bottles of liquor to serve from the back bar shelves," one of the three bojon patrolman growled after finishing his lazy stroll through both the dining and nightclub rooms. "Not payin' those taxes is a serious offense, and servin' minors will get both of you some jail time," he threw in for good measure.

His two companions also had made their way through our establishment, strutting their stuff like hotshot tin soldiers. They positioned themselves on either side of the front door while Carlo and I tried to carry on a sensible conversation with their leader, who, I discovered from a quick scan of his name badge, was a Corporal Stansloski.

"You can't be serious!" Carlo exclaimed, trying hard to hold his temper. "We've never had any problems before. We check all IDs, and everyone knows our liquor suppliers are on the straight and narrow."

"Well, that's not what we heard," chimed in one of the cops standing by the door.

"I'll handle this," Stansloski hotly scolded his fellow officer. "Now, look here," he lectured, turning back to Carlo and me, "We think you guys have gotten careless, and you're hidin' somethin' behind all this fancy decoration, playin' up to these high rollers in their suits and slinky gowns. You guys need to be extra careful. When rumors get started, people start talkin' and we've got to check it out."

"But why at our busiest time on a Saturday night?" I questioned indignantly.

"Well that would be the time when we're most apt to find you guys or your guests breakin' the law," the corporal answered smugly.

"Who authorized you to make this raid? Where'd your orders come from?" I demanded.

"Now listen here you little wop bastard," Stansloski snarled. "We don't need no orders, and if you think you can smart mouth me, I'll run you in right here and now."

I could have decked the son-of-a-bitch with a single punch to the chin, but held back as Carlo stepped between us. Just then, another cop came ambling through the front door. I squinted at his name badge: Sergeant Herman Borgstadt. I thought I recognized him as a dinner customer, or someone who had occasionally occupied one of the barstools.

"Well, well, gentlemen. What do we have here?" the sergeant asked in a clearly contrived tone all-too-cheery for the moment. "Heard from dispatch that there might be a little trouble down here at my favorite restaurant. Everything under control officers?" He looked around the empty restaurant then turned towards Carlo and me. "How are you doing this evening, my friends? How's business?" On his face was a full-blown toothy grin.

"Sergeant, we don't know what this is all about," Carlo turned to face the new arrival who now appeared to be in charge. "As we were trying to tell your officers here, we've never had problems with minors in here before and our liquor stamps are closely inspected. We run a clean operation, and I think you know that, so why are we being targeted like this?" he asked in the most polite and sincere voice I knew he could muster.

"Now, look here boys, no one's targeting you or your restaurant," Borgstadt responded patronizingly. "Just seems that my men here thought it best to check you out tonight. They're real sorry if they came at the wrong time, but we can't plan our work around your busy time, now can we?" Borgstadt declared, the smirk still on his face as he hooked his thumbs in his belt buckle and began his own leisurely stroll through our now vacant rooms.

The Sergeant turned back to his patrolmen, "I think your work is done here for tonight. I want to see your report on my desk before the end of your shifts. Now get back out on patrol," he ordered. When the trio of intruders left and Borgstadt finished his tour, his next orders were issued to Carlo and me.

"I'd like a cup of coffee, if you don't mind." Borgstadt walked over to the bar, tipping his hat to the young, now idle, waitress, and waited to be waited on. I went to fetch his coffee and Carlo joined him at the bar. I heard the Sergeant say to Carlo as I went to the kitchen, "It's been a long day for me, mind if we sit over there at one of those empty tables?"

I grabbed a mug from the kitchen and poured the hot, steaming coffee. I had to pause a moment behind the door to allow my rage to subside. I couldn't understand why, all of a sudden, we were on the cops' hit list. Cops in this town don't bother with trivial crap like inspecting booze bottles and checking IDs. Why now? We knew when we built the addition that the spotlight would be on us from the mob, but why the cops? Was there a connection? Had Jimmy and the boys infiltrated the department to such an extent that our city's finest were doing their dirty work? I wondered if Bravo could explain it. Actually, I was afraid of what his answer might be. My instincts in situations like this were seldom wrong. At last, the cops and the gangsters finally get together, joined in a common cause.

By the time I swung open the kitchen door to join my brother and our unwelcomed guest, the coffee in the mug was nearly cold. I went back to get a hot refill for clearly one of Pueblo's finest. I felt like spitting in the cup. When I finally slid the coffee in front of that brassy bastard he was loud mouthing something else to Carlo.

"You know, I've been outside for awhile kind of watchin' people comin'and goin' but tonight I didn't see my friend Sergeant Bravo, or his gorgeous wife. He's usually here on a Saturday night. Am I right?"

"No," I responded, my anger rising again. "Sergeant Bravo was not here tonight. I haven't seen him in over a month. Why do you ask about him?" I inquired suspiciously, already suspecting where this might be going.

"Oh, no real reason. I just know he's a good friend of yours and hangs around here a lot. You went to high school together, I hear. And I just thought if he was in here tonight or if he's ever in here, he'd make sure things were on the up and up. Isn't that right?" Borgstadt responded sarcastically.

"What do you have on your mind Sergeant?" Carlo asked, his hand clenching and unclenching at his side.

"Oh, I'm just enjoying my coffee. Real good coffee,"Borgstadt chuckled. "There's a chill in the air. Oh, by the way, how's your pistachio crop this year?" He looked at me, grinning again to emphasize his phony interest. "I hope you have a good, long growing season. I love those damn things. I eat them by the bushel, and you can see what's happenin' to me as a result," he chuckled once more, patting his beer belly.

"Crop is good this year." I responded guardedly.

"That's real good. You know we never did catch that scum who torched your place out there. Sure would like to do that. Bravo investigated that for you, didn't he? But never came up with anything, I guess. Never could find his report come to think of it. Anyway, any more problems? Sure would hate for you to have any more problems out there. Love those pistachios," Borgstadt rambled on.

"Sergeant, what is on your mind?" Carlo repeated.

"Now you listen here, buddy boy," Borgstadt suddenly snapped. "I'm comin' here nice and friendly. I'm havin' a nice, friendly cup of coffee, makin' nice, friendly conversation. If you'd like me not to be so nice, I'd be happy to do that too."

Neither Carlo nor I responded.

In silence Borgstadt finished his coffee and rose to leave, but before we had the pleasure of watching him go, he placed his hands on the table and leaned in close to both our faces. "Let me make it real clear. From now on, I'm gonna be watchin' this place real close. I'm gonna be watchin' you here, there and everywhere including out there with your pistachios. Too many things goin' on around here that need fixin', and there ain't the right people aimin' to do that just now. But I'm gonna change that, and I don't think you're gonna be able to run and hide behind your favorite cop anymore. In fact, your favorite cop also needs fixin', and I'm just the man to do that too. You tell him that. Now good evening, gentlemen. You can expect to hear from me again, real soon," Borgstadt promised, his face red and his breathing rapid, his anger rising with each word.

We both stared back into his snarling face without a word. I was holding my breath – his could have killed a small animal. Finally, he turned and strolled out the door. Besides being our newest nemesis, the thing that I hated most about Borgstadt was his fake southern accent. His put-on drawl was a veiled attempt to hide his German accent, but it occasionally leaked through his practiced speech. It was almost comical. I had heard too many Krauts jabbering away not to distinguish Borgstadt's true native tongue despite his overt attempts to disguise it.

Later when Carlo and I emptied the cash registers we discovered that that night's receipts had dropped nearly eighty percent from the previous Saturday.

The second raid occurred three weeks later. A third raid followed within the month. One was on a Friday night, the other again on Saturday. All of them set our customers scurrying to the exits.

I asked Sergeant Bravo to check the files for any reports on the raids. There were none. I also asked him if he had ever filed a report on the burning of the greenhouse. He said he did not. He said that since we had decided not to file an insurance claim there was no reason to have a report on file with the department. Instead Bravo said he wrote and filed a report on the incident with trusted agents with the FBI. In that report he put on record all the evidence gathered plus his true, uninhibited theories about the real perpetrators.

"In this town you don't file written police reports accusing the mob of anything," Bravo reminded me.

I told him what Borgstadt had said the night of our first raid. Bravo wasn't surprised, but he said he couldn't talk about Borgstadt or any of his minions just then. And worst of all he said he couldn't do anything about the bullying. He didn't have the backing of his superiors to stop Borgstadt or even control him. All he could do was advise us to sit tight, do our best to put up with the harassment and he would have an answer for us soon. We suggested going to the chief, or the mayor. Bravo said that wouldn't do any good. Just be patient, he instructed. Things would work out.

In the meantime, we'd lost more than four thousand dollars in food and liquor receipts because of the raids, and we still had to pay the bands that ended up playing to a nearly empty house.

What pleased us most was our customers came back quickly, despite the raids and the harassment. Many of our loyal patrons pledged their support and promised to help fill both rooms even if twenty cops swarmed over them. After the third raid, much to what I'm sure was Borgstadt's utter disappointment; Angelina's remained nearly full for the remainder of the evening.

We broke even that night after paying the band.

Chapter 63
No More Weekend Passes

When I told Herman Borgstadt the night of the first raid that the pistachio crop had been good that year, I was lying through my teeth. It was a fantastic harvest. My grove of producers had expanded to nearly six acres. The hybrids were procreating with an even stronger, more resilient species of offspring. The past winter had been harsh, by all measure, with the average daytime temperature not reaching much above forty degrees from mid-December through mid-March, and only after Easter did it rise to the low sixties during the daylight hours. That below-average temperatures remained until early June.

My trees not only survived, they thrived. I further refined the exterior heating system, and ran a natural gas line network through the groves that supplied the heaters. I installed thermostats to monitor the temperatures to duplicate those in balmier climates. Even though I had a species of tree better adapted to the colder weather, it was best to continue to trick the genes, laid back as they were, to make them think they still harbored in the haven of northern California.

For this latest harvest I recruited migrant farm workers from the nearby lettuce fields to help collect the production. With the bounty, I filled two hundred and fifty, refurbished gumball machines that I had placed in locations in a fifty-mile radius of town. I hired two full-time nut vendors to collect coins and keep the inventory fresh. I had trouble finding good machines until I found a lawyer who represented a bankrupt vending machine company in Idaho who sold me their entire stock of three hundred gumball machines at a bargain basement price.

Somehow the Colorado State College of Agriculture found out about my new super superior pistachio tree and sent a group of students to investigate my grafting and growing techniques. One student decided to write his master's thesis on the exceptional trees, and I spent an afternoon giving him a tour of the operation. He received an A−.

I stopped ordering the saplings from the farmer in Fresno, and soon received a letter expressing his support, but I think he was hoping my success would not infringe on his corner of the market. Pistachio trees are not supposed to grow in the Rocky Mountains, he reminded me in the last sentence of his congratulatory letter.

Maggie's job was overseeing the business side of the nut business, and she and I still enjoyed many of our weekend days off at the farm with our child, watching him grow, along with the swelling in his mother's belly. The planting, pruning and playing with my family were a true delight.

I wouldn't necessarily call our lives at that time tranquil, far from it. In reality all we had done was find a quiet, nurturing place to run and hide for a time. A shelter from the storm, I called it. I liked to think of going to the farm as being granted a wonderful weekend pass from duty in the Army, knowing when the days were through, we would be thrust back into the fray.

Then one Saturday afternoon, maybe a month after the last raid on the restaurant, our haven was invaded. I stepped out the door of the greenhouse and saw Sergeant Bravo's unmarked Ford swing into the driveway of the farmhouse. We met midway in the backyard, by the barn, and walked over to the lawn furniture arranged under the canopy of the huge oak tree. Maggie was checking the irrigation flow through the groves and had not seen Victor arrive. Scotty was covered with mud, content at his mother's feet.

"My friend, I wish I could come with better news," Bravo began solemnly. "Carlo's daughter Julie is missing. She was on her way to a dance lesson near Central Park when a witness saw a man grab her, push her into a white van and speed away. We have as many men on it as we can spare. We found the van about an hour ago parked behind the *Safeway* on North Second Street, but she's gone. I'm so sorry. Carlo and Julia Gail are at home. I think they have been trying to reach you, but apparently you can't hear the phone ringing out in the field." All the while he was talking, his voice had ebbed softer and softer until, by the time he was done, it had reached a level I could hardly hear.

But it didn't matter. The impact of his first few words had numbed me. My breath was gone. My knees buckled. I had to sit down. The muscles in my neck constricted as if I was carrying a yoke with thousand-pound anvils swinging from each end. My ears were ringing, so maybe he was talking louder than I thought. I shut my eyes. There was silence. Darkness.

"Johnny, are you all right?" he gently probed.

And then it erupted from me. "Oh, God. No. Tell me no!" I bellowed from a point in my soul deeper than I thought I could ever reach. "He's done it again."

I turned to my friend, looking for solace, pleading for guidance. "Victor, how do we deal with this? Just like the last time, when he took Scotty, the cops aren't going to do anything. Sure, they'll look around a little until it gets dark and then they'll quit. She's only fourteen. I can't even think about what they might do to her. My God, man, how do we deal with this?" I tried to wring an answer from him as the tears welled in my eyes and my hand quaked. I reached for his shoulder for support. Victor was in control, consoling, stern, trying to dissuade me from the violent conclusions I had already drawn.

"Johnny, we can't jump off right here. I won't let you. We don't know for sure if it is Strawberry. Maybe, and God, I hope this is not the case, it's someone else who isn't connected, or it was random," Bravo offered. "I don't know which would be worse."

"What the fuck are you talking about?" I recoiled, withdrawing my hand, clenching my fist. "Which is worse? If it's random, as you say, some sex fiend, she's probably dead already. Are you saying if it's Strawberry, its better?"

"I don't know, Johnny," Bravo admitted. "I can't imagine

Clemente would let him kill her. At least with the mob, there is control, some checks on their behavior."

"Bullshit, Victor, you know better than that. Sure it's Strawberry, and Clemente will let him do what he wants," I responded with anguish nearly beyond my control. "Plus mark my words when I tell you that Borgstadt's in on this as well. You watch, the patrols will go out, make like their looking around, maybe even question a few of the perverts in town, write their reports and go home and sleep like babies. That's what will happen, and we'll find Julie dumped in the rail yards or somewhere."

Just then Maggie approached. She saw the look on my face, seemed to stumble, and almost fell to her knees. She hugged her belly as if she needed to protect the infant inside. I reached for her and guided her to a chair beside me. Scotty was trailing behind, and jumped up into his daddy's lap.

Victor hardly noticed her arrival, clearly stunned at my reference to the German cop. "What are you talking about? Borgstadt?" Victor's question came back to me with a harshness I know wasn't intended. Then he said, trying to convince himself more than me, "He's stupid, but he's not that stupid. I know he's out to get me and somehow link me to you and Carlo. He wants to bust you guys and bring me into the middle, claiming that I covered up for you. But this goes too far. Way too far. It doesn't make sense."

"You know about the raids at the restaurant and his threats. There's too much of a coincidence," I insisted, "between Borgstadt coming after us and how quiet Strawberry's been up 'til now. That son-of-a-bitch cop knows everything. About Scotty, about the greenhouse fire, everything. If you didn't file reports, how did he know? It's almost like he's been in on all of it from the beginning. Strawberry's got him out front until he finds an opportunity to hit us real hard. Now he's done it. His knockout blow."

Then something Bravo said struck me. "Why is he out for you anyway?" I asked my friend. "What do you have on him and his bunch of lackey cops?"

I glanced at my wife. She was sitting passively, her body crunched over, rocking front to back, her head in her hands. She hadn't spoken.

"Can't talk about it, please," Bravo responded guardedly.

"The hell you can't!" I exploded. "My brother's kid is probably going to die out there, after she's been raped twenty times by twenty different slimy guineas, all because of those two rotten bastards. You've got to tell me! It's got to stop, and we're the only ones who can make that happen! You can't live this way any longer, and neither can we. We've got to figure out what to do," I begged.

Scotty, startled by my outburst, jumped from my lap and into his mother's. Finally Victor opened up.

"You're right Johnny," he began. "But before I tell you this, you have to promise to listen so you understand. I know both of you are desperate for revenge right now. I am too. I would like nothing better than to see those two on a slab at the morgue with bullets in their brains, fired from my gun. But we've got to let the law run its course here. I'm so close to taking them down. I just need more time," Bravo pleaded with us.

"We've run out of time, Victor," Maggie finally uttered quietly. "But of course, we will listen to you. Tell us what you can. Do it quickly. We trust you, but so much of this is out of your hands."

And so Bravo laid it out. He told us all he knew about Borgstadt; his Nazi roots, his checkered past in Chicago, and his suspected quick assent to lead police corruption in our town. He told us about his night ride with that menace with a badge and the barrage of threats he unleashed upon my friend's family.

"How are you planning on revealing all of this?" Maggie asked. She wanted facts; both of us did, with equal intensity. Bravo sighed, reluctant to answer.

"Victor, no holding back. We've got to know," Maggie pleaded.

"Alright," he almost moaned in surrender. "A Special Federal Grand Jury has been impaneled. They've heard the evidence I've gathered thus far and want to further investigate not only our cops on the take, but Strawberry Torino, and they want to go all the way up to the top," Bravo said, and quickly warned in the next breath, "No one can know. You cannot breathe a word to anyone."

"You mean there's finally enough on Black Jim to bring him down and you could get Strawberry in the process?" I asked, a hopefulness sneaking into my voice.

"I don't know how far it can go; how much evidence can be collected. I'm going at this alone. I finally convinced the Feds to lend a hand, and the federal prosecutor in Denver only asked the judge for three months of the jury's time. It's hard to tell what we might get. So much of it so far is heresy. I just don't know." As Bravo talked, it seemed his confidence began to wane. "I'm doing the best I can. These bastards will stoop to anything; jury tampering, outright brides, intimidation, who knows? Even an airtight case against them could blow apart in a second if they can claw their way into that courtroom to corrupt the process. I only hope we can hold them off long enough to get indictments."

"At least this might be a beginning. If only this town knew what you were trying to do for it, for all of us," Maggie offered, reassuringly.

"Thanks, Bravo said, "but I'm no hero. All I'm trying to do is piece together enough to bring it all into the open. When I do, all of them will start turning on each other. They're like hyenas. They will attack each other first. I will say, what we think is that Strawberry has taken charge of fencing stolen goods from a string of damn sophisticated burglaries in town, and we also think there are some men in blue in on it with him," Bravo explained.

"And, you think that bastard Borgstadt might be the ringleader from inside the department?" I interjected.

"Christ, Johnny, I don't know, he might be. Every day I wake up, I think about it. If there's one guy in the department capable of pulling this off, it's Borgstadt, but I can't pin anything on him just yet. I may never get enough to lay him out," Bravo shook his head in frustration. "Oh, Johnny, Maggie, I'm so sorry. Maybe if I had just a little more time, I could have nailed him, before – before he did this." he lowered his head in his hands.

"So in your gut, just like mine, you know it's him. You know Strawberry's got Julie." I spoke with renewed desperation.

"Yea, I know. I know," he responded. "At least it's as clear as it can be who and what we're up against."

I fell silent. All of us did for a moment.

Then with a hardened, cold demeanor, Maggie removed her arms from around her son, leaned forward, into our friend's sympathetic face and finally said, "There's only one thing to do." She then gently placed Scotty on the ground, grasped his hand and slowly walked with him toward the workshop.

Bravo drove off shortly thereafter, promising to report any progress in the search. He also gave me a warning not to act on my own, but I sensed a distinct lack of conviction in his tone. Before he left, he instructed: "Don't you make a move without talking to me first."

Chapter 64
Neurological Damage

Bravo

When Sergeant Bravo left the Danna farm that afternoon, he had no idea where he was going. He was on an aimless trek back to town, straight into the maelstrom created by the child's disappearance. He was unsure of the wisdom of his decision to tell Maggie and me about the Grand Jury investigation and its findings thus far, although he knew he could trust our confidence. Someday, he hoped, he could tell us everything he'd learned while sitting in that closed, locked, and heavily guarded courtroom, listening to testimony that struck his sense of schoolboy curiosity, yet ultimately sickened him.

As he entered the outskirts of the city, having decided, once more, to inspect the site in the vicinity of Central Park where witnesses said they saw Julie thrown into the van, he thought back to the testimony he'd heard. No doubt in his mind, the jury's transcript would read like a well-crafted crime novel.

The lead prosecutor, Michael Bluestein, was a Jewish boy from Boston who grew up in the Back Bay and probably had some experience with the ongoing battles between the

Italian and Jewish mobs. At first, Bravo recalled, he was skeptical of the well-groomed, spit-shined, silk-suited Blue Blood, but soon after Bluestein's impassioned opening remarks to the jurors, Bravo immediately gained confidence in the attorney's dedication to the ominous task at hand. In a speech Bravo though was nothing short of extraordinary, Bluestein began with the background, laying out the facts. After the war, Americans went on a well-deserved buying spree. The 1950s created one big warehouse, exploding at the seams, storing and dispensing to a hungry public every imaginable item. Production of consumer goods rose to all-time highs, he reminded them. The market was glutted, and prices dropped on everything from appliances to shoe polish. Luxury products were produced and sold off at a record pace. Soon after the baby boom began and millions of new households were formed, essential and extravagant items were purchased by a suddenly prosperous middle class on their way to capture a better lifestyle and long-coveted piece of the American pie.

Emerging from their hibernation, like a famished bear after six months in a darkened cave, Bluestein embellished, La Cosa Nostra smelled the feast in waiting and with jowls frothing launched its hunt to satisfy its ravaged carcass. Bluestein was a master orator, in Bravo's mind, but also was an experienced enough lawyer to know his flourishes in poetic prose would not bring a jury to act without simple, straightforward descriptions of the alleged crimes. So Bluestein got to the point. It was an elementary, yet persuasive hypothesis.

"The mob soon discovered that well-executed burglaries by well-organized, skilled professionals would yield major returns on invested capital," he explained. 'There were plenty of both domestic and foreign black market purchasers paying high prices for American-made goods, so what was the problem?" Bluestein asked the jury.

"Storing and moving the contraband once it was procured," he answered for them. "But this was no different than the logistics associated with narcotics trafficking," he pointed out. "Although the end product was harder to store and transport. It's more like the old days of Prohibition. Bigger pieces to haul around, more trucks, more drivers, more expense goods in transport; but those were minor problems for the Mafia. They'd conquered the problem thirty years earlier, so why not now?" Bluestein asked.

"Jewels and furs, crystal and china. Watches, fine suits, keepsakes, all could be transported with little problem. It was much easier than hauling bottles of whiskey clanging around in the trunk of a car, or the bed of a flatbed truck. The mob met the challenge during prohibition, later in the drug trade, and it only made sense that they would rise from the ashes with another scandalous scheme," Bluestein concluded.

Even though the jury knew then that the mob was involved, Bravo was worried about convincing them of the corrupt cops. Had he given Bluestein enough evidence to establish a definite link between the crooks in their suits and the crooks in their uniforms? Bravo was desperate to weld that link together the jurors. His gut told him the evidence against Borgstadt and his cohorts was more that circumstantial. It stacked up rather quickly after he and Borgstadt's night ride in his new cruiser. He had to convince the jurors that his findings were solid.

He had many tiny but substantial bits and pieces of evidence gathered from break-in victims he'd interviewed, whose stolen articles didn't match police report inventories. Such items as a missing twenty-five-thousand-dollar diamond ring never showing up on any cop-produced list for the record. A state-of-the-art tool and die machine stolen right out of a steel mill contractor's storage unit. It was probably worth fifty thousand dollars and took at least five cops to move it, Bravo had speculated. Nothing about it ever hit police records.

There had been case after case of phony reports full of bogus lists, but no eyewitness accounts putting Borgstadt or any of his men at the scenes of the actual break-ins. But Bravo knew they were bound to slip up someday, if he only had a witness. And then he had a break. A mysterious telephone call at his home one night. He didn't recognize the voice. The caller wouldn't give his name, but when he mentioned the suspect German sergeant, Bravo couldn't get dressed fast enough. He sped across town to meet the cloak and dagger man on the fourth hole of the Pueblo Country Club golf course.

It was three o'clock in the morning. Bravo was wide-awake. His snitch would prove to be the rat of a lifetime. Their early-morning shadow-shrouded encounters lasted a month after that. Bravo never saw the man's face during this time. The stranger called himself the Professor, and when they met they stood on opposite sides of a big oak tree lining the fourth fairway, speaking to each other in the blackness. Yet the accounts of Bravo's rat – cultivated, and to his credit, somewhat cultured – were golden. It took Bravo two weeks to convince Bluestein to grant the Professor full immunity from prosecution, and in three hours of glorious testimony in front of the Grand Jury, condensing a month of moonlit monologue, the snitch paid off handsomely. The Professor's accounts provided what Bravo hoped would be enough information for the jurors to indict the whole bunch on twenty felony counts each.

And then, much to Bravo's delight, the Professor, who turned out to be a portly middle-aged mustached man named Rocco Vencenso who looked the part of his alias in his tweed jacket adorned with real leather elbow patches, corduroy slacks, and a silk kerchief dangling from the pocket, dropped the bombshell.

Clear as a church bell on Christmas morning, the Professor said, Jimmy Clemente put Strawberry Torino in charge of implementing the cop-inspired burglary ring and Strawberry had recruited Sergeant Herman Borgstadt of the Pueblo Police Department to run the ring from the inside. Although Bravo was not surprised at the information, he was stunned to have the facts dropped in his lap.

When the commotion in the courtroom finally died down Bluestein asked the Professor why he had chosen to come forward.

In a calm, dignified manner, his voice booming across the room, the Professor proclaimed, "I decided to bring this information to you after my fifth or six long stay at a neurological clinic in Kansas City. You see, ladies and gentlemen, I suffer from chronic migraine headaches and dizzy spells from a never-quite-healed fractured skull. I throw up every time the migraines hit me. You see, they were caused by a blackjack swipe to the back of my head," the Professor explained calmly. "Punishment over firing my .45 one night at a wayward varmint that got tangled up in a trip wire." His voice was eerily tranquil. "He wouldn't let them take me until he finished his Goddamn meeting."

"Who wouldn't let them take you to the hospital?" pressed Bluestein as he delightfully strolled in front of the jurors, his hands clasped behind his back and an I-already-know-the-answer grin stretching across his lips.

"Jimmy Clemente, the rotten son-of-a-bitch."

Bluestein nodded. "Tell us more if you can about Clemente's plan of corruption and his connection to members of the police department."

The Professor said that Jimmy never told his men when or how his ideas germinated in his balding skull, or who might have planted them there, but he was always coming up with new schemes and new teams of minions to carry them out. For instance, at a recent meeting in which he attended in the cavern below the cheese store, the Snitch said Jimmy appointed a new capo to run the narcotics trade to free Strawberry up for his new assignment.

"Strawberry was Jimmy's main man, but Jimmy cautioned his new team leader that night about Borgstadt," the Professor recalled.

"'He's a big ugly Kraut cop who may look dumb, but is shrewd, sneaky, dirty and vicious, and will cut your throat in a second if you turn your back on him,'" the Professor imitated Jimmy.

"As before," he explained, "to smooth out the operation, the mob needed a bunch of crooked cops. The cops would steal the merchandise, move it in small pieces to pre-designated locations for storage, and be paid on delivery. At that point, they were out of the picture. Then, once in safe storage, the goods are sorted and moved out by truck, car, or train to markets demanding those particular items. It was a real simple system responding to an always-reliable theory of supply and demand. The mob sold stolen art mostly in New York; they didn't ship many furs to Florida, except to Miami; gold was coveted in San Francisco; and heavy machinery was needed in Detroit. Hunting rifles went to Montana, or the Dakotas; handguns went to Boston for the fight between the Irish and Italian gangs, and fine clothing made its way to California, to awaiting arms of fledging starlets in Hollywood. It all worked like a charm most of the time."

So you can see," Bluestein cut in. "As so often been the case in decades past, Pueblo was the proving ground; the mob's laboratory. They work out the kinks of the operation here and export the results to cities across the country; particularly to cities in Jimmy Clemente's domain."

As he pulled his cruiser to curbside near the entrance of Central Park, Bravo remembered the shocked looks on the juror's faces when they realized that Pueblo was a major center for Mafia activity that stretched across the country.

After Bluestein drained the ex-capo of every ounce of incriminating evidence in his scattered brain, he was whisked off to Hawaii, well ensconced in the Witness Protection Program, his pockets full of fifty dollar bills, wearing a new flower shirt and sandals too small for his feet.

Chapter 65
Slippers Go Flying

As Bravo's cruiser disappeared from sight, I went to the workshop to find my wife and son. There Maggie was, seated at her workbench with Scotty playing with his wooden blocks at her feet.

I told them both how much I loved them and kissed each on the forehead. Maggie was engrossed in her work. Scotty was engrossed with his blocks. I told them I would return with news, regardless of what it was, and hurried off, driving too fast, into town. The Dannas were home by then. Vincennes had his shotgun near the front door. He would stand a diligent watch. I headed toward Carlo's house, dreading what awaited me.

I found Julia Gail curled in a tight ball lying on the living room couch; hugging Julie's favorite tattered and torn stuffed Easter bunny rabbit. A light dose of sedatives had helped Julia Gail remain somewhat calm although her initial hysteria completely drained her to near exhaustion. She told me Carlo's anger and frustration exploded more than once after the crushing news. He couldn't sit by and wait, so, like a madman, he had stormed out on his own. I imagined him driving recklessly through town and out on to the surrounding back roads, desperately searching everywhere for his daughter.

We closed the restaurant for the night, and Angelina gathered her daughters and husbands at her house to worry and pray. I hit the streets after making sure the rest of my family had congregated and swore to me they would remain together until this crisis had found resolution, be it tragic or joyous.

I probably searched many of the areas Carlo had already been to, and I ventured into plots in and around the city, remote and removed from where I believed Strawberry's kind would hide.

I drove into the heart of bojon town, begging for help. Into the Hispanic section, where, we Italians usually never ventured, and into the tiny black district on the north side. Everywhere I found true sympathy and sincere promises to help. In fact, when I think back, in not one part of town were my urgent pleas ignored. A beautiful blonde, blue-eyed teenager like Julie would be easy to spot, and on that one night, in every neighborhood, on every street, they all came together, one big family united in a single cause. Spontaneous search parties were formed in many of the neighborhoods. Geographic and ethnic boundaries were crossed. Few cops were out, it seemed, but if a whole division had swarmed the city, it would not have been enough for my satisfaction. As so often in the past, it seemed we were alone, fighting by ourselves, but on this night, the people of my town were with us.

I found my brother at about one o'clock in the morning at Karen's All Night Diner, a favorite among truck drivers on Highway 50 West of town. As I entered the establishment I heard him finish an irate one-way conversation with two still-on-duty patrolmen who were sipping coffee and chomping on fresh donuts.

"Get your lazy asses out of here and go find my daughter, you no good pricks!" Carlo yelled from his booth in the back of the diner.

Neither officer said a word to him, instead, rather sheepishly, got up from their stools at the counter and left. Those guys didn't care. I joined my totally spent brother in his booth. His face was buried in his folded arms resting on the dining table. Coffee came but soon got cold. I waited to speak, and instead simply placed my hand on my brother's head like a priest giving his blessing.

"We'll find them and we're gonna kill them," I quietly whispered.

~

Three mornings later, Julie was found.

I sat across from Bravo at a table at Angelina's, which was still closed to regular customers. It was empty inside except for us, with only a bright ray of sunshine warming the room and lighting my friend's face. I looked into his bleary, bloodshot eyes, waiting for his words. Outside, nearly blocking the front door, lay a huge stack of fresh-cut flower bouquets, dozens of them. Stuffed animals of every kind, posters and placards with hand scribbled messages wishing for Julie's safe return home and cards adorned with hearts, colored crudely in red Crayola. A monument to her. There were prayers, sentiments and words of encouragement from all of the neighborhoods, searching with us, hoping for the best.

Bravo smiled. "She'll live." He told me she had been found in the front yard of a woman named Estella Spagnoli, who lived with her seven cats, a good-sized mean-as-hell Billy goat and four chickens near Route 1 South of town.

Victor raced to Estella's house upon hearing the call for the rescue squad over his portable police radio that always sat atop his nightstand. He had returned home three short hours before the call came in for brief rest before returning to the streets and the outlying countryside in a search he feared would be futile. He admitted he had all but given up hope. He never told me this before, but statistics show that after the first forty-eight hours after a kidnapping, if the victims are not found, most experts believe they are dead. He told me he had slept six hours in the last three nights.

When he heard the dispatcher's voice loudly summoning help for an unconscious young, blonde-haired girl, and directing the ambulance to Estella's dilapidated farm, Victor said he leaped from his bed with a spark of hope and sprinted out the door. When he arrived at Estella's, the girl was already in the ambulance with an IV in her arm and Estella refusing to leave her side. He could barely recognize Julie; her face swollen and discolored.

He told me when Estella had walked out her front door, as she did at the same time every morning to retrieve her newspaper, she saw a naked figure, slumped over, propped up against the pole upon which her mailbox was affixed. Estella had told Bravo that the body seemed lifeless at first. There were numerous bruises, deep and purple, and welts down the girl's spine. Her long, blonde hair was matted in sweat and caked in mud. Her clothing lay ripped and soiled, scattered in a ditch beside her.

Then the woman heard the girl mumble something incoherent.

"When she heard the child murmur," Bravo told me, "she wrapped her house robe around Julie and took off. She told me she broke into a sprint like she hadn't in twenty years, aiming straight toward front her door and to the telephone inside." Bravo paused for a moment and chuckled softly. "She offered quite a descriptive picture, saying both her bedroom slippers flew from her feet in opposite directions as she ran. Hell, she was still barefoot at the hospital, and they had to get her a hospital gown to cover her up because Julie still had her robe," he added.

I shook my head in thankful disbelief, wondering out of which heavenly cloud this woman had dropped. Thank God it had been Estella who had found her.

"Jesus, she's a saint," I proclaimed.

"You might say that," Bravo agreed.

Before heading to the hospital, Bravo called Carlo and Julia Gail. He was cautious and caring with Carlo who answered, not wishing to spur his hopes, but told him to gather Julia Gail and get over to the hospital as quickly as possible. Before he hung up the he heard a shriek from the background at the other end of the line.

After I arrived a short time later, I found out that Carlo and Julia Gail had made it to the hospital before the ambulance carrying Julie and Estella had arrived. When the attendants pulled the gurney supporting a nearly unrecognizable little girl wrapped in sheets into his and Julia Gail's full view, Carlo said they nearly collapsed in each other's arms at the sight of her face.

"That's my baby!" Julia Gail had screamed. "Look what they did to my baby!" Only then, Carlo said, when she saw the girl's parents and heard Julia Gail's anguished cry, did Estella relinquish her hardened role of protector of the missing child that had turned up near her doorstep.

The barefoot stranger clad only in her nightclothes, not caring about anything else, walked up to them and said with confidence and compassion, "She's going to be alright."

The doctors rushed Julie to the examining room and prepared the surgical suite, just in case. Much to their astonishment the x-rays revealed a dislocated shoulder, two broken ribs, but no serious internal injuries. There were many cuts and abrasions, but there would be no permanent scars, physically at least. The mental trauma suffered by the child would take much longer to heal, the doctors told her parents. She was unconscious for forty-eight hours before awakening, thirsty, and hungry and reaching for the embraces of her mother and father.

Julie's brain blocked out her three days in hell, so Sergeant Bravo had no solid leads to follow, leaving him only sketchy physical descriptions of the perpetrators. All she would say was there were two, and then three, with the third one being big and fat. The fat one talked only to the others, she would add. He didn't do anything to her, she mumbled, before returning to a soothing slumber.

Estella returned to the hospital each day for first-hand reports, and each day, she was brought in to Julie's room by Carlo and Julia Gail to hug the little bird, as she described her, whom she had rescued after falling from her mother's nest. Estella became part of our family after that.

We knew that Victor's investigation would lead nowhere, and even if Julie could describe those bastards down to the stains on their teeth, her attackers were probably long gone hours after they threw her to the side of the road. They were brought in for a job, paid, and told to scatter when it was done. That's how the mob handled its business.

Julie's life had been spared. Her tormentors were under contract to perform, and their duties had been well specified. Strawberry found his mark. It cut us to the bone, leaving visible scars that we would forever inspect. He executed his plan very well, yet his hands remain clean. Next time he would kill, I was certain. This was his last warning. Had Clemente sanctioned it? We didn't know. We didn't care. He certainly hadn't stopped it from happening. None of them would get away with it this time.

As days passed and we waited for Julie's release from the hospital, I tried to contact Victor for an update on the investigation, even knowing in my heart that each time I would find him at the end of one of many blind alleys. On the afternoon we met at a downtown drugstore soda counter for a cup of coffee, he confirmed the futility of his probe, and then sat back to let me rage. It was difficult for me to control the urge to wantonly strike back. As before it became an obsession; my quest for vengeance had quickly consumed my soul.

Victor was sitting patiently on the stool next to me. Finally I stopped my ranting and looked over at him. His face was drawn, his eyes transfixed in the mirror behind the counter.

"What's wrong? You look like you've been hit by a truck," I said with some sympathy.

"I don't want to tell you this right now. We should still be celebrating Julie coming home, but you've got to know," he responded, dropping his voice.

"Oh, Christ, what now?" I moaned.

"I just got a call from the federal prosecutor in Denver," he said, his voice lifeless. "They've dis-empaneled the Grand Jury. No indictments are coming down. Not enough evidence. Somebody got to them. All they need is a majority vote on a Grand Jury to indict. They couldn't even get that. All that time workin' that case; tryin' to break through. Now, nothing, nothing, nothing at all. They're free to keep going. Nobody can stop them. It's lost." He turned to me, a hopeless look in his eyes.

"No it's not," I insisted, slamming my fist on the counter. "It's not lost. There is a way. But we must prepare."

Chapter 66
Beloved Benefactor

In the months and years that followed Julie's abduction, we marveled at the girl's quest to trounce the demons that threatened to misshape her young life into a distorted, damaged reflection of those who brought their wrath upon her innocence. And she beat her abusers at every turn.

Julie was a tough, very determined child. She was bound to shed the suffering and cast off her ordeal. Her strength came as no surprise. Carlo was the first to point out the similarities between his daughter and her mother. Julie's steps toward recovery reminded us of Julia Gail's emergence from the iron lung. She shared the same determination to overcome a brutal affliction that all the experts agreed would become a permanent disability.

Julie knew the story of her mother's victory over polio. Although Julia Gail downplayed her exceptional fortitude during her battle against the disease, she and Carlo both realized that her example was serving their daughter well as she embarked on the long, cold, cruel road toward recovery. They talked openly and without reservation about those nights she was away from home. They forbid her to feel shame or embarrassment. She was a victim of a senseless act by senseless people, they told her, and she would win because of her un-shattered self-esteem and her confidence in her own abilities. Those were the things she could hold on to. Those were the things that were not violated. No one could take that away from her.

Gradually she began to heal. As was the case with her mother, Julie's trauma solidified her strength, her endurance and her self-assurance. Besides her family, Julie latched onto another powerful pillar of strength to help see her through the bad times. It was Estella. Their bond was never broken. As for myself, I had tremendous respect, admiration and gratefulness for Estella and for what she did and what she kept on doing through the years for Julie, for all of us, actually – until her own infirmities became too much for her to endure. She was a friend, a mentor, a blessing from God. Julie was at Estella's bedside through the horrific bouts with debilitating arthritis until the pain became too much to bear and she surrendered.

Every Christmas until Estella's death Julie would bring her lovely medallions of the head and bust of the image of an angelic nun who became our family's favorite patron saint – Saint Brigid of Ireland. Julie and Estella adored the legendary stories of Brigid; her ties to Saint Patrick and the remarkable breadth of her patronage. Brigid was the protector of many; from babies to blacksmiths, from poets to poultry farmers, but most of all, Brigid, in the eyes of Julie and Aunt Estella, was chosen as their patron saint for her watchful eye over those who rescue and those who must be rescued. The cross of Saint Brigid hangs on the walls of each of our homes to this day.

Chapter 67
Empty Confessionals and Big, Blue Lincoln's

Even though we encouraged Julie to put the brutality behind her, we could not do the same. We could not forget. We would not forget. My loathing for those responsible grew stronger every day. My niece would recover because of her unmatched inner strength, and that strength came from an endless outpouring of affection and support. As all of us in our own way nurtured this sweet child, we knew we would soon become as ruthless as her captors.

Ever since that torturous first night of Julie's disappearance, searching and finding Carlo alone, dejected, defeated; staring into his cold cup of coffee at Karen's, he never said it out loud, but I knew he needed me to act for him against our enemies. Carlo was not afraid. Given the chance he would have gladly eviscerated the lot of them. But my brother was not cut out for a managed plan of attack. He would have been brutal, no doubt, but he also would have been careless. He lacked discipline because his emotions were in control. All he cared about was getting even and that was dangerous to him and to all of us. We could not afford to leave a bloody trail, because that trail, whoever might be following it, including the cops, would lead right back to the father of the victim. So, without a word between us, I took over.

Even though vengeance was inevitable and I was comfortable planning for it, I still struggled with maintaining a sense of righteous self. I guess you're not human if you don't have that struggle. Or you are as equally degenerate as your targets. Are those qualities of human nature forever sacrificed by stepping across that bright line between right and wrong? Did we have a choice? Yes, we did, but no we didn't. Not really. I don't think there was ever a debate, at least a serious one. It was what we had to do to protect our family. That bright line had to blur in our minds and we had to leap across it without hesitation.

We were going to war. We didn't want to. We had been shoved, pulled, jerked —screaming and thrashing – into the conflict. Now conflict it was forced upon us we would embark upon it with a fury. We knew the enemy. It is cloaked in its pinstriped uniform. It is well equipped and supported with regiment-sized forces. It has abundant weapons, refined tactics and a relentless pursuit of its cause. There was no doubt who or what it was, and there was no mistake that evil oozed from every pore in its body.

I had known that kind of enemy once, had already met him; had already met the devil on the battlefield when he tried to annihilate the world. My disgust for him is all consuming, and my revulsion for the new devils in my life is haunting me now.

When I look back on those days and weeks prior to our counterstrike, I find the details difficult to reconstruct. We covered our tracks so well, and our well-crafted alibis became so impenetrable that sometimes separating fact from fiction is not an easy exercise. I do know that it took meticulous planning and preparation. I was responsible for that. The technical part was easy for Maggie. She had plenty of training and plenty of practice at her special craft, and she was riveted to the task at hand.

We would have put events into motion sooner, but we gave time for Maggie's belly to flatten and for her strength to return. A baby girl, eight pounds, thirteen ounces; born one month after they released Julie from the hospital. We named her Rose. She would blossom. After that, some six weeks of relative quiet and calm passed with exception of regular dirty diapers and nighttime hungry yelps here and there. Tranquility prevailed in the early weeks of our second child's life. Soon, we knew our mission would begin in earnest.

The shock back to reality interrupting our brief retreat to a normal life came with the fourth raid on the restaurant carried out by Borgstadt's patrolmen. Again, they failed to find anything, and again failed to scatter our customers. Their leader didn't bother showing up that night to review the good works of his gofers. We waited for Borgstadt with hot coffee brewing. We would have enjoyed the confrontation with him. We could see the detective for what he really was – a cheap, ugly, ramshackle stand-in for Strawberry.

Tying Borgstadt to Strawberry was easy. Stupid cops, playing mobsters out in plain sight, with their capo hiding behind a gold shield pinned to his chest. Their belligerent, harassing raids had become almost comical, but we weren't laughing. The next morning after Borgstadt's no-show we returned to duty with renewed vigor. The complicated part of our plan was deployment. Surveillance of our targets came first. We were challenged with finding, tracking and predicting the routines of our enemies. We turned the tables from being the stalked to becoming the stalkers. That part was relatively easy, since the Apalachin raids Jimmy and his boys had gone further underground, hiding and scheming;

pushing and peddling, extorting and robbing from bunkers in blanketed obscurity.

My Army days helped us pluck the rats from their holes. Tactics and maneuvering skills came back rather once I put my mind to it. When we had the intelligence, and when we decided where to act, the rest was the not-so-simple stage of execution. Our timing had to be perfect to carry out our deed successfully. What we needed on our chosen night were a few extra minutes for added safety. So a time-consuming decoy was in order.

On that night, we watched from afar as the big cars gathered beneath the giant tree. We knew which one he drove. We had been told he would come that night to share his demented wisdom with the others. I felt horrible wrapping that big male raccoon in the trip wire that surrounded Jimmy's compound. I'm still not sure what the slightly built thug did with the angry, snarling animal after he unearthed himself from Jimmy's cave to investigate the noise. Whatever happened between Jimmy's tiny trooper and the squealing varmint, we'll never know for sure, but I do know that Jimmy's guy bellowed louder than our hissing decoy, cussing and moaning all the way back to the trap door entrance to his boss's cavern.

What we do know is that it took him thirty minutes to find the location of the disturbance. And that's all the extra time we needed. That additional half-hour allowed Maggie, dressed all in black and moving through the darkness with stealth precision, to install the device to the undercarriage of the big Lincoln, make the proper connections, and set the timing trigger. She returned to our chosen spot, adrenaline pumping and panting hard, with a thumbs-up. And then we waited in the shadow of a dim moonlight. It was now well past midnight and into the early hours of the morning. Maggie, hard to see draped in her dark clothing, dozed off. I had trouble staying awake myself. Our vantage point was about a quarter-mile away. We kept watch through the highest powered set of binoculars on the market – Army-Navy surplus.

And then, as the sun peeked just above the horizon yet the sky was still a hazy grey, I caught sight of some movement below. A number of shadowy figures emerged. I laid there waiting, tense. Finally, I saw him. The fat man appearing in the dim light. My heart pounding in my chest. There he was at last, carrying his right hand with his left in a strange way as if it hurt him. He walked slowly, a deliberate, plodding gait, with his head down and shoulders stooped. He looked tired, forlorn, and I almost felt a twinge of sympathy. Almost. He arrived, opened the car door and edged his way in. The dome light came on. I could see his face clearly. I hated the sight. A moment later a blinding light.

Maggie didn't care to see. I was glad the guard dog, a German Shepherd, was some distance away when the blast occurred. The animal was not hurt. The flash came first and then the sound an instant later. Maggie turned to go, but I grabbed her arm, taking a moment to gaze at the spectacle, the devastation. We dashed to our awaiting truck, the bright orange ball erupting behind us, racing skyward, consuming the Lincoln and its occupant.

We sped away in the opposite direction of the scene, but did hear the German Shepherd barking hysterically at the flames.

~

Jimmy

Wild Bill told this part all too well. Jimmy knew Strawberry had an all-around bad day the day he died. He told Jimmy when he arrived that night for the meeting that he hadn't slept the night before. Jimmy didn't care.

The meeting carried on well past the appointed hour of three o'clock in the morning. He had plenty of business to attend to. The time spent bandaging the right hand of Spencer "the Dispenser" Donatelli, whose little finger had nearly been ripped off by the fangs of the furious raccoon, plus other annoying distractions put Jimmy in an awfully cantankerous mood as the early morning hours progressed.

When the meeting finally ended, he told Strawberry to stay after the others were asked to leave. Their session that early morning had been a lively and mostly a productive one in spite of the interruptions and Jimmy's nasty temper. The gallery of wise guys heard promising reports on the progress of the fencing operation involving the local cops and on the re-invigorated heroin trafficking, plus the encouraging results of new gun-running activity from Mexico; all of which showed positive signs of success and increasing profits.

They also were told of finally, after many successful tests, being able to export the marketing of the fencing scheme to other select cities in Jimmy's kingdom. He reluctantly gave Strawberry credit for his efforts in recruiting the crooked cops to support the program, but not before complaining about the fat payoffs going to that "Kraut mother-fuckin' sergeant." But Strawberry explained how important Borgstadt had become in maintaining the secrecy and loyalty among those involved in the lower echelons of the police department, and Jimmy knew it was essential to keep as many greedy cops on the payroll as possible, so he allowed Strawberry to assert his position for the continuing education of the others in the room.

"He's worth it, Boss. I have them right where I want them," Strawberry assured him. After the others left, Jimmy's cavernous conference room was quiet. He watched Strawberry's head bob and his eyelids droop as he fought sleep.

Interesting, Jimmy thought, *the man's fatigue is surpassing his usual anxiety over being ordered to stay behind.* It wasn't the first time. Jimmy enjoyed his one-on-one, man-to-man private talks with Strawberry. Jimmy paced around the table, retrieving an empty pasta- and marinara-sauce-encrusted plate left from dinner hours ago and taking it to the sink to be washed and dried by Lizzie later in the day.

Then he returned to Strawberry, standing behind him. He still hadn't uttered a word. Jimmy noticed Strawberry's shoulders tense. With one quick motion Jimmy produced his blackjack and struck Strawberry's bare knuckles resting on the table. He heard his finger bones shatter. The big man howled in pain.

"What the fuck are you thinkin'?" Jimmy began his tirade. "You kidnap that kid out of revenge on people that don't even belong to us. You rape that kid and leave her to die. I should cut your lousy, fat, fucking throat and hang you up like a pig to drain the blood," screamed Jimmy to his blubbering associate.

"Boss," Strawberry cried aloud between sobs. "I didn't rape her. The minute I turned my back on those punks from Phoenix, they got to her."

"You didn't stop them. Why didn't you stop them? You idiot. I should spit on you." And he did, right in

Strawberry's face. The moisture, Jimmy noticed, blended in well with Strawberry's flowing tears.

Jimmy took a deep breath. He was too old for this. Lizzie kept reminding him about his high blood pressure and the doctor's orders to take his medicine on time.

"I don't know what I am to do with you. I can't kill you. You make me too much money," Jimmy declared, more calmly now. "Why do these people hurt you so much? It's been ten, no, twelve years. It's over. Stop. I'm telling you. If the Feds get into this, I may turn you over to them myself."

"Boss," Strawberry gasped between breaths, still desperately defending himself. "They humiliated me. I remind you of that. We are taught *insegnare mai a dimenticare*, never to forget."

The man was spent and in dire need of sleep. Jimmy stroked Strawberry's wet cheek. "She didn't die. That's good, but you've taught them a final lesson. And now you must forget. You hear me? No more. I give you a final order. Do not defy me. Never again. You leave those people alone. Go about your business now. Forget them. I want no more problems. You're becoming a rich man. Think only of that, and only of your loyalty to me. Now go," Jimmy ordered.

He watched the big man stumble toward his car, all the while fumbling and grimacing, gingerly fishing for the keys from his pocket with his good hand. He stood at the door of his new powder blue Lincoln Continental, parked right where it should be, under the willow tree, away from the road and behind Jimmy's underground den. Finally he slipped his key in to the lock and climbed in behind the wheel.

Jimmy made his way to his upstairs bedroom and was eyeing his befuddled capo through the wide window that overlooked his property. The sun was peeking over the horizon. It would be a beautiful day, Jimmy thought wearily.

The wind was calm. He closed the blinds and quietly crawled between the sheets next to his adoring wife. He gently kissed her forehead.

Then he heard the blast, felt it through his bones. It rattled his window, shook his bed and in pure shock, he bolted upright. He ran to the window and stared out across his lawn at the inferno. He shook his head, dazed and bewildered. His first sensible thought while gazing in amazement at the fireball that engulfed the big blue Lincoln was the cops. The last thing he needed was a swarm of good or bad cops buzzing around on his property, playing big shots and acting with authority. He had no idea who had blasted his trusted capo into oblivion, but right now, he had to find help to cover up the evidence and keep the incident quiet.

Lizzie, startled out of a deep sleep, joined him at the window. She looked in his face. She knew fear was reflecting in his eyes. There was no doubt in Jimmy's mind as he stared back at his wife that this was no amateur job. He had seen the destruction and debris caused more than a few car bombs to know that this was the work of a professional. One swoosh and one boom and it was over in an instant. Later, he would worry about who did it. Right now he had bigger problems to contend with.

Within thirty minutes of the detonation, Jimmy had ten men at the scene. He found most of them at Karen's Diner where they had gathered for breakfast after the meeting. After the boy with the nearly severed finger received Jimmy's frantic call, they sped back to the cheese stand for cleanup duty. In giving his orders Jimmy was self-conscience when he heard his voice crack with anxiety and childlike emotion.

The Boss remained inside his house watching his men put out the fire and sift through the smoldering debris. He wanted to be as far away from the rubble as possible. And he wanted it all gone to obliterate the scene that had already begun to haunt him. At Jimmy's direction his men pushed the blackened and twisted metal of the fancy Lincoln into the creek bed. They hurried to cover what remained of the vehicle and its occupant with sand and soil. They didn't bother removing Strawberry's mummy-like carcass from the car. He was left behind the wheel, his broken, barbequed hand on the ignition switch.

Jimmy finally went back to bed around four o'clock that afternoon. He slept with unceasing nightmares.

~

Borgstadt

One night shortly after Strawberry and his car exploded, Sergeant Herman Borgstadt sat in his unmarked sedan near the south entrance of Central Park awaiting his troublesome associate. Borgstadt was worried as he fidgeted with his radio, switching from the police scanner to a new jazz station broadcasting on a FM frequency with stunning clarity and quality.

"Aha!" he exclaimed as the sweet saxophone sound came gliding through the car's speakers he'd installed at city expense. But he couldn't concentrate on the music. His nerves were frayed. Strawberry had never stood him up before.

Borgstadt stewed. Then he grew angry. Then he was frightened that he might have offended the big man, but then again, he was gaining more power every day, and when he stopped to think about it, he wasn't threatened by Strawberry, or even Mr. Clemente himself, if it came to that.

Even though he had never met Black Jim, Borgstadt was so sure of himself that he thought not even the Boss could touch him now. He had control. He was producing twenty, maybe thirty thousand a month in stolen goods, most of it pure profit. They needed him. He was rock solid in the system now, indispensable, and they knew it. He could take on Black Jim at any moment if he gave him any shit.

In the next instant, however, anxiety and fear crept up his spine as he sat there waiting. One hour became two hours; two hours became three. He shifted in his seat. His legs were cramped. He would not tolerate having to wait. Eventually, exhausted, he nodded off. The next thing he knew, his sleep-muddled brain was awakened by a tapping on his driver's side window. His eyes struggled to focus on the source of the noise. When they did he stared into the silenced barrel of a .45 caliber automatic. He recognized the man who held the gun to the window glass. The man smiled but not in a friendly way. Borgstadt knew what was coming next. It would happen quickly. He could not run. He could not hide. He peered back into the silenced barrel, curiously thinking that it looked as big as those Panzer artillery 88s his Nazi brothers in arms fired at America's troops during the siege at Bastogne. Then it was dark forever.

~

Jimmy

Wild Bill took exceptional delight in reporting this.

The next morning, Jimmy read about Sergeant Borgstadt's murder on the front page of the *Chieftain Journal*. The article was highlighted by a gruesome photograph of a shattered, blood-spattered driver's side window and a white sheet covering a body sprawled across the car's front seat. The photo was printed in color. In another front-page story, the paper self-congratulated itself by announcing installation of a new photo color-processing machine. Jimmy suspected the editors decided the Sergeant's murder scene was a perfect opportunity to display the new technology. Great results, Jimmy mused. Bright red blood for all to see.

On page sixteen, under the Crime Beat section, there was a single paragraph mentioning that two days before, a farmer, out on his early-morning chores, reported a loud explosion and ball of flame to the West of Jimmy's property. Police were still investigating, the story said.

Jimmy read both stories with loathing and revulsion before tossing the newsprint into his living room fireplace. He would not allow Lizzie to see any of the trash they were printing. He sat heavily in his favorite chair, but it provided little comfort. For the first time in his long career, Jimmy pondered his next move with uncertainty. He had always given himself high marks for his decisiveness. He always had been systematic in everything he did, but this time, he had to admit that he was hesitant, and uncharacteristically unsure.

Someone had the audacity to violate my inner sanctum, he raged, *my personal property; my hallowed ground, and they did it so blatantly that even my Lizzie was forced to witness it!* This could not be tolerated. Jimmy's instincts for survival and control fought him viciously now, rather than motivated him as they had in the past. He hadn't reached the top without an innate drive for success. And success meant survival at all costs, and survival meant control. Control of those under your command. Loyalty above all. Control kept you safe, protected you among your enemies, and allowed you to strike first, a kill or be killed mentality. When that control was jeopardized, it meant loyalty was diminishing, and you were no longer safe. The tools to strike first were gone. And when that happened you were as good as dead.

Jimmy knew the rules. He felt that armor of invincibility slipping away. For the first time in his tenure, he felt threatened. He was in a terrible quandary. Had his reign come to an end? Did he strike back to retain power or beg off, and ask to retire gracefully? This is more than indecision, he realized; I am at a crossroads.

What if Strawberry's murder had not been in retaliation for the fat man's rampage of revenge? What if it had been a warning sent by Jimmy's own people? He usually avoided dwelling on it, but today, right this minute; the fact that he was pushing seventy came to the forefront of his mind. He had no intention of slowing down, not just yet, but others with the desire to ascend to the helm, a strong desire like he had so many years ago, may have sensed an opening, realizing Jimmy's weaknesses and acting on their own to bring him down. But he still loved his job and he was doing it well. Mandatory retirement was out of the question.

Yet, in the back of his pragmatic brain, Jimmy sat there with the stark knowledge that the old guard was slowing but surely losing its grip. The Genovese Family was being infiltrated and fractured. Vito had died in 1969. The Gambino family was assuming greater power and Jimmy knew he was not part of that inner circle. Joe Bananas, the prick, was giving him great anguish, constantly testing his will, strength and authority. Jimmy knew the New York bosses could remove him at any time, but his gut told him that decision had yet to be made. He could fight back, but was it worth it?

No longer, Jimmy realized, did he have the resources to fight a gang war to protect his turf. His combat troops were spread over a two-thousand-mile span. They were not concentrated within a ten-square mile radius of Manhattan, or Brooklyn, or Newark, like those of his counterpart gangsters in the East. Jimmy felt the disquiet in his bones. He rose from his chair and made his way down into his dark, underground sanctum. When he got there and switched on the light, it felt like a dungeon.

He picked up a deck of cards and dealt himself a hand of solitaire. The days rolled slowly by for Jimmy from that point on. He neglected to call his next regular monthly meeting; the month following the backyard bombing, sending word that he was ill. He kept Lizzie very close, not allowing her to go out alone, for he feared that the regime change by violence would begin with her and end with him.

One night the carefully edited movie version of *Bonnie and Clyde* was featured on late night television. Lizzie had gone to bed before it started. Jimmy watched it until the end and dreamed that night it was Lizzie and him being riddled unmercifully by the stream of bullets flying from barking Thompson machine guns. He woke in a frigid sweat and threw up his linguini dinner.

Lizzy made him lots of minestrone soup. He cancelled his meeting a second time. Then one day while reading the obituaries in the morning paper, he saw the death notice of a friend – a local bar owner who had been Jimmy's trusted associate from way back in the old days. He was a petty operator, mostly running prostitutes and a small time numbers racket, but Jimmy liked him. He succumbed to a ravaging case of lymphatic cancer at the age of fifty-three. Jimmy didn't even realize the poor bastard was sick.

Jimmy decided to attend the funeral. To pay his respects. That's the way it was done. Jimmy was loyal to his friends. He had few, so this act of devotion was important to him. It would be his first venture away from his compound since the bombing.

The morning of the funeral Jimmy dressed in his vintage brown suit, felt Fedora hat, white shirt and pale maroon tie. The only thing unusual about his dress was the black elastic armband he shimmied up over his suit coat arm to encircle his right bicep. He kissed Lizzie goodbye and climbed in his Chevrolet for the drive into town. The 1963 Biscayne was a beautiful brown. To get it, he traded in his 1957 salmon and grey Bel Aire, and when he did, the reliable old Chevy that carried him and Lizzie to the ill-fated meeting near Binghamton had one hundred and twenty thousand miles on it. But it still ran well. Salmon and grey was just too fancy, Jimmy decided.

Driving slowly, as he always did, Jimmy soon spotted his tail, following two car lengths behind. Between the two of them they were backing up traffic at fifteen miles an hour below the speed limit on the recently completed East-West four-lane parkway that circled town. When Jimmy parked in his spot at Saint Teresa's, his tail was close behind and, quite curiously, the occupants of the car let themselves be seen. Jimmy glanced over his shoulder as he exited his Chevy for the short walk to the entrance of the church.

He didn't recognize either one of the boys in their dark suits and sunglasses, and he figured at that moment, in broad daylight with plenty of witnesses congregating for the services, this was not a prelude to a hit. Plus his trackers seemed to expose themselves openly. Jimmy quickly concluded it was most likely the Feds since, instead of a sniper's rifle all they carried were long-lens cameras.

Goddamn, Jimmy thought as he entered the church, *they're takin' my picture and they want me to know it. Outrageous.*

Jimmy sat nervously through the hour-and-a-half-long Mass, alone in a prime spot in a third row pew on the aisle. He heard the hushed whispers of the mourners when he had entered the church and the loud rebuke of a mother to her son when the boy nearly shouted, "Is that him, Momma, the gangster?"

In his own way Jimmy prayed when the priest said it was okay to do so. He hadn't prayed in years, but now it seemed the right thing to do. After all, his heart was not cold. He sought the sort of solace that might be due him from the God he didn't know so well. Maybe next time, confession, Jimmy thought. He didn't dare take communion. When the little girl behind him tapped his shoulder and offered her hand during the "Peace be with you" interlude, he took it and smiled cheerfully.

When the service ended Jimmy waited for most of the congregation to leave. He was tired again. He always seemed tired these days and he was in no hurry to give his stalkers the satisfaction of stripping him naked with their lenses. Let them work for their fun, he thought.

Before he exited the church, he could see them through the doorway, right out in the open not fifty yards away. Jimmy shook his head in disgust as he finally stepped through the sacred sanctuary's front door into the bright sunlight. He could hear the rapid-fire chatter of camera shutters as he descended the stairs. He decided to avoid the gravesite service, having paid his respects to the departed's widow while viewing the corpse in its open casket before the service began. He walked slowly to his awaiting Chevy and drove straight for home, this time at the speed limit, with his photographers on his bumper the whole time.

~

Bravo

Borgstadt's murder was creating so much confusion and chaos in the police department that Sergeant Bravo couldn't get any work done. He sat at his desk and all he heard around him from his chattering fellow officer corps was unrelenting speculation like, "Was it a Mafia hit?" "Or a disgruntled citizen?" "Or was it a jealous husband?"

What Bravo immediately picked up in the conversations swirling about was the definite lack of concern over Sergeant Herman Borgstadt's sudden demise. No one seemed to care that he was gone; his remains on a slab in the morgue with the coroner practicing the latest forensic techniques on his nearly disintegrated skull. No doubt, in his relatively short span of service to my town, Borgstadt made few friends, and many enemies.

His killer left a remarkably clean trail; so clean in fact, that for the level of expertise within the detective division, there were absolutely no leads to follow. As the weeks passed, the frenzy over Borgstadt's murder died down and Bravo noticed less squad room squabble about the ongoing, though futile, investigation. Finally the coroner complained that he needed room in the body cooler.

A woman claiming she was Borgstadt's girlfriend claimed the body, and had it buried in the Rosemont cemetery that very same day. The next thing Bravo heard was that the girlfriend had sued the city for Borgstadt's insurance benefits. Six months later, after a wild courtroom scene filled with tears and screams of lost loved ones and costs of the burial, the judge handling the disposition of Borgstadt's tiny estate declared the girlfriend ineligible for the benefits.

It was at that point that the judge asked Bravo to help find a legitimate beneficiary for the death benefits due from the Sergeant's untimely departure from this world. Bravo knew Lieutenant Weinstein would be more than happy to help. Out of the blue, Weinstein found a "distant cousin" of the murdered police officer who lived in Milwaukee.

She received the surprise of her life when the check and cover letter arrived explaining the ten-thousand-dollar insurance settlement payment. After a thorough briefing from Lieutenant Weinstein, Miss Amy Horowitz, a survivor of the Nazi death camp at Treblinka in Poland, told the judge over the telephone that she distinctly remembered her deceased mother talking about their infamous relative being kicked out of the Chicago Police Department some years before for insubordination stemming from unknown infractions.

Chapter 68
White Truffle Shavings

My town began to change in significant ways after Borgstadt and Strawberry were gone. I don't think many people could see the change at first, but we all began to sense it as time went on. Some of the change was good, some of it not so good.

The economy was changing for one thing, and not for the better. The Industrial Age was morphing into the Technological Age, and demand for steel was declining. A world economy was yet to blossom to create an international market for America's precious metal. That would be twenty-five years into the future, and the steel mill in Pueblo couldn't be sustained that long. Cutbacks in production led to cutbacks in jobs. The steelmaking infrastructure at the mill was old and dilapidated. Mr. Rockefeller wasn't around this time to bail it out; and neither was the government. Skeleton crews were formed to meet miniscule production quotas, but that didn't last long either. As the early 1980s rolled around, we all looked around for a solution. When none was found, eventually the old mill was shut down for good.

One morning, years later, I picked up the newspaper and read about Jimmy. It was all there, like it had never been a secret; the mysteries that had built a secure, impenetrable mote around his life had been drained. The sources for the story were wide-open FBI files, down to the most intimate details of his existence, and his demise. The story said that Jimmy had died in his rocking chair after finishing just the third chapter of Mario Puzo's *The Godfather.* His wife found him slumped over, the book on the floor beside him. According to the autopsy report, his high blood pressure finally blew out his aorta. There was no foul play. He hadn't liked the book so far, according to the reporter's account of his subsequent interview with the deceased don's wife.

Like the steel mill, Jimmy became old and dilapidated. His infrastructure was gone; the market had changed. Vito wasn't there to bail him out, or help him transition to the new age. The Mafia would go on, but without Jimmy and those of his lost era. Lizzie Clemente told the reporter she would be closing the cheese stand for good.

I put down the article and considered the irony. Jimmy Clemente's last notion, the final thrust of information into his brain, was planted there by Mr. Puzo through his romanticized, stylized, unintended version of Jimmy's own life. Mr. Puzo portrayed the Mafia world in all too realistic detail. He entertained those who read his work with graphic renderings of the lives and times of the Corleone family, a Mafia fiefdom, its members presented in fascinating fictional profiles. A true work of literary art, however, Jimmy would not have been amused, I speculated.

The subject matter hit too close to home. Jimmy had actually lived Mr. Puzo's tales. And in his brief reading, I was willing to bet that he was not entertained or amused. If you ask me, he died scowling and cursing at every word on every page. You see, the mob succeeded in the shadows, but when its deeds and its doers come to light, it fails; its leaders reduced to comical characters subject to ridicule, scorn and Hollywood's un-holiness.

The Mafia rules by fear, and if exposed to a public who sees it for all its faults and vulnerability, its time abruptly ends. Jimmy's end had come, and I believed he died disappointed, dismayed, and disillusioned. At least I hope so. The article made my mind wander, reaching back to those who Jimmy had touched; his presence always hurting but his reach never lasting. I thought of Julie.

Julie became a state champion gymnast in the vault and floor exercises; and later made the 1968 U.S. Summer Olympics team as an alternate. She graduated summa cum laude from Boston University with a degree in biology, and rather than going on to medical school, she joined an upstart pharmaceutical company selling laboratory chemicals and reagents. She bought stock early, and retired at forty with a two million dollar buyout package. She and her husband, a chemist, had four children. Carlo and Julia Gail visit them often, but they really don't like the cold winters and hot, muggy summers of Massachusetts. Maggie and I enjoy traveling to the East much more than my brother and his wife, and we spend many wonderful vacation days with Julie and her family.

When Aunt Estella died a few years back, we buried her with a cross of Saint Brigid that Julie had hand-stitched and placed lovingly in her hands laying across her lap.

And then there is Nicole. She married the lawyer within a year. He fell in love with both her and her children. After a successful stint in private practice, her husband quit to run for District Attorney. Nicole earned her law degree attending night school while raising her family. She never practiced law; instead, she ran her husband's campaign, which they won on the first try. He served four consecutive terms before retiring in the early 1980s. They had two more children together. She kept most of the money from Silvio's

bank accounts and established a college fund for their offspring.

As for my town, the people of Pueblo began their fresh start, one without the two pillars that had supported the economy and woven the fabric of society for so long. Both the mill and the mob had rotted away. And it was good, at least the mob part. I'm proud to say my brother and our families helped prompt that change, but we had to do it without Angelina. She left us within a month of Jimmy's departure. But she knew Jimmy was gone and was glad of it. She cried tears of joy when I told her while visiting her at the Cresthaven Nursing Home where she had resided since suffering a stroke mid-way through the preparation of a fine dish of piping hot polenta ladled over cold mascarpone and topped with shavings of white truffles. We kept her last dish on the menu for a month in her honor.

She was lucid and coherent to her final days. All of her recipes were published under the joint authorship of Maggie and Julia Gail a year after her death. They sold one hundred and thirty thousand copies of the book worldwide, with sales in Sicily reaching more than twenty thousand. The book went into its second printing a year ago after a New York publisher paid advance royalties of fifty thousand dollars.

Sergeant Victor Bravo became a lieutenant, then a captain, and then a deputy chief of detectives. The city elected its first majority Hispanic city council the same year as his final promotion. He could have been chief but declined the offer. He could have run for mayor, but declined that, too. Victor and I still find solace in each other's company and spend time together, mostly at my A-frame cabin that I built in the mountains west of Walsenburg, or on Bravo's boat, fishing for browns on the man-made reservoir Northwest of town.

Perhaps, with the exception of the Mafia, generations change as conditions change. The generation coming behind Carlo and me struggled like those before us. Pueblo still tries real hard to keep her young citizens in her grasp. Our children and grandchildren loved the place, and hated having to leave it, but they knew they could not thrive with the lack of opportunity here. I hope that will change, but for now, they scatter like the blowing dust. Even the pistachio business couldn't sway my children to stay. When we sold it, the groves spanned one hundred and fifty acres. We had five greenhouses and two thousand gumball vending machines in locations as far away as Lawrence, Kansas. I'm told my trees have become a phenomenon of sorts in the annuals of horticultural science, and today are studied in graduate-level botany classes.

My granddaughter keeps two samples of my antique gumball machines proudly displayed on her fireplace mantel in her home. She tells me they are regular conversation pieces at her frequent dinner parties. Investment earnings from the sale proceeds from the pistachio business are sent to my children, and will send my grandchildren and their grandchildren through college from the family trusts that we created.

Scotty bought me a snooker table for Christmas one year and put it in his basement. We play occasionally and he still hasn't beaten me. Rose gets bored with the game when she's there for family dinners, with her husband and two children playing with Scotty's three in the living room. In her spare time Maggie tinkers in her workshop, but not with dangerous toys. She likes fixing microwave ovens for some reason. We have five around the house. Cecil and Julia Gail breed horses on a small ranch outside of Canon City. I have no idea why; neither of them ride, they just seek a perfected blood line of prime show Appaloosas, and when I seek an explanation for their passionate pursuit, they remind me of my pistachios.

I think I have a few years left to ponder the past, seek forgiveness for my wrongs, cherish the rights, and strive to set the record straight for what may lie ahead when I hit the dirt for good. I am satisfied with what I've done and harbor few regrets. There is no guilt; rather a wish that it not need to have happened in the first place. The nightmares are gone, replaced by dreams of placid fields and flowering hedgerows populated with buzzing bees instead of soldiers flinging bullets. My son beckons me to return to the scenes of battle when our country celebrates those anniversaries and Ronald Reagan weeps before the pasture of crosses and Stars of David at Normandy. I will not go. I will not re-live what I saw and what I had to do. Once in a lifetime is enough.

Today, Angelina's Fine Italian Restaurant is a chain bookstore, sporting a coffee shop serving machine-made scones and bagels, pre-packaged in Kansas City and shipped in once a week. The coffee comes from Seattle. Copies of Angelina's cookbook sit prominently in the front display window.

Recently, heavy spring rains washed away a creek bed embankment near a huge willow tree standing west of town. The rapid erosion exposed the rusted carcass of an unidentified big, old car lying on its side, encased in the mud. Inside it they found a diamond pinky ring, and the remains of human bone. They called out the coroner who scooped up the bone fragments in a plastic bag and put the ring in his pocket. Not enough evidence for an inquest.

The End

www.ingramcontent.com/pod-product-compliance
Lightning Source LLC
Chambersburg PA
CBHW020453020726
47493CB00001B/10